FALL OF
EDONIA

Published by Author Academy Elite
PO Box 43, Powell, OH 43065
www.AuthorAcademyElite.com

Identifiers:
LCCN: 2022915595
ISBN: 979-8-88583-114-7 (paperback)
ISBN: 979-8-88583-115-4 (hardback)
ISBN: 979-8-88583-116-1 (ebook)

Available in paperback, hardback, e-book, and audiobook

Book design by David Alderman.
Cover design by Kimmo Hellström. Map design by Arturo

FALL OF EDONIA

By J.J. Johnson

This book is dedicated to Kynleigh Rae&Baby on the way.

May you both dream up incredible stories that will ignite the imagination of others. -Love Dad

TABLE OF CONTENTS

ACKNOWLEDGMENTS

To all of you who have helped make this dream a reality, thank you! This includes you the reader who has chosen to select this book and embark on a journey placed in my mind and heart years ago. To my wife and daughter, I want to say I love you. Without your patience and sharing of time I would have never been able to write this book. Thank you to everyone who helped bring this book to life through the Kickstarter campaign. Without your generosity this story would not be what it is today!

To the others involved both in editing and proofreading your tireless hours helped shape this story. This especially includes my forever beta reader Ann Brown. The professional editing credit goes to Sheena Crosby at Stellar Media. I'd also like to acknowledge all those who helped in the formatting and artwork of this book. Especially Kimmo Hellström who has been an amazing cover artist for me since A King's Return! Thank you is also due to David Alderman who did the interior design for Fall of Edonia. Last but most importantly I thank my King, Jesus. He who has guided my life. You above all other names are worthy of my time, effort, and greatest passions. If this story can further your kingdom even an inch forward, I pray it does so.

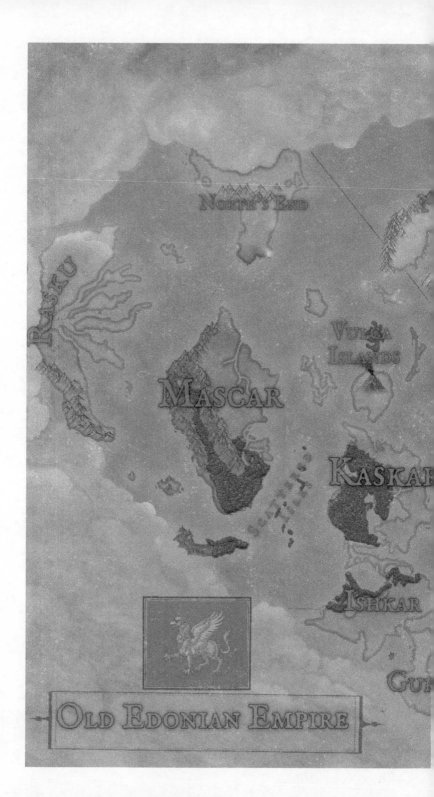

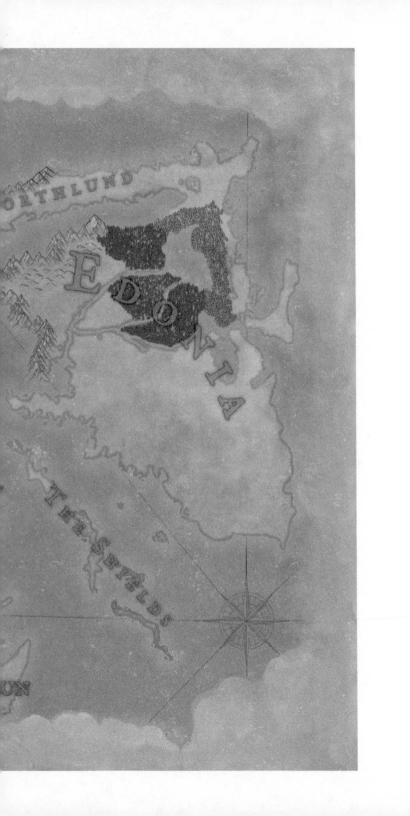

PRELUDE

T
HE GRAND AND pompous cityscape of Edonia tore at the sky ahead. Arthur rubbed weariness from his eyes as his journey downriver had finally come to an end. A sigh of relief left his lips as the mighty Edon River carried his royal vessel to the banks of the pristine city. Edonia's vaunted, bleached towers capped with gold dominated the view. Buildings of commerce, governance, and shelter crowded every inch of the coast ahead. It was the city that ruled the world, or so it claimed. Edonia remained defiant of the reality that its once vast empire was now reduced to a regional power. With each passing decade its iron fist had rusted away little by little. Edonia and her army were still the greatest military force that walked the world. Arthur had no doubts about that. Only her reach was hampered by the decades of less than capable leadership.

Thoughts like these were dangerous in the Edonia now ruled by the emperor. Once, the ruler of such a powerful empire had been selected by his cunning and strength. Now blood determined the ruler of the throne. That blood had diluted Edonia's past strength. Arthur shook these thoughts from his mind as he stepped onto the dock. A royal envoy stood ready to greet him. Their scarlet armor gleamed in the midday sun. Etched on their breastplate was the griffin of Edonia. The sigil that carried either dread or pride, depending who looked upon it. Wherever it was displayed one would know the might of the Edonian empire had come.

"Welcome, Duke Arthur," said one of the guards as he bowed.

Arthur returned a courteous nod as he motioned for the envoy to lead the way. Without a word the royal escort took formation, pushing aside a cluster of gawking citizens. The guards led their distinguished guest with pride through the bustling streets. Passing through the raucous crowds Arthur observed the mass commotion that surrounded him. Endless faces streamed restlessly by him. The occasional passerby stopped to see what royalty had greeted them this day, but in a city that claimed for itself a title like center of the world what was one more royal visitor to them? He had chosen to walk the length of the city this visit. Perhaps it was to stretch his legs after days on the deck of a boat. More so he desired to see the state Edonia was in. Rumors reached as far as his home in Fenikia of discontent among the populous. Arthur was determined to see for himself if the rumors were true.

He passed a corner of men and women who laughed and danced without a care in the world. Such a scene was a rarity these days.

Little do they know, Arthur thought to himself.

His visit was more than a casual trip to the city of Edonia. It wasn't just the stirrings in the capitol city that disturbed the emperor. Great threats loomed on the southern edges of the empire. The region of Hunan was planning to rebel, or so was the word whispered on the lips of royal courtesans. The desert kingdom of Hunan was said to have broken free declaring for themselves a new emperor. Arthur's own mind was skeptical. Hunan was nothing more than an outlier within the empire. Sure, they had a vast population for such a desolate place, but what were numbers compared to what the empire held? Besides he knew of other tales. Ones that spoke of the growing paranoia within the heart of the empire. Those were rumors he could believe to be true. An angry voice shook him from his reflection.

"Ungrateful dogs," muttered a guard in Arthur's escort.

"They don't know what keeps an empire going," responded another in their ranks. Arthur turned his attention to the source of their agitation. A small symbol of a griffin plucked of its feathers and in a drunken state was plastered on an adjacent wall. Underneath it read, *Drunk on the Blood of the People*. The two guards who voiced their complaint moved to harass the citizens gathered beneath it. "You know who did this?" one of them barked to the crowd.

PRELUDE

Fearful glances looked away, hoping not to be singled out from the crowd. One guard shook his head in disgust before he began snatching individuals to interrogate. The other guard with him ushered Arthur on, not wanting a dignitary of his status caught in the mess. The sound of a growing disturbance faded behind Arthur as he escorted further down the street.

What would become of the bystanders? he wondered as the sounds faded in the distance.

It was a fleeting thought stolen away as the small company rounded the street and was greeted with the marvel that was Edonia. With the outer slums now at their back an endless stream of glistening white structures spread out before them. Each building weaved together like a garment washing out the sky above. It left Arthur feeling suffocated under its daunting shadow. The street level was no different. Thousands upon thousands had taken up residence in the capitol of the world. All were a mix of complexions blurred together in the hustle of everyday life. The very nature of Edonia could leave the uninitiated feeling disoriented.

Thankfully, as they plodded on, the mass of buildings began to dissipate until only one remained. The palace of the emperor. Its magnificence and grandeur set itself apart in a city built on such claims. The breathtaking view filled Arthur's vision. The Edon Mountains cast their shadows on a distant riverbank filling in the backdrop of the scene. Beneath them flowed the Edon river, its banks carrying countless passengers out to sea. Even set against such a scene the domed structure of the palace caught the eye. Hints of sunlight reflected off its golden craftsmanship. Every inch was covered in artisan's skill. Each proclaiming the glories of the empire. White columns of enormous size lined the entryway. All of them displayed with detail the image of the mighty griffin. Every step toward the palace was littered with sculptures, towering arches, and armed guards.

All of it stood as a testament to one thing. It was here that the world's greatest power reigned. Arthur followed his guide up the familiar white marble stairs. The oversized steps led to a vast portico.

Beneath its covering towered two bronze doors engraved with the menacing griffin. Its talons clutched the victims of all who dared stand against it. With silent demeanor those who stood sentinel ushered them in. Behind the doors was a circular room with a vaulted ceiling. The tile floors were finely decorated alternating pieces of gold, crimson, and white. They all streamed to the middle of the floor where a beam of light cascaded from a hollow dome above. The light rested on the familiar sight, a regal and defiant griffin. Once more displaying the symbol of the empire's absolute authority.

Arthur listened to the clattering of footsteps coming from an adjacent hall. A host of guards marched with another royal guest, Thegn Lucian of Kaladin. The thegn was a youthful figure dressed in decorative robes of jade complexion. Embroidered on his chest was the proud eagle of his house. His sandy blonde hair was combed back and his face finely trimmed. His jade eyes creased with a smile at his familiar friend.

"Duke Arthur, you've arrived," Lucian said as they embraced.

"Have the others arrived for the summons already?" asked Arthur.

Lucian gave a somber nod. "They arrived yesterday. Some preliminary councils were had and Emperor Septimus is…" he paused. "Well, you'll see."

Lucian turned to the guards. "Please, the duke and I can find our way from here."

The captain and his men remained resolute. "Our orders were to deliver you directly to the emperor."

So, Septimus really has become that paranoid. Arthur thought.

"Very well. Lead us then," Arthur said motioning the captain of the guard forward.

With quickened pace they moved toward the emperor's throne room. Through the halls covered in portraits of ancient heroes and rulers they pressed until a stunning section of open space greeted them. Within, a fountain bursting with clear streams flowed into small channels across the floor. Lush vegetation filled with delectable fruit dotted the room. Golden hues from the sun's rays filtered through silk curtains.

With no time to drink in the calming scene they were brought before the massive throne room doors. They creaked open to reveal the room that put all others to shame. Gleaming Edonium decorated the lavish dwelling. Intricate detail was woven into every inch. An epic depiction of a griffin devouring a serpent rested before the throne in a circular mosaic. Treachery will not overcome the empire was its tale. Not to mention all the other creatures that lay slain near the griffin's talons. No beast, no nation, no person will prevail against her strength. Above it sat Emperor Septimus painted in golden light on his ebony throne. Septimus straightened his posture as Arthur and Lucian entered the room. A small cluster of royalty standing at the base of the throne turned to the new arrivals.

Arthur's eyes remained on his emperor. Crimson robes embroidered with a white griffin clung loosely to the man's flesh. Septimus' silver hair was groomed and tucked back, his beard sharing the same coloring only it remained unkept. The sapphire eyes set within his wrinkled face squinted at his guests with distrust. Resting on his head was a majestic crown made of Edonium. It seemed to weigh heavily on his wrinkled brow.

"Welcome to my court, Duke Arthur and Thegn Lucian," Emperor Septimus said in a cold greeting. Both men dropped to a knee before him.

"Rise," Septimus said in exasperation as if every sign of loyalty should be greeted with mistrust.

Arthur fixed his gaze on the others who had answered the summons. Before him stood Duke Volkmar, the only other man to lay claim to that title. His sharp, narrow, face and dark eyes twisted into a formal smile. His thin locks of ebony hair were brushed back and resting just above silver robes sporting a black raven. Beside him was Baron Holger. A husky man whose tunic always looked to be bursting from the seams. The Baron kept his hair long and decorated with elaborate beads and braids as was Bjønen's custom. His rosy cheeks and round face burst into an obnoxious greeting.

"Greetings Duke and Thegn!" he roared in his baritone voice.

Volkmar rolled his eyes at the informality of addressing his superiors first. "Yes, greetings my fellow Duke and comrade Thegn."

"Where is Thegn Oswald?" Arthur asked eyes searching the group.

"He has fallen ill and has remained in Venhorn," Emperor Septimus said with a scowl.

Arthur and Lucian fell in line as they finished their formal greetings. Each set of eyes quickly returned to the emperor who sat impatiently atop his throne.

"Now that we are all here, we can finally discuss the pressing issues of the empire," Septimus said.

Arthur could sense the tension in the room. Something had the man shaken. As if on cue Octavian, the emperor's head advisor stepped beside the throne. His sharp features and clenched jaw fit the description of most high-born citizens in the empire. Adding to this demeanor was his finely groomed hair. Its black strands with streaks of silver were combed back tightly with firm control. Few would know the man was of foreign origin. Arthur was positive Octavian wished to keep it that way. Octavian had gained the emperor's undying trust, one of the few in Edonia who could make such a boast. He carried a proud demeanor as he straightened his crimson garments. Clearing his throat, he took his place beside Septimus.

"Tell them, Octavian," The emperor ordered.

"I speak for the emperor and all Edonia's subjects when I say that our very civilization is being threatened," Octavian stated.

"How so?" asked Volkmar.

Octavian licked his lips before speaking, "The kingdom of Hunan, once loyal to our empire, has declared independence from our rule."

"Let them. A bunch of desert rats can do no harm to Edonia," Baron Holger bellowed.

"Are you as dim as you are fat?" snapped the emperor. Holger blushed with embarrassment but knew better than to reply.

"Holger speaks crudely, my lord, but his words are not false. What could Hunan possibly gain by doing this?" Arthur asked.

Septimus' face grew grim. "Continue, Octavian."

The head advisor nodded. "Our scouts have warned us that Hunan may have somehow found a way to manufacture their own Edonium weaponry."

"So the rumors are true…" mused Lucian.

Septimus' gaze weighed each of their intentions. "This will not stay hidden for long. That is why we must act swiftly to find out if Hunan really can produce enough weapons to threaten us. If so, we need to get ahead of this before panic spreads in the streets."

"Do we know how many they possess?" Arthur asked.

Octavian cleared his throat, "Only a handful. Even if they do possess knowledge to fabricate Edonium weapons, an Edonium Blade is not easily forged. It takes time to mass produce let alone acquire the necessary metal. We've already sent out what spies we have in the capitol to find where they are getting their raw materials."

"A traitor under our nose selling our most valuable resource," roared Septimus as he slammed his fist against the throne. A fearful silence choked the room.

"Emperor Septimus and I have devised a plan to assault the kingdom of Hunan before they can rise in strength," stated Octavian.

Septimus spoke once more with restrained rage, "You will gather as many fighting men as your kingdoms can spare and send them here. Then we will sail along the southern coast wiping out any Hunan outpost in our path. Let them see the cost of resisting the empire."

Volkmar gulped before speaking, "Your Majesty, you have our swords, but why call us in person for such a message? Would we not have been able to respond quicker had you asked this of us before we arrived?"

"Wise words, Volkmar. I called you because I suspect a network of traitors in our lands. Loose words on parchment cannot be trusted in times such as these. Only words heeded in council."

The emperor's eyes pierced each of them from his throne. "Even still my trust waivers. What have I done to deserve such treachery? Have I not provided peace? Stability? Ungrateful…"

"The emperor desires that this council remain hidden from the

7

public," Octavian said directing them back to their purpose. "He also desires that Lucian and Arthur would lead our forces in battle."

"Us?" asked Lucian. "You know we will serve at your pleasure but..."

"Yes, yes you will," interrupted the emperor leaving the matter at that.

"We will bring you a swift victory," Arthur replied sharing a nervous glance with Lucian.

"What of me?! You send these limp armed warriors to fight and not a roaring bear?" groaned Baron Holger.

"You have your own problems to account for. Did you not think I would hear of this rebellion in the north?" chided Septimus.

Once again Holger's cheeks flushed at the scolding. "John and his merry band of woodland folk are nothing but a flea. Give me but a short time and you'll hear of him no more."

"We shall see." The piercing sapphire eyes of Septimus bore down on the Baron as the words left his lips. Try as he might Holger couldn't help but squirm under that gaze.

"What of me, Your Majesty?" asked Volkmar.

"You and Thegn Oswald will serve as my council in the matter of these traitors. Return home, send your troops, and from there see if you can help unravel this knot we are tangled in. Also another matter."

Septimus nodded to Octavian who pulled out a small parchment from his tunic. "Here is a formal letter I would like you to pass on to the Duchess on my behest."

Volkmar bowed in response. "As you wish, Your Majesty."

"So the emperor decrees. You have your tasks, gentlemen," Octavian declared.

"Now be gone and return quickly," grumbled Septimus. Before they could dismiss themselves they were stopped by the growling voice of the emperor.

"And remember, no one must speak a word of this."

The four of them bowed before quickly shuffling from the room. As the doors closed behind, Arthur turned to Lucian and motioned for him to remain a moment.

PRELUDE

"The emperor is clearly shaken by this news, but Hunan can't possibly be able to create their own Edonium Blades can they? That secret is hidden beneath the palace in vaults even we cannot access. Only master blacksmiths know the secret, and they are never given permission to leave."

Lucian sighed as he weighed the question in his mind. "This is strange news indeed if proven to be true. The emperor's foul mood doesn't help the matter either."

"Silence, Lucian, we are but steps away from his court! Talk like that…"

"I know, I know. It's best we end this war quickly and be done with it."

The two of them turned to follow after the others. As they passed through the decadent halls Arthur couldn't help but feel a sense of dread rise within him. Whatever was happening to the empire he doubted it would end quickly.

1

JOHN OF THE WOOD

A KALEIDESCOPE OF COLORED leaves painted the Northern Darkwood. John winced at the crunch each of them made beneath his feet. Today was the day. The day he and his merry band of rebels would finally get what they needed to stand a chance against the tyrant Holger. A small, armed caravan treaded on high alert through the columned trees just ahead. Men armed with spear and axe scanned the surrounding foliage. John inhaled, letting the breath leave his lungs as he nocked his arrow.

Another breath, and just as the air left his lungs, he released the fletching. The bolt zipped past oak and pine until it sank deep into the neck of an unsuspecting guard. A battle cry burst from the woods all around sending the caravan into a frenzy. A host of a few hundred lightly armored warriors rushed forth, battle axe and dagger in hand. John could see the guards around the caravan fight back the fear rising within them at the sight.

What could a few dozen do against so many? Yet, they had one advantage. Unlike John and his men, they were equipped with patches of plated steel. Some may even be fused with the precious metal Edonium. He looked on as the first wave of his men swarmed the caravan. Sparks ignited as steel weapons did their deadly dance. He nocked another arrow, quickly lining up his next victim. The man never saw it coming. His corpse dropped with a sickly thud, and those around him moved on to find another foe.

John prepped to send a third arrow when a voice came behind him, "John, I've got urgent news!"

"It best be, Maggie, I was just about to take another shot," he said with slight annoyance.

He turned to face his companion and part-time lover. Her bleached blonde hair was pulled back and tightly woven for battle. The round shape of her face and its soft features could easily fool a stranger into thinking she was just like all the other village maidens of Bjønen. Little did they know hidden beneath her innocent form was a deadly warrior. Meeting her caramel eyes, he knew she was serious.

"Our scouts just sent word. The baron and his men are on their way. He's caught wind of our attack."

"How far out?"

She reached beneath her worn leather jerkin, pulling out a small parchment. "Not far."

He took it in hand and scanned the contents. Tucking the note away he let out a sound of disgust.

"It's too late. We need this shipment of Light Bringers."

"But if the baron arrives!" Maggie protested before he cut her off.

"If he does, we'll deal with him. These swords are our one shot at forging a kingdom of our own."

Maggie placed her hands on her hips as she surveyed the ensuing battle. "Come then, we best finish this quickly."

John cracked a smile. "I thought you'd never ask."

He followed her example and nocked another arrow to his bow. The two of them let loose striking two more guards to the forest floor. Perfectly in sync. That described their relationship most days. Besides the occasional spat, he knew Maggie would always have his back. The one person in the entire Edonian Empire he could trust completely. That trust didn't hurt their bed sharing either.

He pushed such thoughts aside as several remaining guards took note of the deadly duo raining bolts down upon them. With raised shields they charged in their direction. Maggie causally placed her bow on her back, withdrawing two bearded axes from her side. John followed suit pulling his short sword free from its sheath. With unified cry they rushed to meet their attackers.

Maggie let fly the axe in her left hand. It found its mark in the shin of the closest warrior sending him to the forest floor. John took advantage removing the man's head with one swift blow. He turned to see Maggie leap into the air and land on top of the other man's shield. The momentum sent them both tumbling to the ground. The only difference was Maggie regained her composure. Leaping to her feet she pounced on the dazed guard, finishing him off with one swing of her axe.

John moved toward the two enemies that remained. One of them thrust his spear catching John's left arm, thankfully striking hidden chainmail. Before the spear could retreat John took the shaft in hand jerking it free from the man's grip. Maggie read John's mind and let out a violent screech drawing another of the guards' attention toward her. Seeing the man was now distracted John sent the spear in his hand whirling into the man's back. Only one remained. Behind the helm was a face filled with terror. John smirked as Maggie moved to his side.

"What are you two?" mumbled the remaining guard.

"Your doom," John whispered.

They moved in one swift motion cutting the man down with ease. With the job done the two of them took stock of their victim's possessions. Moving to one of the dead guards Maggie bent over to retrieve the axe she'd thrown. She clicked her tongue as she did, "You'd think they'd learn to send better soldiers to protect such a vital resource to the empire."

John watched as the few caravan guards that remained fled into the depths of the Darkwood. A cheer rang out from his men as the quick work of raiding the caravan began. He motioned for Maggie to follow him. As they drew near, one of the captains came forward shaking his head.

"What is it, Huldwin?" John asked as the man approached.

"They're not here, sir," Huldwin replied.

"What do you mean?" Maggie asked.

"The Light Bringers. They must have moved it or heard we were coming. It's a dummy caravan, sir."

John let out a cry of frustration as he grabbed a nearby helmet and rammed it into the ground.

"Holger that shantz. He knew we were coming."

"John," Maggie said clasping his arm. "The note."

His mind cleared in an instant at her words. She was right, there was no time for his temper tantrum. Holger was coming, and he had set the whole thing up. Suddenly, the sound of a bellowing horn rumbled through the surrounding trees.

"Form battle lines! Hide the archers in the trees!" John cried.

"Sir?" Huldwin asked in a panic.

"It's Holger. He's here."

"But…but…that's why we came for the weapons. So we'd have something that could stand against him. Without it…"

"We don't have that luxury right now, Huldwin!" John snapped. "Remember, Martha? Your daughters? Your sons? Do you remember what the Baron did with them when your crops didn't yield what you'd hoped?"

"Of course," Huldwin said with a look of shame.

"Well now's your chance to do something about it." Without another word he faced Maggie who knew what to do without command. Skills built by years on the run, she quickly vanished behind a set of pine trees. In fact, as John glanced around, over half his forces had disappeared within the cover of the woods. They knew their moment for revenge and glory had come. Mustered around him were the designated few he had picked to stand as a decoy for such a trap as this.

He could hear the thundering sound of hooves drawing near and shortly after he could see the beasts of war break from the tree line ahead. Leading them was the fat baron on his steed. His hair hung loose in auburn braids over a leather tunic embroidered with the bear of his clan. Hanging at his side was what gave him his true power, an Edonium Blade. A weapon that could tear any man in half with a single swing. While all knew such a blade weakened with each taste of men's blood, many a killing blow could be served before it became like all the rest.

"John of the Wood, I see you have made a fine mess of my caravan. Although I suspected more of you to survive against such a pathetic guard," bellowed the Baron.

"Baron Holger, I see you've grown even larger in your trip to the south," John shot back. "The food must be an especial delight in Edonia."

"Enough, petulant *boy*. You've done enough carousing in the woods. It's time you let the adults deal with the problems of Bjønen."

"Ha! You speak of solving problems, yet that is exactly what I am doing. I'm getting rid of you."

"Silence! I have heard enough of your pathetic droning. My men have waited many years to wipe your blight from Bjønen."

"Let us see if you are up for the task, my baron."

With that Holger let out a flustered grunt before issuing the order for his men to charge. A host of lightly armored calvary streamed forward. Their plated armor glistened from the beams of light peaking through the forest canopy. Behind them five squads of troops armed with sword, spear, and axe followed.

"This will be interesting," John muttered.

"Sir, we can't possibly stop them," Huldwin complained beside him.

"Enough of your cowardice, Huldwin. If you wish to turn tail and run, be my guest. Though I doubt you'd make it far."

The captain gulped and mustered what courage remained in him. John narrowed his eyes watching for the precise moment he would give the order. The pounding of hooves tearing at the earth grew in strength with each heartbeat. Still, he waited.

"Sir, are you going to give the order?" Huldwin asked, voice shaking.

"Enough, Huldwin!" The man was so dim witted at times. Several more seconds passed until the riders reached the destroyed caravan. Just as the first of their ranks reached the broken-down carts John cried, "Now!"

A storm of arrows showered through the dense woods. The crossfire of bolts struck down beast and rider alike sending them into a panic. The riders in the back had no time to halt their mounts and found themselves crashing into their dying companions. Some were sent flying off their steeds, while others found themselves impaled on the splintered wood of the earlier assault. John smiled with glee at the sight of their most dreaded enemy devastated in one fell swoop.

"Fire!"

The order sent another hail of bolts crashing into those that remained. Even the plated armor couldn't protect their foes from the number of arrows being thrown their way. Men slipped on the blood of fallen allies as they scrambled to break free. It was all too perfect. A command rang out for the dismounted troops of the Baron to move forward. They rushed in the direction of arrow fire hoping to dislodge John's carefully placed archers.

In reply, John's men sent a volley toward the Baron's incoming troops. Arrow pierced tree and man alike as they whistled through the forest. Foot soldiers stumbled forward over fallen peers. The sharp steel in their hand ready to seek revenge.

"Archers!" John cried hoping for one last volley to cut down their pursuers. Muffled cries mixed with the whoosh of arrow fire followed. Some of the baron's men were able to reach John's archers before they could release their shot. Chaos soon enveloped the field of battle. Men reached for axe and spear to fend for their lives. What was once neatly drawn lines blurred into fury and chaos. Even with the success of a surprise attack John knew they were outnumbered. Only one option remained.

He rushed to secure a nearby horse that had lost its master. With a thrust of his sword he cut down a soldier that tried to stop him. Just as he mounted, he heard the cry of Maggie's voice behind him.

"John, what are you doing?"

"Finishing this," he said, spurring his horse forward. The forest was a blur as he brushed past any who tried to stop him. Through the thick of combat he could just make out the plump Baron surveying the battle on his steed. His greedy eyes gleamed as he must have felt victory was now assured.

"Baron!" John roared as he drew near the man.

Holger gave a smug smile as his hand moved to the sword at his side. His expression quickly morphed to panic as a single bolt sank into the throat of his steed. The horse reared unsteadily as he ordered it to turn, but the swift motion along with the horse's imbalance sent the Baron crashing to the ground. Holger's horse attempted a gurgled shriek as it capsized. John watched in amusement as it bucked and squirmed until it succumbed to its wound. Its massive weight pinned Holger to the ground leaving him exposed. Holger wrestled to break free, eyes filled with animalistic terror at John's swift approach. Without fear for his dignity Holger wiggled free and fled as John pressed toward him.

Just as John was about to sink his thirsty blade into Holger's flesh, one of the baron's knights rallied to his aid. The plated soldier moved to block John's pursuit. Other knights seeing the event unfold moved to join in protecting their master.

"Get me... get me out of here!" panted the horrified Baron.

The lead knight nodded. "You heard him! Give him a mount."

One of the others dismounted allowing Holger to climb onto the steed. Without hesitation he spurred the beast back in a wild panic toward Bjønen.

"Retreat! The Baron's retreating!" came the cry across the battlefield. Soon Holger's forces melted away into the thick of the forest. The knights now paid no mind to the rebel leader before them. As the baron's forces fled John felt the presence of another move beside him.

"You're welcome for the arrow," came the voice of Maggie.

"I always knew you could read my mind," John said with a smile. "Should we give chase?"

"No..." John replied narrowing his eyes. "Something feels off."

"Then we will have wasted the lives of countless men! No dead Baron and no Light Bringers!"

"Not a waste," he replied, half listening. In a blink it all made sense.

"John?" Maggie asked. "What's got a hold of ya?"

Ignoring her, he dismounted and moved toward the spot where the baron had collapsed. Resting discreetly beneath the Baron's dead mount was a glimmering object. He quickly pushed the beast aside and to his utter joy his suspicions had come to fruition. In his hand was Bear Paw, the Edonium Blade of Bjønen. A sword that laid claim to Bjønen itself and was only matched by those who held great power in Edonia.

"Is that what I think it is?" said Maggie in reverent awe behind him.

John turned with a sly grin, "We have won more than a token victory today, my dear."

The tavern was dimly lit, but John needn't see its occupants' faces to know they were full of joy. Sounds of laughter and revelry reverberated off the walls. He rested at the bar, Maggie at his side. The return journey to Laketon was the easiest they'd ever made. It wasn't long before each man found himself at the famous Lucky Fish tavern. A night of celebration must occur with the vital blow they had struck on the Baron and his men. With such a defeat John could rest at ease of any prying eyes of the Baron's spies in the sleepy fishing town.

He felt Maggie stir beside him, her marvelous caramel eyes surveying the room. She felt his gaze and turned with a seductive smile.

"The men sure look to be enjoying their victory," she said ruefully.

"As they should," John proclaimed in an inebriated tone. Maybe he had celebrated a little too much.

"We've not won yet, John. The baron still lives."

"We will deal with him soon enough, Maggs. With this!" He tapped the sheath at his side that now housed the vaunted Edonium Blade.

"You know that sword makes you a marked man now?"

"Ahh my dear you needn't worry," he said with a sip of ale. "Besides, wasn't that our plan all along? To steal the empire's precious

Light Bringers to forge an army of our own?"

"You and I both know we'd hoped at best to come away with more Light Bringers than dead. From there we'd see where we stood."

"Yet here we are with a weapon that brings terror to all who look upon it. Even better, we have made our fat little bear of a baron toothless."

"So what are you thinking, John? What's next?"

Maggie's words captured his thoughts. For so long he had dreamed of this moment. A moment to free Bjønen of oppression, to seek revenge on those who had taken so much from them. As he searched deeper there was another thought that came unguarded to the surface of his mind. For once there might be a chance for a commoner, a man of the people to have the say in how things should be ordered. Not some royal bureaucrat or wealthy patron who had never struggled a day in their life. This was a moment he knew that would shape the histories and he was the center of it.

"John?"

Maggie's voice shook him from his daydream. "Sorry, Maggs, I was just...dreaming."

"That doesn't answer my question. What will we do now that we've got that fancy sword?"

His face broke in a wryer smile. "We grab ourselves a kingdom."

Those caramel eyes gleamed with delight at such an auspicious future.

"Does that mean I get to be your duchess, my duke?" she said with a mocking bow.

"Ahh Maggie, my dear, don't think so small. You could someday be Empress with such beauty as yours," he proclaimed.

A blush filled her face. "John, don't mock me. I was being serious. Besides you got to make me an honest woman first."

"I know how to make you a dishonest one," he said rising to his feet. "A drink for all on me!"

He slammed a bag of coin down onto the bar as a wild cry filled the room. After, he offered a hand to lift Maggie from her stool.

"Come, Maggs, I know a place where we can celebrate."

Maggie giggled taking his hand in her own. The two of them scurried out into the midnight air. As if in a dream he could hear Maggie's giddiness beside him, but his focus was somewhere else. It was that thought that gripped him earlier. A long-buried seed that was now coming to bloom. Maybe, just maybe he would be someone to remember after all.

2

LEO

DULL GREY LOOMED over the misty Raven River below. Gothic spires leaped from palace terraces, clamoring for space in the sky. Leo let out a tired sigh as he kicked his dangling feet over his bed. His father had been gone for so dreadfully long. He'd been called once again to answer to Leo's grandfather, the Grand Emperor of Edonia. Nothing exciting happened during the days of his father's absence. Rather than tales of his family's deeds or the bark of his father's command, the halls echoed with servant gossip. All a waste of words that clung to half-truths. Leo found them all so boring. There was a certain freedom people carried with them when Volkmar was gone. He had to admit he didn't mind that so much. In fact, he rather liked not having his father's looming presence roam the halls at times. It was just... well... he wasn't sure. He knew his father didn't much care for him. That was plain but something inside Leo yearned to prove himself, to show that he was worthy of his father's affection and that could only happen if his father was around.

His mind drifted again to the host of activities that were planned that day. Some studies in the ancient language of Edonia perhaps. He dreaded those. Why did he need to learn a dead language? Shouldn't he know one that would actually be useful? If he timed it right maybe he could distract his mother with a different request. The idea brought on more questions and more schemes.

It all depended on when his mother would return from her meeting. His mother, Duchess Beatrice, was known throughout all of Edonia. Not just for her pedigree but her wit as well. That cunning often left him feeling stupid and three steps behind when she spoke. Regardless she had always taken special care to never make him feel inferior to her. He loved that about her. Something his father could learn from.

A ship on the horizon snatched him from his musings. The ship's dark bow broke through the fog of the Raven River to reveal a mast bearing the symbol of a raven adorned on a wine-colored field. His father had returned! Without another thought he jumped from his bed, just remembering to snatch his cloak as he went. Swiftly he slipped on his boots and dashed out the bedroom door, dodging quizzical looks from maid and servant alike. He just reached the end of the hall when a voice stopped him in his tracks.

"And where does the royal son think he's going?" came the voice of Crumwald, his mother's chief aid.

"Now, now, Crumwald, be easy on the boy. I suspect he is eager to greet his father," replied the silky voice of his mother. Duchess Beatrice now appeared behind the wrinkled old face of Crumwald. No woman in all the land matched her beauty. Long curls rested on a violet form-fitting dress. Her sapphire eyes fixed on her mischievous son.

"Isn't that right, Leo?"

"Yes, mother," he said restraining his frustration at being caught. He'd hoped to have his father's attention first before everyone else stole it away from him.

She moved beside him and placed a delicate hand on his shoulder, "Come, we shall greet him together."

Leo gave her an eager nod as she motioned for him to follow. Through the winding and dim halls they went. Nothing about the place felt cozy or welcoming to Leo. Vast and monumental designs were woven onto elevated ceilings. Each of them left him feeling small no matter the room. Strange creatures and staring eyes crafted into their design met him around every corner. He'd never liked the palace. One time he brought this to his father's attention. All it left him with was a feeling of shame followed by chastisement for being such a coward. His father's disgust at his softness had always been made clear. That wouldn't stop Leo now, he'd show his father he wasn't the weakling Volkmar imagined him to be. As they reached the palace entrance an entourage of guards stood ready to welcome their duke home. A heartbeat later the doors swung open revealing Duke Volkmar.

"Father!" Leo cried as he ran to embrace him.

Duke Volkmar lifted his eyes from a parchment he carried in response to the outburst. Leo tried not to notice the embarrassed expression that Volkmar carried at the sight of his son.

"I missed you, Father," Leo said wrapping his arms around Volkmar's waist. The duke gave a hesitant pat to his head.

"Yes, yes, it is good to see you as well, Leo. But please, I have returned with some important business to take care of."

Leo felt the cold stiffness of his father's slight embrace before ushering him away. So, it would be this father who had returned to him. Leo watched with growing sorrow as his father casually greeted the duchess with a kiss before moving with his entourage to a nearby meeting hall. Not long after, he felt the presence of his mother move beside him.

"Don't worry Leo, he does miss you."

"He sure knows how to show it," Leo muttered.

The duchess let out a slight sigh in reply. "Come now, let's prepare for dinner. I am sure many guests will be joining us tonight."

Frustrated, he stomped toward his room in defiance. "Sure, and all father's attention will be on them."

The clanging of dishes filled the air as the dinner guests worked at their meal. Leo's appetite had left him since the rejection of his father earlier that day. Still, he was captured by the news of the war with Hunan.

"Yes, I understand the emperor's concerns but does he really need that many of our men?" complained the councilor Vladimir seated beside Leo's father. The councilor was an aging man. His long strains of jet black hair had become peppered with gray, and his face was creased with wrinkled skin. Leo pitied the man after the passing of Volkmar's father. Vladimir had once been an esteemed voice in Varnas' court or so Leo had been told. Now he had become nothing more than a token voice in his father Volkmar's court.

"Do you want to tell his majesty that we won't be sending him the troops he's requested?" jested Volkmar.

A blush came over Vladimir's face. "Certainly not."

"I am just glad to hear my father is well, circumstances not withstanding," said the Duchess moving another piece of food to her mouth.

"Yes, he misses you both dearly and has even requested that you accompany me on my next journey," Volkmar said not lifting his eyes from the plate before him.

"We can see grandfather!?" Leo blurted.

His father's eyes turned to him with that all too familiar agitation.

"The emperor, my dear," corrected Beatrice.

"As I was saying. It should not take more than a month to gather our forces and return to Edonia. Duke Arthur and Thegn Lucian have already rallied their men and will be leading an assault any day now."

"Surely the commanders will need more time?" replied councilor Vladimir.

"What do you say, Commander?" Volkmar asked, turning his gaze to Rowan seated a few chairs away. The commander was all lean chiseled muscle. His hardened face carried with it a frightening pale scar that ran down his left cheek. The cropped cut of brunette colored hair dusted with red that he wore contrasted sharply with his black cloak. Rowan had always given Leo an ill feeling, but his father trusted the man above any other in Varnas.

"For the emperor? Anything," Rowan replied with a mocking grin.

"See?" Volkmar sent a reassuring smile toward the nervous Vladimir.

The dinner grew quiet as something unsaid seemed to hover over the room. Leo once again couldn't help but feel that dreaded inferiority creeping up on him. What did they know that he didn't?

"I beat William in swordplay this past week. My instructor says I have grown immensely in my handling of a sword the last month."

His father's gaze remained steadfast on his plate as he silently chewed. Clearing his throat Leo tried again.

"Would you be willing to come witness a sparring tomorrow? Maybe you could even give the headmaster a dual?"

"Enough, Leo!" Volkmar snapped.

Shame turned to red splotches around Leo's collar as all eyes in the dining hall fell on him. He fought back the hot tears that threatened to break free. With unkept fury he flung his seat back and stormed out of the room. Just behind him he could hear the voice of his mother call out. In reply the stern voice of his father told her to return to her seat and let the boy go. The tears flowed now. With his sleeve he covered his face moving with reckless abandon down the palace halls until he reached his room. Flinging the door open, he collapsed onto his bed weeping.

"I hate him!" he screamed into a pillow. He beat his fists in a wild rage against the duvet covering his bed. He continued on in his anguish until he was drained and left only with his sorrow. Just as sleep was about to take him, he felt a gentle hand run through his smooth ebony hair. He turned with a sniffle to see the face of his loving mother.

"I won't apologize," he said defiantly, before turning back to his pillow.

"I won't ask you to," she said stroking his hair.

"Then why have you come?"

A deep sigh left her lungs, letting silence hang between them for a dozen heartbeats.

"Your father... he wasn't always this way."

"He has been for as long as I have known him," Leo sniffed.

"Yes, that is the travesty."

His mother remained silent as if peering into a painful memory.

"What is it, Mother?"

Beatrice met his eyes and mustered up a weak smile. "Your father changed the day we lost your brother."

"You mean my twin?" Leo inquired.

"Yes, that loss… it broke your father in a way and he's never quite recovered."

"He thinks Ivan would have been a better heir. He wishes I would have died instead."

Beatrice waited a moment before she spoke again. Her words weighing heavy in her mind.

"Your father cannot know what could have been. You will make a good ruler someday, my sweet Leo."

"Nothing I do pleases him. How can I prove to him that I'm worthy? I try so hard…"

"Your father is a wounded and ambitious man. He wields both with little restraint. Don't let his flaws ruin you, love."

Leo turned to meet his mother's eyes. Nothing but kindness was in them. No manipulation, no disdain, only a mother's warmth.

"You think I will be a better ruler than father someday?" he asked.

"Certainly, my dear. I have no doubts you will be the greatest among men when it is your time to rule. You are both kind and thoughtful. Something we need more of in the halls of power." A smile stretched across her face as she said the words.

"What… what should I do about father in the meantime?"

She pondered his question for a moment, "You may still be young, Leo, but you are also the emperor's grandson. Go to him in the morning when emotions have cooled and speak with him as one future ruler to another."

"Truly, mother? Won't that make him angry?"

"It will be a good test for you. You mustn't let fear of your father hang over you forever."

Leo mulled over her words. She was right. Why should he let his

26

father's cruelty rule his emotions? He gave a curt nod of affirmation.

"I'm proud of you, love," she said stroking his hair one last time. "Now get some sleep."

As she rose from his bed he couldn't help but smile. She always knew how to bring him back from the depths of sorrow. He curled up in his bed wrapping himself in the duvet. Visions of the ruler he might someday be formed in his mind. Proud, strong, loved, and respected. All the things his father demanded from others. But Leo could be more, he must be. He wouldn't lose the qualities that mattered most kindness, compassion, and wisdom. As sleep took him in its grip he drifted off to a land where he was emperor and his father's cruel ways were no more.

The next morning greeted him all too early. The sun broke over the horizon sending beams of light reflecting off the golden Raven River. Letting out a sigh, Leo raised his arms in a long yawning stretch. His throat felt scratchy and dry from his outburst the night before. Much of the vigor and courage had vanished with the morning mist as well. Regardless, he wouldn't back down now. He mustn't if he was to step into who he wanted to be.

Jumping from his bed he moved swiftly across the room snatching a pair of trousers from a nearby rack. Next, he found and put on his favorite surcoat, a midnight-colored fabric embroidered with a cluster of silver ravens. Finishing the final fastenings, he turned to a mirror hanging on an adjacent wall. He fixated on the small boy staring back at him.

The deep violet pools carried a new fire on his youthful face. He took his hands slicking back the loose locks of jet-black hair. Giving himself a curt nod, he mustered up the strength to face the man he feared the most. With determined pace he threw open the bedroom door. If any eyes fell on him he didn't notice. It was with laser focus he pressed down the hall, past clamoring servants preparing for another day in the royal chambers.

In a matter of moments he found himself standing before his parent's room. Sucking in a deep breath, he mustered up every ounce of courage he had and threw it open. With a thrust of the arm the door swung inward nearly crashing into the wall. The room sat empty. Its only contents were royal furnishings and neatly framed paintings of his family. That's when the voice of Crumwald sounded behind him.

"Looking for your mother, young master?"

Leo swallowed down the flutter of panic at the abrupt question. Turning he met Crumwald's stare.

"No, my father... actually."

Crumwald gave him a quizzical tilt of the head, but decided not to investigate further.

"I believe he is in his private study with Commander Rowan, young master."

"Thank you." Leo didn't wait for a reply as he burst down the hall. He didn't want any questions or advice draining him of what courage remained. Through the stone halls filled with the all too familiar statues and daunting spires he went. His father's study rested within the tallest spire of the royal keep. Leo followed a host of twisting stairs that stretched upward until they reached a plain wooden door set within the narrow tower. At the top he rewarded himself with a small catching of his breath. he rested a hand against the cold stone wall his legs burning from the flights of steps. Everything felt as though it was working against his courage today. His gaze turned toward the dreaded door of his father's private chambers. A thin bit of wood was all that held him back from his father now. That's when the sound of aggravated whispers caught his ear.

"You know what happens if we don't act now, Rowan!" came the stern voice of his father.

"My Lord, I understand but if we can't get all the captains on board, we can't hope to..."

"It won't matter if we don't act now. If word gets out about the little rat and the emperor's decision, all our plans will be for nothing."

Rowan's reply was muffled by the scuffling of a chair.

What are they talking about? What did a rat have to do with anything? And what had his grandfather decided? Leo pressed his ear closer to the door straining to hear.

"We march in a month. I want no more arguments. Edonia's armies are away, and we have others on our side. We will never have another opportunity like this again. Get as many loyal men as you can and that will have to be enough. Do you understand me?"

"Yes, Duke."

Loud footsteps thundered toward the door and suddenly it flew open to Leo's horror. It sent Leo falling backward on the stairway. Slowly he raised his eyes to meet the mortified face of Rowan now standing over him.

"Uh… uhh father I wanted to…" Leo stuttered as he looked beyond Rowan into the room.

"What did I say about disturbing me in my study, boy!" Volkmar raged behind the mortified Rowan.

The commander turned to Leo's father, giving him a look that made Leo's skin crawl.

"I will deal with this, Rowan. Go." Volkmar said with a dismissive wave.

Rowan bowed curtly before taking his leave, not giving Leo the slightest glance as he stepped around him to descend the stairs. Leo turned his eyes back to his father. His dark pupils burned with disdain.

"What do you want, Leo?" Volkmar hissed.

"Uhh…I want…I want…"

His father let out an agitated sigh. It was that sigh. That all too familiar displeasure that gave Leo the fury he needed. He rose to his feet, cheeks flushed with anger.

"I wanted to tell you that I will not be treated as a creature to be endured any longer. I know you despise me, father, but I have come to tell you I will not take it any longer. You may not love me, but you will respect me. I am not some dotting toddler anymore. So… so if you have anything you wish to say to me from now on you best remember these words."

He'd done it. He had actually stood up to his father. Something even more miraculous happened. Volkmar smiled. No, not just smiled, he burst into a roaring laughter. With uncontrolled heaves Volkmar bent over raising a hand for Leo to wait. Leo didn't know if this made him more angry or confused.

Finally, Volkmar regained his composure.

"Son, that may be the finest thing you have ever done," Volkmar said wiping away a tear.

"Really? You're not... mad?"

"It's about time you fended for yourself rather than take shame like a fine garment to wear. No, I am proud of you. I respect that you came to me with this."

Leo couldn't believe it. He stood paralyzed. Searching for words and finding none. Thankfully his father spoke again.

"I have just one question for you."

"Yes, Father."

"Did you hear anything when you approached. If so you're not in trouble, but you must know royal secrets must be guarded with the utmost care. Can I trust you to tell me the truth? Can you handle that kind of responsibility?"

The question came rushing at him like a hidden dagger. Leo fought to keep panic's tendrils from claiming him. With one swift breath he released the words.

"No, I did not."

Volkmar's eyes weighed him. As if searching for any deceit that could be painted on Leo's face. As if appeased Volkmar nodded his head slightly.

"You said something about a sword match last night. When was that again?"

Leo couldn't fend away a grin at his father's words. Somehow his plan had worked.

3

DUKE ARTHUR

THE SMELL OF SALT water filled Arthur's nostrils as mighty ocean waves rocked the boat beneath him. All of Edonia was made for such travel. Every large river passage weaved its way through open fields and dense forests to find its way home at sea. Arthur inhaled another round of the wondrous air.

A fleet of massive proportions encompassed the sea around him. Their wooden flanks displayed the colors of the empire, crimson and gold. Each mast proudly bore the griffin ready to strike terror into its enemies. Below the symbol that united them all flapped the lesser claims of the men aboard. Dotted throughout the fleet flew a plethora of colors representing all the individual regions that lay under control of Edonia.

Some hoisted the soaring jade eagle of Kaladin, others the black bear of Bjønen. Then there was the scarlet phoenix of Arthur's home known as Fenikia. The wine-colored raven of Varnas and the brown moose of Venhorn were few if any among their ranks. In his haste to squash Hunan the emperor had demanded an immediate assault on the first of their defenses. This left Arthur and Thegn Lucian feeling more than a little apprehensive. By all estimates the first of their targets, Kita Fortress was guarded with nothing but a few garrisons. So they had been told.

"Estimates…" Arthur let out a chuckle as he mulled over the word. Over a decade of warfare had taught him how useless "estimates" could be. He was stirred from his musings as Sir William approached from the deck behind. The grizzled vet plodded across the forecastle in his fully plated armor. Its color was polished iron tinted scarlet. Outstretched wings of a soaring phoenix were etched into the breastplate. Arthur caught William's steely eyes as his long-time companion took his place at Arthur's side.

"What's the word?" Arthur asked.

Sir William stroked his prickled chin. "Small scout boats just returned. Say we may have underestimated Hunan's forces. Seems they had more time to prepare for our coming than we anticipated." Arthur looked as William's eyes fixed on the horizon where Kita Fortress would soon come into view.

"Have all our forces departed Meridon Fortress yet?"

Before William could answer the clattering of footsteps behind them drew their eye. Thegn Lucian was barreling toward them with his trusted guardian Sir Kain just behind.

"Have you heard, Arthur?" Lucian shouted in an exasperated tone as he drew near.

"Military estimates have always been suspect, Lucian," Arthur said with a shrug of the shoulders.

"But not like this," Lucian replied lowering his voice. The Thegn's eyes shifted from the deck crew back to Arthur and William.

"Word is Light Bringers and Edonium infused arrows were spotted on the ramparts."

"So, the rumors are true," Arthur mused.

"We may have more than a simple skirmish on our hands. Why did the emperor insist we depart without the full force of Venhorn and Varnas at our sides?"

Arthur placed a hand on Lucian's shoulder. "You know the emperor has a soft spot for Varnas. Seeing as his daughter and grandson roam its keep. Baron Oswald is an old man prone to taking his time whenever he can. I'm sure the emperor's..." Arthur paused thinking carefully for the proper word, "His... eagerness drove him to this decision."

"Even still. Must our men pay the price for his nepotism and impatience?" Lucian complained. His youthful face was flushed with anger. Arthur understood the sentiment. It took years of bloody battle and countless military mistakes to weed it out of you. Lucian was an untested warrior. He'd soon come to understand the way wars really worked. The dance of compromise and loss in order to achieve your goals. No war was without sacrifice. The only question that remained was who would be making it.

"It seems so," replied Sir William, his voice nearly a sigh. The cold eyes of the veteran confirming Arthur's thoughts.

"He's right, my lord," said Kain.

Lucian turned to his trusted companion. "Always the realists, you two. Can't I believe in a more optimistic world?"

"Only an opportunist's world, I'm afraid," shrugged William.

"Come now, gentlemen, no need to grow fatalistic here. We still have the might of Edonia with us. Many of the emperor's own banner men join us. Do you really think a tiny fort on the edge of Hunan will stop us?" Arthur said.

"Stop us? No, these desert dwellers, even with ten Edonium Blades, couldn't stop the full force of the empire. But if they can hurt us enough… Well, others might start getting ideas," Kain replied.

"You mean the Kaskarians?" Arthur asked, amused.

"Not just the island nations but Northlund as well. I've even heard stirrings of farther lands wondering if the once mighty Empire of Edonia is ripe for the picking."

"Arthur's right, enough of the fatalism, gentlemen. We have a war to win. No need to drift into conspiracy theories on a day like today," Lucian said shaking his head.

"Right on cue," came the gruff voice of William. His stare had returned to the Sunset Sea's horizon. Peaking over the glistening waters stood a single red-roofed pagoda. A warning horn shortly followed the sighting.

"Fortress ahead!" Came the call from the crow's nest.

In response, the deck sprang to life with men rushing to their assigned battle stations. Drawing near to Kita Fortress the marvelous and bone-dry ruby sands of the Crimson Desert now came into view. Arthur drank in the dying moments of the tranquil scene. Soon it would erupt into the chaos of battle and all its beauty would be marred by the violence of men. A breeze whisked across his face, and for a moment he thought he could just make out her voice. An image flashed across his mind. Platinum hair splayed across decorative pillows. Serene turquoise eyes. A creased smile. The picture vanished just as quickly as it had come.

"You alright, Duke?" Sir William asked raising a hand to Arthur's shoulder.

"Yes, it's nothing," Arthur said shaking free of the haunting memory.

"Best focus my friend, no daydreaming when the battle comes. I prefer to have my friends alive," teased Lucian.

"Of course," Arthur said giving a curt nod.

He could see out the corner of his eye the shrewd gaze of William. The long-time guardian and friend knew when he was lying, but he must have decided to let it go as he strolled casually after the departing Lucian and Kain.

Arthur squeezed his eyes closed, straining to regain focus. The trance lifted and the strange feeling of her presence faded with the wind. He was ready now. Ready to bring glory and victory to the empire. He stepped forward to join the others, doing all he could to repel old memories from creeping back again.

Ballista darts sent ribbons of water streaming onto the deck as they whizzed past. Arthur's ship was close enough now that he could see the banners bearing the blood orange tiger of Hunan on the ramparts. They thrashed in the eastern wind, matching the fury of the fortress' defenders. Another wave of fire rained down, tearing apart the deck of a ship beside them. The beach landing the fleet aimed for rested below the sheered cliffside that housed Hunan's fortress. How all their ships would dock on such a small beachfront was beyond Arthur. That was the first of their problems. Their second was the sheer cliffs of desert rock that kept the fortress at arm's length. Those who made it onto the beach would have to ascend a heavily guarded pass before they even reached the front gate. All the while Hunan's defenders would have ample opportunity to rain death down on them.

Once again a wave of bolt fire descended on them from the fortress above. Several of the projectiles zipped past Arthur as he braced for the incoming fire. Glancing over his shoulder he could see one found its mark as it protruded from a nearby deckhand. Water fountained up from several other places where the bolts had collided with the deck. The streaming water sent the ship's crew into a frenzied panic.

"Abandon ship!" cried the captain.

"We're so close!" Lucian yelled in response. "Can't we make it?!" Arthur peered toward the shore. The targeted beach was only a small distance away.

"We won't make it!" barked the captain as he tossed a comrade overboard.

Another loud crash came, and more water burst onto the deck.

"Come, sir," said William placing a hand on Arthur's shoulder.

Shaking his head Arthur began unbuckling the scarlet armor he'd strapped on for the fight. The heavy steel crafted just for him would soon become a treasure lost to the sea. Only the Edonium Blade remained strapped around his waist. He would risk his life over parting with something so precious. Following William's example, Arthur leaped from the deck and plunged into the frigid water below. The depths rushed to meet him desiring to pull him under. With a burst of strength he kicked toward the surface. Blurred by the salt water, he could just make out other shapes plummeting into the water all around. Gasping, he broke through the surface and filled his lungs with precious air. The chaos above surpassed what lurked below. Sinking ships and floating corpses littered the sea around him. Men foolishly leapt into the water fully armored thinking little of the consequences. Cries of the dying roared in a haunting chorus. The ships that remained afloat now jockeyed for a space along the shore.

"This is madness," Arthur muttered. It was a mistake as salt water nearly choked him.

Some distance away he could see a bobbing head call for his attention.

"Duke Arthur!" came the voice of William.

Motioning with a hand William called for Arthur to follow him to shore. Fighting the tossing of the waves Arthur expended precious energy to reach his companion. Nodding to one another they both began the arduous swim to shore. The current wrestled his every stroke as he pressed toward the safety of dry land. The whiz of the occasional arrow also found time to hound him in the midst of it all. Just as it seemed the sea would win, a break from the current finally came. The momentum of the surf vomited him onto the beach. With the little strength that remained, Arthur sprawled onto the coarse sand feeling it stick to his face. Panting he let out an unrestrained sigh of relief. Eyes closed he soon heard the exhausted groans of William beside him. Both clung to the silent reprieve as long as they could.

"Great start," William groaned, rising to a knee after some time.

Arthur returned a gargled choke in response.

"Did you happen to see Lucian or Kain?" he said finally able to recover his voice.

William gave a sorry shake of the head.

Beside them the first of the assault ships burst onto the shore. Dozens of Edonian soldiers began to leap from its side hungry to avenge their fallen. Among those still on board, Arthur could see Lucian still fully armored with Kain at his side. Lucian spotted them from the top of the ship and barked an order Arthur couldn't hear. The beleaguered duo returned a weak waved. In one swift motion Lucian leaped from the deck and rushed to meet them.

"How?" was all Arthur could mutter as Lucian and Kain approached in their glimmering armor.

A mocking grin stretched across Lucian's face. "We hitched a ride just before ours collapsed. You shouldn't have been so hasty to abandon ship!"

"Come, gentlemen. Are we planning to lounge on the beach all day or gain a victory for the emperor?" mocked Kain.

Arthur turned to see the rolling eyes of William. "Let's go before these green glory hounds get an even bigger head."

With only his Edonium Blade to protect him, Arthur clamored his way up the beach. Clothes dripping, he spotted a host of soldiers beginning to form rank for the coming assault. Following Lucian he took his place at the company's head just as the thegn began to rally the gathering troops.

"Men of Edonia! We are first to breach, last to leave, you hear me?" Lucian cried raising his sword, its silver metal radiated a dazzling light upon its razor-sharp edge.

"For the emperor and the Empire!" was the soldiers' reply.

"Very good. Now, march!"

He shot Arthur a quick look before moving with the rest. "Just an Edonium Blade huh? You must like a challenge."

Ignoring the jest, Arthur patted the trusty sword at his side. "Phoenix's Flame hasn't let me down yet. I don't expect her to do so today."

Lucian gave him an unconvinced look but moved on without another word. It didn't take long before Arthur found his boast undone. Half a dozen of his men soon came offering him their armor. Reluctantly he took his officer's set knowing the man would not let him refuse. Now, fully armored in common plate, he set off with the rest for the cliffside pass. As the scouts predicted, armed towers lined the road ahead. Hunan warriors stood ready to greet them with ballistas ready. Unfortunately for them it was time Edonia showed her strength. Several small ballistas of their own had been offloaded from the ships and armed for such an occasion. With normal bolts they posed little threat but these were Edonium arrowheads. Forged in the fires below the palace and mixed with the strongest metals known to man. Edonium forged correctly could shatter any fortification or defense. Even diluted arrow tips could chip away any structure in little time. A material that never rusted, never dulled, and could only be destroyed by those who knew its secrets. It was the weapon that had built an empire. Now, it would be the weapon to crush any ambitions of a new one.

He watched as the small ballistas let loose their first round of fire. Rather than bouncing off the tower stone, each arrow chipped away at the meager defenses. Soon the unstable rock of one came tumbling down as the fortification was eaten away by Edonium arrow fire. Even with this display of might, the remaining Hunan defenders did not flee. Instead, they returned a hail of darts in defiance. Arrowheads glistened in the sun as they came tumbling down to meet Edonia's forces. Steel chipped and splintered while other bolts found flesh. Arthur looked down at an arrow protruding from the ground in front of him. Covered by dirt but still shining beneath rested the milky white substance of Edonium mixed with steel.

"So it is true..." he muttered in amazement. This changed everything.

"They have Edonium!" he warned, falling back behind a cluster of rocks. The instinct made him laugh.

There was nowhere to hide with Edonium being hurled at them. "So, this must be how our enemies feel," he chuckled to himself.

The news seemed to confuse some and enrage others within their ranks. With a burst of energy, the army at Arthur's back moved forward to take the next tower. The vicious struggle of return fire repeated until a trail of bodies and broken towers lay behind them. All that remained in their way of victory was the fortress itself. A hoard of Edonia's finest drenched in the gore of battle now stood eager to bring Kita's gate crashing down. A pause in the fighting left the two sides in eerie silence. Among the Edonians only the sound of distant reinforcements marching could be heard making their way up the cliffside. Those remaining of Hunan's defenders stood sentinel glaring wordlessly from the fortress' ramparts. Each of their faces sat expressionless as they waited. Arthur could see in their unyielding eyes a readiness to die.

"And so they shall," he thought.

The glistening Sunset Sea now rested below the sheer cliffs to his right. Already the day was waning, as if the sun was weary of watching bloodshed. Well enough, there would be plenty more of it before its rays would greet them again. As he focused on the sea an image once again flashed before his eyes. Blonde strands mixed with sticky crimson. Too much of it… He had never seen so much…

His fists tightened as he fended off the haunting image. Relief came with the firm clasp of a hand on his back. Looking over his shoulder he saw the face of William motioning for him to follow. Relieved by the distraction, Arthur followed the man to an outcropping of dark sand stone. Lucian and Kain sat waiting for them around a small cook fire.

"I see you didn't catch a stray arrow," Lucian said, lifting his gaze from the flames.

"Funny I didn't see you at all during the fighting. You sure you didn't miss it?" Arthur asked with a smirk.

Kain shot his master an amused look of his own. "Careful Arthur, the thegn can be sensitive."

"Enough, you two!" Lucian said waving a dismissive hand. "While you have been resting, I took the initiative to send some scouts around the eastern cliffs."

"And?" asked William.

"And they report the Hunan defenders are almost out of their precious Edonium stock."

"Can we even trust the reports anymore?" William scoffed. "I count more dead on the beach than we've lost since the war in Mascar."

"They've given me their word," Lucian said.

William let out a disbelieving grunt.

Arthur turned to his companion, "Calm, William. The fortress isn't large. I doubt they have enough storage for a week, let alone a siege."

"A siege? Is that your plan?" Lucian asked, disdain tainting his tone.

"Careful, Lucian. Duke Arthur is the commanding officer here. Not you." William said, in a low growl.

"Both of you, enough. Lucian, do you have another suggestion?"

Arthur asked.

"Yes." his eyes shifted from William to Arthur. "We need to take this fortress as fast as we can. If we get bogged down in a siege it will give more time for the other fortifications to prepare for our coming."

"I have to agree with Lucian, my lord," Kain said.

"Of course you do," William chuckled.

Arthur shot William a stern look. "We will lose a lot of men with an assault."

"We already have lost more men than the emperor would care to know. But we have the potential to lose more men than Edonia has seen since its founding if we don't put an end to this conflict quickly. Every day we give Hunan is another day to produce Edonium weaponry," Lucian replied.

Arthur stroked his chin in thought. Lucian was right. Hunan with Edonium was a threat unlike any Edonia had faced in a millennia. If they couldn't crush Hunan quickly who knew how long the war could drag on.

"We cannot let the fringes of the empire see weakness. If they sense blood in the water the very fabric of our empire could come undone. We must end this now… whatever the cost," Lucian said in hushed tone.

"Whatever the cost…"Arthur chewed on the words. He had heard those words before many years ago. It had been another war that seemed so important at the time.

"Sir?" asked William.

"Yes… prepare the men for an assault. Tonight."

A slight smirk crossed Lucian's narrow face. "Yes, commander."

Kain gave a solemn bow as the two of them set off to give the order.

"Good soldiers will die needlessly today," William sighed.

"Good soldiers die every day, William. Blood is the fuel of the empire," Arthur said turning to his friend. William's face was stone. Hiding behind his cerulean eyes was the secret knowledge of Arthur's pain. The pain that colored his whole world. With an obedient nod William stepped away to give the order.

Ash wafted downward beneath a midnight sky. Heat radiated off the burnt remains of Kita Fortress causing Arthur's blackened skin to sweat. The sickening sound of steel pulled from flesh rang out as Lucian removed his blade from a dying man's chest. The reports had proven true. Barely any Edonium remained within the fortress. It didn't stop the lasts gasps of Hunan resistance from spilling more Edonian blood. Another groan released as William thrust a spear of mercy into a dying foe.

Corpses from both sides littered the charred remains of the fortress road. The carnage filled path ushered them forward to their final destination. They continued their weary jaunt up the fortress' path until it reached the fortification's highest peak. A single building rested at its top. Before them crackled and whined the wooden remains of a keep. On its steps bloodied and dying lay the Hunan's fortress commander and the remains of his guard. Their faces were black with soot and behind their thin hazel eyes burned defiance. As the four of them approached, the finely decorated Hunan commander rose to his feet. Blood streaming down his arm until it found its resting place on the cold dark stone.

"Welcome, mighty conquerors," the commander said mockingly in the Hunan tongue.

"Speak the tongue of the empire, you rebellious dog," Kain barked.

A bloody smirk stretched across the commander's face, "Did you find what you were looking for?" he asked in broken Edonian. "There is more to come..."

A blur of milky white suddenly flashed toward them. With reflexes only gained from years of combat, William grabbed the desperate commander's arm forcing the white dagger from his grip. With one smooth motion he sent the man crashing to the ground.

A gargled noise left the commander's lips as his broken body met cold stone. The others with him moved to act but with one quick motion were cut down. Weapons drawn, Arthur and the others stared at the commander bleeding out before them. The man belted out a discomforting laugh in one last act of defiance. The gargled sound faded away as he took his final breath.

Arthur looked to the others. The same thought was painted on their face. Whatever the days and months ahead held, one thing was certain. The force of the empire behind them or not, this wouldn't be a simple jaunt into the heart of Hunan. These men were willing to die for their cause, every last one of them.

4

JULIET

FLICKERING CANDLELIGHT danced across the ancient timber betable of contentsams of Venhorn's hall. Timber beams stained dark stretched and bowed high above Juliet as she entered the room. The scent of dwindling cook fires and stale ale saturated the air. How Juliet cherished her cozy home tucked away in the Edon Mountains. Her pale eyes rested on her father seated upon his humble wooden throne. The aging face and greying beard could not hide the glimmer of joy in his eyes. Only a small fraction of Venhorn's clan remained within the hallowed hall feasting at such a late hour. Their merriment not yet satiated before the coming task.

Thegn Oswald's voice bellowed off the timber walls at the sight of Juliet, "Ahh my lovely daughter wishes to join the festivities now that they are coming to an end?" A familiar smile cracked beneath his thick beard as he stood. With surprising grace for his age he descended the throne's steps and wrapped her in his arms. The feel of leather and smell of pine was the familiar comfort of her father's embrace.

"I'm sorry I'm late," Juliet said, tucking back a blonde strand of hair. "The hills of Kaladin were against us on our hunt."

Oswald squeezed her again before stepping back to examine her. His crystal eyes were full of amazement. "How'd my daughter grow to be a full-fledged woman already?"

"Father, I've been a woman for some time now. It's only your memory that is fading."

"You'd be right about that my dear," he said, smirking.

Juliet turned to examine the hall. The few who remained were sprawled across the floor or tables in a stupor.

"How are the spirits of the men?" she asked.

The jolly face of her father hardened. "The men of Venhorn know their duty. They will answer the call of the emperor with all valor."

"I'm sensing a 'but,'" she said, eyeing him.

The burly chest of the thegn heaved as he let out a sigh. "It's an unsavory business I've been given. A rumor of treachery has spread across Edonia."

The words gripped her. "Treachery?" she asked, leaning in.

Her father peered around the room and stooped low, speaking in a whisper, "Septimus fears someone has given Hunan the key to forging Edonium weapons."

Clasping a hand to her mouth she held back a laugh. "Father, that secret's been hidden for over a thousand years. You really think Hunan of all kingdoms would be able to acquire it?"

Oswald remained still but for a slight shifting of his feet.

"What are you not telling me?"

"I got word this morning. Duke Arthur and Thegn Lucian sent their first report from the frontlines of the war. Hunan wielded Edonium weapons in the fight."

Jaw dropping, she didn't know what to say.

"Please don't tell your mother or your brother. The last thing I need is them worrying about traitors in the empire. You hear me, Juliet?"

"Father, they aren't…"

"Listen to me, Juls," but he couldn't keep the sternness in his voice. "Why do I even bother," he said shaking his head. "Just trust me. It's easier this way."

She gave him a glare but didn't press further. "So what does that mean for you?"

"I have been given the undesirable task of finding this mole. Whether someone is leaking the forge's secrets or slipping Hunan the weapons. The emperor has tasked Duke Volkmar and I to find out and report back to him."

"Does this mean you're going to Edonia?" she exclaimed. "Father, the journey takes weeks! And your health is…"

"What am I to do? When the emperor sends orders there isn't a question mark."

"I will go."

"Now that's funny. You want me to send my only daughter to investigate the greatest treachery in all the empire's history by herself?"

"Yes."

"This isn't funny, Juliet."

"I know."

Her father's pale blue eyes fixed on her for a long while before speaking again.

"Juliet… What will I tell your mother?"

It took all her strength to restrain her sudden burst of joy. "You'll tell her the emperor required a royal representative of Venhorn to present our army for the war. It's not a lie and seeing as I am one of Venhorn's finest fighters…"

"Careful now, Juls. Venhorn has many fine warriors with many notches on their shield."

"And I just need a chance to add a few of my own to prove how inferior they are," she said with a smirk.

He sighed but it could not mask his amusement. "Come, you've been gone a week. I'm sure your brother and mother are anxious to see you."

Down an adjacent hallway they went. The start of a new day peered through the clear windows on either side of them. Distant snow-capped peaks belonging to the Edon Mountains glistened with hues of orange and pink. Life subtly began to stir within the keep. Servants and royal emissaries awakened to join with the symphony of a new day. She imagined her mother and brother still laying nestled beneath a pile of warm furs. They never were admirers of the morning. Not like her father and her. After swerving through a half dozen halls, they finally approached the large oak doors of her father's room. Just as Oswald laid a hand against the handle a voice cried out from down the hall.

"Sister!" came a young boy's voice. The slender frame of a dirty blonde came dashing toward them. With one smooth motion Juliet scooped her brother up into her arms and swung him in the air. A burst of laughter left him as she gently returned him to the ground. Slowly turning the corner after him was the regal form of her mother, Gwen. Her curved frame was graced with snow white hair that fell past her shoulders. Dazzling turquoise eyes creased with a smile at the sight of her daughter.

"Finally home, are we? Liam just couldn't wait to hear of your grand adventures in the wild."

Juliet glanced down at the giddy face of her brother. "Is that so?" she asked, tickling him.

"Did you catch any wild beasts?" Liam asked through bursts of laughter.

"Ahh yes, I nearly brought back a wild drake for you, but he just got away."

"Sister, drakes are a myth. Even I know that," Liam said, catching his breath.

"Come now, Liam. I am sure your sister is weary from her journey," Gwen said, beckoning the boy.

"I am actually off again. Tomorrow."

The face of her mother grew stern as her eyes swerved to Oswald.

"Come now, Gwen. She's a grown woman. If she wasn't so feral she could be a commander of a fine battalion."

Juliet shot her father a glare at the half-insult.

"So, it means she should leave for Edonia just as she returns from another dangerous task given by you?"

Here we go again… Juliet thought.

"You know I can't travel these long trips anymore, dear. Besides when was the last time she visited Edonia? On top of that, seeing the emperor. It's an honor".

46

"I wish none of us had to visit that dreadful city or that emperor ever again."

"Gwen, you mustn't talk like that!" her father scolded.

Ignoring his warning Gwen turned her gaze back to Juliet. "If you are leaving so soon then we should make the best of it. Come, I could use some help in the garden this morning."

With a sigh Juliet nodded in obedience knowing it was better not to resist. It wasn't long before her hands were soiled and her back aching. How she dreaded gardening and... her mother. Maybe dread wasn't the correct word. But their relationship had never been like the one with her father. Words seemed to always be taken wrongly. Her motives and desires questioned. More than anything it felt like work.

It had been hours now under the sun. Liam had long given up his invisible quest of wrangling a drake and now wandered elsewhere. How Juliet wished she could join him. No words had filled the silence between her mother and her as they dug. Maybe that was for the best. After placing the last of her plants Gwen stood to her feet, dusting off her knees.

"I know why you are going," she said suddenly.

Juliet shot her a quizzically look.

"Your father is a kindhearted man but not a subtle one."

"So... are you going to stop me?" Juliet asked.

Her mother's eyes drank in the surrounding garden as she spoke. "I have spent countless hours cultivating this place. Hard work, sweat, even some blood," she said with a faint chuckle. Juliet waited silently for her to continue.

"Servants thought it was beneath me. Your father didn't understand my obsessive desire for this place. But now, any who come to visit us always comment on how much they love this portion of the keep."

"What does that have to do with me going to Edonia?" Juliet asked curtly.

A faint smile creased Gwen's face, "People may not understand you, Juls. They may tell you that isn't your place. They may even try to stop you." Gwen's glimmering eyes now locked with her own.

"But when it's all said and done, they will see what you see. They will know why it was all worth it."

Juliet found herself dumbfounded at her mother's words. In response Gwen knelt down wrapping Juilet in a slight embrace.

"Just make sure you spend some time with Liam before you go. He admires you more than you can imagine." With that she stood and walked away. Leaving Juliet wide eyed on the manicured grass.

The morning sun just peaked over the Edon Mountains entering her room. Rising with an exasperated grunt Juliet tossed her bedding aside. Arms raised high she worked to release the weariness from her aching muscles. Life in the wilderness the past few weeks had left them feeling stiff and sore. How lovely it had been to rest in her own bed, even for a night. She lingered a moment longer savoring its comfort. Reluctantly she rose and found her tried and true leather tunic embroidered with the lumbering moose of her house. She had no desire to adorn herself in finery like the many dignitaries in Edonia. She'd save that unpleasant moment for when she absolutely had to. Then and only then would she resign herself to the torturous fate of wearing lace and silk.

Gently closing the door behind her she entered the hall outside her room. Adjacent her room stood her brother's. With a soft touch she pressed his door open to reveal the still sleeping Liam. His light brown wavy hair sat disheveled from a night of tossing and turning. The rhythmic rising and falling of his chest was slow and peaceful. With delicate care Juliet knelt beside him, whispering in his ear.

"See you soon, baby brother. Remember to guard Venhorn while I'm gone."

Planting a small kiss on his cheek, she stepped away from the bed, stealing one last glance before turning down the sunlit hall. It was silent within the keep until she drew near its exit. The sound of gruff voices and busy motion greeted her as she passed outside its vaunted doors. A large grey wall encircled the keep's courtyard. Ancient fortifications of generations past. Looming in the distance towered the vast array of snow capped peaks belonging to the Edon Mountains. Their dark stone like jagged teeth protruded from the ground tearing into the morning sky. Worn and weathered cobblestone made up the surrounding courtyard surface. All around her was filled with commotion as the commanders and captains of Venhorn took final stock of supplies and barked out their orders. Juliet's eyes darted to and fro in anticipation at the prospect of joining such an important journey. From the mass of people came a booming voice calling to her.

"Ah Juls, you've finally risen," said her father separating from the others.

"Yes, because it is so late," she said rolling her eyes.

He returned a toothy smile. "I have something for you. For your journey."

Her ears perked up at the suggestion of a gift. Her father's generosity was not easily earned but when shown it was found to be more than generous. Thegn Oswald reached down into a small pack at his waist. Tenderly he lifted a piece of fabric from the bag.

"This here is a cloak made of dry weave. I've been meaning to give it to you for some time but you're always on the move."

She rolled her eyes again but gestured for him to continue.

"Not a cloak like it in the empire. Keeps you absolutely dry in the rains, warm in the cold, and cool in the heat. It has been in our family for generations. It won't do me any good any more on account of…" Oswald touched his protruding stomach with a chuckle.

"It is more than a fine gift, father," she said taking it in hand. Two golden clasps in the form of stars cinched the dark green cloak to her tunic.

With teary eyes she wrapped her arms around him, taking him aback. "I will miss you."

Oswald laid a gentle hand on her head. "And I you."

He stepped back taking a misty-eyed look at her. "I am so proud of you, Juls. Now, do this old man a favor and listen just a moment," he said as his pale eyes peered into her own. "I've watched you grow from a capable warrior to one of the finest huntresses and rangers Venhorn has seen. Even still what you are about to walk into... Well it's the griffin's lair."

His pale eyes grew stern as if straining for her to understand. "When I told you of the treachery in Edonia yesterday there was one thing I failed to mention. This rot may run as deep as the emperor's inner circle itself. Trust no one. You hear me?"

Juliet hoped her nod was sufficient to convince him that she had. As if satisfied her father cracked a smile once more.

"My own daughter rooting out the greatest threat to the empire in ages. Who would have thought. Send the emperor my regards and tell him more men are on the way."

For some reason as the words left her father's lips the task became more surreal. A hefty weight now tugged on her as she turned toward the stables. It was too late to voice her concern as the horn ordering the men to march bellowed out from the courtyard.

"Looks like it's goodbye for now, Juls," her father said with a sorrowful expression.

She fought the lump in her throat as she turned to join the others on the long march south.

5

OCTAVIAN

C RIMSON LIGHT FROM stained glass windows painted
the throne room floor. A council of advisors had gathered
this day. They wore robes of white silk and elaborate
patterns, a display of the empire's refinement and luxury. Each
advisor stood relieved to hear good news had finally come from the
war with Hunan. The first victory of the empire had been secured.
This fair message was lost to the emperor. His aged and wrinkled
face fixed into a disgusted frown at one detail in particular.

"So it's true," Septimus said with deep disdain. "The pale
skinned Hunans have Edonium."

All stood silent unwilling to bring the wrath of his majesty upon
themselves. No one but Octavian, that is. Octavian cocked his head
fixing one eye on the emperor to his left.

"Even with such weapons Hunan has proven incapable of
standing against your might, Your Majesty."

Septimus let out a snarl. "Just wait until Kaskar gets word of this
or the Northlund folk. Ahhh by my father Septima himself, the
whole of the empire may turn once they know Edonium can be
acquired outside Edonia."

Boldness pressed Octavian to speak again, "But in that sentence
lies the key, Your Majesty. Acquire perhaps, but not fabricate. If we
can find the source of where these weapons come from then we can
stop the leak. In fact Thegn Oswald is sending us someone for the

task, I hear."

"He should have sent someone two months ago," grumbled Septimus. Despite his harsh tone Octavian could see behind the emperor's sapphire eyes that the fire of his rage had cooled.

"See to it that the man who has betrayed his empire is captured soon. He will know the proper treatment for such a betrayal. I don't care how or who does it. Get it done."

The advisors squirmed uncomfortably at the command. All of them knew what fate awaited the man accused of such crimes.

"On to the next bit of business," the emperor said tapping his figures on the armrest of his ebony throne. "Bring him in." In response the grandiose throne room doors swung open, revealing a weary and disheveled Baron Holger. A slight smirk crept up Octavian's face at the Baron's pathetic appearance. Holger cautiously shuffled across the vast room, careful not to catch the gaze of those in his peripherals. His thick brunette hair hung in loose braids to cover his shame and bounced with each plodding step. Dropping to his knees, Holger began to grovel before them all. Octavian found it amusing that the Baron had placed himself on the symbol of the griffin that sat before the throne. Ironically Holger had kneeled at the very spot where a bear laid slain within the mosaic. It stood as the symbol of Bjønen's submission a millennia ago.

"My... my emperor... I beg your pardon... If only I were given more men. I could take back..."

"Enough!!" Septimus roared. His voice pierced the silence that hung over the room.

"You have been given more than any man of your status deserves. When your uncle passed away there were plenty to take his place, but your groveling and gold convinced me you were fit for the task. Yet you cannot even handle a simple peasant rebellion. Not only can you no longer supply me troops for our campaign in Hunan, word has reached me this self-proclaimed John of the Wood now wields your Edonium Blade. I have no more patience for your failures while I deal with threats all across my empire."

A familiar painful silence returned as all awaited the emperor's final judgement. Every eye fixed itself on the downcast baron. Holger's every fiber was trembling now. Octavian struggled to muster any pity for the man. He'd warned the emperor that this day may come. No amount of gold or honey-dipped words could make a man fit to rule. Holger was an obnoxious and arrogant beast, and no amount of gold and flattery could fix that.

"So, what shall I do with this, man?" asked Septimus with a devilish smirk.

None among the advisors dared to voice their opinion. Likely, they feared a similar fate could be pronounced on them one day if they should fail. Only one voice was unafraid to share their council.

"The same way all failure is dealt with, Your Majesty." The cold words left Octavian's lips with ease. He had trained himself all these years to speak without expressing his true feelings of how the empire operated within the presence of the emperor. It was how he survived, how he thrived in such a place. Holger's reaction was instant. Snot and tears mixed in an undignified display of pleading.

"Pick this pathetic creature up off my floor before he stains it with his piss!" Septimus snarled.

A host of guards dressed in crimson armor and white cloaks marched forward. The blubbering Holger fought their grip as they lifted him from the floor.

"Your Majesty, please! I will serve wherever, however, you desire. It need not come to this!"

"Your filth has tainted this empire long enough, and I suspect your greed and ambition will not keep you content for long." With the slight tilt of his head the order was given. How often had Octavian observed the cool calculus of the empire? Too long now. He knew how it always ended. Either bestial panic or violent resistance. Holger seemed to be the latter. The baron reached for the axe at his hip but it only took a blink for the cold steel of the guard's sword to gut him where he stood.

The grotesque gargling of the man reverberated through the decant hall. A strange and juxtaposed scene to the uninitiated of court proceedings in Edonia. Years at the emperor's side had taught Octavian differently. It was acts just like this if not more gruesome that had built the beauty surrounding him. Strength, discipline, intolerance of failure. All of this and more were the violent necessities of power. If you couldn't stomach such things, then prepare to bend the knee or join those already in the grave.

The cold, lifeless eyes of the baron stared up at Octavian as he stood perched beside the emperor. They looked as they if they were still pleading for mercy even in death. Mercy? Holger would find no such thing in this court. Not while this emperor sat upon the throne.

"Get this mess off my floor," the emperor barked.

Just as quickly as the baron had been ushered in, his lifeless body disappeared from their sight.

"I believe that finishes this morning's council," Septimus decreed.

Finally, another voice from the crowd spoke up, "What of Bjønen, Your Majesty?"

"Ahh, yes. The pitiful woodlands to the north. What to do with this John of the Wood?"

The emperor's sapphire eyes flickered across the room until they settled onto Octavian standing at his side.

"This rebellion needs to end, now. I don't need a conflict in the north and the south. There is no other among my advisors I trust more than you. Take what you need and finish this. After you're done pass the title to Holger's cousin, Theodwin, like I should have done many years ago."

Me? Octavian thought. *This could complicate things...*

"Of course, Your Majesty," Octavian replied.

"See, this is a servant you all should follow. I command and he says yes."

The room burst into a series of panicked nods.

"I serve at the pleasure," Octavian said, coolly.

"You are dismissed," Septimus ordered with a causal wave. The room's occupants obeyed with swift motion. The host of the emperor's advisors soon clogged the elaborate doors. Each of them eager to be out from under the emperor's shadow.

"Stay, Octavian."

Octavian turned, giving the emperor a curious look.

"I want to show you something." With no other explanation Septimus stood and retreated behind his throne. The sudden movement left Octavian briefly disoriented. Taking delicate care in smoothing back his silver-streaked hair he followed the emperor who'd now entered a small doorway. Deep shadow clouded the hallway inside. The emperor cared little for visitors to his private chambers and the dark entry created a certain aura of seclusion.

Octavian himself had only visited his majesty twice within these walls and that because of a near fatal sickness some years ago. Octavian could hear the jingling of keys as the emperor moved to unlock a blood red door before them. With a loud click they were granted access. Moving into an octagon shaped room Octavian worked to reorientate himself. Eight walls with eight simple doors lay before them. Guarding each of the doors stood a silent sentinel. Men born and raised within the palace walls. Each of them bred from the beginning of life for one thing, to give sole devotion to the empire and its emperor. Their final commitment to such a grand honor as the emperor's secret guard? Mutilation.

Underneath the silver masks they wore, hideous faces could be found. Both tongue, beauty, and reproduction had been taken from them. No secrets, no vanity, and no passion. Or so the empire had preached to them. Octavian pitied the sorry lot. Standing in their honorary crimson armor, polished and gleaming before his majesty were the sorry husks of men. Their devotion's only reward to serve in a dark room and a life of solitude. Sure, they knew nothing different but what a world they missed outside of these oppressive halls.

Septimus approached the door resting northwest of them. Without word the guard moved to the side allowing Septimus to pass. With another rattle of keys the door unlocked and the two of them pressed further in. The paranoia of the emperor had grown over the years since the death of his wife and the departure of his daughter.

Whereas his chambers once sat with a luxurious view of the Edon River, now he preferred the dark and dank dwellings underneath the palace. A spiral staircase lit by torchlight led them deeper underneath the grounds above. Cool air welcomed them as they descended, leaving Octavian with a shiver running up his spine. It felt as though each step led them further into the mouth of a beast. The slick, wet walls like a throat closing in on them the further they went.

After some time, the stairs ended leading them to one single door within a small waiting room. The door was made of bronze and encrusted with glimmered flecks of Edonium. A metal so precious men would sell all they had just for one sliver. Here in the palace it had been used for decoration with little thought to its value. Just another show to all of Edonia's wealth and power. Octavian heard the sound of one last lock being opened, revealing the elaborate chambers of the emperor.

Gold, silver, and crimson covered every corner of the room. A bed that could fit a family rested with a canopy draped above it. Crimson sheets lined with gold were neatly laid as its dressing. An oversized tub sat in the corner of the room. Surrounding it was every fine perfume and spice one could obtain within the world of the empire. A host of robes and attire lined another wall. Garments set for each occasion. While the room was ornate because of all the exotic decor that filled it, it left one with the sense of disorder. Things that should be displayed within the grandest quarters sat carelessly on the floor. Clothes, books, and other objects sat scattered across tables in an unorganized heap.

The emperor showed little care for the mess as he moved quickly toward a wall to their right. A smattering of portraits and objects of unknown significance hung on it. Reaching toward a small painting the emperor lifted the image and suddenly the wall whisked away.

"Few men in their lives have seen this place. Even fewer live to tell of it," came the emperor's voice in a deadly serious tone.

"What… what is this place, Your Majesty?" Octavian asked, stuttering.

"Come." With that the emperor turned, taking a small torch in hand that had rested within the hidden chamber. A blast of cold, damp, air whipped across Octavian's face from the tunnel opening. Slick, grimy rock replaced finely plastered walls within the tunnel's confines. It wasn't long before a faint light could be seen up ahead. Without warning the emperor extinguished the torch as the two of them reached the tunnel's end. With breathless wonder Octavian found himself entering a massive cavern.

Stalactites fifteen feet long hung from the ceiling above, like sharp needled teeth ready to devour its prey. An underground lake was present to his left. Its frigid, dark waters a still sheet of glass. The sounds of a blacksmith's shop reverberated off the cavern's walls and Octavian could see the faint glow of a smelting fire. More incredible than the hidden cavern was the amount of Edonium piled up before him. Enough to make at least fifty pure Edonium Blades.

"It's… incredible," Octavian whispered.

The emperor gave him a bemused look. The kind only bred with familiarity to the spectacular.

"There is something else I wanted to show you," Septimus said turning toward a descending path.

Following like a child in wonder, Octavian descended the small zig zag path to the cavern floor. Passing through the stacks of Edonium they reached an area with a few blacksmiths hard at work. Their blackened faces were marked with an 'e' displaying their slave status. As Octavian moved among them a few shot unmoved glances at their unexpected visitor. In each of their hands were the typical tools of their trade. The simplicity of the operation took Octavian aback. Was there no secret equipment to forge such mighty weapons? As if reading his thoughts the emperor spoke, "Our enemies for so long have tried to conjure up some way to forge an Edonium weapon. All manner of tools and sacrifice have been made in countless vain pursuits."

A smug look crossed the emperor's face. As the smiths returned to their work Octavian suddenly heard a faint murmur leave the men's lips. They were singing, no not singing. It was something different, a rhythmic tune like song but firm in its command.

"It is the power of the ancient tongue that can forge such a blade. When such commands of the old tongue are wielded correctly that is."

Words? Octavian thought. *What kind of madness is that?*

"You're telling me countless men have given their lives to forge such blades and all they needed to do was know a few magic words?"

The emperor began to burst into a raucous laugh, "So simple, isn't it? Mere words having that kind of power."

Calming himself, Septimus met the eyes of Octavian. "But it is not merely words spoken. It is how they are released and who is releasing them. The simple utterance can forge nothing. It is the force, one may even say the belief, that drives them."

"Belief?" scoffed Octavian. "What belief?"

Septimus gave him that bemused look again.

"Come, there is one last thing you must see," Septimus said waving Octavian onward.

Shuffling past the heat of the forge the emperor moved to the far end of the cavern. As he approached, faint runes sparked to life in the shape of a door across the cavern's blackened wall. Octavian watched as Septimus stepped forward, stone melting away to reveal another chamber. Not wanting to fall behind or be left alone in such a strange place, Octavian chased after his emperor. They now stood to Octavian's amazement in the largest library he had ever seen. Shelves of books stretched beyond sight nestled into cold stone. He could just make out in the far distance shelves of wood merging with those carved from the cavern's walls. As if the library itself expanded in layers.

"Here lies the knowledge of the ages. Every record that has been written under the sun. No event, reign, or disaster unrecorded," Septimus said waving with a grand gesture.

Octavian was speechless. What could one say to such a place? Without waiting for a response, the emperor moved to a small wooden table near the closest shelf of books. Octavian remained a moment to drink in the sight. What the library lacked in sophistication it more than made up for in size. Yet, its low ceiling and cramped selves still left one feeling more than a little claustrophobic. Beside the table where the emperor had seated himself stood a brittle woman. Her aged face was streaked with wrinkles and the skin hung loose from her cheeks. As Octavian approached, the woman bowed in reverence.

"It has been some time, Your Majesty," the woman said. Drawing near, Octavian could see that the woman was blind. Her grey hair was pulled tightly back into a bun and her faded white robes clung loosely to her sagging skin. No doubt she was a librarian of sorts but her blindness astonished him.

"Did you find it?" Septimus asked. An assumption that revealed the emperor had planned this moment.

For what reason? Octavian mused.

With a polite bow of the head the woman presented an ancient-looking tome. Septimus gently set the fragile pages on the nearby table. A cloud of dust puffed into the air causing Octavian to stifle a cough. Delicately, Septimus turned the browned pages until he found what he was looking for. With a motion of the hand he ushered Octavian to his side. Peering over the emperor's shoulder a strange and horrifying image captured Octavian's attention. Within the tome was drawn an elaborate illustration. It was of a foul looking creature, the color of blackened smoke that welded dagger like teeth. Its silver eyes shone through the page with glee as it prepared to devour a host of men.

"What is that monstrosity?" Octavian asked.

"He is an ancient creature. Far more ancient than the empire itself," replied Septimus.

An eerie silence hung over them as Octavian found himself unable to look away from the horrifying image.

"He was a man...once. One of the first men in fact. Given great power and purpose by the First King of our world. Yet the tales say it was not enough. He along with six other rulers of the world reigned in peace over the kingdoms of men. They shared a common tongue that held power over the very fabric of creation itself. But Maluuk grew discontent with the limits to his power. Fear gripped him in his old age. You see, all men fade from this world when their time has come, but Maluuk was not ready to face that hour. Legend spoke of hidden pools of water scattered across the world. Water that had been blessed by the First King with the power of unending life. It was told that the first to drink of these waters could possess the ability to offer it to others."

Octavian stared at the emperor in disbelief. Why had Septimus brought him here? Why show him these fanciful tales?

The emperor continued, "Maluuk ignored the other restrictions in the legend. Only one was said to be worthy of this power and that it was the First King alone who should wield it. It was said any other who possessed it would poison this gift to men, turning them into creatures shaped after their base appetites. Ignoring such warnings Maluuk set off to find this hope of immortality. Decades of bloodshed, lies, and betrayal finally led him to what he was seeking. With the discovery of the pools of life he was able to claim immortality for himself. With such a power in hand his ambition grew and soon after he moved to overthrow the other kings of old."

The emperor breathed in deep as he flipped over the page revealing a new set of images. "For many ages the race of men either partook of Maluuk's gift joining in his ranks or were made enslaved by him. That is until the blessing of Edonium was revealed. Men enslaved to the mines of Edon were given a new source of power. Maluuk in his greed sought to use this new resource to secure his reign forever. Little did he know it was the one thing that could undo it. With the ancient words remaining in their hearts the people of Edonia began to forge weapons that could stand against this Felled King. Thus, my ancestors rose up to lead the world against Maluuk. They named the weapons born from their labor Dawn Blades. Weapons to usher in a new day like the days of the First King. With them they rebelled against the forces of Maluuk. Little by little Maluuk and his darkness was beaten back until the foul creature was forced to retreat into the far shadows of the world. The warriors of Edonia were heralded as the saviors of men and so we were."

Septimus turned to a new page once more, sending a fresh cloud of dust into the air.

"The reign of Edonia was a golden age. For nearly a thousand years all lands prospered. Some even prophesied that the First King would come again through their reign, but as you know well our empire has receded like the tide. Little by little our strength has waned. Men no longer sought to be ruled by us, to their detriment."

The emperor closed the book with force, shutting away the image of an ancient map of the empire. A testament to its once expansive reach.

"It's why I must show no mercy to men like Holger. They are a disease to our once ancient glory."

Octavian stood silent for a moment before speaking, "I understand your harshness to the baron, Your Majesty. What I don't understand is why you are telling me these fantasies? Do you truly believe these myths and legends? Is it not all propaganda of the empire?"

The emperor's face grew still. "I… I once thought them mythical stories myself. But this shadow that encroaches on us. Does it not feel different? The waning of our great empire is just the thing this Maluuk could be waiting for. If he isn't the instigator himself."

For the first time in his life Octavian could see fear behind the sapphire eyes of the emperor. It caused him to take a step back.

"Your Majesty, you're just weary. Kingdoms rebel. They grow tired of tax and labor. It is the woes of empire. Hunan's rebellion and all the others are nothing special."

"I don't need words to tickle my ears, Octavian. I brought you to this sacred place for a reason. No one but the emperor and those sworn never to leave this cavern have witnessed what you see now, not in a thousand years. I brought you here to witness it. To see that a place like this can make the myths and the legends seem more possible. It can cause one to believe there is something more in this world than the cold calculated will of men."

"Perhaps more possible, Your Majesty, but not less fanciful."

"Perhaps," Septimus said, growing visibly weary. "But even after men have taken the truth and forged their own purposes from it, its residue remains."

"The empire makes its own truth, does it not? One built on blood, wealth, and strength. That is the truth, Your Majesty."

Septimus let out a calloused laugh. "You've stayed in my council too long, old friend. Even you believe the propaganda."

Senile old man, I am not your friend. I speak the truth. You and your ilk have carved up the world and now you don't want to pay the price, thought Octavian. Instead, he said nothing.

"Come, I suppose you've listened to the wild rantings of an aged emperor long enough."

Indeed I have, Octavian thought, following Septimus in silence.

Turning back to the door they moved out from the ancient library and back into the massive cavern. Runes sparked behind them closing off the sacred tomes behind stone once more. The sounds of the forge resumed as they passed it by. They brushed past Edonium and ascended the path carved into the dark stone of the cavern. At the top Octavian stopped for one last glance at the mystical place. Surely, the legends couldn't be true? Drinking in the scene he felt a small bit of doubt seep in. If a place like this existed, what else could be true?

No, he thought shaking away the feeling. *I won't get sucked into a delusional scapegoat for this empire.*

With that he turned to start the journey back to the hall above.

Stopping mid-pace Octavian's mind raced as he stared down at the empty parchment resting on the table. What was he to do? The hours of reflection now ate away at his earlier confidence. Ancient evil, Dawn Blades, and the complete trust of the emperor? Was he putting them all at risk? No, he must continue. He knew the emperor trusted him. That was his plan all these decades. Trust. A knot formed in his stomach as the word endlessly churned in his mind. Could he really do it? Could he really betray the emperor?

In all his years of captivity he had been treated well. At least once he was seen as valuable. The evening so long ago now flooded his mind for the thousandth time. Flames licked at the walls with the wails of women haunting the night. Flashes of steel and pain like hasty strokes of a paint brush blurred his vision. His mother's brunette strands bloody in his hands. His father fighting to the last breath before a spear was driven into his chest. Octavian could still hear the gasp leave his father's lips as he fell limp to the ground. What happened next was a flurry of broken images. Men bearing the griffin sigil grabbing him as he fought. His home nestled in the mountains of Mascar burning in the distance as he was ushered away.

He hated this dreaded empire and all it had stolen from him. His was the cry of an untold number throughout the ages. Only now, he had the power to do something about it. To repay this emperor and empire for all they had done. A tinge of guilt rose within him once more. The wrinkled face of Septimus and his sapphire eyes peering into his own. Septimus was the man who had taken everything from him in the empire's pursuit to keep Mascar. Yet, he was also the man who first noticed Octavian's cunning and skill. Septimus had allowed Octavian to rise above the rest simply on merit. He'd even went so far as to hide Octavian's foreign identity so no questions would arise. The emperor was also the man who trusted Octavian with his children and now his grandson. Could he really betray that man?

Octavian balled his fists to stop them from shaking. Another image arose in his mind. It was the face of his parents. Their pale eyes crying for justice. Justice for the life robbed from them. Their silent petition was the resolve he needed. Taking a deep breath, he put ink to parchment. Thoughts of the life that could have been theirs fueled his strokes. A life stolen from him. Vengeance was finally at the door, and it was time to let it in. Stopping with a flick of his quill he paused to read the last line.

The time is now. It read. And so it was.

6

JOHN OF THE WOOD

SUNBEAMS GLISTENED off the golden hilt in John's hand. Its craftsmanship was beyond compare. The face of a snarling bear rested in the center of its gold tinted cross guard. Dark brown leather weaved itself around the smooth metal to provide its user grip. John's eyes followed down to the pummel where a bear paw was imprinted in the fine metal. It was a weapon few others in history had possessed, and now it was his.

Only the most powerful of men in Edonia wielded an Edonium Blade. A strategy of the elite to instill fear and dominance over commoners. There was Iron Fang wielded by Oswald of Venhorn, Edon's Bane belonging to Lucian of Kaladin, Raven's Claw for Volkmar of Varnas, Phoenix Flame the weapon of Duke Arthur of Fenikia, and Griffin's Dread held by the emperor himself. And now there was him. John of the Wood, common man from Laketon, possessor of Bear Paw.

"I'm starting to get jealous of the way you look at that sword," said Maggie breaking him from his trance.

With only a slight agitation he slid the glowing sword back into its sheath. The world seemed strangely dimmer now that the faint light of the blade was gone.

"Don't worry Maggs, she's the second prettiest lady in my life."

Her caramel eyes smiled at the compliment. "So what do you think? Should we make our move?"

John turned his attention past the woods that surrounded them to the city walls in the distance. From the small outcropping of rock and pine in which he hid, he could just make out Baron Holger's home, Bjønen. Bjønen remained the only major city left within Edonia to still keep a wooden palisade rather than stone fortifications, an over confidence by the rulers of the city. Nestled away far within the empire's interior who would consider it a target? Now its pride would become its downfall.

"We can light a section of the wall on fire and repair it quick enough for our own defenses," John said examining the structure.

"That is if we can keep the fire under control," Maggie muttered. "Still we don't want to scare the people, John. They need to know we are their liberators, not the next iron-fisted ruler."

She was right. Shantz, why was she always right? he thought.

"It can never be simple, can it?"

"With you?" she smirked.

John took another long look at the city fortifications. The whole of their forces rested close by ready for his order. The time to attack would come soon but everything must be perfect. Perhaps one more day of scouting would reveal the weakness they needed. That's when he heard the loud blast of mourning bells. A large tower peeking over the city's defenses began to play its sorrowful tune. A chorus of horn blows confirmed the occasion and suddenly things became very clear. Just beyond the tree line headed toward the city moved a large caravan. Ebony banners flapped in the wind atop a host of black-robed travelers.

"Is that what I think it is?" Maggie asked.

Leading the procession was a large wooden casket. Draped across it was the banner of Holger's clan. The sigil of a mighty black bear.

"That can't be him?" Maggie said, astonished.

Just then Huldwin came breaking from the woods behind. "Sir, the scouts just south of us report the funeral is for the baron. Apparently his trip south ended differently than he had hoped."

"I'd say," John grinned. "Prepare the men. We strike now."

Both Huldwin and Maggie stared in disbelief. "Are you two deaf?"

"It's just, sir. It is against all sacred laws to attack a city in mourning."

"Shantz, Huldwin, are you dimwitted? This is the perfect opportunity. The city's gates will be wide open and her defenses down."

Maggie gulped but rallied to his aid. "He's not wrong, Huldwin. We may not have another opportunity like this, but…"

"The men won't like it," Huldwin complained.

"Their feelings will recover, especially once they find themselves the new rulers of Bjønen."

With a hesitant nod Huldwin departed to give the order.

"Remind me to find a new captain when this is over, Maggs. Huldwin has proven his cowardice is stronger than his courage."

"He has been loyal to you since the beginning, John, and I happen to share his concern."

John's eyes hardened as they met hers.

"The way you come to power matters. If you want the people of Bjønen to see you as legitimate you need to honor their laws," Maggie said extending a hand to the city before them.

John spit out a disgruntled noise. "It's those very laws I'm trying to destroy, Maggs. The laws placed by powerful men who only care for themselves. As for the people? They respect power, and I have that right here," he said patting the sword at his hip.

"Do you not hear the contradiction in terms, John? If anything, you sound like Holger."

He fought the swell of rage at her words. "The baron was a fat, greedy monster. He used his power to benefit himself. I know what it's like to live under men like him. So don't you ever question my motives for the people. I know what it is to be one of them!"

He felt a tinge of guilt as his anger receded. Maggie gave no reply but from the flushing of her cheeks he knew he had hurt her. Opening his mouth he was going to speak again but the sound of troops coming stole his attention. It was Huldwin with a few hundred men ready for battle. Putting aside their tension, John stepped forward to address the men.

"Men of the Wood! Our time has come. Now, some of you may

feel an unease at what we are about to do. But make no mistake, we are doing Bjønen and all under her charge a favor."

A stillness hung over them as they listened to his words. Many faces still carried a sense of unease.

"Listen! How many of you have loved ones resting in an unmarked grave because of that man?" John asked pointing to the funeral procession. "How many of you have grieved a thousand times over the lives, homes, and lands stolen from you because of Holger?"

A faint murmur rose from the watching faces.

"Now is our time to get some solace for all that man wrought. Bjønen and its ruling family may grieve a little today but let them taste the sorrow we have endured for decades."

A rallying cry now reverberated through the crowd. John's face broke into a smirk at the reaction. For a brief moment he caught the caramel eyes of Maggie beside him. Hers were not so impressed by his rousing speech. Regardless, she would come around. Now it was time for vengeance. Withdrawing Bear Paw he raised the Edonium Blade high above his head.

"For a new day and a new dawn!"

The men echoed his cry and with that they were ready. It didn't take long before the funeral procession reached the city gate. Its fortifications now stood wide open to receive the mourners and, unwittingly, a rebellion. With the signal horn blaring John and the others rushed from the tree line making haste for the vulnerable gate. Panic quickly spread across the funeral procession as they saw John and his men approach. The city's warning bells now rang in his ears giving him more motivation to quicken his pace.

Just as they drew near to the main gate, archers perched in wooden towers above loosed their arrows. A few of John's men collapsed from the fire, arrows protruding from their now still forms. John barked an order to return fire sending a few of Bjønen's defenders to an early grave. The panicked mass of the funeral procession frantically fought one another for entry into the city. Their panicked state worked in John's favor as the city guards were unable to seal John's men out with the crowd rushing in. John felt a self-satisfied smirk creep onto his face. It was all working just as he had hoped.

He and his fighting men weaved their way into the huddled mass taking care to only slay those who opposed them. Like water bursting through a dam, John and his fighting force soon found themselves breaking into the city in an unorganized stream. A smattering of guards rallied into loose formation to oppose the city's invaders. Expressions of pure malice painted their faces. John rushed toward the unorganized force loosing Bear Paw upon its first victim. Those who didn't fall by his hand fled deeper into the city. Giving chase through frantic streets John led his force after them.

One fool who chose to oppose him found out how deadly Bear Paw truly was. John didn't even try to dodge the man's blow. Instead he carelessly raised his Edonium Blade, watching it sheer the guard's weapon in two. It only took another heartbeat before the fight was over, leaving John's opponent as a lifeless corpse on Bjønen's trodden street. Bear Paw sung in his hand at the victory secured. John felt an energy radiate up his arm from the weapon, giving him a sense of endless vigor.

This is what true power feels like, he thought in awe.

Two more guards soon met a swift end by his hand before they could even react. Their armor and flesh melted like wax before the Edonium Blade. As more of the earlier procession fled into the city their panic soon spread across every side street and alley. John watched as families abandoned store fronts and belongings in an attempt to find safety. His men had been given strict orders not to touch the commoners, but John feared battle fury may soon take over if things didn't end quickly.

This in mind he pressed forward cutting down the few remaining guards in his path. Giving the order for his forces to continue deeper into Bjønen John paused hoping to catch sight of Maggie. The slight terror that something might have happened to her soon faded as she came into view. He found her a few streets behind kneeling beside a weeping child. Her face was serene as she tried to calm the boy who was crying out for his mother. Seeing him approach, Maggie shot John a cold expression as she took the young boy in her arms.

"Can... can I help?" John asked.

Softly shushing the boy Maggie looked up at him. "I think you've done enough helping these people today already, John. Just go finish this." He didn't appreciate the calloused tone in which she said the words.

"How did you think this would end, Maggs? You knew from the beginning our plans to take Bjønen from the Baron and his ilk. You even suggested an attack!"

Her soft face hardened as she peered into his eyes. "Our plan was to kill Holger and rescue Bjønen, not terrorize its people."

He shook his head in frustration. How could he explain it? Everything had a cost. To kill Holger would just allow another of his kin to sit on Bjønen's seat of power. All of it needed to be uprooted. A new order had to be installed and John? Well, why should he not have a say in it all. Without him uttering any of it, Maggie's eyes read his every thought. He'd shared them with her hundreds of times before.

"Don't let the reality of it all stop you now, Maggs. We are so close."

"Go, John. I'll take care of the mess you leave behind."

It wasn't the words he wanted to hear but there was no more time to sit and argue. What would it change anyways? Jumping swiftly to his feet he weaved his way through the timber homes and cobbled streets until he reached the frontlines of the conflict. The battle had come to where all roads in Bjønen led, a single open square in the heart of the city. Resting at the back of the empty square was a humble looking keep. Its oak beams curved into the shape of a steeple that towered over the conflict. The building was a relic of a time when the vast expanse of the empire hadn't yet occurred. A small row of protruding spikes had been erected around the keep in an effort to stall an invasion. Perhaps John's rebellion had made Holger paranoid after all.

Approaching his men, John found Huldwin standing by with the others for their next set of orders. Behind the keep's thrown together defenses paced the remaining city guard. Their makeshift armor made of scavenged plate and ragged furs no longer felt intimidating to a man wielding an Edonium Blade. John could see leading the city guard was a man distinguished from the rest. He donned a long drooping beard that hung down to his chest. Within its braids were woven elaborate beads of various metals. His coarse brown hair and tattooed face told the tale of a seasoned warrior. In his thick and sinewy arms was a heavy two-handed axe. The man's dark eyes planted in his stern face met John's.

"John of the Wood, you dare defile this day?" the grizzled leader bellowed.

"Theodwin, come to take your cousin's throne so quickly?" John mocked in return.

"A throne that was rightfully mine from the beginning," Theodwin said, in a low growl.

"That may be an issue between us." John said, raising Bear Paw for Theodwin to see.

"Take your filthy commoner paws off that sword."

"See, that's the problem with you lot. That word 'commoner' - you say it like it's an insult." A satisfied smirk crept onto John's face knowing Theodwin had given him the moment he so desired. Lifting his voice John spoke over the sound of the masses so the surrounding homes could hear.

"People of Bjønen, for too long your rulers have seen you as lesser folk. As if you existed to serve them! I am here to tell you a new day has arrived. One where you, the people, will have one of your own to lead you. Not as a tyrant or a cruel master but a friend. A commoner just like you."

John could see the peering eyes now springing from their windows as they looked onto the city square.

"Search for yourselves. We have not harmed any who did not raise a weapon against us. We are here as liberators not raiders."

"Sir," came the interrupting voice of Huldwin.

"What is it, Huldwin! Can't you see I am in the middle of rallying this city to our side?" John hissed. The glory of the moment faded with each heartbeat.

"There is something you need to see, now."

"Truly? It cannot wait?"

Bursting onto the scene came the deep and menacing laugh of Theodwin.

"What's so funny?" John snarled.

"You. Little 'John of the Wood' thought he could make a name for himself. Don't you know, John? Stick your neck out and its sure to be chopped."

"What are you on about?"

"I may know, sir." said Huldwin nervously.

Real dread now washed over John. "What is it?" he asked in a whisper.

"You'll want to see for yourself," Huldwin said nodding his head toward the city gate.

Quietly John skirted away from the prying eyes of the city and followed Huldwin back through the corpse strewn streets to the gate. An eerie hush had fallen over his men as he passed them by. What could have crushed their spirits on such a momentous day? He soon reached the palisade. Below it Maggie waited leaning against the base of a watcher's tower. In her caramel eyes John could see dread swirling.

"Maggs, what is it?"

"They're here, John."

"Who's here?"

"Edonia."

His whole body went numb. How was that possible? Without thinking he flew up the rickety ladder desperate to see the truth for himself. Reaching the watchman's platform he stared out and onto the open plain. Spreading across the vast farmland stood a host of two thousand fully armored soldiers of Edonia, each with a Light Bringer dangling at their hip. The banner of the Griffin, the mark that had brought terror to untold number, now had come for him. He felt the terrified presence of Maggie take its place by his side. Both of them gazed at the sight of their impending doom.

"What do we do, John?" she asked.

For the first time, in a long time, he had no answer.

7

LEO

A SLIGHT YAWN ESCAPED Leo's mouth as he stared out at the throng of spires below. Perched atop a palace tower he felt the cool wind brush across his face. Rays of the sun's warmth burst through floating clouds above. He loved days like today. The weather was balmy making it a perfect outing to bask in the noonday sun. The city of Varnas teemed with life beneath him. Men scurried through the streets like tiny ants among the ebony buildings. Just across the glistening Raven River swayed an endless sea of pines. Drinking it all in, he drew in another breath of the fresh air.

Allowing his gaze to wander it eventually settled onto Varnas' port. More than two dozen ships sat docked and ready to take his family and all his father's fighting men to Edonia. Battle never had appealed to Leo. Why send those you love so far away to never return? Could talking not bring peace? Were adults that unreasonable? He would have thought his father one of those unreasonable men not long ago, but something had changed.

Ever since he had taken a stand against his father's harsh treatment things had become strangely different. The duke had even taken the time to visit one of his sparring matches. Leo remained unconvinced on how long it would last, but he would enjoy it while he could. A deep sounding horn bellowed from the harbor. Its haunting tune engulfed the city. It signaled that Varnas' army would be departing soon. Loved ones would be standing teary eyed as they watched their beloveds sail off to war.

Varnas' docks would soon be turned into a place of grief. It was something he wished to avoid until the bitter end. Partly because the journey would be one of excitement and adventure for him, and he wanted nothing to dampen that. His last journey to Edonia had been several years ago. Only faint images remained of the trip in his mind. But what did still took his breath away. Enormous towers that never ended. Structures of unrivaled craftsmanship. Libraries so full of books one would die before reading a third of their wares. To see the undying city once more caused his pulse to rise in anticipation. Being the emperor's grandson had perks of its own. No place was off limits, at least for the most part. He would be given priority wherever they went. No waiting like the common folk he'd seen crowding the streets. His mother had warned him not to let it all go to his head when they arrived, but how could he not? They were different and there was no reason to deny that fact.

"Sir Leo, I suspected I would find you here," came the voice of Crumwald behind him.

Slight agitation gripped Leo as he recovered from the startling voice. He quickly pushed it away and turned to face the old man. Crumwald leaned against the frame of the tower's slender doorway. Behind him was nothing but blue skies. An expression of restlessness exuded from Crumwald as he tapped his foot impatiently.

"Does my mother request to see me?" Leo asked.

Crumwald bowed courteously before speaking. "Yes, it is time for the royal family's departure."

Leo rose to his feet, dusting off his black trousers. "Give me one moment and I'll be right down."

"Do hurry, young master. Your mother impressed upon me that this was an urgent request."

Of course she did, thought Leo. He gave an obedient nod to Crumwald to satisfy the man. Accomplishing his task, Crumwald scurried off, likely to fulfill a whole list of other tasks. Leo stood alone once more on the tower's perch. He found himself drinking in the view of his home one last time. Who knew when such a perfect day would come around again? The weather of Varnas was much like the attitude of his father. One day temperate, another stormy.

Turning with a sigh he made his way down the spiraling stairs after Crumwald. He reached the first of many connecting platforms that ran between the two highest peaks in the palace. It was there that something caught his eye. A door sat slightly ajar within the narrow corridor. It was a room reserved for his father's private messenger birds. By his father's command it was ordered to remain locked at all times. Leo never understood the restriction. It was just birds? What could they do? Leave a few droppings in the palace? It might do the place some good he chuckled to himself. Besides a servant could clean it up easily enough.

Now curious he took a step toward the open door. Perhaps there was more to this room than his father had let on? Scanning the corridor he saw no guard or servant in view. Carefully he crept toward the opening, barely peeking inside. He could make out nothing impressive from its contents just metal cages housing several of Varnas' famously trained ravens. The door creaked ever so slightly as he opened it further. If anyone asked, he just wanted to see the ravens.

The room stank of droppings and stale hay. The beady eyes of the midnight-colored birds followed him as he meandered through their dwelling. Maybe there was no mystery after all? Just as he turned to leave, a black raven swooped in from a small window. Trained to perfection the bird perched itself onto a handle just above a reading desk. Wrapped ever so carefully around its leg was a scroll impressed with the emperor's seal.

Now that was interesting. Extending a cautious hand, he gripped the parchment. His eyes met the dark pits of the raven's. It stared at him expectant of Leo to release the binding around its leg. With tender yet shaky hands he loosened the tightly woven strap, freeing the raven of its burden. The raven cawed in satisfaction before flapping over to a nearby cage. Leo turned his attention to the note. In his hands was a message sent from the emperor's palace itself. The urge to open it churned within him. The wrath of his father was sure to come but was he not going to rule someday himself? The same blood ran through his veins. In fact, his was a superior breed. Not only was he born from the house of Varnas, but he also had the emperor's bloodline within him.

Looking down at the seal made of cherry red clay marked by a griffin, he made his decision. With a satisfying crack the seal broke. He rolled the parchment across the reading desk clamping down the edges with a nearby weight. It took all his schooling to pool together the message.

Midnight,
Have the A ready when you arrive in Edonia.

"The A?" he asked aloud. He put the question behind him as he quickly scanned the rest.

There has been a development of great interest you will want to know of once you arrive. I have made all necessary preparations here. All that awaits is your arrival. Make haste for we may not have another opportunity like this. Our hour has come. The time is now.

"What was this about? Preparations for the war with Hunan?"

Something felt off. The letter itself remained unmarked by a signature. A clamor of muffled voices suddenly came from the corridor outside the door. In a clumsy panic Leo tucked the letter into his tunic and dashed out of the room. He just managed to quietly shut the door as Crumwald turned the corner. This time accompanied by his mother. A look of disapproval painted her slender face.

"See I told you the boy was still up here," sighed Crumwald.

"Leo, we are going to be late. You know how your father gets when things don't go precisely how he envisions."

"Yes, mother I was just... I was just taking in a final view of the city. You never know when it could be your last."

The two of them stared quizzically at each other. It took all Leo's strength to fight the blush he felt creeping up his neck. Being late was one thing but sneaking where he didn't belong…

"Morbid," Crumwald said shaking his head.

"I cannot for the life of me understand where you get some of these things," Beatrice said shaking her head. "Come, child."

She extended an arm to her side. A command more than a gesture. Leo knew not to test her grace any further as he scurried to take his place beside her. Glancing up, he could see one of his mother's eyes probing him. How he desired to tell her the truth. Of anyone she would understand, maybe even applaud him if the note turned out to be of importance. But he knew now was not the time. It needed to be in secret and a place where they had privacy. He would wait and soon enough the opportunity would come.

Days upon the Crystal River had finally brought them to the mouth of the mighty Edon. The fair weather in Varnas had thankfully followed them on their journey. Leo leaned against the ship's railing, observing the glistening water flow steadily beneath. The tranquil waters and picturesque scene of the countryside had taken his breath away. Just upon the horizon he could see the peaks of the Edon Mountains rising into view like tiny, razored teeth just beginning to spring free. Soon the vast city of Edonia would greet them. Its outskirts were a welcoming parade that lasted for hours before their final destination. Not many had the privilege afforded to them to dock in the royal harbors.

Looking up from the river Leo glanced around the deck of the vessel. Sailors busied themselves with routine work. Upon a tiered deck his father was busy mulling over final arrangements with his commander, Rowan. They likely discussed the sending of Varnas' army and all the logistics that would follow. Leo found himself gulping as he worked to muster up the courage to speak with his mother. In the following days no opportunity had shown itself to reveal the secret letter he'd found. That was until now.

The Duchess was refreshing herself privately within her quarters after a taxing day of travel. He knew this was his best chance, yet a strange apprehension kept him from moving. What if his mother was angry with him for sneaking where he shouldn't? What if she told his father? More than anything one question haunted his mind. What if the note was something more sinister? What if it was a code for darker purposes? A small wave lapped against the ship's side causing him to stumble. Glancing around, Leo brushed himself off pretending to be unshaken.

I must act no matter what. It's what a good ruler would do, he thought.

Balling his fists he embraced the courage needed to act. With an air of false confidence, he strode across the deck. Sailors stopped and smirked at the young boy walking with such a stride. He dodged their glances knowing one look might send the fragile strength he'd found slipping away. Just as he reached the door that led below the ship a voice cried out to him.

"Leo, my boy."

Leo's eyes looked above him to the raised platform overhead. A grinning Volkmar peered down at him.

"Come up here a moment," his father said, with a wave of the hand.

All Leo's newfound courage waned at the beckoning. Perhaps his father had found out. With a sullen march, Leo ascended the stairs to his left taking his place at his father's side. To his disbelief the duke wrapped a comforting arm around his shoulder.

"It's a beautiful day isn't it, Leo?"

"Uh… yes, Father. It is."

Volkmar gave him a quizzically look. "Why the apprehension, son? Don't you know Edonia draws near? Has the grand city given you some anxiety?"

So he doesn't know, thought Leo relieved. "Yes, I suppose so."

"Well, fear not. Edonia intimidates many. It can be a dangerous place when its leaders are... distracted."

Was he speaking ill of grandfather? Leo wondered. He found his voice. "Does Grandfather have something weighing on him?" he asked.

Volkmar's face morphed slightly. Leo wasn't sure if it was anger or something else.

"Your grandfather is a busy man. I only mean that it's not possible for him to know all the affairs that happen beneath him. Especially in times of war."

Volkmar's eyes focused on Leo now. "We are going to help fix Edonia, my boy. It has been many years since I thought that possible but now..." His father trailed off, not finishing the thought.

What did he mean by fix? What was wrong with Edonia? Was the war doing something to his grandfather? Surely Hunan could do little harm to the might of the empire?

"Are the tides of battle not in our favor? Will Varnas' army help?" Leo prodded.

Volkmar face creased into a weak smile. "Yes, I do believe our army will help. Edonia will be rid of what plagues it soon enough."

An uncomfortable silence hung between them. His father's eyes fixed on the tiny sliver of white now coming into view. It was likely the reflection of their final stop before Edonia. The outpost known as River Watch. Volkmar sucked in a breath of air.

"I'm proud of the boy you've become, Leo. Ever since... well it's best not to talk about such things. I just hope you are proud to call me your father. I know I've been harsh on you, but it is only because I believed you needed it in order to fulfill our destiny. You weren't what I expected in a son, but I see growth in you."

What a strange statement, Leo mused, not taking his gaze from the growing fortress ahead. Since when did his father care what he thought? Volkmar's lavender eyes met Leo's. A sense of sincerity Leo had never felt before stirred behind them.

"Of... of course, Father."

Volkmar turned to look over the horizon once more, now possessing a content expression.

"Go on. I know you wish to speak with your mother."

A blush gripped Leo as new wave of panic washed over him. *Did he know after all?* Leo fought to keep panic from showing as he gave an obedient nod. As fast as stealth would allow, he descended the stairs and moved once more to the door that led below the ship. As it shut behind him, he clutched his chest. Taking deep breaths, he wrestled to ward off the anxiety that threatened to swallow him.

He doesn't know. He just saw me coming down here. It's logical, Leo, he said to himself. Still several moments passed before the beating of his heart lessened. Underneath the deck he could feel the magnified swaying of the ship. He used its gentle rocking as a calming presence he sorely needed. That rocking wasn't so calming for others. As he turned the corner he was met by the ailing face of Crumwald. The normally pale skin of the man had become a shade whiter. With unsteady hands he propped himself up against a passageway wall.

"Young master," Crumwald said with a nauseated bow.

A sick enjoyment came over Leo at the sight. The normally proud and proper Crumwald reduced to such a form was humorous indeed. Seeing the flicker of enjoyment in Leo's face Crumwald's own expression darkened.

"Are you here to visit your mother?" he asked with a bit of annoyance now in his tone.

"I am," Leo said fighting the smile that yearned to burst onto his face.

"Go on then. Though she specifically requested no visitors." Crumwald's eyes sharpened to warn Leo not to make this an extended visit. With that Leo squirmed past the hunched advisor and made his way to the decorated door behind him. Golden edging surrounded carved ravens on the ornate door. Placing a hand on its handle Leo pushed it open. He was greeted by the light of a dozen flickering candles. Even with a small window at the back of the room extra illumination was still needed in the dim quarters. The chamber was humble in nature, at least for royalty. A small bed fit for two sat surrounded by a few cabinets and shelves, each anchored down with various straps. His mother was seated before a mirror inspecting the lines on her face.

She turned with a cool smile to greet him. "What is it my dear?"

He scurried across the room wrapping himself in her embrace. "I have something I need to show you, mother." He looked up into her violet eyes. One of many features she had inherited from the late empress. Her silky blue dress felt soft against his skin. Even in a simple traveler's dress his mother was radiant.

"Go on," she said.

"I have been waiting to share this with you, Mother. I found it... exploring."

A wary look crossed her face. "Exploring you say? What kind of 'exploring'?"

"The kind that would normally get me in trouble, but what I found is important!" He scrambled beneath his black and gold tunic until he found the hidden parchment. Pulling it out he offered it to her.

Beatrice's eyes met his extended hand, carefully looking over its contents. "This has the emperor's seal. Where did you find this?"

"I may have discovered the door to father's private courier birds open."

"Leo! Do you know how upset your father will be? Stealing a royal message is an offense punishable by..."

"Look inside it, Mother." He shook the coarse paper gesturing for her to take it.

Hesitantly she took the parchment in hand. Her eyes moved thoughtfully as she examined each word. After a moment they rose from the parchment to meet his own.

"Does your father know you have this?" she asked.

"No, of course not! Would I be on this ship if he did?"

She rolled the letter up tucking it away in her dress. "Speak of this to no one."

"So... what do you think?" he asked. "Was I right? Was it not important?"

"Lower your voice, Leo. Yes, you have done a good thing," she said, shaking her head slightly at the thought. "Well let's say you did a bad thing, but it has worked for a good purpose."

A slight grin cracked across his face at her affirmation.

"But you must know we are in a very dangerous predicament," she warned. His smile immediately vanished at his mother's words.

"How so?"

For a moment a conflicted look passed over her, as if debating whether she should say what was on her mind.

"Come, Mother. If I am to be guarded against this danger, I must know what to protect myself from."

Exhaling a tired sigh she nodded. "Fine, but you must not utter a word to anyone. Not even Crumwald."

Like I'd tell that old badger anything important, Leo thought.

He nodded eagerly for her to continue.

"There is more to you going to Edonia than visiting the emperor."

He cocked his head wondering what more there could be.

"Your grandfather… my father, he is nearing the age in which all men must pass from this life."

"Grandfather is dying?" Leo asked with little restraint in his voice.

His mother's eyes shot him a cold rebuke for the outburst before continuing, "His mind is degenerating in its old age. He knows it but none speak of it for the fear it might induce."

She was silent for a moment. Her face caught in serene reflection. "He has finally come to terms with this fact." Her eyes slowly returned to Leo. A heaviness pooled behind them. "He has named you, Leo, to be his successor."

Leo stood dumbfounded. Him? Emperor?

"Why… me?"

"Because, my dear, you are his blood. The only one to carry on his lineage." She rested a hand on his shoulder. Her grip firm but comforting.

"You must understand this is not a game. Men across the ages have killed for much less than the opportunity to become emperor."

Leo gave her an understanding nod but he found her words barely reached his mind.

"Me? The emperor?" he repeated again to himself. The thought made him nauseous and thrilled all at the same time.

"That includes your father."

The words hit him like a bucket of ice water. "What do you mean?"

"Our marriage," his mother paused before releasing the words like a burden loosed. "It was one based more on strategy than affection."

She waited to see Leo's reaction before speaking again. Sadly, her words didn't surprise him. His father was cool, calculating, and ambitious. Why should his marriage be any different?

"The emperor believed by marrying me to Volkmar he could keep tabs on his more aspiring rulers. Volkmar saw our marriage as his path to the throne. Things perhaps could have been different but after the loss of your brother... well your father never looked at either of us the same."

Leo could see the weary sorrow in his mother's eyes as she recounted the distant memory.

"Why, Mother?"

"Why what, my dear?"

"Why did you agree with Grandfather? Why marry a man who you didn't love?"

She let out a pathetic chuckle as she spoke, "Marriage for the great houses is rarely about love, Leo. Someday you may sadly find out this truth for yourself. But not all of it has turned out rotten." She tussled his hair as she said the words.

"Above all we must keep this little fact a secret between you and me. I fear your father may not have your best interest in mind. You see, the emperor tested him. He was to deliver the news of your ascension to me. Yet, in all his time home he has failed to mention it."

"So how did you find out?"

"Your grandfather and I have our own ways of communicating when the need arises. Away from the prying eyes of others."

"It all made sense now," Leo thought. His father's sudden change in mood. Was it all just one big ruse to deceive him? Could adults truly be that cruel? His father could. That Leo had become convinced of. Like so many others in Volkmar's life, Leo was just one more piece he could use for his own gain.

"I will do it, Mother."

She cocked her head questioning him, "You'll do what, love?"

"There is much I don't know of the world and the ways of empire, but with your help I will become Edonia's next emperor."

Beatrice's radiant smile broke through her somber mood. "Of that, my boy, I am sure."

8

DUKE ARTHUR

WEARY AND HARDENED faces surrounded Arthur as their vessel rocked gently with the ocean waves. Months of campaigning had turned new recruits into seasoned warriors or left them dead in the desert sands. The men of Edonia had proven their vicious reputation once more. Behind them remained the ruins of half a dozen Hunan fortresses and cities in their wake. One by one Hunan's cities and defenses would fall. Kita Fortress had only been the tip of the iceberg. At every stop whether few or many, the Hunan army had fought to the last man. What had inspired these warriors to such madness? Arthur couldn't understand why they resisted. Didn't they know it was futile? Still opposition met them at every turn even as Hunan's Edonium infused weapons dwindled.

Arthur looked his men over once more. Hunan may not have the victory, but their resistance had taken its toll. Thousands of soldiers had paid the ultimate price and many more still would. His prying gaze stopped on the blank face of Lucian. The thegn's eyes carried the same hollowness of his companions. Arthur wondered how much more the man could take. Kaladin's army had been hit especially hard. Yuan and Hideo's defenses had turned into a killing field for many of Lucian's men. Even now as Arthur numbered off the remaining troops, he could find less than two dozen Kaladinians in their ranks.

Pulling at the back of his mind was the urge to say something, anything, to his grieving friend. Words felt futile. What could bring

85

comfort to the loss of one's own comrades? Words would be cold comfort in the face of all the loss still to come. To add insult to injury, the reinforcements from Venhorn and Varnas still had not arrived. The delay meant more Fenikians, Kaladinians, and natives of Edonia would pay with their own blood.

"Don't look so somber, you'll kill the mood," came the scratchy voice of Sir William behind him. The grizzled face cracked a rare smirk at his own joke. William took his place beside Arthur looking up at the overcast sky.

"This shantz weather is doing the mood on ship a lot of good as well." Arthur said, letting out a mocking laugh. "It seems this war is wearing on all of us, even the sky."

"The men will come around. We've been on the war path before. It's nothing new."

"I'm not so sure, William."

The trusted knight gave him a curious look. "Strange talk coming from you, Duke. You used to be the one cracking the whip on feeble-minded men."

Yes, he had been that man. A lifetime ago. Back when campaigning for the empire meant glory and prestige. Before his loyalty had robbed him of peace. Arthur squeezed his eyes shut fighting with all his might the image of golden hair flickering in the setting sun and sweet giggles serenading the summer night.

A pang of guilt crossed William's face. "Sorry, sir. For a moment my words betray me."

"It's fine," Arthur lied, knowing it would leave him with the flash of painful memories for the rest of the day.

"I suppose we best coordinate with Lucian. We should be arriving at Saki Island soon enough, William said. Arthur could tell when his long time friend was changing the subject for his own good.

"I suppose so."

Arthur turned, striding across the misty deck toward the moping thegn. As the two of them approached Lucian perked up. His gloomy face remained the same but Sir Kain at his side greeted them with a welcoming expression.

"Come to tell me how I must send more of my men to die?" Lucian asked.

Arthur shared a look of concern with William and Kain.

"What Thegn Lucian means," Kain began to say before Lucian cut him off.

"This thegn means exactly what he said."

"We will hold off the remaining forces of Kaladin for the assault. My men and I will lead the siege this time," Arthur said hoping to appease Lucian's foul mood.

William shot him a questioning look. Likely disapproving what Fenikia's already depleted forces would have to endure.

"We are so close to ending this. The men will be motived," Arthur said answering the unspoken protest.

"Look around, Arthur. There is anything but motivation on this damnable ship," Lucian growled gesturing with an unsteady arm.

"Watch your tongue, Lucian," warned William.

"Are you drunk?" Arthur asked narrowing his eyes. Only now did he catch the scent of ale that permeated the air.

"If I am? Don't you worry yourself, Arthur. I have all I need to kill a few more of those narrow eyed…"

"Enough! Kain, make sure he sobers up before I see his face again above deck. The men don't need this kind of display from their commander," barked Arthur.

Kain nodded in hesitant obedience, his eyes darting toward Lucian.

Lucian's already gloomy demeanor grew cold. "You think our men don't feel the same as me? We've been left out to dry by our beloved emperor. No reinforcements for months. At every stop we report weapons infused with Edonium and what do we get in return? Nothing. Sure, let's worry about honor among the commanders, Duke. I'll savor each accolade as I send more of my men to die on a forsaken beach with their guts spilled from a Hunan blade."

"It's time to get some rest, my lord," Kain said tugging at

Lucian's arm.

The thegn reluctantly stood to his feet. "You know better than any of us what our service costs us, Arthur. Yet you would continue on?"

"Now," Kain said, more stern than Arthur had ever heard the man.

Lucian tore his arm free and moved toward the lower deck, stumbling as he went. With a mouthed sorry Kain turned to follow after.

"He's starting to crack," said William. His voice shook with restrained anger.

"Let's just hope he can keep it together a few more weeks."

William wagged his head in doubt but Arthur had no choice. There was no turning back. Once Saki fell they could finally set the stage for their final assault on the city of Hunan. After that? Well, then they would make the long journey home. That thought created more fear in him than what awaited on the battlefield. At least in war he had no time to stop and think, to remember. Home was a battlefield all on its own. Halls haunted with memories he'd rather forget. Chilling reminders around every corner of what once awaited him there. Rooms now abandoned that were once filled with joyous laughter. Home, a place he'd hoped he could leave forever. It wasn't that he wished to die on the battlefield. The cold steel of another's blade was not an experience he desired to encounter. It was the dread that awaited him in the silence. Another part of him knew he had thousands of men relying on his leadership as well. To abandon them because of his own pain was to fail as a commander. Yet, the faint hope of a stray arrow or the surprise ambush of a hidden foe lingered in his mind. He shared none of these thoughts not even with William. They were the monsters stalking him in the dark of night when all other voices grew silent. Pushing their dark allure aside he turned to William.

"I will speak with Lucian in the morning. Make sure he is ready for the task."

"If not?" William asked.

"Prepare to wield Kaladin's Edonium Blade."

The sun had barely risen when Arthur found Lucian tucked away in a quiet place on the deck. Rag in hand Lucian moved it smoothly across the glowing surface of Edon's Bane, the feared Edonian Blade of house Kaladin. Lucian's jade eyes flicked up at Arthur before quickly returning to his sword.

"You want an apology?" Lucian asked.

Fighting back his rising frustration Arthur took a seat next to his friend. "I want to know what put you in a such a state last night."

Lucian let out a dry chuckle. "You mean the loss of all my men? All the fatherless children and widows of Kaladin are not enough for you?"

"I know this is your first conflict for the empire. Now you see what the true cost is."

A faint sigh left the thegn's lips. "It's just... we give all of this to maintain the empire and protect this emperor and for what? Cheering crowds, waving banners, and showering the emperor with honors that belong to us? All because of another war against another land who despises us. Perhaps rightly so."

Arthur straightened as he spoke. "Careful with your words, Lucian. Men have been executed for much less."

"By an emperor who clings to power like a scared child."

"Lucian," Arthur warned in a whisper. "You are like a son to me but if any of the men hear your words how am I to stop them?"

"I know," Lucian said with a defeated slump. "I'm just weary, Arthur. Weary of sending my men, my friends, to die in this war. All so some decrepit emperor can hold onto power. Our men deserve the fame and the wealth from such a campaign. Not the man who has it all already."

"Glory and honor. That's what you seek?" Arthur asked.

"Only that those who truly earned it would receive it. My men paid with their blood. Do they deserve less?"

Rusted trinkets of time, Arthur thought. *I would trade them all just to see…* Best not to dwell on that now. Besides he needed the proper motivation to turn Lucian back to their cause. He stood to his feet catching the thegn by surprise.

"If what you want is glory and honor for those who truly deserve it then I suppose we best put on a show the empire cannot forget."

"What do you mean?" Lucian asked.

"We end this. Not dependent on the emperor or his reinforcements, and when the dust settles we proclaim the names of who truly won this war. We make sure the empire knows who really defeated Hunan, and we make sure they receive their reward."

"That's dangerous talk," smirked Lucian.

"I thought you said you wanted glory for your people? All glory hunting is dangerous."

The eager eyes of Lucian smiled at the jest. "My Duke, I was just making sure you were prepared."

It had been a lie. Arthur knew at the end of all this no glory awaited them. He found himself staring at the planks of wood above his berth. A handful of commanders snored in exhausted sleep around him in the tight quarters below deck. A sleep that eluded him. It had been a long time since he had a genuine rest. Perhaps since their deaths… He wrestled to push the nightmares away, but he found he had no strength left tonight. Resigning to his fate, he let his mind drift back to the days of his youth.

Lucian had been too young for the previous grand campaign of the empire. He was lucky. A few more years and he could have had a lifetime's worth of nightmares. Practically the whole world had belonged to Edonia once. But the reach of Edonia's power had receded, leaving the empire desperate to retain its holdings. Mascar, a continent to the west, had taken its turn in joining the waves of rebellion. Arthur had just come of age then and like any young man was eager to prove himself. He retraced the hours he'd spent drilling in the art of combat. His young mentor and captain in his father's army, Sir William, pushed him to his limits.

Dust clouded the arena as Arthur traded blows with his sparring partner. That was the day he first laid eyes on her. Gabriella, her sapphire eyes watched him with playful candor. She rested her delicate form, adorned in a thin pale blue dress, against the banister above the training grounds. Tucking back a loose blonde strand that had been caught in the breeze, her eyes moved to meet his own. That's when Arthur felt the crack of a wooden training sword against his rib. He crumpled to the ground from the blinding pain that streaked up his side. The wide-eyed Gabriella vanished in a cloud of dust.

"All my memories lead back to you," Arthur mumbled to himself as he traced the same plank with his eyes for the fiftieth time. Refocusing he returned to the memory of his time in Mascar. It was a dreadful continent filled with dense jungles and rain year-round. The western coast was a wall of impenetrable mountains. Where the two met... well he wasn't sure a worse place existed in the world. Upon arrival the army landed in the eastern marshlands with the orders to split into two forces. One to the south and the other to follow the mountain range north until they reached the capitol.

He had been lucky for his lineage. Most new recruits had been ordered south, likely the veterans knew what awaited them there. Tales of unimaginable horrors spread through the war camps about the southern campaign. At first Arthur didn't believe a word, figuring the commanders made them up to scare men away from desertion. But when not a single man returned to reinforce them on their final assault on the capitol of Mascarda? How could the rumors not be true?

Squeezing his eyes shut he begged for sleep to come. A vain hope to avoid remembering what happened next. Mascarda, the grand capitol of Mascar sat enshrined within a deep mountain crevasse. Vertical cliffs of dizzying height stood on either side of the city walls.

Thick, black smoke rose from the besieged metropolis. Edonia's army had held the city's residents at bay for nearly a year, yet no sign of victory had come. For every man they killed ten Edonians fell with them. It had become a massacre without end. Every soldier sat huddled in his tent at night wondering when his unit would be called to dash their lives against Mascarda's ramparts. All the naive excitement had been drained from Arthur then. Each day that passed brought his mind to only one thought, his young bride back home. Her smooth skin, radiate smile, wisdom…

"No," Arthur said to himself withdrawing her image from his mind. He put the grim scene of Mascarda before him once more. Somehow its horrors seemed easier to face. The news of the army's demise in the south created a desperation in his commanding officers. A suicidal order came down the ranks. The army was to begin an all-out assault. Images from that night's attack still haunted him. The limp body of a child. The horrendous screeches in the dark. Corpses piled on top of each other until entire roads became inaccessible. Crimson liquid flowed like rapids down the cobbled streets. Among the smoldering ruins of Mascarda he wandered. Even now he could put himself on the palace's street in his mind. The smell of burnt flesh, the deep weariness in his muscles, it all remained like a recent memory after so many years.

Those that survived from the Edonian forces began ransacking the dwellings of the royal monarch. Numb, Arthur wandered the palace halls aimlessly while others released their frustrations in acts of violence and theft. Was this what war was about? There was no glory here. No honor, just pure animalistic fervor. Kill or be killed. Not a tale for the cheering crowds back home. A particular scream jolted him from his stupor. Moving swiftly, he found the room where the cry had come from.

As he turned to enter, a spear grazed his steel helmet. An older, thin, brunette woman lay splayed on the floor, her wounds fatal. A young man nearly the same age as Arthur sat on the floor stroking her hair. His hands were stained with the woman's blood and hot tears streaked down his blackened cheeks. Another man fully armored in Mascaran plate raged at the Edonian soldiers within the room. One Edonian fell to the Mascaran's spear but the thrust by another caught the Mascaran in the chest. Defiantly the man roared at his killers before succumbing to his wound.

The two remaining Edonians moved toward the weeping youth, bloody blade in hand ready for more butchery.

"Enough!" Arthur found himself shouting.

The two men looked perturbed at his interrupting of their sport. "He's fighting age," One of the soldiers said.

"Shantz on your butchery, he's just a kid."

"Like you?" one soldier mocked.

The other laughed as Arthur hardened his gaze. "You really want to spare him? Fine, but you do him no favors. He'll get shipped off to the labor camps or worse. By the time he's done he will be begging for death and cursing your name for stopping us."

Arthur looked down at the young man. His wide eyes were filled with shock as he continued to stroke his mother's hair. Seeing Arthur wouldn't relent, the two men grabbed the boy by the arms.

"Up you go. Seems fate has other plans for you."

The young man whirled into an animal like panic. Clawing, biting, and squirming to break free. One of the soldiers cursed as he fought to restrain him.

"You take him," the man said throwing the Mascaran youth toward Arthur.

Arthur clutched the youth's arm but found his strength was not enough to hold him. Just as the Mascaran was about to break free a pummel came crashing down onto his skull, a small ribbon of blood sprouting from the wound.

"Really?" Arthur snarled.

"You were about to lose him," said the soldier, shrugging.

Arthur knelt putting the young man's arm around his shoulder. He began to drag the Mascaran out into the hall, ignoring the mocking laughter of the two soldiers as he struggled to do so. He couldn't remember how long it took him to leave the city. It all blurred into an endless stream of time moving from one desolate street to another until the arched city gate came into view. Even then it had taken him until sunrise to remove enough corpses to slip through the disjointed gates. Exhausted beyond his imagining, he stumbled through the war-torn pasture outside the city. Peeking over the horizon was a blended sky of coral, crimson, and indigo. A wave of sobs washed over Arthur as his little remaining strength waned. The young man's body crashed to the ground, his eyes closed from exhausted grief. Arthur lifted his gaze to the face of the Mascaran at his side. The face he'd one day come to know as Octavian.

Stirring from the memory, Arthur wondered if anyone else knew Octavian's secret. Perhaps the two soldiers if they left Mascar with their lives. Not many had. Why had he revisited all this pain again? That's right, glory. He let out a mocking chuckle as he lay in his uncomfortable bed. The campaign of Hunan and its "glory." If glory was a trail of bodies left behind them perhaps they were glorious after all.

When did I become so gloomy? he thought sighing to himself. Many years ago, he assumed. Finally, sleep's embrace gripped him as he rolled over. Just as his eyes closed, a warning horn sounded in his ears. All around men shot up from their bunks, weapons already in hand. Arthur groaned fighting the irritation that sleep would allude him once more. Sitting up he watched the mad dash ensue as soldiers scrambled to equip their armor and prepare for whatever was approaching. Arthur eventually did the same, finding his replacement suit awaiting him in the small armory below deck. The fine armor was decorated with edges dyed crimson. Intricate patterns of a phoenix bursting through flames were etched into the breastplate. Snapping the last of his plating into place he reached for the matching helmet. A steel dome with two spread wings on each side. A sheen of red bled onto their tips.

Ready and equipped he followed the stream of soldiers onto the deck. Already waiting up top stood Lucian and Kain.

"Where is Sir William?" Arthur asked as he approached.

"Here, sir," came a voice just behind them.

"What do we have?" Lucian asked.

"Hunan? I thought the scouts said they had no ships docked at Saki," Arthur said.

"Not Hunan," Kain said raising a finger to the coming vessels.

Swaying under the moonlit night was a green and yellow banner adorned with a viper wrapped around a spear. The banner of Kaskar.

Arthur couldn't believe his eyes. "Kaskar? That means..."

"It means the other realms taste blood in the water," William said.

"It means more men to slay," Lucian snarled drawing his sword. Dozens of flaming orbs suddenly blanketed the night sky. Arthur watched as they crashed into the ocean's surface just ahead of the fleet. Water sprayed onto the deck soaking a cluster of nearby soldiers. Soldiers roared a battle cry and the command for return fire clamored from the ship's helm. The sea around Arthur morphed into chaos as splintered wood and flames engulfed the once serene waters. Arthur rushed to the captain's helm, desiring a better view of the growing conflict. The two opposing fleets sped toward one another. The mass of ships soon became a tangled web of sails and flame. Arthur's own vessel veered and whined as the wake of other ships crashed into its hull. Resting a hand on a nearby railing he fought to regain his balance. Equilibrium found, he once again took stock of his surroundings. That's when he saw a Kaskaran ship armed with a ram smash into the starboard side of their vessel.

Arthur heard the muffled cry of William at his side just as the impact came. Men were tossed into the air from the blow. Their flailing arms searched for security but only found the frigid and murky depths of the sea. Shards of wood came mere inches away from spearing Arthur as they jettisoned from the hull.

Clarity was washed away as the boat reared from the collision. Stumbling to his feet amongst the debris of the ship Arthur searched for his companions only to find a host of Kaskarans now pouring onto the deck's remains. A faint golden glimmer captured his attention away from the scene. A few feet away rested his Edonium Blade loosed from its sheath. Just as he moved to retrieve it, a Kaskaran clamored up the stairs toward the helm. The man was clad in sleeveless leather armor. His light brown skin the familiar Kaskaran tint. Sharp features hardened as the man's eyes locked onto Arthur and then the sword only a step away. Neither hesitated as they leaped for the Edonium Blade. In a mad scramble Arthur reached for the sword's hilt now mere inches from his grasp.

The two of them collided, sending them both rolling across the deck. An animalistic tangle ensued as Arthur fought for his life. The Kaskaran unsheathed a dagger at his side and sent it crashing down at him. It dug into the wood grazing Arthur's cheek. In return Arthur sent his now helmet-less head crashing into the Kaskaran. Fighting back the stars from the blow Arthur kicked the dagger from the man's loosened grip. Snarling, the Kaskaran wrapped his thick fingers around Arthur's throat and let out a vengeful roar. Vision fading Arthur did the only thing he could think to do. Tucking his chin, he bit down with all his strength onto the man's hand. The taste of blood gushed into his mouth followed by a terrified scream.

The Kaskaran reeled, gripping his blood-soaked hand. Arthur scrambled for the dagger the man had dropped a heartbeat before. With one swing the sharpened edge found its mark. Gasping Arthur shoved the lifeless Kaskaran body to the side. The warrior fell limply to the ground, dagger protruding from his neck. Finally able to breathe Arthur stood to his feet with a ragged cough. The battle continued to rage all around him. Stumbling he moved to recover Phoenix Flame. The familiar sword hummed happily in his hand. As if it had been awaiting eagerly for his return. Weapon now returned, Arthur cut his way through several more Kaskarans on his way to the main deck in search of his allies. The quick work with an Edonium Blade renewed his gratitude for possessing such a weapon. It wasn't long before he found Lucian, William, and Kain with swords drawn leading a counter onto the enemy ship that had smashed into their own.

Surveying the damage Arthur could see their vessel was lost. The others must have seen this as well and were working to commandeer themselves a new one. Arthur could see William cock his head as he caught a vision of him moving their way. With a wave of the hand the loyal knight beckoned Arthur to them. The remaining Kaskarans aboard attempted to flee at the sight of the glowing blade in his hand. Some took their chances diving into the sea rather than face such a weapon. Arthur couldn't blame them. For those less fortunate or too afraid they met their fate by the edge Phoenix Flame's sharpened edge. Enemy dealt with, Arthur found his way aboard the Kaskaran ship.

"The ship's finished," Lucian said as Arthur approached.

"It was smart of them, attacking by sea. Helped offset their lack of Edonium," added Kain.

"Let's appreciate their strategy later. When we aren't about to die by it!" Arthur shouted over a loud crack from an adjacent ship.

"So what's the plan to commandeer this ship?" William asked.

Lucian turned to survey the Kaskaran vessel. Edon's Bane let off a faint golden glow that illuminated his stern face. "We kill them."

He rushed forward not waiting for the others. Arthur shared a concerned glance with Kain and William but didn't waste any time in chasing after the thegn. Edonium Blades sang as Arthur and Lucian made quick work of any who dared approach them. Kain and William, both master swordsmen of their own, cut down their foes with ease. It wasn't long before the Kaskaran ship was turned to a graveyard. The surviving Edonian troops soon poured onto the Kaskaran ship. In a mad scramble they tossed over all the belongings that they could from their rapidly sinking vessel. Arthur watched as the last of the hull slowly submerged into the murky depths. A strange sorrow gripped him at the sight. Typically, he tried to remain detached from trivial things such as emotional connections to objects. Yet, seeing the ship that had carried them all this way sink… He'd rather not dwell on the way it made him feel.

The battle continued on into the night, but they faced a different kind of challenge now. Their new ship was trapped within the wreckage of surrounding hulls, masts, and debris. Each of them worked tirelessly to create a path of escape. Dripping with sweat and weary beyond memory Arthur tried his best to ignore the sound of the dying men all around. Still, he found himself watching the world around him burn. It was an eerie feeling to be peacefully adrift while others fought for their lives. As the battle ensued a soldier pointed off in the distance as a Kaskaran ship collided with an Edonian vessel. Both slowly sank as the men aboard fought unaware of their pending doom. How many out there would drown by the end? Would either side have an army left when daylight finally arrived? Feeling the weight of tragedy he returned to work, determined this time not to stop. It was the early hours of a grey dawn that finally revealed an answer of the army's fate. Amongst the flickering embers and driftwood two dozen of Edonia's fleet remained.

"That can't be all? Can it?" William asked. The veteran's face looked especially weary this morning. Soot covered every inch of his weary figure. His baggy eyes and wrinkled brow scrunched in disbelief as he surveyed what remained. William glanced at the Edonium Blade in Arthur's hand. "Looks like you'll be needing to carry the load more than you thought with that thing."

Arthur stared at the sword in his hand. "I'm not sure how much more blood she can spill." The sleek silver blade still put off a radiant light but any wielder of an Edonium Blade knew each death had a cost.

"We've survived," Lucian said, raising Edon's Bane in a victorious pose as he approached.

"That's about all we did. Have you looked around you?" William asked.

Lucian's eyes sharpened. "Watch your tongue, Sir William. You do remember your rank, don't you?"

Arthur could see the red creeping up William's neck but fortunately the grizzled vet bit his tongue.

"He's not wrong, my lord. Less than thirty ships remain," said Kain following behind the thegn.

"It's not enough men to take Saki and Hunan. Even the fleet we departed with was only meant to get us as far as Saki. From there we were to stage our final assault," Arthur said trying to hide the exhaustion from his voice as he rubbed his forehead.

Lucian was silent a moment, hand stroking his chin. "Then what if we bypass Saki?"

"And what, drift at sea?" asked William. Arthur shot him a warning not to press the thegn further.

Lucian ignored the remark as he paced across the deck. "The plan was to use Saki as a staging ground for our attack on Hunan, like you said. But what if... what if we go for Hunan directly?"

"My lord, even with a fleet of a hundred ships that would be a feat, but thirty?" Kain stated in disbelief.

"He's right, Lucian. It's madness," Arthur agreed.

"This is our chance, Arthur. If we wait for reinforcements on Saki the emperor will claim this victory as his own. He will claim he had to rescue us from the jaws of defeat. All our men's sacrifice and all we have suffered, gone. But if we take Hunan there will be no way to stop word from spreading about our deeds. All our sacrifice will be worth something."

"This is insane! You can't consider this plan, Duke," William spat.

"Silence, knight. When your superiors wish you to speak we will say so."

Arthur examined Lucian carefully. Something had changed in the man. He was young and eager but never cruel, not like this. Beneath his emerald eyes swirled a look of desperation. A look all too familiar to Arthur. A look that got men killed.

"We need to get off the seas. Either way we are in no shape to sail for Saki or Hunan. Send the command to retreat back to Yuan. From there we can decide what our next move will be."

A look of relief passed over Kain and William, but Arthur could see a flicker of resentment burn within Lucian's eyes.

9

JULIET

J ULIET HUDDLED IN her newly gifted cloak. Her father hadn't lied. The dark green fabric was thick and sturdy like leather, but it had kept her cool underneath the blistering sun. Now with the cold sea air whipping down from the Edon mountain peaks, she experienced its ability to keep in heat. The early signs of fall created an unpredictable time for weather in the lands she called home. At a moment's notice scorching heat could turn to frigid winds. The army would be leaving the familiar fields and mountainous slopes soon. A final marker testified to that fact. Tucked away into the western mountain chain was Ironhall.

The fortress had been constructed long ago by the forgotten names of her ancient kin. It was a fortress unlike any other in Edonia. Its keep was forged into the mountains themselves. Thus, rumors spread that it was infused with Edonium making its walls impenetrable. Protruding out from its mountainous defenses like a spear head was the outer wall, a mass of stone nearly half the height of the mountains it guarded. Shadows from its ramparts darkened the valley below it like a looming predator. Ironhall had long been a source of pride for her people. It was a shame that the empire had staked its claim over the fortress in the age of its conquests. Still, the worn remains of old Venhorn lay etched within its stone.

A faint sigh left her lips as they passed by the dormant place. Its proud status had been reduced to a warehouse kept only for dire need. Venhorn was not alone in its faded glory. All the kingdoms dwelling in Edonia once stood proudly on their own, but that was more than two millennia ago. A time long lost to those in the empire. Identities merged, cultures mixed, and few remembered the old ways. Even she was not immune. Her father's encouragement to read the ancient histories had not kept her from seeing the world with Edonian eyes. How could it?

A world of power, glory, and, at times, security. A world in which she now marched to defend. The days passed by with little to note. A few grey foxes at play had captured her attention, along with the rare sighting of a white elk grazing. But nothing other than the natural beauty of the landscape and its inhabitants were worthy of song. It was only at the rounding of the mountains did new life move through the military columns. Glistening in the distance stood white pillared towers capped with crimson and gold. The western shore of Edonia now in sight.

New vigor pushed the army forward until the outskirts of the city were just before them. The western shore of Edonia was large enough to be a capitol in and of itself. Its chalky-colored roads bustled with life as both merchant and civilian hustled to wherever the current of business took them. The thunderous footsteps of the army at her back brought this daily life to halt as those who crowded the road parted before the intimidating force. A mix of hope and dread filled the eyes of the people as they watched their defenders pass by.

A strange way to greet your soldiers? Juliet thought as she led the army onward.

Her father's commanders seemed to pay little attention to the people and so she did her best to follow suit. A war horn blew as they neared the western city's docks. Soon after, another answered its call. Buildings parted before Juliet revealing the astonishing city across the bay. Structures of varying shape stretched upward into dizzying heights as far as the eye could see. Their stature stood as a testament of man's attempt to defy his limits. Marvelously decorated ships floated sleepily downstream on their way out to sea. It had been some time since her last visit to the capitol city. How could she have forgotten what a sight it was to behold? Juliet looked to the army's commander, named Gudbrand who rode at her side, his face twitched with annoyance at her obvious gawking.

"Come, our transport is this way," Gudbrand said steering his steed in that direction.

Juliet felt the flush of embarrassment creep up her neck. It took all her strength not to steal continued glances at the marvels around her. Soon orders were given for the men to load into the ferries to usher them across. The fleet of transporters carried them across the narrow end of the bay and down toward the southern end of the city. Children lined the coast waving banners and crying out as the army passed. Juliet smiled and to the amusement of a few returned a wave of her own. None of the other soldiers seemed to notice the onlookers onshore as they awaited their destination.

After some time adrift, a large platform came into view. Shortly after, the order was given to dock. Juliet watched as her own transport slowly waded its way to the platform's edge. As the ferry landed, it thumped the platform's edge catching her off balance. She caught herself ungracefully and dared a glance to see if anyone had noticed. Two soldiers snickered at one another across from her, their eyes meeting her own.

"Great," she mumbled to herself, turning away before her cheeks turned bright red. With planks dropped for crossing, the soldiers of Venhorn slowly offloaded and sorted into formation. A host of citizens had gathered on the platform eager to catch a glimpse of the arriving army. Ornate and ancient structures encircled the place and upon seeing them Juliet remembered why. It was Valen's Plaza, named after an emperor of old.

It had another local name as well. What was it? She wondered to herself. *Oh yes… Widow's Departure.* The plaza had become the place where all of Edonia's armies sailed to go to war. Leaving a trail of widows in its wake, thus the name. It was a sad tale. No wonder she'd forgotten it.

Surrounding the plaza stood a commemorative stone balcony overlooking the growing mass of soldiers. Turning with little excitement, Gudbrand beckoned for her to follow toward it. Trailing after she was amazed by the detail etched into the ornate structure on which the balcony rested. Carvings of past wars lined every inch of the cold stone. One in particular caught her attention. It was the memorial of Venhorn's conquest. To celebrate the victory a carving of Venhorn aflame had been crafted. A stream of gloating soldiers bearing the spoils of the city's treasury emerged from the ruins. Above the scene was the emblem of a griffin holding within a pair of bloody talons a slain moose. The event depicted was ages ago. She likely wouldn't even know the thegn's name that ruled in that time and yet her stomach churned at the wretched scene. Keeping her eyes from wandering to any other atrocities she marched forward after commander Gudbrand, eager to put the moment behind her.

Passing under the shadowed portico they were greeted by a small entourage and directed to ascend a spiral stairway just ahead. It led them to a darkened room overlooking the arriving troops. A panicked shock fell on Juliet as she climbed the last of the steps. Waiting within the room's shadows stood the emperor himself surrounded by his royal entourage. She felt the air leave her lungs as Emperor Septimus turned to greet the new arrivals. For the first time in her life she was about to meet the most powerful man in the world. Even with a thegn for a father, an audience with the emperor was a rare occurrence. It had become a privilege the cautious ruler granted few.

The emperor's sapphire eyes seemed to weigh his new guests, as if searching for some hidden motive. The royal guards standing sentinel at the top of the stairs ushered them to enter the room. Juliet became astutely aware that she was still dressed in her traveler's clothes in the presence of the emperor. The emperor's eyes drew upward as he seemingly took note of this fact as well. Just as quickly, his heavy gaze flicked away in the direction of Gudbrand.

"Go on," The emperor said evenly.

"I bring 10,000 men to the aid of the empire, Your Majesty,"

Gudbrand said bowing low.

"I see you bring more than that." The emperor's eyes fell to Juliet again. She only hoped the terror she felt wasn't showing on her face.

Gudbrand stood, uncertain of what to say. "It… it was at the behest of Thegn Oswald, Your Majesty. He believes she may be of some aid to you."

"Is that so?" the emperor asked. "How can a young thegn's daughter assist the ruler of the world?"

The dark eyes of the man standing behind the emperor narrowed at the words. His posture was proud, and his thick black hair was slicked back with precision. The sharp features of his face left him with a look of cold certainty.

"I believe Oswald has sent his daughter here because of her uncanny ability to find the truth," the dark-eyed man replied.

How does he know that? I don't even know who this man is, Juliet thought, dumbfounded.

"I swore that I spoke with you about truth already, Octavian. It's not easily found, if it even exists," the emperor said in a mocking laugh. "Still. I could use a bit more 'truth' around here." The emperor's piercing gaze seemed to stare right through Juliet, melting away any confidence she might have had.

"Can you speak? Or is your muteness part of these 'abilities' you have?"

Juliet became painfully aware that the emperor was speaking to her directly. As in, he wanted her to actually speak! A murky cloud hovered over her mind as she searched for words.

"I… I believe I can help you find your traitor," she finally said, stuttering as she spoke.

Septimus rumbled out a deep laugh. "Ahh you think so? Thousands of trained spies and political savants at my disposable and you think you can do better?"

She stood paralyzed, unable to speak or to defend herself. *Come on, say something, Juls!* she yelled to herself.

"Perhaps a fresh perspective could shed light on what we have been blind to, Your Majesty," said the dark-eyed man named Octavian.

"So be it," said the emperor throwing up his arms in exasperation. "Edon knows the rest of you are as useless as they come. Why not let a little girl have her try."

Wearied, the emperor moved to overlook the army forming ranks on the platform. Juliet found herself still unable to move, frozen in embarrassment. She could feel the hot tears begin to well up in her eyes. That would be a shame she wasn't sure she could recover from. Before the first tear fell a gentle voice spoke up.

"The emperor can be... stern," Octavian said giving her a slight smile.

"That's one way of saying it," she said sniffing.

"Come, I will show you what we have so far." Without waiting Octavian moved back toward the spiral stairs.

Juliet glanced toward Gudbrand and realized he had already abandoned her to speak with the emperor about the arriving troops. Turning back she couldn't find Octavian. Realizing this she chased after this peculiar advisor. Juliet caught him at the bottom of the stairs and she found herself strolling silently along an empty walkway. A line of arbors ran overhead that formed a maze-like path to the emperor's palace. Vibrant colored flowers weaved their way through the arches soaking up the late day sun. Quiet gardens and lavish fountains filled the various courtyards on either side of their path. Looming a short distance ahead was the emperor's palace. It stood as a massive block of marble and granite that towered over all its competitors. As if the structure itself was inadequate, several smaller administrative buildings encircled the walled courtyard that the palace called home. Octavian led her down a path to the smallest of them. As they reached the building Octavian gestured for her to enter. Opening the bronze-covered door, Juliet was greeted with the choking taste of dust. The room and its contents sat in disarray as if a researcher had finally snapped and gone mad, leaving his work abandoned in the process.

"What is this place?" she asked.

"It is my research center of sorts. I have been researching for some time now those who might wish harm against the emperor."

"That's a long list," she chuckled.

"Indeed," Octavian replied with a smirk.

"How did you know the reason my father sent me? I've never met you," Juliet asked cautiously eyeing Octavian.

Peering down at her from his towering height he spoke wryly, "It is my job to know everything about the empire, but in your case, Oswald sent word ahead of time."

"Then why did the emperor not know it was me that my father was sending?"

Octavian sighed at the question. "The emperor has many things demanding his attention. Thus, he has me for lesser matters."

"Oh…"

Seeing she had no more questions, Octavian turned to the contents of the room. "This is all we have on the possible sources of the Edonium leak. I suggest you get started right away."

He turned to leave before Juliet grabbed his arm in disbelief. "You're leaving me alone with this mess?"

Octavian warily looked down at her hand gripping his arm. "My dear, the emperor has given me another task. One that is going to take me far away from the city for an extended time. You should see it as an honor that he leaves you with this invaluable mission. I wish you the best of luck."

Without allowing a reply, he ripped his arm free and shut the door behind him sending up another cloud of dust as he went. Stunned Juliet stared at the mass of disorganized parchment covering the room. She wanted to cry, to scream, to find the nearest ferry to take her back to the western shore where she could take the northern road home.

"No," she said inhaling a breath. "Father sent me here for a task. I have faced wild animals, thieves, and deadly storms. I will not lose it over a few tomes and pieces of parchment."

Finding a nearby chair she sat down. Its uneven legs left her tilted in the seat. With an annoyed grunt she snatched the nearest parchment and set to work.

Juliet's eyes blinked open to reveal a tome covered room painted by the early morning sun. How long had she slept? Yawning she raised her head from a drool covered page. Wincing in disgust she sent a hand through her blonde hair to discover how disastrous it had become. She'd spent two weeks now in this cramped little study. Two weeks and finally the pieces were coming together. Just before she'd fallen asleep…

Among all the names, lists, and places she found something of note. A growing group known as the People's Justice. They claimed to bring peasant issues before the emperor. Their motto was to advocate for the people on their behalf. Behind the scenes however things appeared more sinister. Octavian's notes spoke of several protests that had grown violent over the last few months. Protesting was a dangerous prospect in an empire built on stability and control. Several of the leaders had been killed, and the note left by Octavian was that the group posed little threat now that they were gone. She wasn't so sure. On her occasional break she would walk the city streets near the palace complex to drink in the sights and sounds of the capitol.

It felt as though every seedy alley or crowded market was covered with painted propaganda from this People's Justice. All of their ire pointed at the corruption of the emperor and his war. Understandable. Only the emperor's private circle understood why they had to stop Hunan. If the secret leaked that Hunan now possessed Edonium, rebellion would spread like wildfire in the empire's expanded territories. To the people in the city however it all looked like another pointless bloodbath.

That was the piece of the puzzle she still needed to fit together. If this People's Justice wanted to stoke a rebellion, why not expose the leak now? What were they waiting for? All she could find were discontented whispers in every run-down tavern and decrepit inn.

Nothing of substance had come to surface… yet.

All she knew was something was stirring in the city's under-world. Each face she passed on the streets bore a sense of unease. Everyone was on edge and whatever the cause, it was happening right under the emperor's nose.

How could Octavian have missed this? she wondered.

Perhaps it was because the royal court had spent more time in their ivory towers than on the streets. She was taken aback by that thought. This People's Justice propaganda was seeping into her own mind now. How easy would it be for them to manipulate reality to the discontented masses?

Slowly she rose to her feet grabbing her cloak from a nearby ta-ble. Its usual dark green fabric somehow blended with the cherry table on which it rested. A strange occurrence she'd noticed a few times now. Shrugging the thought away, she wrapped the cloak around herself and tapped at her hip checking for the familiar feel of her trusty dagger. Taking a small strip of cloth in hand to tie up her loose strands of hair she made for the door.

The cold marble of the palace was splashed with a soft coral hue from the rising sun. Gold intricacies woven along the surface spar-kled with radiance from the morning light. It was a sight that took her breath away each time she saw it. Breathing in the morning chill she was greeted with the sound of nature waking from its slumber. In the exotic trees and well-trimmed shrubs of the palace garden birds let out their morning song. It was a faint reminder of the things she loved most about home. Nature's chorus was never far away in the rolling hills and untouched wilderness of Venhorn. She never imagined she'd find a touch of it here in the city.

Breaking the peaceful moment was a deep and menacing drill horn near Valen's Plaza. Likely a call to the forces of Varnas that had arrived not more than a day ago. She found it strange that they drilled rather than prep for their departure to Hunan. However, her curiosity was not strong enough to probe further. She dared not go chasing another situation that would bring her near the emperor again. Not until she proved him wrong. Nodding to the posted guards she passed under the final gate of the palace complex and into the city proper.

It took her some time to maneuver through the fine administrative and merchant buildings that surrounded the palace. They were a place reserved only for the city's royalty and high-ranking officials. It was a space where the voices of the people rarely were heard. There she was again thinking like this People's Justice. She turned a corner and was once again amazed at how quickly the city morphed into different world. Only a few streets were all that divided the bureaucrat homes and the real Edonia. The finely paved roads turned to mangled cobblestone. Polished and painted walls were now replaced with grime-stained plaster. Unhealthy looking algae seemed to find a place between the ever-growing crevasses. The deeper she pressed the more she found the walls caving in on her. Streets became narrow enough that only two could pass at time. The sun vanished beneath a smoke and plaster filled sky. Strange gases rose from grates beneath her, the smell causing her to gag each time she passed one.

In this portion of the city even the faces of the people grew more stern. Lines creased weathered expressions on both young and old. They told of hardships tucked away from the decadent lives of Edonia's rulers. The familiar painted slogans of the People's Justice lined the alley walls. One of them in particular repeated itself: *Drunk on the blood of the people.* Observing the insignia drawn, she felt a pair of watching eyes on her. Glancing over her shoulder she took note of a frowning man observing her.

Skin crawling, she threw up her hood, careful to tuck away any loose strands of hair. It became abundantly clear that not many of her station wandered these parts of the city. Following the trail of graffiti she found herself within a tiny market square. Lines of drying clothes wafted from the overcrowded complexes above. Children played among the small open space while older women sat content at their humble booths. She eyed one woman in particular whose sharp eyes wandered to and fro, as if pacing. The merchant raised an eyebrow in curiosity as Juliet approached.

110

"What's a pretty little thing like you doing around here?" the elderly merchant asked, extending a vein riddled hand.

"I'm looking for something," Juliet said taking the woman's hand in hers.

"Ahhh a fine dress? I have plenty. But I doubt it would suit royalty such as yourself," the old woman said with a smirk.

Sudden panic washed over Juliet. "You know who I am?"

"Ahhh, lass, you're in the under-city. Knowing is what keeps you alive in a place like this. News came not long ago of the thegn's beautiful daughter visiting our city. The young men haven't shut up about it. Hoping to steal a kiss they say. HA! A dead toad wouldn't even offer them such a gift."

The casual nature of the woman didn't help reduce Juliet's panic. If this woman knew who she was, who's to say the People's Justice hadn't spotted her already as well? The merchant woman seemed to take note of Juliet's rising concern.

"Not to worry, lass. They call me Mama Thelma. It's my job to keep our little corner of the city informed. As far as I know, your identity is safe with me," Thelma said with a wink.

"Informed you say?" Juliet asked.

"Yes, nothing passes by this little burrow that Mama Thelma doesn't know about."

"Then perhaps you could help me?"

"Depends," said Thelma.

"Depends on what?"

"What a rich little girl like you has to offer me."

The sweet demeanor of the woman evaporated before Juliet's eyes. "I suppose you travelled with some fine wares on your way to the big city."

Juliet narrowed her eyes at the old woman. "I don't know what kind of person you think I am, but I can assure you it is not the pampered princess many would assume."

Showing her seriousness Juliet tucked back her cloak revealing the hidden dagger at her waist. Thelma burst into a laugh. So much so that tears began to run down her cheeks. Juliet flushed with anger at the woman's mockery.

"Oh, lass I can see you have some vigor in you. Reminds me of myself many moons ago. I'll tell you what. You pay an old woman enough coin to send me home for the day, and I'll tell you what you want to know."

Begrudgingly Juliet believed this would be the woman's final offer. Digging into a small bag at her waist she pulled out two golden coins stamped with a griffin bearing a crown. Encircling the edge it read Long Live the Empire, Long Live the Emperor. The old woman took the coins and bit down on them.

"Legit coin, lass. Now that's my kind of deal."

"You better not waste my time, old crone," Juliet said crossing her arms.

"I shan't fail you, my lady. Now tell me what it is you want to know."

"I'm looking for a group. They call themselves the People's Justice. Do you know where I can find them?"

"Dangerous folks you're looking for, lass. I doubts you'd be wantin' to sniff 'round their lair."

"That's for me to decide. Now tell me, do you know where they stay?"

"'Course old Thelma knows! She wouldn't be here if she didn't."

Juliet stood impatiently waiting for the woman to continue.

"They's holed themselves up in an old warehouse by the under-city docks. Little thing. Easy to go unnoticed from prying eyes."

"How can anything along the bay go unnoticed? The empire patrols and regulates all of it."

"Ahh, yes. The griffin is diligent. But at night many a thing can slip the empire's gaze."

"Have you heard if they possess any Edonium?"

"You paid for a location, lass, and that's all you get. They hear I helped you go snooping around and my neck might be next."

"Fine. Where is this warehouse?"

The old woman sniffed. Craning her neck she looked to see if the other vendors were listening, "South end of the city. Near the last gate. Real run down. They like to use the seven-pointed star as their symbol. They mark it on all their stuff."

That's interesting. The symbol given in the prophecy of the New Dawn? Juliet thought. "That's an empire propaganda symbol. Why would they use it?"

Thelma shrugged her shoulders. "As if I'd know? Us folk down here are desperate for a new ordering of things, lass. Suppose they think they can bring some sort of change themselves."

"Interesting."

"Now get on. Before someone sees us together that shouldn't." With that Thelma turned to busy herself by sowing a half-finished garment.

Let's see if what you say is true, old woman, Juliet thought moving to make the long trek to the southern end of the city.

Her journey south led her through the heart of Edonia. It was a peculiar sight, seeing so many variations in one place. Neighborhoods divided into all creeds and colors. People from the far reaches of the empire had set up shop within the walls of its capitol. Each street she passed seemed to offer a new smell or aesthetic. The aroma of spices found in far Gurun collided with the loud shouts of Ishkar's fruit vendors. Beyond them was a more exotic variety. Surprisingly a whole sector of the city was occupied by the recently rebellious Mascarans. Their bronze skin and darkened hair helped them blend in with those in Edonia, but here... a whole different culture enveloped her. Quaint shops dotted each corner surrounded by marvelous streets made of tiny colored tiles. Sculptures and fountains sprang up at various intersections. All that paled in comparison to the fact that she couldn't understand a single word being spoken. The Mascaran tongue rang out from every overhang and open window. The empire in which she belonged was a world foreign to her own. By the time she reached the southern end of the city she felt as though she'd crossed into another world and returned once more. It stirred in her a desire to explore the lands outside the comfort of home. Unfortunately for her she had work to do.

As she approached the southern coast of the bay, she could see a dark-colored building huddled among the others. Paint chipped off its walls and its windows were broken within their frames. No sign of life stirred within. In fact, no one roamed the street around it either. In all her time within the city not once had she seen a completely abandoned street until now. A small drawing caught her attention above the abandoned building's door. Chalked in white was a simple seven-pointed star. She felt a satisfied smile creep onto her face.

With soft footsteps she tried peering into a nearby window with no success. Wooden planks blocked any prying eyes from peeking in. A loose board happened to catch her attention, however. With the force of her boot she broke the plank free. The gap gave her the leverage she needed to send the other planks in the window clattering to the floor. Her way now unimpaired she slinked into the dimly lit room. Deep shadow fell over a cluster of several dozen crates. Each of them similar in size and shape. The room was void of life, giving her the perfect opportunity to see what contents the crates held.

She pulled out her trusty dagger and used it to pry open the closest container. The wood creaked as it gave way. She tossed the lid aside examining the contents. Inside lay a layer of straw which looked to cover something. She worked to remove it, and in little time all her suspicions had been confirmed. Resting before her was a crate full of Light Bringers. Her senses jumped to high alert as two voices came from the window she'd entered through. Looking around she surveyed the best place to hide. A stack of three-foot-high crates was her best bet. She leapt behind them just as the sound of a lock opening echoed off the warehouse walls. Her heart pounded in her chest as she pressed herself against the stack of crates. That's when she noticed something strange. Where her cloak touched the wood its color seemed to merge until fabric and plank were indistinguishable.

"It blends with anything it touches," she said in amazement. "This truly is a fine cloak, Father."

Just as the two voices moved in her direction, she pressed against the ground draping the cloak around her frame. She watched in amazement as the fabric turned a dark brown. Outside the cloak she could just make out what the two men were discussing.

"They're dead! Are you not hearing me?"

"I'm sure it's just a mistake. He promised us a revolution if we gave Hunan the weapons they needed."

"Listen to me! They used us! All he wanted was for us to create a war to distract the emperor. We were pawns. Now hurry up and help me get the proof before they find us."

A cascade of footsteps suddenly sounded from the road outside the warehouse.

"There they are," a deep voice bellowed. A whizzing sound reverberated inside the warehouse followed by a sickening gargled noise. A shadowed form fell beside Juliet and she felt the ooze of sticky liquid cling to her boots. Mustering all her willpower she fought to keep her panic from growing.

What in Edonia is happening? she thought.

The sound of drawn blades rang in her ears. "You lying shantz!" cried a voice.

Footsteps clacked against the floor and soon after she heard the same thrumming sound. A heavy thud followed and then the room fell silent.

"Come on. The duke said the weapons would be inside," said the deep voiced figure from earlier. A dozen men's shadows danced on the walls around her now. Soon after the sound of splintered wood and creaking boards filled the room.

"They are searching the crates!" she thought panicking. Slowly she slinked to the floor. Peeking through a narrow fold of her cloak she weaved her way through the stacks of crates. The doorway was just ahead. As she was about to escape a foot stepped in front of her blocking the way. Fear left her frozen between a narrow line of crates. She remained still long after the man had left, completely unaware of her presence inches away. She didn't know how long she waited. Time passed without meaning as men scurried back and forth around her. Even after all the commotion had died and the room was cleared she found herself unable to move. Unaware of the hour, she slowly rose to her feet.

Two corpses lay face down on the floor a few yards away. Pools of blood gathering under their arrow ridden bodies. The door to the warehouse lay in a shattered heap beside its frame. A few empty crates and straw remained tossed across the floor. She knelt beside one of the men feeling a rage rise within her. To be so close to finding an answer... and now.

A symphony of cries burst outside the warehouse walls. Shrieking women and children mixed with the roar of angry men. She rushed to the street noticing thick black clouds of smoke rising in the distance. Finding the nearest path to the bay she hastened to discover a better vantage point. Opening like a window before her was the Edonian Bay's glassy surface. Reaching the coastline, she turned north. All along the shore pillars of smoke billowed upward choking out the powder blue sky. Squinting, she could just make out the flash of steel among a mass of blurred motion. Slowly she lifted a hand to her mouth in disbelief. The great city of Edonia was under siege. It was in that moment of realization she felt the cold bite of steel press against her neck.

10

OCTAVIAN

A SMATTERING OF FLUFFY clouds hung in a pale blue sky overhead. The sound of a thousand clattering hooves echoed around Octavian as he fixed his gaze forward. It was all just a blur of senses to him at the moment. His mind was preoccupied with all that was to transpire back home. Of all times the emperor must usher him away. Dread lurked in his thoughts as well. The Duke of Varnas was not to be trusted. Any man who would trade-in his own kin for power was dangerous to deal with. Octavian had no doubts Volkmar would not hesitate to slip a dagger into his back should necessity demand.

"All the more reason I should be in Edonia," Octavian grumbled to himself.

Aaron, his trusted commander perked up at his master's voice. "What was that?"

"Nothing, at least nothing we can change now."

"You're worried about Duke Volkmar, sir? I doubt the snake would have the stomach to turn on us so quickly."

Let us hope so... Octavian thought.

"What of the girl? Think she'll discover the truth?"

"She's an untested child, Aaron. What could she possibly discover? And even if she did it will be too late."

"She could warn the emperor."

It was true. There was little comfort when trying to hold a conspiracy this grand together. He had his contingencies if things were to go sideways. The personal army at his back being one of them. It had taken him years of hard work, bribery, and rumors to corrode the confidence of a few commanders within the current regime. Being the emperor's representative in most matters presented him with the opportunity to meet all manner of people within the empire, especially those disgruntled with the status quo. It became the perfect chance to garner a personal army loyal to him alone. One couldn't be too careful in times like these. Getting into bed with traitors, kin-slayers, and foreign powers meant you needed some contingencies. Octavian's was two legions of Edonia's finest at his beck and call. Turning his attention forward Octavian could see a worn structure posing as a palisade just ahead. Squinting he could just make out tiny shapes scampering across its ramparts.

"Seems we may have a fight on our hands," Aaron said.

"We shall see."

Octavian spurred his mount onward, confident with the full might of an Edonian army at his back. As they drew near, the figures on the wall became defined. Waiting for them was not the forces of Theodwin but a band of ragged-looking woodland folk. Octavian's eyes fell to the city gate next. A smattering of bodies lay dead in the open field. Many of them city guard, but from what he could see a few civilians as well. Arrows protruded from the defenses and a few small pillars of smoke rose from behind the wall.

"Seems Bjønen has run into a little trouble," Aaron said taking in the scene.

"Indeed it has," Octavian mused.

"How would you like us to play this, sir?"

"Let's see who exactly it is we are dealing with."

Octavian found himself adjusting his silver polished armor. He never had been comfortable in a warrior's attire. His role was that of the politician. Whispered words, fine pleasantries, and diplomacy were his specialty. The brutal life of a soldier never had appealed to him. So in the times he was required to wear the warrior's garb it left him feeling awkward and clunky. Like a man pretending to know a matter while accompanying experts in the subject. Shrugging his shoulders in a vain attempt at finding comfort he pressed forward.

The host of Edonia's forces marched until the city gates towered over them. Waiting to greet them was a decent looking peasant who distinguished himself as a leader. His sandy blonde hair was cropped short and disheveled in a way that still portrayed a rugged charm. Beneath his worn leather and chainmail was a figure made of lean muscle. The kind formed from a life of hard labor and struggle. At his side was a young woman. Her blonde hair was nearly white, a more common trait in the north. Her rounded face and soft features left her with a sense of compassion even as she branded a stern gaze. She adorned herself in a similar fashion to the other woodland folk surrounding her. Simple leather draped over time-tested chainmail.

Octavian trotted forward on his midnight steed to address the motley crew. "By order of the emperor himself I have come to see the crowning of a new baron in the land of Bjønen."

"Has his majesty also sent you with reparations for the devastation brought upon these lands by the previous Baron?" the leader replied with a confidence Octavian couldn't help but admire.

"He has not."

"Then I suppose he has no desire to take into consideration the people of Bjønen's choice for its next ruler?"

Octavian paused for a moment. A sense of political opportunity unfolding before his eyes. "He does not."

Before the man upon the wall could speak again Octavian raised a hand to silence him. "But I am."

"Sir, what are you doing?" Aaron whispered beside him.

"Hedging our bets."

"What ability do you have to stand against the wishes of the emperor?" The man upon the wall asked.

"John of the Wood, I presume?" Octavian asked.

The man nodded.

"You see, John. Things are about to change in Edonia. Many

119

would say for the better and as head advisor to his majesty I have been given certain privileges. So I will make you an offer on behalf of this changing empire."

A faint smile crept onto John's face. The woman beside him however remained unconvinced.

"I'm listening."

"I find it best if we talk inside… privately," Octavian said nodding toward the gate.

The woman beside John stirred uneasily. "John, I don't think…"

"Quiet, Maggs." Was all Octavian could hear before John turned to address them again.

"The army stays outside."

"Of course," Octavian said smiling. "I would like a small contingency of guards to accompany me. You understand, don't you?"

John nodded his approval and barked an order to open the gate. The timber doors creaked as they pushed aside the corpses that stood in their way. Octavian, Aaron, and a dozen guards led their mounts underneath the welcoming frame. Octavian found himself averting his gaze from the carnage around him. Another aspect of the warrior's life he wished to avoid. It was a necessary part of running an empire but seeing it firsthand was something he'd always taken special care to steer clear of.

Within the city walls rested a muddy squalor of streets and timber homes. Bjønen was the last of Edonia's major cities to cling to the old ways of life. Supposedly it had its charms, but for a man raised on the streets of Edonia it left little to be desired. John and his companion Maggs, as he called her, ushered them into a nearby home. It was dimly lit and whoever had dwelt in it before must have left in a hurry. Scattered across a small dining table was a half-eaten meal and many of the room's belongings lay disheveled on the floor. John stretched out a hand inviting them to take a seat.

"Eat whatever you like," he said with a smirk.

Octavian wasn't sure if he'd managed to refrain his disgust, but from the reaction of the others with him he figured he was doing just fine.

"So what is it you have to offer?" John asked taking a seat.

"Straight to the point? Fine, I don't mind leaving as soon as we can," Octavian said glancing around the room.

"Don't come down from your highborn perch too often, do you?" John asked.

"And you don't know when another holds your life in their hands, do you?"

John's eyes sharpened at the threat, but his bravado didn't flee.

"Here is my proposal, John of the Wood. I was sent to crown Theodwin as Baron of Bjønen. I have no special affection for the man, and as I mentioned before things are changing in Edonia."

"What kind of change?"

"Now that, my friend, is not your concern. Here is what should matter to you. I am happy to make you Baron if that is your desire. All I ask is when the time comes you and your men will answer to me."

"I don't like a deal when I don't know the man I'm gettin' in bed with, John," said the woman named Maggs.

"I suppose after the first few times you tried, it left you with some vile disease," Octavian sneered.

"You shantz!" Maggie shouted reaching for her dagger.

The host of guards with Octavian grabbed their hilts ready to strike. John raised an arm across Maggie stopping her from doing anything foolish.

"I don't know too many highborns who'd speak to a woman like that, peasant or no," John snarled.

"Then you haven't met many," Octavian replied coolly. "Let's get back to business, shall we? It's a simple offer, John. I leave here with my men, and you are made Baron. Or we have a quick skirmish where my men slaughter every last one of you, and your people are left under the rule of Theodwin. You don't win in that scenario. I'm offering you a chance to have all you've ever wanted, and all I'm asking in return is for you to answer when and if I call."

The room fell silent for a moment. John's face grew thoughtful as he contemplated the offer. Octavian tightened his jaw in disbelief that the man was even giving the offer a second thought. Meeting Maggie's eyes John stood from his seat.

"You have yourself a deal," he said extending a hand.

Octavian rose to his feet, suspicion permeating from his demeanor. "Quite a bit of hesitation for such a generous offer."

"Well, I just proclaimed to the people I was one of them. Hard to swallow becoming just another one of the empire's servants, but better that than dead."

"Indeed. I know what it's like to serve a master. You'll get used to it."

With that Octavian took John's hand in his own.

"What of Theodwin? Will you dispose of him yourself?" John asked.

"Well, John, as new baron of Bjønen I suspect all usurpers of your title are yours to deal with. Do with him as you like. All I ask is that no more disturbances come from Bjønen for a time."

A childish grin crept onto John's face. "We can handle that."

"I'm sure you can."

Octavian turned to Aaron and the others. "I believe our work is done here."

Aaron nodded and motioned for the guards to lead the way. Their small band waded through the debris-filled streets back toward the city's entrance. Peering eyes of the common folk fixed on them from their hovels. A fleeting moment of compassion fell on Octavian as he met some of their gazes. It would be men and women like this who'd pay the price for the games they played.

Passing under the city's gate he felt Aaron move to his side. "You sure about this John fellow? Would it not have been easier just to install Theodwin? I'm sure the men will be disappointed they won't get to spill a little blood."

"It's good for them to curb their bloodlust from time to time. Keeps them disciplined. As for John, no, I don't trust him. But Theodwin and his kind have been loyal to Septimus for many years and that loyalty was about to be rewarded. Those kinds of bonds are not as easy to break."

Octavian turned to Aaron with a smirk. "John is chaos. A young man eager to make something of himself. That drive can be dangerous if mishandled but given the proper target it can become a useful tool to our purposes."

Aaron's face showed he was less convinced, but he nodded regardless. A new ally in the north was an unexpected bonus to this journey. Perhaps making it a useful endeavor after all. Octavian turned inward, reflecting on what was to transpire in Edonia as the order rang out for the army to return its long march home. Only the slightest bit of doubt remained but it was that sliver that kept him awake at night.

The rod cracked against the headmaster's hand. "I told you slaves the emperor demands extreme etiquette. Do you want to end up in the Edon Mines?!"

The harvesting had finally come. The time when all the royal members of Edonia were forced to offer up their best slaves for the emperor's consideration. A fellow slave near Octavian named Drakul had failed the proper line of greetings once again. The man shuffled anxiously among the row of his comrades under the headmaster's abuse. Shantz fool, he was going to fail them all. Octavian had worked too hard for that. His days in the royal courts of Mascarda had prepared him for such trials as these. Other royal members turned slaves were not as lucky. Being born and raised under the thumb of the empire had taught his people many of its customs. It took more than simple knowledge of facts, however. One needed to see every angle to survive in the politics of the empire. Something this Drakul clearly lacked. The man stood dumbfounded, scratching his head in search of an answer for the waiting headmaster.

"It's not in there," Octavian said, smirking to himself.

The headmaster moved down the line of slaves shaking his head. "Is there any of you worth presenting to the emperor? I was told you all came from royal families."

He stopped in front of Octavian eyeing the display of tableware properly aligned before him. The headmaster's eyes moved to examine Octavian's attire. Every button meticulously fashioned. Each crease weeded out of the fabric. It was an example of perfect form, or so Octavian had come to believe.

"You know the proper way to present yourself and your facial structure speaks of regality but how is your mind?" the headmaster asked.

"In excellent shape, your grace," Octavian answered, emotionless.

"Your grace is a bit much, but flattery will help you. What was the driving force behind our sending troops to the kingdoms of Mascar?"

It was a trick question. *Shantz this headmaster*, Octavian thought.

"The purpose was to quell the insubordination and rebellious nature of its kings. Men who refused the rightful demand of their emperor for both troops and supplies during the war with Ishkar," Octavian said hiding his true feelings on the matter.

Those feelings were more like… "The men of Mascar stood against a bloodthirsty emperor whose only desire was to send others to die in a war over pride. Now, shantz off kindly, would you?"

"This one impresses," the headmaster said. With a wave of the hand he motioned for the scribe that had been following him to pay attention.

"Mark this one for training in his Majesty's banquet hall."

"Yes, sir," said the scribe taking down the note on a piece of parchment attached to a board.

Octavian restrained a smirk. How long had he waited for this moment? Years toiling away as some lesser bureaucrat's slave all for a chance to meet "His Majesty." Finally, the emperor's greed would catch up to him. The weeks of preparation and training passed in a blur. Endless instructions followed by rigorous rehearsals eventually gave way to the moment he'd waited so many years for. Servants bustled around a ginormous glistening marble kitchen in preparation for the evening's feast. Plump slabs of meat and fine fruits rested on shining golden platters. Each of them had been lined along a bleached counter ready to make their debut. The smells made his stomach churn nearly distracting him from his cause. But no matter how delectable the food might be, it would not deter him from this moment. A moment that would likely never come again.

A clap sounded in the kitchen shortly followed by servers gathering in a line on the shiny polished floors. The headmaster from the harvesting barked out the order that the time had come to serve the meal. Before joining the others Octavian quietly slipped a small, serrated knife beneath his sleeve from a nearby counter. The cook preoccupying the space remained blissfully unaware. Placing arms at his back Octavian stood with straight posture for the headmaster's final inspection. The plump man eyed each of them dusting off even the slightest fleck attached to their attire. Following a dissatisfied grunt from a loose button, it came to be Octavian's turn for examination.

"Impressive, again," sniffed the headmaster. "You will serve the emperor's table tonight. Perhaps you can even impress him, though I doubt it."

Octavian's heart leapt. The final barricade had been removed from his path without his having to lift a finger. His heart pounded in his chest at the idea that his life was likely forfeit after this night. A small bell rang and the headmaster ordered plates to be put in hand. It was just the distraction he needed in order to calm his nerves. With systematic precision each servant stepped out the kitchen doors and into the banquet hall armed with the evening's delicacies.

It was a staggering sight. Tables stretched all across a massive room forming a tiered rectangular shape. A hearth rested in the middle roasting a boar of enormous size. The finest guests had reserved their seats to witness the beast up close. Eloquent dancers floated around each table with seductive smiles shot toward the most distinguished guests. Each of them were of various shapes and skins tones. Likely women hand-picked from every continent as far as Rasku. Scanning the room's contents Octavian wouldn't be surprised if every duke, thegn, baron, and nobleman was in attendance tonight. Each of them had been sectioned off by their respective realms, their leaders seated up front and center. With a hushed order the headmaster beckoned the servants to set out on their carefully planned course. Each of them moved with precision, dressed in their fine white coats. Some disbursed to house Fenikia and others to house Varnas, Kaladin, and Venhorn. The lesser servants would serve the smaller houses of Edonia, those of Bjønen, and the desert clans of Hunan. Then there was him. On the far side of the room seated at an elevated table all his own was Emperor Septimus accompanied by his family.

The emperor's sapphire eyes watched his dinner guests with a cold cunning Octavian could admire. This was a man who knew how to play the game. With dishes in hand Octavian weaved his way with eloquence toward his target. The prestigious guests didn't even spare him a glance as he passed them by. To them a servant was only visible when needed. He didn't mind that tonight. Just as he approached Septimus' table the next round of entertainment began. Lamps dimmed and a hush fell over the crowd. Darkness blanketed them until a faint glow of florescent lights flickered beneath the tables. The vibrant and mystical colors brought out a constrained gasp from a few of the guests. A single figure stepped out from the darkness and into the hearth's glow. She was more breathtaking than any Octavian had ever seen. Olive skin glistened in the dim light of the hearth. Her dark eyes flirted with each guest they met. With trained ease she danced to the growing murmur of music. A perfect form performing with perfection. All eyes in the room locked onto the provocative performance. Using the cover of darkness Octavian moved behind the emperor's table into his assigned position. While all eyes remained glued to the performance, his watched the family of the emperor.

A delightful glee radiated from Empress Anna. Her violet eyes watched with anticipation of each move. Septimus however sat like stone, unmoved by the display. The emperor's mind seemed elsewhere. Calmly Octavian stepped forward placing each dish before the imperial family. He took care to lay the cutlery and plates just right, all the while feeling for the cold steel beneath his sleeve. As the dishes were set before Septimus' daughter, Beatrice, she looked up at Octavian with a grateful smile. She'd been the first to acknowledge his existence the entire night. He returned a gentle toothless smile of his own before returning to his place behind the imperial family.

He stood alone in the place reserved only for the servant of his majesty's table. He became aware of the presence of the fully armored guards at his left and right. Their sentinel eyes stood unmoving as they peered out over the vast crowd. Patiently Octavian watched as the evening waned. The royal etiquette called for him only to move when called upon. Any uncertain flinch brought the potential for disaster. Something strange happened in that waiting. In his observation Octavian could see the emperor made of stone melted when his gaze fell to his daughter. The girl who could be no more than a few years Octavian's senior seemed to warm the frigid emperor. Confusion began to swirl inside Octavian. The joy in Beatrice's violet eyes swelling up a culpability for his plans he'd never considered before.

Could he really take the life of this man? The price of another child left without their father? He fought his doubt remembering how many had died for this man's greed, lust, and desire for power. How many had become fatherless or worse because of this man? Another doubting question broke through his defense. Would any of his victims have acted differently given the same chance as this emperor? Would he? Violet eyes spoke a different tale about this emperor. One of a loving father much like Octavian's own. One that was taken from him. He clutched the knife beneath his sleeve. The slight movement stirred the guards beside him but after a moment the armored figures relaxed once more.

Frustration gripped Octavian as the evening continued to drone along. The emperor still had not ordered another request. How would he make his move if this emperor sat content all night? A sudden raising of the lights drew his attention to the hundreds of faces in the room. That's when they fell to a table directly across from the emperor's. A dark-haired man with a fine tunic embroidered with a crimson phoenix. It was the duke's son, Arthur, seated next to his pregnant bride. Arthur's eyes fixed on Octavian as if fighting to recall how he knew him. Octavian gulped feeling the weight of those eyes. Recognition flickered in Arthur's expression after a long pause. He had come to realize what Octavian knew already. This duke's son had saved the Mascaran now before him some few years ago. Arthur rose in his seat drawing a curious glance from his bride.

"No, shantz you fool, you'll ruin everything," Octavian muttered under his breath.

Just then the headmaster stepped forward addressing the crowd, "We hope tonight's dinner was all to your liking, my lords and ladies. Especially you, Your Majesty." The headmaster bowed as he addressed the emperor, "Now if you will allow, our servants shall come to remove your dishes to make room for the final course." The headmaster bowed his head once more giving the order.

Now! Now is your chance, Octavian screamed to himself. Slowly he approached from behind the emperor taking the man's dish in hand while readying the knife in his left.

"Father! Wouldn't you say tonight's servant has done exceptionally well?" came the voice of Beatrice.

With a tooth-filled smile the emperor turned looking up at the mortified Octavian. "I would say so. The last man writhed like a fish anytime he approached the table."

"Thank you, Your Majesty," Octavian said dumbfounded.

"Where are you from, son?"

Son? Octavian repeated in his mind.

"I...I am from Mascarda of Mascar, Your Majesty."

The emperor's face morphed into a look of unease. "Nasty business that. You're a royal son then?"

"It was more than that. The commanders should be hanged for

what they did," protested Empress Anna overhearing the conversation.

Octavian stood speechless.

"You alright?" the empress asked turning to look at Octavian's pale expression.

"Yes…yes I am. I apologize." He fought to quickly gather up the dishes before his tears broke through. Why hadn't he been able to finish this? Picking up the leftover cutlery, he gently slipped the knife from his sleeve onto the table. The sole gesture of strength he had left. If he couldn't take the emperor's life then his should be forfeit. Turning he moved as fast as he could despite knowing that no distance would keep him safe now. A voice halted him.

"What is your name?" Asked the emperor.

Octavian turned with streams of tears running down his face. "Octavian."

In his hand the emperor held the simple serrated knife. His eyes scanning the weeping servant before him.

Octavian kneeled, ready to receive his punishment. "Do what you must, Your Majesty."

The rest of the room missed the scene. Their eyes were already glued on the coming dessert. All of them that is except for a duke's son named Arthur. Still some distance away he watched the scene unfold as he fought through the crowd of servants to reach them.

"I will," said the emperor stepping forward. The guards at his side moved to unsheathe the swords at their hip, but Septimus waved them off with a hand.

Slowly Octavian lifted his eyes to see the hilt of the small knife pointed toward him.

"There is not a man an emperor can trust more than one who could take his life and chooses not to."

"You know my intent was otherwise."

"Perhaps, but you had all the reason in the world and still you didn't."

"That makes you trust me?" Octavian asked.

The emperor kneeled, a gentle smile on his face. "Trust is a strong word, but perhaps there is a future for you within in my council."

Octavian stared in disbelief. *What kind of man is this emperor?* he thought.

Taking the emperor's hand in his own Octavian rose to his feet. For the first time since that dreaded night in Mascarda a flicker of hope stirred inside of him.

The dream faded into a cold sweat as Octavian found himself back in his white canvased tent. The dark of night still surrounding the slumbering Edonian army.

"Why that memory?" he griped to himself as he sat up.

It had been many years since that evening. Back when the emperor had more to live for. When the great love of his life was alive. Still that all too familiar doubt crept at the back of Octavian's mind. The same conviction that had haunted him on that evening so long ago. He hated himself for it. It had stopped him then. It would not stop him now. He forced himself back down onto his uncomfortable cot. He wrestled with his doubts until a dreamless sleep would overtake him.

One more night, he thought. *And this will all finally end.*

A pale blue sky hung overhead as the city of Edonia came into view. Billows of smoke rose into the air clouding the city's skyline.

"It seems Volkmar just couldn't wait," Aaron said in annoyance.

"I only hope it's not his pyre filling the sky," Octavian replied somberly. Internally he could feel a sense of dread rising. Why? Either way the city would be his today. Yet, the uncertainty that awaited them still nagged at his mind.

"Let's not waste more time than needed." Octavian said spurring his horse onward.

Aaron gave a nod before turning to the army. With a lifted voice he issued the order to march. The sound of a thousand footsteps in unison soon followed. They chose to cross the river north of the city, a safer measure than being left adrift via barge. As the last of the army crossed, a signal was given for the column to continue onward toward the city's gate. As Edonia neared, Octavian could see the rising smoke from before was contained to the emperor's district. A good sign.

"At least Volkmar hasn't destroyed the whole city," Octavian said breathing a sigh of relief to himself.

As the words left his mouth a lone rider came darting from Edonia's gate in their direction. The rider's surcoat was the typical red, white, and gold of the city watch. Distraught the messenger brought his mount beside Octavian and Aaron.

"My Lord Octavian, it is good that you return when you do!" the guard panted. "Duke Volkmar and his forces have attempted to take the city and the emperor's life."

"Attempted?" Octavian thought.

"Has the duke been dealt with, soldier?" Aaron asked.

"No, commander. His forces even now assault the palace. They will break in soon. We feared the worst but now that you're here…"

The man trailed off as he observed the shared look between Octavian and Aaron.

"Sirs?"

A swift flash of Aaron's sword cut the man from his mount. The messenger's eyes remained frozen in shock as his body hit the ground.

"We march on the palace!" Aaron barked. "For a new emperor!"

"And empire!" returned the legions at their back.

Again a strange sensation washed over Octavian as he took one last glance at the dead city guard. This is what he had dreamed of for so many years. Why now did it feel so hollow? Looking up he could see Aaron was already on the march leaving him behind. Pushing his doubts away Octavian spurred his mount forward to follow. Passing through the north end of Edonia, Octavian could see it remained relatively untouched. The only change being the normally crammed streets now sat empty. Every peasant and commoner must have chosen to hide in some stained crevasse of the city to avoid being cut down in the street.

"Unable to reap what you have sown," Octavian mumbled to

himself as he passed a nearby graffitied wall. On it was the picture of Edonia's proud griffin plucked of its feathers and in a drunken state. Underneath was inscribed the words *Drunk on the blood of the people*. It wasn't wrong. Only it wasn't Edonian blood that had been shed. That was still to come.

The slow plotting through the city dragged on as they maneuvered toward the palace. Moving a force their size through the city took time, but the heat of the day made the affair miserable. Eventually the main road opened before them and soon after it brought them to the emperor's palace. The city morphed into a battleground as they drew near. On the side of the road sat scattered corpses and debris. Both men dressed in the violet and black of house Varnas and the crimson and gold of Edonia laid slain among the corpses. Just before them a group of raven clad men with stone faces busied themselves by hoisting the dead onto an already burning pyre.

"Volkmar must be eager to clean the city for his grand procession," Aaron mocked.

The working men issued a curt nod as they approached. "The duke and his men have been waiting for you," said one of the soldiers. He was a gruff looking fellow with a long milky white scar that ran down his cheek.

"Perhaps the duke should have waited for his allies in the first place," Aaron replied.

The soldier shot him a scornful look but turned back to his grisly task.

They, along with the army, moved on following the road until it led them to the palace gates. Inside, the once pristine grounds now housed thousands of Varnas' men. From the look of it they had forced the emperor's remaining defenders into the palace where they awaited their fate. Talking with a group of men was Duke Volkmar and his second in command Rowan. The two men turned in their direction, Volkmar greeting them with a delighted smile.

"I was hoping you'd return soon," the duke said as he approached.

"I was hoping you would show a bit more patience," Octavian

replied with restrained annoyance.

Volkmar's face shifted to a casual dismissal. "I had no choice. The emperor was eager for our men to set sail, and if I had delayed any further he would have grown suspicious."

"We can't change what's happened, but now we can determine what's next together," Rowan added.

"Fine. What is the situation?" Octavian asked dismounting.

"Rowan," Volkmar said inviting the man to answer.

The commander nodded. "We arrived with close to 7,000 men of our own. I suspect the city watch including what the emperor had on hand was half that when we sprang our trap."

"And those sympathetic to us?" Octavian asked.

"Many of them were shipped off with Venhorn to support the war effort, we didn't have much to rely on for our assault. The element of surprise aided us, however. Can't say more than 1,000 remain held up in the palace."

"And your forces?" Aaron asked.

"We took some unexpected loses," Volkmar said, perturbed.

Rowan bowed his head in a shameful gesture. "Some of our men missed the signal and got cut down by the emperor's personal guard. We have some 4,000 remaining after everything."

"So what's the problem?" Aaron asked looking toward the palace.

"My men have spilled much of their blood in the conflict. They were hesitant to walk into a trap-infested palace without more reinforcements from our... partners."

"You mean they wanted to wait for us to be their fodder for the emperor's traps," Aaron snarled.

"That's a crude way to put it. I prefer to look at it as mutual investment," Volkmar said observing a fine ring on his hand, likely stolen from a dead bureaucrat.

"Come Aaron, if he wants us to put our own blood into this coup we'll show them how Edonians handle their business," Octavian said glaring at the pompous duke.

"Men! Form up to assault the palace!" Octavian barked. It felt good to give a military order.

With wordless obedience the soldiers loyal to him moved into formation. Rowan followed suit shouting his own orders to the waiting Varnas army. Gleaming silver plate adorned with crimson and gold tabards lined into rows next to their violet and black brothers-in-arms. They were all men hardened by service and disciplined beyond any other force that walked the world. It was a surreal moment. To see the very soldiers called to serve the empire standing ready to assault its heart. Octavian took in a breath to appreciate the moment.

The familiar decadent gardens had morphed into a wasteland. Manicured grass was now torn by a thousand soldiers' feet. Shrub and tree alike sat wilted from abuse. Even the finely sculptured fountains carried a ruinous look to them. Many sat half-emptied from thirsty warriors. Others were stained red with the blood of the dead. Small fires spit out their blackened cough into the powder blue sky. Garnishing it all was the sight of the Edonian's sworn protectors being the perpetrators of it all. A task no foreign army had ever been able to achieve. Still the deep satisfaction he longed for alluded him. If anything, a sense of dread seemed to stir within his chest. Aaron looked to him for the final command. Octavian issued a curt nod, and with that the forces of Edonia descended on their emperor.

11

JOHN OF THE WOOD

H E'D DONE IT. HE HAD finally made a name for himself. Turning Bear Paw over in his hand he admired the fine details of its hilt once again. His eyes finally came to rest on the blade. John stared in amazement at the ominous glow that seemed to radiate from the sword's edge. It truly was a weapon fit for a ruler. A clearing of a throat brought him back to reality. It was Maggie who stood, hands on hips, a disappointed expression on her face. She'd had that look more often of late. It was beginning to wear on him.

"What is it this time, Maggs?" John asked annoyed.

She let out an exasperated scoff. "How dare you be irritated with me, John," she said pointing an accusing finger at his chest.

"I thought all this was about winning Bjønen its freedom from tyrants. Not becoming one yourself!"

"It is," John said coolly.

"Then what was that!" she said with restrained frustration.

John glanced at the door in which the empire's head advisor had departed not long ago. "It was survival, Maggs. What would you have me do? Get us all killed?"

"I'd like to have seen you at least put up a fight before putting on the empire's leash. So what now? Instead of Holger it will be you who sends Bjønen's sons to die in another pointless war?"

John stood to his feet in a rage. "This was always about removing the baron. He was the source of Bjønen's pain. You really thought we'd never have to compromise with the empire, Maggs? Are you delusional?"

"But what of all your talk about emperor and empress, about changing things?" she asked.

"It was bed talk, Maggie! Are you that dim?"

Even as the words left his mouth he regretted them. Maggie's face turned cold. No, frigid. "Enjoy your coronation, John. I'll leave you to finish your business with Theodwin."

She turned to leave but stopped, resting her hand on the doorframe. "If you are wanting some 'bed talk' later to celebrate I suggest you find someone else."

With that her slender frame vanished from view. John sent a fist slamming down onto the table beside him. "Shantz, woman. This should be a day of rejoicing and she's gone and soured the mood."

Huldwin now appeared just outside the door. Likely waiting for the lover's quarrel to end. With a courteous bow he entered.

"When do you want to deal with Theodwin, sir?"

"Now," John hissed rising to his feet, Bear Paw still in hand.

The pale blue sky from earlier had turned a dismal grey. Perfect for an execution. John followed as Huldwin led the way through the main street. As they passed, townsfolk began to step outside their hovels. One man even took the leap of enquiring from them what was to happen to Bjønen now. Another called after them raising his voice above the growing chatter.

"Has the empire departed, my lord?" the man cried.

My lord? John could get used to that. "They have." Pivoted John to address the man. He'd never been afraid to turn a moment to his advantage. "And not only that! But they have granted me, John of the Wood, the title Baron," he proclaimed.

More faces now appeared from windows and doorframes. "Good people of Bjønen, a new day has dawned for all of us. No longer will you be led by a ruthless tyrant out of touch with your realities. As baron, my door will always be open to you. My hearth always burning and banquet hall ever flowing."

The man from earlier steeled himself before asking another question, "That's nice and all, my lord. But what of crop taxes? City repair? A city watch free of corruption?"

"Yes, yes, we will take care of all these as well," John said waving a calming hand.

The man seemed less convinced as he turned to enter his home once more. He waved a cynical hand as he went. Others in the crowd looked to carry a similar disenchantment.

"People of Bjønen! As a sign of my good faith I offer you this harvest season a taxation of a mere five percent!"

That got their attention. A small murmur stirred through the gathering crowd once more and John could see the surprise in many of their expressions.

"John," whispered Huldwin before John cut him off.

"Baron," John said.

"Baron," Huldwin sighed. "We can't feed our fighting men with that. Let alone stock up for winter rations and pay our share to the empire."

John placed a hand on Huldwin's shoulder. "My dear Huldwin, look at the people? Do you want to ruin this moment with the worries of logistics? The grain will come. We will find it somewhere. As for the empire. I have a suspicion they have much more to worry about than grain shipments from Bjønen."

John moved to address the people once more. "Now, good citizens, march with me to end the tyranny of Holger's clan once and for all!"

A host of townsfolk gathered around him raising up a chant, "Baron John! Baron John! Baron John!"

John basked in the praise. How he had longed for this day. With a triumphant raising of Bear Paw he ushered the people to follow him. Through dusty streets they marched until Bjønen's keep towered before them. The standoff between John and Theodwin's forces still remained. John's men stood entrenched around the barricaded structure patiently awaiting orders to come. Theodwin and his men meanwhile peered out nervously from the makeshift fortifications. Their eyes narrowing with caution at the growing commotion.

"Theodwin of Bera come out and face your judgment," John declared in a loud voice.

The burly man stepped onto a small platform to overlook the gathering crowd. "What is this nonsense, John? Shouldn't you be preparing for the swords of Edonia to come cut you down?"

"Ahhh Theodwin, dimwitted as usual," John said smirking. He looked back at the jeering crowd. "Who's going to tell him?"

They began to rain insults down on Theodwin. Some even began to throw whatever object they could find. Theodwin's cheeks flushed with fury at the insolence.

"You ungrateful rabble. You think a group of peasants can stand against the swords of Edonia? When they come I'll have them cut you down..."

Just then one of Theodwin's men tugged at his arm. Bending down, Theodwin's face twisted to panic at the whispered words. His eyes slowly turned to meet John who stood grinning amongst the "rabble." Theodwin cleared his throat addressing the mob once more.

"Good people of Bjønen," he began before the boos cut him off.

A chant started to rise. "Down with the house of the bear!"

Like a dam about to burst, the mob of Bjønen began to tear away at the rubble keeping Theodwin and his men protected. Debris flew into the air as a roar of human frustration flooded the square. It was all too perfect. Never in John's wildest dreams had he envisioned this day going so well. A loud crack sounded followed by the toppling of the barricade. The people of Bjønen rushed through the opening in a mad dash to grab the city guard. Terror seized Theodwin's men as hundreds of hands pulled and tore at them. In the chaos John could see a group working to seize Theodwin from his makeshift perch.

The man swung at them with his sword but soon the platform began to shake. With a desperate leap, he jumped over the defenses into the now half empty plaza. He hit the ground with a bone-crunching thud. Theodwin lay still a moment before rising to a knee with a groan. Underneath dirtied trousers John could see the bulge of a broken bone. Gloating, John stepped toward the burly man.

Theodwin's dark eyes seethed as he looked up at John. "You think you've won, John of the Wood, but you're just a peasant. Look around you. A ruler is supposed to bring order, law, control to his people. You've sown the seeds of chaos, and soon it will come crashing down on your head."

John cocked his head as if something rather important was being spoken somewhere else.

"You little shantz! Heed my words you…"

John took a knee, matching Theodwin's gaze. "No, Theodwin, I don't think I will. You see, men like you. Men of power. They think the world belongs to them. That it is their right to rule. But heed my words."

John's eyes seared into Theodwin's with unbridled hatred. "You have reaped what you've sown and soon every one of you will come crashing down from your ivory towers."

Bear Paw slipped with ease into the man's spine as John spoke the words. A faint gasp left Theodwin's lips before his head wilted onto the cold stone. His dark eyes fading into lifelessness. John rose to his feet drinking in the scene around. The crowd burst from the keep carrying shiny trinkets in hand. Corpses of the old city guard lay strewn across the plaza. Some men running by John wore their armor in mock tribute. Only one thing was missing in this glorious moment. A certain presence was absent from his side.

John glanced around hoping he'd catch a glimpse of platinum strands within the mob. But no, Maggie was nowhere to be found. He sighed. Why should she ruin his victory? If she wanted to mope about, then by all means let her. Deep down, however, he knew all that he'd accomplished felt slightly hollow without her at his side. Sucking in a deep breath he shoved those feelings away, putting on a celebratory face. Finding a cask of mead being rolled from the keep's wares he joined the men procuring it with a triumphant shout. Those with him raised a mug in tribute to the new baron as the golden liquid poured out.

"Let tonight be a night of revelry," John cried as he raised a newly filled mug. The others joined him in a celebratory cheer. Long after the sun had faded, the town of Bjønen continued to bask in their newfound freedom. No matter what was to come he was confident that the day of Baron John's coronation would be long remembered.

12

LEO

L EO WAS ALL SMILES as their ship came to dock at the royal plaza of Edonia. Standing patiently on the platform to greet them was the emperor himself. Septimus' wrinkled face and sapphire eyes lit with recognition at the sight of his grandson. A retinue of guards surrounded Leo's grandfather as he waited for his newly arrived guests to disembark. Leo stared in awe of the royal guard's shining crimson armor, ornate capes, and deadly sharp Light Bringers. Each of their faces was hidden behind a helmet designed to look like a griffin's face. Only the elite guard were given such a privilege to don that particular armor. Leo had heard tales that in order to join their ranks all of them had sworn to protect the emperor at all costs. Even so far as cutting out their tongues in order not to betray the emperor's trust. He'd hoped it was only a rumor, but the guards' wordless stares left him squirming under their gaze.

Soon I'll have my own guard that is devoted to me, he thought to ease his mind.

It was technically true that he had one now. But men in boring chainmail and simple steel didn't light his imagination like the elite guards and their devotion to the emperor. A sudden thud of wood on stone shocked him back to reality. Several large planks had been laid onto the plaza, signaling it was time to deboard. Leo looked up into his mother's violet eyes. Her soft face smiled back at him. Taking her hand in his they moved to cross the wooden plank onto the plaza. As they crossed, he imagined below was a thousand-foot drop into shark infested waters. Each step was a treacherous one as he held his breath. Crumwald who followed behind them gave a less than amused look at the game but allowed it to continue until they finally placed foot on dry land. The swooshing of many robes followed as the emperor in his grand attire moved to welcome them.

"My dear Beatrice. How long has it been?" Septimus asked forsaking royal dignity as he wrapped her in an embrace.

"Too long, Your Majesty," Beatrice said gently pulling away.

"Enough, I am your father, am I not?" Septimus protested.

"In private, yes. Out here?" Beatrice said waving a hand to the watching soldiers. "You need to be as stern as you've ever been."

The emperor's face grew serious for a moment but soon broke from its shell once more as his eyes met Leo's.

"My boy!" he proclaimed with extended arms.

Leo ran at a sprint into the embrace. "Grandfather!"

"Your Majesty," corrected his mother.

"Come now, Beatrice. Let the boy speak as he will."

"Father, I am telling you there is much for us to discuss."

"Yes! Indeed!" came the voice of Leo's father, Volkmar, behind them.

Leo felt his mood darken at his father's approach. As if this private moment between family was now being intruded upon by an outsider. He fought to restrain his disdain at the man who cared for little more than his grandfather's throne.

"Your Majesty, I hope all is well," Volkmar said bowing.

Septimus shot Volkmar an unamused look as he rose to his feet. "'Well' is not exactly how I would describe Edonia at the moment, but we shall soon have some relief. Especially now that you have come."

"I must apologize for the delay. It took longer than expected to gather our full force."

"Yes. Yes, it has. Fortunately the lack of reinforcements hasn't stopped our progress in the war. News has reached me that Yuan fell not a fortnight ago."

"Truly?" Volkmar asked. Leo swore he saw a strange sense of panic cross his father's face at the news.

"Yes, at this pace I suspect the duke and thegn will steal all the glory from us," Septimus said with an empty chuckle.

Leo looked up at his mother who was eyeing both men. "Come now, must we talk of bloody war and logistics the instant we step off the ship?"

"Beatrice is right. Come, I have your rooms prepared in the royal palace," Septimus said waving a hand to follow.

"If I may, Your Majesty, I must speak with my commander, Rowan, about a few preparations for the army before I join," Volkmar requested with another bow.

"Go," Septimus said waving a dismissive hand.

Leo watched as his father presented another gesture of thanks before slinking away. All the fake posturing seemed so obvious now. It infuriated him. What once looked like the highest courtesy from his father now gave him the impression of a common street vendor. It was a facade that was willing to say or do whatever was necessary, all so he could get what he wanted.

Good, Leo thought. *I like it better when you're not around.*

"Come, Leo." He suddenly felt the brushing of his mother's hand in his hair. "Stay here to help the others would you, Crumwald?"

"As you wish, my lady," the head advisor said bowing.

Leo turned with giddiness to follow after his grandfather. Their small entourage strolled across the plaza encircled by a retinue of the royal guards. Passing under the portico at the plaza's edge Leo found himself on one of the shortcuts reserved for the emperor. It was just one of many perks he'd come to enjoy when visiting the capitol city. The tucked away path was lined with green shrubs that towered overhead. Among many of his probing questions Leo had come to find their leafy columns weren't just for aesthetics. They also served to protect the emperor's movement from any prying eyes.

After some time, the hidden path opened up revealing the palace courtyard. Its lush grass and never-ending gardens were full of unique structures. It was a vast kingdom in which Leo longed to play. He'd often run off to pretend to be a royal guard fighting against the enemies of the empire. He knew the inaccuracy of the tales he weaved, yet they were a joy to him all the same. Royal Guards never marched with the army, but their finely decorated armor enamored him. So, in his tales of conquest their crimson plate joined the ranks of the army.

The small company of guards with them halted as they reached a small unassuming door at the palace's base. Only a fraction of the patrol continued with them as the door creaked open revealing a dimly lit tunnel. His mother broke the silence of their journey as the door shut behind them and a torch was lit.

"I'm glad to see the increased security. I fear there may be more danger to your life than you know."

"There's always danger to my life, my dear," Leo's grandfather replied. Beneath the bravado Leo could see concern in his eyes.

"Besides, Thegn Oswald, has sent me his very own daughter to look into our leak," he said in mocking tone.

"I've heard of the Lady Juliet. She is young and unproven but do not underestimate the power of a determined woman," Leo's mother said with a playful smirk.

"Indeed. I've had a lifetime of them." Leo's grandfather shot her a knowing look as he said the words.

A silence hung among the party for a time as they moved through the damp tunnel. Leo wondered if he should say something but felt a strange unease in both his mother and grandfather. One that was slowly seeping into himself. Did it have to do with that mysterious note? A doorway filled with light finally greeted them ahead. Beyond it was a circular room tinted by crimson curtains. A stream of checkered tiles met at the center of the room where a beam of light shown onto a symbol of a griffin. The beast always frightened Leo. Especially its eyes. Sharp and menacing slits that peered at him wherever he went. He was grateful that they quickly moved out of the room and toward their quarters.

"May we speak in private?" Beatrice asked as they entered the hallway lined with bed chambers.

"Of course." The emperor turned to the four guards accompanying them. "Leave us."

The men stopped immediately without reply. Their masked faces revealing no emotion. The emperor motioned for Leo and his mother to follow. Septimus led them down the endless hall until they stood before a huge oak door. Leo watched as his grandfather pulled out a pair of keys. One slipped perfectly into a small hole within the lock. A satisfying click sounded and with that Septimus pushed the grandiose doors open.

The contents of the room were a familiar sight to Leo. It was the chamber his parents often stayed in on their visits to the capitol. While it had been some time, the memory of the vast room had cemented into his mind. How could it not. Upon entry, one was greeted with a marvelous fountain of fresh spring water. It flowed into channels within the floor until it cascaded down from the terraced room into a grotto below. The terrace itself was a large octagon that encircled the small grotto. The opening in the middle did nothing to take away from the size of the living quarters. To the right a bed that could host ten sat with silk sheets and plump pillows. Ornate mirrors, dressers and other niceties littered the room. While many had come from various places in the world, they seemed to meld into one pleasing aesthetic. The colors of the room were made of cream complexions illuminated by soft light. Of all the accessories, Leo enjoyed the smooth slab of stone that slide into the crystal-clear grotto below. He quietly tiptoed in its direction before the stern voice of his mother stopped him in his tracks.

"This is not the time, Leo."

"But mother!" he protested.

"You must learn your responsibilities come first. Today is to be lesson number one in that regard."

Downcast he joined his mother and grandfather who had moved to a table in the corner of the room. As the emperor sat, his mother grabbed a bottle of wine from a nearby rack and filled two glasses with the dark red liquid. Gently she set the gold rimmed glasses on the table before them.

"You are sure no one can hear us in here?" she asked.

"Positive. I often hold secret councils in this room. The fountain and grotto are not just to please the eye."

Beatrice nodded as if satisfied. Reaching into her dress she pulled out the letter Leo had given her days before.

"Leo found this in Volkmar's rookery."

Septimus took the parchment in hand, noticing the emperor's seal as he did. His eyes darted to and fro as he scanned each line.

"This… this sounds like treason," Septimus muttered as he finished.

Beatrice sat silently. Her violet eyes cold and unyielding as they fixed on her father.

"I knew Volkmar was covetous of the throne, but *this*." His grandfather paused weighing his next words carefully. "Clearly this note comes from someone inside my own palace. What preparations could they possibly make that I would not know of?"

"Have you considered Octavian?" Beatrice asked evenly.

"All these years and now you want to accuse him? He had a chance long ago and many since, why now?"

"Perhaps he's had enough of being a slave?" she said shrugging her shoulders.

"Slave? He's treated better than most royalty in this empire. No, it cannot be him… Perhaps Darius. His council has been rather poor of late."

"You've grown a softness for Octavian, Father. His leash has been a little too loose for my liking. I've even heard he has free rein in the investigation of our Edonium leak."

"Watch your tongue, Beatrice. I am still emperor, and I will not have my judgement questioned. Yes, the man has some delegated authority. I couldn't run this empire without such methods. He's been loyal to me at every turn, so I did not think to question him in the matter."

Leo was amazed at the way his mother was addressing his grandfather. He'd never seen her like this. More than once he'd been scolded by her for breaking formality with his grandfather and now she spoke like this? Was she really that concerned?

"I can have Crumwald investigate the matter further," she said taking the glass of wine from the table in hand.

"I told you, it's taken care of. Besides, that little maiden from Venhorn is handling the matter now."

"So where is Octavian?" Beatrice pressed.

"Up north. Handling another issue my royal council seems unable to fix."

"I see," Beatrice said, taking a sip from her wine.

"Perhaps we could interrogate Father?" Leo said braving to make his voice heard.

Both Septimus and Beatrice fixed their eyes on him.

"Perhaps so…" Septimus murmured.

"Before we confront him directly we should gather all the facts we can," warned Beatrice. "Volkmar is a clever creature and without proper evidence, he could try to frame this all as a mad conspiracy on your part."

Septimus weighed the words as his eyes still remained on Leo. "It's good that you are here my boy to see what it's like to rule. The crown you will soon wear is a heavy one, and it feels as heavy as it's ever been."

"Your grandfather is right, Leo. This trip will not be a leisurely one. I suggest you rest while you can. You're about to receive a baptism by fire in the fight for emperor."

At her words the heaviness of it all washed over him. Was he really ready for all this? Biting his lip he mustered up the little courage he had. He was going to have to be ready because there was no going back now.

"Alright, Mother. I will get some rest, but please, I don't want to be left out of anything important."

Septimus smiled at him. "The boy's grown from last I saw him."

"Indeed he has," Beatrice said tussling his hair. "Sadly, quicker than I would have liked."

The attention caused a flush of embarrassment to creep up Leo's neck. Wordless he slid his chair away from the table and hopped to his feet. With a polite bow he moved toward the ginormous bed ready and waiting for him. Tucking himself beneath the comfortable sheets he listened for a faint moment to quiet murmurs of his mother and Grandfather. Their voices now muffled by the trickling stream and bubbling grotto. Soon that familiar friend named sleep wrapped him in its embrace.

"Young Master, wake up," said a voice stirring Leo from a deep sleep. Darkness morphed into a blurred face leaning over him. Vision focusing Leo now recognized the face of Crumwald stooping over him.

"Young Master, I must insist that you wake up," Crumwald said again his tone insistent.

"What is it?" Leo said rubbing sleep from his eyes.

"There has been an incident. Many incidences in fact within the city, and I must insist you follow me to safety."

"Safety? Are we in danger?" Leo asked suddenly alert.

Crumwald tried to mask his concern, but his eyes gave him away, "All I can say is your mother ordered me to bring you to her at once."

"Where is she?"

Crumwald took his hand. "In the throne room with your grandfather. Now come."

Crumwald yanked Leo from the comfort of his bed with more strength than Leo anticipated. With shaking hands Crumwald hurriedly rifled through a stack of clothes on a nearby dresser. Settling on a matching set he gestured for Leo to change quickly. Now fully dressed in a dark grey tunic with black trousers Leo realized how starving he was. Steam rose from a meal that sat prepared on the wooden table. Crumwald, reading Leo's expression, shook his head.

"I'm sorry young master but there isn't time. Perhaps your mother can fetch you something once we join her." Crumwald didn't wait for a protest as he ushered Leo forward until they both were moving through the halls at a quickened pace.

"Crumwald, you're scaring me. What's going on?"

The head advisor's face was unyielding as stone as he ushered Leo through the palace halls. Leo began to become increasingly alarmed as the eerie quiet haunted each hallway they passed. A sense of doom seemed to hover in the air. Not a soul could be found even as they drew near the emperor's throne. As they turned the final corner to the throne room a rhythmic pounding greeted them. Hundreds of royal guards dressed in crimson armor marched with determination in the direction of the palace entrance. A captain followed behind barking out commands.

"Barricade the entrances! I will not have this fight brought into the palace. You hear me, soldiers?!"

Fight? What fight was he talking about? What was happening? Leo's mind spun.

Crumwald's grip tightened around his wrist as he pulled Leo past the host of guards. A brief moment later they found themselves before the throne room. Two guards wordlessly opened its doors to allow them access. Crimson light flooded the elongated room. The familiar smell of the bay greeted Leo along with something else. Burning. His eyes fell to his mother who stood beside the throne, her face deeply concerned. Next to her sat the emperor in a barely restrained fury.

"How did you not know about this?" Septimus raged at a captain of the guard.

"Your Majesty…"

Before the man could finish, the emperor flung the cup of wine at his side. "Did I not warn you all to keep an eye on him?"

What was Grandfather talking about? Leo's eyes widened.

A nearby curtain fluttered in the wind revealing a glimpse of the surrounding city. All around pillars of smoke were rising in the air.

"Mother, what is happening?" Leo said voice quivering.

Beatrice turned, just realizing he had entered the room. "Leo, my boy!"

She sprinted from the dais wrapping him in her arms. The throne room's door suddenly burst open behind them revealing a panting guard.

"Your Majesty! They've surrounded the palace. I suggest we move you to a secure location."

"No," Septimus said in a low growl.

"If Volkmar wants to steal my empire let him come," Septimus said as he rose to his feet. In his hand rested the Edonium Blade, Griffin's Dread. Its polished golden hilt was carved with intrinsic detail. The pommel was shaped like a griffin's talon clasping the sun. Its cross guard was formed into the shape of two golden wings fully extended. Crimson leather weaved its way around metal to provide its grip. The deep silver blade extended out several feet, its edge glowing with white light.

"Father? This was father's doing?" Leo whimpered into his mother's chest.

Beatrice stroked his head for a moment before raising his gaze to meet her own.

"Do you remember what I said about trusting no one?"

Leo sniffed. "Yes."

"Your father has proven how desperate he truly is. He's made an attempt to take the city. His intentions are to show how weak the emperor has become, but we won't let him, will we?"

Leo stared into his mother's violet eyes. There was a calm there. One he wished he could capture for himself.

"Okay…" Leo said gripping her tight. A thunderous noise filled the air. A battle cry of several thousand strong shook the walls around them.

"They're in the palace!" Came the cry of a guard peering out a nearby window. Leo could hear the noise of battle begin on the floors beneath them. Sounds of shattered glass and clanging steel echoed down empty halls. A squadron of guards in disciplined march took position in front of the throne room doors ready to stop any who'd dare to assault them.

"In formation!" A captain barked. Each of the royal guard locked oval shields together creating a barricade between them and the adjacent room. Leo looked up examining his mother once more. Her eyes grew serious, but no hint of fear could be found within them. Turning to his grandfather, the only thing he could see was rage. Septimus' sinewy arms tightened revealing thick veins as he gripped his sword.

"Father," Beatrice started, her voice tender but firm.

"No need, my morning song," said the emperor. "I know."

It was a strange moment. Leo had never heard his mother called that before. A silent exchange passed between the two of them. Something that could only be shared between the bond of a father and daughter. Time crawled in eerie silence as all waited for what was to come. Leo examined each face, both those of the royal guard and the emperor's council. It was a mixed company. Cold expressionless faces intertwined with dread. To Leo's shock even Crumwald held a weapon. A simple Light Bringer shined in the aging man's hand. The head advisor breathed deep, his eyes meeting Leo's for a brief flash. Cries of battle drew near now. Leo felt his blood pounding in his ears as the adrenaline kicked in. His vision narrowed to the tiny space above the royal guard's shields. A host of faces, blood stained and wild eyed appeared from a far off hall. Leo could see the mixed sigils of the griffin and raven marked on their tabards.

"Spears low!" barked the captain in preparation for the coming swarm of soldiers. Leo watched in awe as the two forces collided. A memory of waves smashing against the high cliffs of the Edonian Peninsula flashed before his eyes. Only now the sight before him was not sheer cliffs and ocean. It was flesh, blood, and steel. The royal guards' formation buckled as an endless tide poured in from the palace interior. Swords now drawn, they hacked and slashed at any weakness they could find. Men fell by the guards' blades only to be replaced with another. The room adjacent to them was now cluttered with the living and the dead. Warriors on both sides fought for every inch of ground. A faint hope rose up in Leo as the royal guard began to regain ground.

Perhaps they can do it! he thought.

A sudden glow in the room beyond caused his heart to sink. Turning the corner was his father, Edonium Blade in hand. Raven Claw radiated with the familiar white light all Edonium Blades shared. Its hilt was dark silver, almost black. A raven's head adorned the pommel while the crossguard was decorated with the outline of a raven in flight. At its heart was set a dazzling ruby. Volkmar's face twisted into a sickening satisfaction at what he saw.

White hot light flashed as he swung his blade at the defending line of royal guards. Pieces of armor and flesh flew into the air like an eruption spewing debris. They tumbled to the ground in a cascade of pure horror. Another slash from the blade cut a hole through the emperor's defenders. Even Leo could see it was over now. With the guard now exposed Volkmar's men poured into the room. By sheer numbers they overwhelmed the remaining defenders, either cutting them down where they stood or forcing them to kneel. Beatrice pulled Leo back forcing them to retreat behind his grandfather who stood at the bottom step of the throne.

The room was consumed by a sea of menacing faces. Many of them common men eager to see their ruler brought low. In the center of it all, encircled by his men was Leo's father. The Edonium Blade in his hand flickered with light as if it was trying to speak. Volkmar's eyes met Leo's. Something similar to disdain hovered behind them.

Volkmar quickly turned his attention away meeting the emperor who stood defiantly before him.

"So you think you've done it? You think you've won yourself a throne?" Septimus asked.

"Think? Look around you, old man. It's already mine," Volkmar said raising his arms to the army around him.

"I knew you were ambitious, Volkmar. But this? You will cripple the empire. Word will spread across the world and when it does!" Beatrice snarled.

"Enough, Beatrice. I married you for your beauty and your ability to give me this throne, not to be lectured by your lack of insight."

She stepped forward, furious. But the raised arm of the emperor stopped her. "Enough, Volkmar. Your men may have won you the day but let us see if you can stay alive long enough to enjoy it."

The emperor brought Griffin's Dread before him, its light reflecting on his weathered face. It was a strange sight to Leo. The ancient figure of his grandfather holding the weapon. Many would likely mock the scene in ignorance. He knew better. It had been many years since Septimus' fighting days, but in those times he had stood unmatched. There was a reason his grandfather was the son who eventually sat the throne. Now, Leo would get to see those long-lost tales in action.

The two men stood frozen, weighing one another. As the sun waned outside, their swords filled the darkening room with pulsating light. Cold faces basked in the light eagerly awaiting the first move. Volkmar twitched sending his blade flashing toward Septimus. It looked as though Septimus' aged form would crumple under the blow. Leo watched in amazement as his grandfather raised his blade stopping the descending sword in its tracks. With ease Septimus shrugged Volkmar's sword away sending him stumbling backward. Volkmar moved again, this time attacking to Septimus' right.

Septimus side stepped the swing with a nimbleness that caught all off guard. All but Leo's mother. He looked up at her, a cool smirk stretching across her face.

Has she known all along? he wondered.

The two men continued their deadly dance across the room. Sparks flying as the two Edonium Blades collided. After a brief skirmish Volkmar withdrew, panting. Leo could see in his father's eyes the faintest bit of doubt begin to settle in. Now it was Septimus who pressed the attack. He sent a flurry of strikes that continued to beat Volkmar backward. Septimus didn't relent. He drove Volkmar to the entrance of the room causing the duke to trip on a slain corpse. Raven Claw betrayed his grip, clattering to the floor several feet away. The emperor lowered his sword its hungry edge now resting on Volkmar's chest.

The satisfied smirk that had once belonged to Volkmar now rested on Septimus' face.

"Is this the kind of emperor you all would serve? A weakling beaten back by an old man?" Septimus asked the crowd of soldiers. Each of them grew pale, knowing the answer.

A sudden flash of light swept across the emperor from the nearby entrance. Septimus let out a howl of pain as both arm and sword clattered to the floor. Leo looked on in horror as a finely dressed man stepped forward looming over his grandfather. The figure gracefully lifted Volkmar's once fallen blade above the emperor. The light of the sword revealed the face of Octavian. Octavian's dark eyes hardened as they fixated on the wounded Septimus at his feet.

"So it is true," Septimus said behind clenched teeth. "You are the traitor."

Leo could feel his mother tense at his side.

"After all my father has done? This is how you thank him!" she shrieked across the room.

Leo watched as Octavian's face morphed at the sight of her. Was that doubt that Leo saw in the man's expression?

Volkmar let out a wild laugh from the floor. "Are you that dim witted, Beatrice? Done for him? Really?"

Octavian stood frozen blade in hand. All eyes watched as Beatrice drew closer. As if in a panic of her stopping him, Octavian moved the sword as if to send the finishing blow.

"Grandfather, NO!" Leo screamed as he raced forward.

The cry stopped Octavian's arm from its descent, his eyes shuttering as if he'd seen Leo for the first time.

"I…I…" Octavian mumbled.

"Ughh!" came the gurgled cry beneath him. The faint glow of an Edonium Blade now protruding from the emperor's chest. Leo stopped in horror. His mother let out an ear-piercing scream. Following the blade up to the wielder's arm, Leo met the face of his father. A sickening smile curled on Volkmar's face as he pulled Griffin's Dread free.

13

ARTHUR

THE BLARING OF THE watchtower's horn jolted Arthur awake. It was almost half a fortnight since the ambush on the Sunset Sea, yet his body still ached from the attack. Groaning he rolled from his wooden cot to peer out the stone cut window a few feet away. The island fortress of Yuan hosted little comfort, but it did come with some spectacular views. Placing a hand on the sunbathed frame he searched the shimmering crystal horizon. Two dozen ships dotted the sea. Their sails bore the moose of Venhorn and the griffin of the empire. Reinforcements had come. Another horn bellowed, signaling the ports to prepare for their new arrivals. Arthur found his eyes naturally fall to the port below. Scanning the docks he ran the logistics in his head for the space they'd need. It wasn't too difficult. They lost more ships than they'd initially realized in the ambush. The once full harbor was close to half empty after their fight for survival.

All the better they arrive now, he thought to himself.

Scanning the docks one final time something peculiar caught his eye. Every dock where the ships of Kaladin should be sat empty. Lucian had been avoiding him since they made their retreat back to Yuan but he wouldn't be so foolish. A sudden knock at the door caused him to jump.

"Excuse me, my lord," Sir William said bowing as he opened the door. "It's urgent."

"I know of the ships' arrival. I will be down to greet them soon. Another matter though, has there been a report on Lucian?"

"That is the urgent matter, my lord. Some men spotted the ships of Kaladin setting sail late last night. They were headed in the direction of Hunan."

"Curse you, Lucian," Arthur muttered under his breath.

"And these men thought it fit to tell us this now!" Arthur said with disdain.

"Lucian bribed them a month's wages to keep their mouths shut. But the threat of punishment for negligence of duties got them talking."

"It's more than a threat. Have them strung up and call the men to prepare for war."

"My duke?"

"You heard me, William."

"But the forces of Venhorn and Edonia have just arrived. Their stores need to be restocked and they'll need some time onshore to recoup before they are battle ready."

"Tell them to remain on ship. Have our men prep what they need and load it as soon as they can. We sail today." He didn't wait for William's protest as he stormed out of the room. His mind raced back to his last conversation with the hotheaded thegn. A nagging guilt rose in him for not doing more to prevent something like this from happening.

"How dare you make me look a fool in front of our inferiors!" Lucian raged in Arthur's private quarters. The faint flickering of candlelight was all that illuminated the dark room. It amplified Lucian's already fiery expression.

"That was not my intent," Arthur said calm but stern.

"No, you just wish to father me forever? How will the men learn to respect me if you constantly patronize me?"

"They will learn to respect you when every decision isn't based on emotion and glory seeking."

"Was it not you who told me I should seek out glory? That it was the only way to make loss of my men count?"

The truth of the words stung. His lie to motivate the young

thegn now coming home to roost. Arthur let out a tired sigh before speaking.

"You have nothing to prove, Lucian. We practically pushed the enemy to Hunan's doorstep all by ourselves. That is something to be proud of."

"Yes, how grand! How song worthy! Thegn Lucian, subordinate to Duke Arthur, famed warrior of Edonia, takes the island of Yuan. How the heralds will proclaim the tale."

"Is that all you care about!" Arthur said letting his frustration grow.

"You've had your day in the sun, Arthur. You've led armies, won glorious victories. Your house will be remembered. What of mine? A father killed in a pathetic skirmish with Northlund pirates? Drying coffers? A decimated army? If I do not return home with glory what will my people say? What can I tell them when I deliver the news that their sons are dead?"

"You can tell them they served their empire well."

Lucian broke into a mocking laugh. "Ahhh, yes. The empire. What a relief that will be to a newly made widow."

"Don't pretend this is about widows and mothers, Lucian. Your father carried the same ambition I see in your eyes. An ambition that drove him to poor decisions. Decisions that drove him to face a fleet twice his size. Decisions that got him killed. I won't let you do the same to us."

Lucian's face darkened at the words. "Never speak of my father that way again if you value your life."

"Stop acting like a child. Our men are counting on us to make the decisions that save their lives and you would throw them away for what? A parade in the capitol?"

Fuming, Lucian moved to the door. "You may think you can replace my father, but you will never be him."

The door slammed as the thegn exited the room leaving Arthur alone in the dim candlelight. He felt the weight of regret weighing on his chest as he released the memory from his mind. How he had chosen his words poorly. He was responsible for driving Lucian to this madness and now it was up to him to make it right. The image of marbled floor stained with blood flashed before his eyes as he descended the tower's spiral stairs. A tidal wave of regret, grief, and rage all washed over him with irresistible force. Lifeless sapphire eyes stared up at him from the cold floor. Her blonde strands splayed across his lap. His thoughtless decisions had cost him dearly before. He leaned against the spiraled stairway wall bracing himself. It took all his strength to fight the feeling of nausea rising in his throat. "Not now, not here," he told himself behind gritted teeth. Delicately he removed his hand from the smooth stone, steeling himself.

Just keep going a little farther, Arthur. He wasn't sure he could but he would die trying.

Gulls cawed as they circled overhead searching for their morning meal. Men busied themselves offloading and loading crates from the newly docked ships. Standing before a recently placed plank was Venhorn's commander, Gudbrand. A disgruntled look was plastered on his youthful but scraggly face as he waited with hands on hips.

"I hear word you would have us set sail immediately with no rest for my men. Do you know how many days we've been at sea? Has the war scrambled your mind, Duke?"

"A bold way to speak to your superior," Arthur mused.

"You speak the truth. I would have this of you and your men," Arthur turned as if to end the conversation but stopped abruptly.

"I suggest you take a different tone with your superiors from now on. Hate to have you forget who's actually been fighting this war."

Gudbrand soured at the words. "You can't hide the truth from us, Duke. Word's already spread about the renegade thegn. Seems you'd have us all killed chasing after this fool."

Arthur whirled on the man. "Listen, Northlander. The day Venhorn blood is actually spilled on the field of battle you may share your council, but until that day comes you listen to my orders. Are my words clear enough? Or is the tongue of the empire still a foreign sound in your quiet little village back home?"

Several passersby stopped, fixating on the commotion. It was a rare occurrence for the men to witness the sight of Arthur's rage. Had he gone too far?

"Come, my lord," said William who had remained silent at Arthur's side until now. "This is not the place."

Reluctantly Arthur nodded. "Just have your men ready to go."

Gudbrand said nothing but turned to join the others on the deck of his ship.

"That could have gone better," Arthur muttered under his breath. A swell of emotions had him in their grip. Emotions he had kept at bay until today. Until that fool Lucian had to go off and court death.

"That was not wise, my lord. If I may speak so boldly," said William.

"It seems everyone is speaking boldly today, why shouldn't you?" Arthur hissed. William knew him well enough to brush off the frustration in his tone. Instead, he fixed his stern eyes on Arthur.

"Lucian has made his choice. We are neither prepared nor recovered enough to assault Hunan head on. You know that as well as I."

He was right, but... an image flashed before Arthur of a little girl sweetly smiling. The same image swiftly morphed into something more sinister. It fuzzed, turning to dark shadow and crimson. Arthur shook his head in an attempt to flee from the haunting scene.

"I can't let him die, William. I can't."

His loyal companion stood contemplating, eyes searching for answer. He had every right to strip Arthur of his command. He was leading the emperor's army on a whim. Using his majesty's fighting force for his own personal agenda.

"For Sir Kain," William finally said.

"For our friends no matter the cost," Arthur smiled in return.

Sails stretched capturing the wind. Cloth decorated with an out-stretched phoenix spurred Arthur and his men across the Sunset Sea. A nervous pit rested in his stomach as he constantly scanned the horizon for both friend and foe. They would throw all they had into this assault. Half as prepared as they should be and barely recovered. But he wouldn't lose Lucian, he couldn't. The man had come under his care and for that reason alone he'd not abandon him to his fate. The thegn may be reckless, arrogant, and ambitious, but Arthur wouldn't lose another person he cared for, not without a fight. As he eyed the horizon a thin stretch of desert came into view.

Crimson dunes of sand as far as the eye could see all converged to form an endless expanse of coast. As their ships drew closer something else came into view. Tucked within a sheered cliff inlet rested a mass of structures. Decorated buildings covered in red tile stretched skyward in a cluster of vertical lines. As his ship moved to round the second protrusion of the three-pronged inlet Arthur caught a better glimpse of the manmade marvel.

The city was unlike anything Arthur had ever seen. Each structure was built with a uniform shape and design. Not one building broke from the perfect symmetry. Their thin frames rested on tiered platforms built within the sheer cliffs themselves. Towering to dizzying heights some buildings even surpassed the surrounding clifftops. The city widened at a slope until foundation met sand. A daunting wall encompassed the base of the city, creating no avenue for assault from the beach before it. It would become a killing field for any who dared to attack. And so it had become already. Arthur was struck with horror as their ships entered the confines of the narrow passage. Half a dozen shipwrecks sat tossed broken and battered in the surf. The few intact vessels that remained dotted the beach ahead. Littered on the blood-soaked sand were the corpses of a thousand men. Their once shining armor and glimmering white swords now covered in the gore of battle.

Not battle, slaughter, Arthur thought as he took in the wretched scene.

The men around him stood dumbfounded at the sight. A whole legion of Edonia had been decimated with ease. In their haste no scouts had been sent to warn of what awaited them. Arthur felt the presence of William move next to him. He turned to see Gudbrand hovering as well.

"We cannot lead our men into this. It will be a massacre," Gudbrand said pointing a finger at the slaughter.

Arthur met William's eyes. The same thought was evident on his old companion's face. Arthur stood frozen, searching for a solution that wasn't there. Maybe Lucian was still alive among the dead and dying? How could he leave him now that they'd come this far? Looking around him, he took in the face of each man. Their eyes pleaded with him not to send them to their doom.

"Turn back," Arthur muttered.

Gudbrand gave a curt nod and turned to give the order. Arthur waited to hear the raised voice and the shuffling of men to turn their vessels around as soon as possible. It didn't come. He looked up to see the terrified expression of those behind him. His eyes followed their distant stares. Rounding the bay and covering the sea was a vast armada of ships. Their sails bore the viper of Kaskar and others the crouching tiger of Hunan.

"We're trapped," Gudbrand said mortified.

"Saki must have had more forces than we imagined," William said gawking in disbelief.

More than double their own fleet hemmed them in. The enemy's armada moved to create a curtain cutting off any hope of escape.

"We're doomed," Gudbrand muttered as he dropped to the deck.

"We could send all our forces to a spot in their blockade. Perhaps a few of us could break free and make it to live another day," William suggested.

Arthur contemplated the plan for a moment. "No."

Gudbrand and William shot him a quizzical look.

"If we are to fall this day it will be in the streets of Hunan, not drowning at sea."

"Are you mad? Some of us may survive if we escape now. If we turn toward the city we're doomed," Gudbrand protested.

"We are doomed either way, and I for one would rather die fighting than fleeing like a coward."

The truth was less noble. He didn't want to escape any more. The longing to pass from the grief of this life had him in its grip. The faint hope of survival the others clung to seemed a bitter cup to him now.

"Is that your order, my lord?" William asked unflinchingly.

"It is."

Gudbrand shook his head in disgust. "You have doomed us all."

"We move to take the city!" William barked to the ship's crew. The sailors remained frozen until the seasoned warrior moved to draw his sword. With shaky hands and panicked eyes the men scrambled to maneuver the ships toward the decimated shore of Hunan. As they drew near, mauled bodies began to welcome them in the surf. Men stripped of armor floated with haunting, lifeless stares. A curious wound on one of the men caught Arthur's eye. Across the man's face was a deep gash. More in line with a wild beast's claws than a weapon of war. Before he could examine it further the corpse drifted out toward the sea. Soon after, ship met sand and begrudgingly men tossed themselves onto the beach preparing to be cut down as they did.

Strangely no arrows greeted them. In fact, as Arthur scanned the defenses of the city no Hunan soldier could be seen. As far as was visible the wall sat eerily still. No noise could be heard from within the city confines. Not even the song of the local birds filled the air. Only the rhythmic crashing of the surf kept up its timeless tune.

"What is this?" Gudbrand asked as he took his place at Arthur's side.

"My lord, you will want to see this!" a soldier cried some distance away.

Accompanied by William, and Venhorn's commander, Arthur disembarked the ship to join the growing cluster of soldiers gathered on the beach. As they approached, he could see a unit of men had gathered around a cluster of mangled bodies.

"The duke has seen violent deaths before, men," William said with distaste.

"Not like this, sir," one of the men said pointing to the sand covered corpses. Arthur followed the man's finger to one in particular. He was right. The dead man's plate was ripped to shreds. Steeling his nausea Arthur bent down to inspect the victim for himself. The dead soldier was covered in deep needle like wounds, their shape similar to teeth marks.

"Could Light Bringers do this, sir?" one of the soldiers asked.

Arthur gulped wondering what kind of beast could tear through steel with such ease.

"This isn't the work of any weapon I've seen," William said inspecting another of the dead.

Gudbrand shuffled nervously behind them. "Duke, I hate to remind you, but we have an entire armada ready to pin us from behind. I suggest we find shelter in the city. That is, if this isn't just another Hunan trap."

Arthur rose to his feet with a groan. "He's right. Keep moving toward the city, but don't let your guard down."

He eyed the foul wounds once more before joining the others. "I hope whatever this is hasn't gotten you too, Lucian."

Surveying the beach ahead he kept a careful eye out for the fine jade armor that Lucian bore. To his relief it was nowhere to be found. Drinking in the scene caused another revelation to dawn on him, however. None of the men on the beach had been slain by arrows. All of the bodies lay in mangled heaps similar to the men he'd inspected.

"No, arrows," Arthur whispered to William.

"Something foul has happened here, my lord," replied William. The seasoned warrior marched a few feet ahead, drawing his sword.

"Eyes up, men. We don't know what awaits us in the city," William barked.

Arthur followed suit, drawing his own weapon. Phoenix Flame radiated a warm light on those around him and the soiled beach beneath. The crunch of a thousand feet reverberated off the sheer cliffs on either side as the army made their way to the city wall. Banners whipped in the wind carrying the nervous mood of their company. As the wall drew near, Arthur gave the command to have a small scouting party accompany him to look ahead. Treading carefully, William and Gudbrand joined him with a few others. They approached the city gate and, to their surprise, found a strange hole cut into it. It was just taller than a man and wide enough for a fully armored soldier to pass through. Arthur ran his hand along the smooth surface of the cut.

"An Edonium Blade did this," he said in quiet contemplation.

"Thegn Lucian could be alive then!" William said excitedly.

"Perhaps..." Arthur mused. New energy surged within him, pushing back the gloom he'd allowed to take hold.

"William, commander, tell the men to get this gate down. Have our forces line the walls, archers first, to cover our troops still docking on the beach. Have those waiting start gathering the dead."

"Sir?" Gudbrand asked noticing Arthur's sudden energy.

"We can survive this yet," Arthur said. "Whoever. *Whatever* did this doesn't seem to be around anymore."

He turned looking up at Hunan's keep. It rested atop the city, distinguishing itself by its breaking of uniformity. It was adorned with crown molding in the form of Hunan script and guarded by a large statue of a tiger. The gaudy features set it apart from the simple refinement of other structures within the city.

"I will take Sir William with me along with two companies to the Keep. Maybe we can find some answers there."

"And Lucian," he hoped.

Bowing his head, the Gudbrand departed to give the order.

"Seems he's caught whatever has a hold of you," William said chuckling.

"Let's use it while it still remains, shall we?"

It didn't take long for the companies Arthur requested to gather. The largest obstacle was funneling their troops through one city gate before the armada at their back grasped what was happening. Thankfully they still remained content to only blockade the bay. Arthur motioned for his men

166

to follow him into the heart of the city. The eeriness remained as they passed through a number of abandoned streets. The occasional straggler could be found cut to ribbons but strangely the city seemed void of life. The beauty of the pagodas was juxtaposed to the anticipation of terror they all felt. Arthur found his eyes darting from window to sliding door waiting for an ambush to break the stupor hanging over the place. Reaching the city center they followed the main road that ascended upward in a steep climb toward the upper levels. The street formed into a zig-zag shape helping alleviate the hike. As they continued their ascent Arthur couldn't help but feel dumbfounded.

"Where are all the people?" he muttered in disbelief.

Timber beams of surrounding structures creaked, and scattered banners flapped with the occasional wind. Heavy footsteps bounced off the buildings around them. An ominous sound in a city of such size. Sword still in hand, Arthur led his men up the final ascent that led to the keep. Rounding the corner he was greeted by the architectural wonder. The immense construction rested on a sheered edge platform that overlooked the city. The pagoda-shaped keep reached a dizzying height that surpassed the surrounding cliffs' edges. Its form widened at its base leaving any visitor feeling engulfed by its enormous presence. Detailed statutes adorned each corner of its tiered roofs and windows were molded with marvelously designed script. It wasn't the majesty of the place that struck Arthur, though. Piled at the keep's base were thousands upon thousands of corpses. Some of them smashed from the crowd, others torn to pieces. A river of blood streamed from the disgusting mass of mangled flesh and bone, rushing like a rapids over the platform's edge like a perverse waterfall.

"By all that is good, what could have done this?" William said stupefied.

Arthur had no words. It was a nightmare beyond his imagining. He had witnessed battle, even the kind that turned to slaughter. But this, this was something else entirely. The men at his back jerked to a halt at the sight, none daring to take a step toward the wretched scene. As the shock faded the next terror gripped him.

"Was Lucian in this mass of humanity?"

His eyes darted around, looking for the image of a jade-plated figure mangled among the others. Thankfully it didn't appear. Instead he noticed something peculiar among the huddled mass of bodies. A tiny gap had been carved out of the wall not far from where he stood. Strange enough a pile of corpses had broken free from the rest leaving a path cleared into the carved opening.

"There," Arthur said raising a finger to the spot.

"You want to go in, my lord?" A nearby soldier asked shakily.

"We must find Thegn Lucian." He turned to address his men, all panic stricken at the prospect of even nearing the horrid scene. "I thought you fighting men of Edonia?" Arthur scowled.

Only one carried the same resolve to go forward, Sir William. "Very well, the rest of you cowards stay here. Sir William and I will find our lost thegn."

The soldiers around him feigned shame, but none stepped forward to join them.

"Shall we?" Arthur asked.

William's face looked extra worn as he nodded his head. How many battles had those tired eyes seen? The greying hair spoke of decades of long conflict. A nice scar running down his nose told of a near death encounter. Yet, Arthur had never seen the man so weathered by war.

"This isn't war," Arthur thought correcting himself. "This is extermination."

The two men cautiously moved toward the tiny gap carved into the wall. They were forced to climb over a small mound of bodies in the attempt, nearly toppling them over into the gore. A memory he surely wouldn't forget. Arthur did all he could to avoid the gaze of the dead looking up at him from the sickening pile. Their lifeless eyes cried out in agony about their grim fate. He had all but succeeded in avoiding their gaze until a loose arm caught his leg. It sent him reeling into the keep's perimeter. Groaning he lifted himself up accidentally locking eyes with a little girl.

Her complexion was pale even before death. Thick dark hair had been woven into two braids at each side of her head. Narrow brown eyes stared at him lifeless. Gulping he tried to break free from her gaze but those eyes pulled him in. They morphed into sapphires, black hair bursting into the color of a sunbeam. The soft face transformed but remained frozen in pain. He felt his own hot tears stream down his cheek.

"Who could have done this! Who!" he screamed.

"Caiah, my love…who…"

A gentle hand touched his shoulder. "You alright my lord?" William asked with a quizzical look.

He was back now in that dreary place. A foreign land where the same old pain of the world had been wrought on a different family. He rose to his feet. "Let's go."

William nodded and the two of them entered into the large bronze doors of the emperor's pagoda. The halls were dark, the grey sky gathering outside not helping their cause. Only the faint glowing light of Phoenix Flame guided their path. Pressing forward into the ever-darkening hall they found a few guards slain at their post. Their bodies were mutilated like all the rest. Searching the place, they found what looked to be a stairway that led to a major section of the keep. Perhaps the throne room itself. Banners bearing the tiger of Hunan draped either side of a narrow path. Reaching the final step they were greeted with a vast entryway. Dozens of white sliding doors offered a different path to the vast complex. At their center sat the grandest of them all. A carved tiger protruded from two towering bronze doors. The marvelous craftsmanship was bordered with a traditional looking pattern all along its frame.

"Think that's it?" William joked.

The two of them drew closer. The throne doors only seemed to grow in immensity as they approached. It left Arthur feeling like a child as he looked up at them. He chuckled to himself. "I suppose a self-proclaimed emperor would have a superiority complex."

Thankfully the doors had been left ajar. Approaching the small crack, a sight they had been dreading came into view. The top half of Sir Kain lay wedged between the two frames. With a wild cry William collapsed at the corpse's side.

"No…my friend. No…" His voice trailed off fighting back a sob. The reaction left Arthur sick. He'd never seen William demonstrate sorrow like this. The man had been a rock all his days, but even he was breaking in such a place. It was Arthur's turn to place a comforting hand on his friend's shoulder. The grizzled vet quickly rose to his feet.

"Let's find whoever did this," he growled.

With careful reverence they moved what remained of Kain out of their way, placing him just outside the doors to bury later. Entering the throne room they were met by a ceiling of dizzying height. Looking up felt as though the room itself reached for the stars. Bodies of the Hunan royal guard lay scattered across the room's mosaic floor, their blood seeping into the crevasses of the marvelous design. Tiny colored stones all worked together to form the image of the emperor's tower crested with a rising sun now stained red.

Arthur held his blade ready expecting the culprit of this nightmare to strike at any moment. Cautiously he and William crept toward the dais at the end of the room. As they drew closer he realized how massive each step of the dais truly was. Each stone block protruded two feet from one another, causing them to step awkwardly as they ascended the throne. Reaching the top Arthur leaned over breathless, his heavy armor having burdened his every step.

Weary lungs choked at what he saw as he raised his head. A crumpled form rested beside the smooth red and cream strata throne. The jade armor looked torn in several places and a small pool of blood had gathered underneath. Arthur couldn't stop the tears from flowing as he knelt beside his collapsed friend. Delicately he turned Lucian onto his back. The jade eyes that had once carried so much ambition now sat poignantly empty.

"Why Lucian… why did you have to go and be a drakon fool," he bellowed out into the empty chamber. Looking into Lucian's eyes nearly broke him. He felt the weight of guilt and sorrow threatening to pull him under. He let it happen again. Why was he so pathetically weak? Why was he so powerless to protect the ones he loved most?

The real horror of it all began to settle in. He was the one who had caused this. It was his words that had pushed this young, naive thegn to madness. Words that he would never be able to take back.

William's eyes scanned the chamber attentive for danger but beneath their surface a similar sorrow stirred. Arthur was unaware of how much time had passed before he finally rose to his feet. William had left his side a while ago to investigate the room further, likely an attempt to give the duke his privacy. As he slid his sword into its sheath something strange caught Arthur's eye. A stream of blood trailed off from Lucian's body beyond to a doorway behind the throne. Perhaps it was a vain attempt to stave off his guilt that caused him to rise to his feet. He pulled Phoenix Flame free once more as he followed the trail. Reaching with his unarmed hand he carefully pushed the door open. The room was dimly lit by a line of red stained glass windows to his right. In the faint light he could just make out something stirring in the shadows beyond.

"Have you come to finish the task?" asked a heavily accented voice. Its sound was tainted with the hoarse tone of a gravely wounded man.

A faint glow suddenly illuminated the figure. It was an elderly man of Hunan descent. His face was marked by several wrinkles and sleek black hair that hung disheveled near his shoulders. His chestnut eyes still carried a defiant fire within them. As Arthur's vision adjusted to the dark more of the man came into view. He wore regal clothes. In fact, his garments were fit for an emperor.

"If so you forgot something," the self-proclaimed Emperor Tao said raising Edon's Bane before him. Arthur could see a fresh stream of blood trickling down the man's shoulder until it joined a larger pool at his feet.

"What's happened here?" Arthur asked.

Tao gave him a blood-soaked smirk. "Betrayal. That's what has happened to us."

Suddenly the Hunan ruler collapsed. The Edonium Blade in his hand clattered onto the floor. Arthur rushed beside him checking to see if the fallen man was still alive. Tao let out a pathetic cough producing more sticky red ooze. Arthur examined the shoulder. A clean cut more than likely made from an Edonium Blade.

So you dealt the killing blow to Hunan after all, my friend, Arthur mused to himself. His gaze turned back to meet Tao's eyes.

"What do you mean betrayal?" Arthur demanded.

A gargled laugh churned in Tao's throat. "A promise broken…" A fit of violent coughs overwhelmed the man as the words left his mouth. It wouldn't be long now, Arthur could see.

"Speak plainly before you pass from this life!"

A satisfied smile crossed Tao's face. "Doom… coming… Thank… new… emperor…"

And with those words Tao faded from this life. The war was over. Arthur sat in the deafening silence still clinging to the robes of the now dead Tao.

What had it all come to? he thought. The war had ended but what remained for him? Numbness washed over him as he sat in the stillness searching for answers he knew didn't exist.

"My lord?" came the voice of William behind him.

Arthur turned seeing the recognition in William's eyes at who laid before them.

"So it's over."

"Not yet," Arthur replied. The reality of their situation returning to him. "We still have to deal with the armada outside."

William nodded. "We should tell the men what we've found. Perhaps it will steel their courage."

Arthur nodded his head, extending Edon's Bane to his longtime companion. William clasped the sword gratefully and the two of them departed the dark room. Tenderly Arthur placed Lucian over his shoulder. The added weight strangely evaporated as he descended the throne's stairs. As if knowing the truth that Lucian had placed the final blow released some other burden he hadn't known he was carrying. William in Arthur's absence had gathered Kain's body together and made it ready for transport. Carrying their two companions they made their journey back to the army in silent reverence.

A dull sky greeted them as they finally broke free of the oppressive confines of Hunan's keep. A host of captains stood anxiously within the gated complex waiting for them.

"Seems they mustered the courage to at least climb over the bodies," Arthur murmured as they approached.

The highest-ranking captain among them sprang to action as they came into view. With a quick but proficient bow he spoke, "My lord, there… well there is something you should see."

"It's been a long day, captain, can you not just tell me?"

"Sir, it's best you see."

Annoyed, Arthur nodded for the man to lead them to whatever it may be. Bowing the captain then motioned for the others around to assist with the bodies of Lucian and Kain. Companions taken care of they made their way toward the breached wall. Arthur was thankful some initiative had been taken to clear a path. His eyes wandered, searching for the little girl from earlier but she was nowhere to be found. Stepping out from the keep's defenses they were met with a high overlook of the city and the narrow inlet below. That's when he saw it. A fleet of untold ships brandishing black sails. He watched as the last of Hunan and Kaskar's fleet evaporated before the might of the mysterious armada.

"Who?" Arthur gawked.

"We don't know, sir. Their markings are unfamiliar to all of us," the captain said staring at the scene. "I'm just grateful we've seemed to avoid their attention."

Arthur watched in awe as the unfamiliar armada began to fade over the horizon. As the last of them vanished from his sight, he could just make out a marking painted on the blackened mast of a ship. It was the sigil of a blood red moon.

14

JULIET

THE DAGGER WAS AT her throat just seconds after she lowered her hand from her mouth. Her gaze was still fixated on the pillars of smoke in the distance and the flash of soldiers' steel as they clashed within the city. The voice of a young man growled from behind.

"Are you with those Varnas skrills," he asked pressing the dagger slightly closer to her skin.

Closing her eyes she drew in a breath to calm herself. She could feel the man's hot breath against her neck. He was taller than her by a few inches or so she guessed by the way he held the dagger. Listening she could hear no click of plate or chainmail with the subtle shifting of his feet. Her eyes shot open knowing exactly what to do. Raising her foot she sent it slamming into the man's knee. At the same time she brought her right arm up toward the dagger at her throat. Grasping it she twisted around just as the impact jolted her captor's knee. The man muttered a curse as she now held him with knees to the ground and wrist twisted. The dagger left his hand clattering on the cobbled stone.

"I think I will ask the questions now," she said to the smarting fool. "Who are you and what do you want with me?"

Still in pain he glared at her, anger burning in his hazel eyes. "You kill my companions and you think you have the right to ask me anything? I won't speak a word to a traitorous shantz like you.

Go on and let me join my friends."

Now able to see her assailant she assessed who she was dealing with. He was thin but had lines of muscle, likely from manual labor, that peaked out from his shortened sleeves. His hair was chestnut and disheveled set atop an oval face. A hint of a beard was growing in around his clenched jaw line.

"Like what you see?" he hissed. Her eyes shuttered realizing she had been staring at him.

"I think you have me confused," she said.

"How so?"

She released his arm to his amazement. "I came here to find The People's Justice for answers not to slay them. I was ambushed by those Varnas soldiers just like your men."

The man rubbed his sore wrist. "Why were you looking for The People's Justice?" A hint of distrust tainted his voice.

Juliet weighed her next words carefully. If this man belonged to them he was no friend of the empire. Glancing over her shoulder she drank in the scene unfolding near the palace.

That is if there still was an empire, she thought.

Her eyes turned back to the man now rising to his feet. "I assume you are with The People's Justice?" she asked.

"Depends," he said.

"Depends on what?"

"How you answer my question."

She pursed her lips. "Fine, I wanted to see if The People's Justice was behind the leak of Light Bringers to Hunan."

"And if they were?" the man said raising an eyebrow.

She looked over at the emptied warehouse. "I doubt they will be any longer."

The man's face soured at the comment, but he quickly followed it with a sigh. "I suppose not."

"So, you are with them?" she prodded.

Now it was his turn to weigh his words. A moment of silence passed before he spoke again. "I was. I suppose the empire has bigger problems to deal with now," he said, pointing a finger to the pillars of smoke.

"Why? Why betray your own empire?" she demanded.

The man let out an annoyed snort. "The empire betrayed us long ago. We only sought to return the favor."

"Seems you've reaped what you've sown," Juliet said nodding her head back to the warehouse.

"Listen! I don't need chastisement from you. You highborn are all alike. Sitting in your lofty palaces while the rest of us get trampled by your greed."

How did he know I am high born? she wondered.

"Your cloak," he said, confusing her.

"You're wondering how I know who you are," he said, pointing at the fine fabric draped around her.

"Something that fine could only belong to one of the great houses. What are you? Child of a thegn or baron?"

She gripped the fabric, frustrated it had given her away so easily. *Just as good at revealing who I am as hiding me,* she thought.

"Daughter of Thegn Oswald."

"Just like a highborn to come here thinking she has all the answers."

"Now you listen!"

"See you do it without thinking. People, to folks like you, are cattle to be ordered about. You're oblivious to the fact that we also may have an opinion worth valuing!"

Her face flushed at his words. He was wrong. Her father was a kind ruler. She would not stand for... A host of cries sounded only a few blocks away, their fear likely from the Varnas troops she'd encountered earlier.

"Listen I would love to stick around and enlighten you on the blights of the people, but I'd prefer to survive this day so..." the mysterious man began back peddling slowly. Just as he turned to sprint, she caught his arm, dropping him to his knees once more by grabbing a pressure point on his wrist.

"Okay... okay not so rough would ya," he said, slowly rising.

As he rose a tuft of hair moved revealing a branded 'e'on his forehead.

"You're one of the emperor's forgers!" she said in amazement.

The man's eyes turned sorrowful at her discovery. "A life I'd rather forget."

"How… how did you escape?"

A crowd of people now streamed down the road in their direction.

"Listen, I'll tell you everything you want to know about me and about The People's Justice. Can we just get out of here first?"

She weighed the offer in her mind. He'd already tried to run once, could she really trust him to keep his word?

"You are willing to stand trial before my father for your crimes to the empire?" she asked.

"Sure," he said rolling his eyes. "Now can we hurry? I don't suspect these men will have much love for those loyal to the empire either."

"One last thing."

"What?" he said exasperated.

"What is your name?"

He gave her a look as if he'd never expected a highborn to care what his name was. "It's Mateus."

"Well, Mateus, I suggest we get going."

She picked up the dagger from the ground pointing behind him. "You first. We need a path to take us north of the city. If we can get to Hornhall we will have entered my father's lands."

"If that's the case…" Mateus paused surveying the shoreline south of them. "I suggest we commandeer one of those."

He gestured to a small ferry boat used by peasants to transfer civilians back and forth between the two sides of the city. She had watched the vessels with curiosity countless times during her weeks of study. How any of the rickety vessels stayed afloat across the bay was beyond her.

"You want to take that?" she asked, hiding her dismay.

"What? Not good enough for a highborn in the midst of coup?" he chided.

"Stop calling me that. It's fine, I just wanted to make sure."

He shot her a doubting glance before moving toward the vessel. The small ferry appeared to be in worse shape up close. Chipped blue paint crusted and peeled over half rotten wood. She could even see patches of a tar like substance had been used to patch old holes on the small standing platform. Mateus jumped in rocking the tiny vessel violently.

"Come now, Your Majesty, we don't have much time."

She glared at him as she tenderly set one foot onto the deck. The shouts of the crowd were just behind them now. Taking an oar in hand Mateus pressed it against the dock sending Juliet floundering forward. Chuckling he offered her a hand. She slapped the offer away as she dusted herself off.

"You wanted me to fall in, didn't you?" she snarled.

"Would have made my escape easier," he said coolly. "How is it you plan to keep me as your captive on our long journey north? I see no bindings. Who's to say I won't run away in your sleep?"

"Perhaps I should make you a cripple?" she stated lifting the small knife.

A flash of panic crossed Mateus' face. "Now that won't be necessary."

He was right though. How would she keep him from bolting the second he found an opening? She eyed him as he confidently paddled them across the choppy bay. Eventually her gaze fell toward the emperor's palace in the distance. She could just make out forms of men moving across the complex. Some fled toward the vast armada that rested at the emperor's personal docks. Others collided with one another leaving behind a fallen foe. How had it come to this and why? Once more she looked at Mateus who stood confidently at the small vessel's head. The soldiers she'd encountered belonged to Duke Volkmar, and he had mentioned Varnas as responsible. Could it really be true that the duke was moving to take the throne for himself?

"You mentioned Varnas earlier. Is Duke Volkmar responsible for this?"

Mateus' face soured at the name. "And others."

"Others?"

"Yes, many a fool has played his part to make today possible, I among them."

He didn't elaborate further, leaving them in an awkward silence broken only by the occasion stroke of a paddle.

"I'm surprised you aren't happy. From what I could tell this is what The People's Justice wanted isn't it? The fall of the empire?" she said, breaking the silence.

"Foolish woman, you don't know anything about what I want," Mateus snapped keeping his gaze ahead of him.

"What do you want?"

He sighed in exasperation. "Some peace and quiet for our journey."

Annoyed, Juliet turned back to face the eastern side of the city. Clearly, pressing him wouldn't produce more answers. The remainder of the trek across the bay was a silent one. It took nearly an hour in their tiny boat before they finally made landfall on the western shore. Mateus steered the vessel to an open slot within a dock occupied with similar ferries. As the two of them disembarked Juliet was careful to keep him in front of her. Mateus motioned for her to follow. He led them out of the docks and through the winding streets of West Edonia with smooth confidence. Entering the city, they came under the shadow of the ever-expanding skyline of the western metropolis. Decades ago many had left the eastern banks of the Edonian Bay to start a life here.

Basically, a capitol of its own, West Edonia became the little brother of both trade and influence to the city across the bay. The same tall structures of pearl, crimson, and gold lined every corner and street. Unlike Edonia proper, the western city remained lightly populated in comparison as many remained content to stay across the bay. For all those who came to start a new life here old ties often dragged them back east.

Moving from the sides streets they joined a small crowd that walked on the city's main road. Off to their right a stirring of voices rose in crescendo as they neared the city's northern gate. Many pointed out the sight of smoke rising in the east. A panic spread through the crowd as confusion took hold.

"Is the great city burning?" one voice cried.

"It's the end, it's the coming of the end," said another. A baby's wail sounded as it felt the terror of its mother clutching it close.

"We need to go, now," Mateus muttered under his breath.

Juliet looked at him with curious eyes.

"The city will be panicked soon. Meaning, they will lock down the gates and try to keep control of those inside," he said nodding his head to a cluster of guards poured into the street as if on cue.

They bore a mix of polished plate and leather. In their hands were newly crafted spears. Each of their faces remained hidden behind a lifeless mask. For the first time it all felt so sinister to Juliet. The panic, the fear, the ruthless control. She wanted to escape it all and quickly.

"What should we do?" she asked.

The slight panic in her words seemed to take Mateus by surprise. Turning toward the gate he assessed their options. "There," he said pointing to several horses tied down in a nearby guard's stable. "We can take them for the road."

"You mean steal?"

"Listen Highborn, do you want to get out of here or not? You didn't think we'd walk all the way back to Venhorn did you?"

She frowned mainly because she hadn't thought of how they were going to get back home. Only that they needed to. It also made her uneasy how well this Mateus knew what to do. He continued to stare at her as if waiting for approval. "I'm sure the poor fellow whose horse we steal can be reimbursed by your father. That is if he's alive at the end of this."

"Fine," she said crossing her arms. "But when this is all over we find a way to return the horses with payment."

Mateus rolled his eyes motioning for her to follow. Approaching the stable they looked for any who might spot what they were doing. The small hovel sat abandoned, its guardians likely off gawking at the scene on the eastern shore. With the speed of a trained thief, Mateus unwrapped a pair of reins, tossing one to her.

181

"Come, we need to hurry." He leapt onto the mount spurring it toward the gate. A sudden panic struck her. She had given him the perfect opportunity to escape! She forced her mount to give chase as Mateus set off toward the city gate. His steed whipped past the dumbfounded guards who stood watch. In a blink Mateus was gone from her sight.

"You fool, Juls," she muttered to herself.

She quickly darted past the host of guards and toward the crest of a hill outside the confines of the city. As she reached the top she was shocked to find Mateus patiently waiting for her on the other side.

"Wanted to get out of the city guard's view," he said with a shrug. He took a bite out of an apple he had somehow managed to procured. Rummaging through one of the saddlebags he found another tossing it to her. She reached for the apple, nearly falling from her horse. She could see an amused grin painted on his face from the blunder. It sent a flush of red up her cheeks, infuriating her.

"Come, I'd like to find a place to sleep before night falls," she said pushing down her embarrassment.

Mateus gave a royal bow motioning for her to lead the way. The next few hours of their journey were taken in relative quiet. Nothing but chirping crickets and the rustling of the wind. Evening was fast approaching and they didn't have supplies for a fire. It was another hour or so before a cluster of dried trees came into view that they could use. She gestured for them to stop and gather the dying limbs and make camp for the night. Mateus, seeing the spot, gave an agreeing nod. Perhaps the first one he'd given her in their brief time together. They only had to wonder for a short time how they'd fell the trees. The owner of the horses had conveniently left a traveling axe in one of the saddlebags.

Mateus took the axe in hand as if to start cutting, but Juliet with smug pride ripped the tool from his hand, "Don't want the city boy to hurt himself," she said with a satisfied smirk. He shot her a frown but didn't protest further. It wasn't long before they sat around a crackling fire, the night sky a canvas of glimmering gems above. She fidgeted in the uncomfortable silence. The hazel eyes of Mateus peered into the crackling fire in silent contemplation. She felt her stomach growl, unsatisfied from the apple she'd eaten earlier. How she wished there was a tasty rabbit roasting above those flickering flames.

"Why didn't you run?" she asked, hoping to find a distraction from the hunger pains. Mateus lifted his gaze from the fire to meet hers.

"Perhaps I wanted to see the inside of a Highborn's palace? Or maybe it's because I am a glutton for capital punishment?"

She scowled. "I was being serious."

Mateus drew in a deep breath. "Perhaps it's because I'm tired of living on the run only to be hunted like a feral dog. Running wouldn't do me much good any more anyways." He pointed to the small brand on his forehead.

"You said you wanted to see a highborn's palace, but didn't you live in the emperor's palace? That's as highborn as it gets."

Mateus broke into a sarcastic laugh. "Yes, yes, the dank caves beneath the palace are the life of luxury. Come visit the blazing hot forges, the cold stone bed chamber. If those can't keep you around then the emperor's vow of secrecy will."

Embarrassed Juliet looked away. "I'm sorry. I didn't know."

"Most don't," Mateus replied, now with less venom in his voice. "I'm actually surprised you knew what my brand meant. Other than I was a slave of the empire."

"It's the symbol itself," she said pointing. "For those... highborn, we are taught what each distinct mark of the slave symbols mean..." her voice trailed off realizing the validity of his point.

"I don't blame you, you know," he said after a moment of quiet. "How could I?"

She looked at him curiously. His eyes met hers, a look of pity in them. "Those born into the life you have rarely see what it takes to maintain it. You travel to the finest places. Your caretakers are careful to avoid any... unpleasantries. In fact everyone within Edonia, highborn or not, is guilty of this in some way."

"How so?" she asked adjusting herself to a more comfortable position. As she did a crackle of wood sent tiny embers fluttering into the air above them.

"Think about it. Have you ever been to Mascar or Kaskar? Let alone Ishkar or Gurun? Why do you think the empire has to put down so many rebellions there?"

She contemplated the question, not wanting to answer hastily with a line he could retort. "They grow weary of their state under the empire?"

"Exactly."

"But that is always the story of the vanquished. Edonia cannot help if she has the power to dominate other lands? Would they not do the same to us if they could?"

Mateus made a click with his tongue. "That is the issue, isn't it? Men scramble for power and crush those who'd oppose them. All the while the poor, the weak, and the foreigner survive on the fringes."

"So why condemn Edonia? Is the world not guilty as well?" she asked accusingly.

"Because…" he said drawing out the word. "At one time they knew a better way and forsook it."

"What do you mean?"

Mateus' eyes fell to the fire as another burst of embers shot into the night sky. "My mother told me of it."

"Is she a scribe in the palace?"

A smirk crossed Mateus' face at the question. "One could say that. Do you know of the ancient library? Buried beneath the palace?"

"You mean the Grand Hall of Learning where all scribes go to train?"

"No, what I speak of is far more ancient and far more dangerous."

"I've never heard of such a place."

Mateus' expression grew thoughtful as a memory passed before him. "I suppose the forge and the library are the two greatest weapons gifted to Edonia. An emperor would want to hold such things close to the chest."

"How does this have to do with your mother?" Juliet pressed, unsure of what to make of this mysterious "library."

"You see all forgers of Edonium are born into the trade. A family secret of sorts. Seeing as we aren't allowed to leave our little dungeon, there's a select breeding pool."

He paused, tending the fire with a stick. "The ancient library is attended by a host of female scribes. One such blacksmith and one such scribe... well." He made a motion with his hands bringing them together and bursting them into an explosion.

"Thus I was born. Chosen at birth to be a blacksmith of the second most powerful weapon in the world."

"And the first?" Juliet asked, wondering what could be stronger than an Edonium Blade.

"The truth," Mateus' eyes grew hard as steel as he said the words.

"My mother took that second one very seriously. So much so she divulged secrets to my father and me. Secrets that by no means should leave her circle of scribes."

"So what happened?" Juliet asked leaning forward now engrossed in the tale.

"Nothing, at least for a few years. Over time she shared some of Edonia's most ancient tales with me. The stories she told transformed me from a simple forger of Edonium into a holder of Edonia's great purpose."

He shook his head dismissively. "How great the mighty have fallen."

"I don't understand all your cryptic talk. Speak plainly."

"Very well."

"The histories you've been told about Edonia are false, or rather they are inaccurate. These great weapons, these Edonium Blades, as you call them were not forged from the superiority and might of the empire. They were a gift. A gift given long ago by something or someone far more powerful than a mere man, the First King. The First King had something stolen from him, another kind of 'gift.'"

Mateus' face turned grim as he became lost in thought.

"And? Come on you can't stop the tale there," Juliet complained.

Hesitantly he continued. "Let's just say there are far more sinister things in this world than the wickedness of men. A darkness spawned from a heart of rebellion in an age nearly beyond records.

It feeds off the seeds of discord, seeking for an opportunity to grow wherever it may be planted."

A shadow seemed to fall over their small campfire, as if an outside force in the surrounding night was listening. Juliet shivered as a cold prickle ran up her spine. In Mateus' hazel eyes she could see true dread.

"This being has roamed our world seeking to build a kingdom of his own. It nearly succeeded too, until a greater power intervened."

"You mean the one who helped Edonia, the First King?" Juliet asked.

Mateus gave an approving nod. "He gifted the men of Edonia with the power to forge Dawn Blades, what we call Edonium Blades. And with them they beat back the darkness to a far corner of this world."

"I've heard very little of this," Juliet confessed. "The tales I was told as a child spoke of Edonia ruling the world. How the lives of men were enriched by our rule until they grew fat, discontent, and bored."

"That's not wrong," Mateus said thoughtfully. "There was a time of golden years. But as the ages passed, the hearts of men grew discontent. The old ways began to seep into their hearts once more. Weapons used to fight darkness had become the tools to propagate it and now... well. You saw for yourself today."

"You're trying to tell me the attack on Edonia has to do with this dark being?" she asked in disbelief. "I'd say it has more to do with traitors and liars. Greedy men who put their own interests before others." A faint hint of accusation seeped into her tone.

"Is that not what the empire has been for some time? Is that not the definition of evil?" he asked.

She had no retort. How could she? The very empire she had given her life to protect and uphold was being questioned and she... she was beginning to see this man's point.

"So what's your solution? To watch it all burn?"

Mateus snorted at the accusation. "Hardly. I was doing something. The People's Justice wasn't about a power grab. It was about the truth. The truth of what the empire was and who they should be." A tired sigh left his lungs as he seemed to slip back into deep thought once more.

"Until I was too blind to see who I'd hopped in bed with. Perhaps I'm no different. I so desperately wanted to bring change but now…"

He lay down on the cold ground wrapping himself in his cloak. "I've spoken enough of these things tonight. You have your answers, now let me sleep."

"One last question, please," she pleaded.

He closed his eyes muttering for her to ask.

"How did you escape the forge and start all this?"

Eyes still shut he replied, "With the blood of my parents and a deal with a fiend."

With that he turned away leaving her alone with her thoughts for the rest of the night.

15

OCTAVIAN

O CTAVIAN WATCHED IN horror as the sapphire eyes of Septimus burst with surprise. A stream of blood now trickled from his mouth.

"No, I didn't." Octavian glanced down at his hand. The Edonium Blade within his grip hummed without the faintest hint of blood on it. A scream rang in his ears as if it was a great distance away. The room spun and a deep sense of dread twisted in his gut. The sickening sound of steel pulled from flesh burned into his mind. Shortly after Septimus' body collapsed into darkness. A sense of motion without clarity overtook Octavian as the room morphed into a whirlwind of images and muffled sound. He was trapped in a nightmare of his own making. It all threatened to overtake him. Squeezing his eyes shut he waited for the feeling to pass.

How much time had passed? Octavian wondered to himself. Hours? Perhaps days?

He stood in the midst of the throne room. The chamber sat in impenetrable darkness under the cloak of night. Guards stood sentinel on either side with flickering torches in hand. The faint light they emitted painted sections of the room in a sinister hue of orange. It had happened again. Revenge had been in his grasp and he failed to take it. And now his opportunity was gone forever. Motion drew his attention toward the throne. Volkmar sat atop it, face masked in thought. Octavian's stomach lurched. Who had he helped ascend to the throne? How was this man any better?

No, Octavian, he thought chastising himself. *This isn't about restoring Edonia. This is about letting it all burn.*

Something strange gnawed at him, however. The story of Edonia's great purpose that Septimus had revealed to him months ago. Could that tale really be true?

"Nothing but a lie the empire tells itself to justify its rule," he muttered to himself.

"Octavian," came Volkmar's voice calling to him. With somber expression Volkmar waved a hand ushering Octavian to draw near. Octavian rose to his feet, hesitantly moving to the throne.

"You look tired, friend," Volkmar said with a surprising amount of compassion. "We have much to discuss about our future empire. You should get some rest."

"Yes…" Octavian said voice trailing off.

Volkmar gave him a sidelong glance. "You're not angry about earlier, are you? I didn't mean to steal the final blow, but your hesitation could have ruined everything."

Shaking his head as if escaping a daze, Octavian looked up at the duke, no emperor. "You did what I could not."

A satisfied grin crossed Volkmar's face. "And the heralds shall sing of it. But without you I would not be alive. For that you have played a critical role. It's not done either. Together we can forge an empire worthy of its name once again."

"I think I'll take the sleep first," Octavian said wearily.

"It would be wise," Volkmar said weighing him. No other word was given so Octavian bowed and moved to leave. He wandered the halls to his chamber as if in a drunken stupor. The day had drained him, that was all. Yet, the nagging, the guilt, threatened to pull him under. His bed was a refuge from it all. A friend he was thankful to find at the end of such a day. Falling into it with a thump he closed his eyes. A dark dreamless sleep overtook him. A sleep he'd desired for a long time.

A beam of morning sunlight stirred him from his slumber. A new day was eager to begin. A day Octavian wished he could delay forever. He knew what Volkmar would ask of him and he was already tired of death. Who was he fooling? There would be plenty more to come. He'd asked for it, desired it even. So, why did he feel… well, like this?

It always leads to death. It will never stop, he thought to himself. *Why should I expect it to ever stop?*

Death. It was the thing that drove all men. The endless pursuit of power to take life and keep it. Men chased it, sacrificed for it, killed for it. Then what? After all the blood is spilled and your hands are soaked crimson what do you have? Another war to avenge those who have fallen? Families divided and cities in turmoil? Allies turned to hated enemies? Why did men seek such things?

"They can't help themselves," a voice seemed to say. He sat up searching the dimly lit chamber. All was still in his finely furnished room.

Had that been his voice?

Shaking away a lingering apprehension he arose and dressed himself in a pristine crimson jacket. Golden buttons lined the middle, clasping at his cleanly shaven neck. He slicked back his thick black hair observing the handiwork in a mirror. With a swift tug at the bottom of the jacket he stepped out into the hall. Servants buzzed about likely hoping to please their new master. No doubt Volkmar encouraged them to earn his praise in such a manner.

Reaching the throne room doors he was met with two men dressed in violet, colors of house Varnas. Giving them a curt nod, Octavian stepped through the open doors. Much of the council already stood ready at the sides of the room. More men jockeying to earn the new emperor's favor, no doubt. Had he done anything to rinse these lands of Edonian filth? He marched forward arms behind back. A confident stride, one he had carried all his years as Septimus' advisor and now…

His eyes met those of Volkmar who stood grinning eagerly beside the throne. At his side, bound, stood Duchess Beatrice and their son, Leo. The boy's blood shot eyes carried dark bags beneath. His finely tailored coat and jacket were ruffled and torn. Beatrice still displayed a defiant look even in her tattered dress. As he approached, Octavian could see another figure beside them. Crumwald, the Duchess' trusted confidant.

"You look refreshed, my friend," Volkmar said extending a welcoming hand to Octavian.

"Thank you, Your Majesty," Octavian replied taking his place beside Volkmar.

Volkmar gave an approving nod before turning back to his wife and son. "Now that all my advisors have arrived, I suggest we get started. Royal members of the court I present to you Duchess Beatrice, her grand advisor Crumwald, and my son, Leo."

Octavian drew in a breath waiting for the pronouncement to come. He hated the fact that his gaze couldn't move from the trembling boy at his mother's side. The boy who'd stopped him not a day ago now standing beside the woman who had stayed his hand many years before. Beatrice pulled the fearful Leo close, not wanting to give any satisfaction to the gloating Volkmar.

Volkmar raised a hand containing a crumbled piece of parchment. "I have proof here that my wife and son knowingly collaborated with the late emperor to feed weapons to our enemies in Hunan."

A faint murmur fell over the crowd as Beatrice's eyes grew wide. "You snake! Can you not even accept your own treachery."

Volkmar ignored her, turning back to the other councilors. "Through a known terror group named 'The People's Justice' they worked to distribute Light Bringers to our enemies in the south. Some have even rumored that the leader of this group is an escaped member of the royal forges."

"Why?" one council member cried in dismay toward Beatrice. "Why would your family work to undo our empire?"

Beatrice opened her mouth to speak but Volkmar spoke again, "This news is disturbing, friends. Upon investigation, though I believe my men have discovered the reasoning, great wealth was recently found in the mines of Hunan. A wealth our late emperor did not wish to share with the empire. So, he set up this war all in a vain

pursuit to pursue his greed."

"Shantz on your name!" Beatrice said, sending a wad of spit onto Volkmar's cheek. He wiped the spittle away with shaking hand. Rage consumed his demeanor. Surprisingly Volkmar kept it restrained as he continued on.

"Keeping this information quiet so we could have the element of surprise, I brought our forces here in a front to help the war effort."

He turned to Octavian. "Head Advisor, Octavian, could not stomach what he had seen from the emperor, and so he helped feed us information from within for the good of the empire. Together we marched on the palace to win freedom back for the people of Edonia."

The room erupted into a clamor of voices. Some demanding more information. Others enraged at the betrayal. All of it a lie. Octavian scanned the faces of the room noting the cool expressions on Volkmar's men. Weathered hands rested on hilts ready to be used if needed.

He would slaughter them all if they do not accept his rule, Octavian realized.

His eyes fell to Aaron, the general who had accompanied him to Bjønen and who still pledged loyalty to Octavian. Aaron's eyes narrowed at the deceit coming from Volkmar, but he remained merely an observer in a darkened corner of the room. Rowan, Volkmar's captain of the royal bodyguard moved to whisper in the new emperor's ear. Volkmar nodded, discontent now plastered on his face. He turned to address the crowd of councilors once more.

"Good men of Edonia. I ask you what would you have me do with those who have betrayed our trust so badly?"

Councilors looked at each other as if stunned. They knew the penalty for treason, but would Volkmar have his own wife and child publicly executed? The room fell silent as no one dared to raise their voice. As if cued, a Varnas guard stepped forward.

"For a betrayal such as this there can be nothing but blood," he declared to the room.

The man began to chant, "Blood for betrayal, blood for betrayal."

Others glanced at one another looking for a consensus to join

in. Soon more picked up the cry until the room was filled with a call for the duchess and her son's lives. Volkmar turned, hiding his pleasure at the verdict.

"You fools!" Beatrice cried. "Can you not see this man is deceiving you? He seeks the throne for himself." She pressed her hand beneath her gown causing some in the audience to blush. As she pulled her hand free, in it was a parchment with a broken seal from of the emperor. Octavian fought the rising panic within him. It was his note.

"It is Volkmar who has betrayed our empire, and here is a letter sent from the palace itself."

Volkmar took the note in hand eyeing its contents. A flash of fear briefly crossed his face. Slowly his gaze rose to address the waiting council members. Octavian watched as Volkmar's hesitation suddenly vanished.

"Good men of Edonia. You see this letter?" he moved to hand it to the nearest councilor, giving him a reassuring nod.

"Whose seal is on it?"

"The emperor's my lord," said the councilman.

"Precisely, and in whose hands did this letter come to us from?" Volkmar's accusing stare now turned to Beatrice. Her violet eyes hardened as they met Volkmar's.

"You treacherous worm. Is there no lie you won't spew?"

"You see, my friends, she has no retort. Only baseless accusations to turn her own vague letter against me," Volkmar said with a satisfied grin.

Octavian could see the defeat growing in Beatrice's violet eyes. She drew in a deep breath as if mustering the strength for one last attempt to clear her name.

"My father recognized his mind was fading," she said, voice downcast. "His entire life he fought to keep Edonia safe from both foreign rivals and inner rebellions." As she said the words her gaze moved to the gloating Volkmar.

"In his final days he had decided that this man before you was unworthy to lead our people. Instead, he chose our son, a child, over you."

Her last words made Volkmar flush with anger. *Could they be*

true? Octavian thought.

"It was our emperor's final wish in his old age that you of all people would never sit on the throne," she hissed.

The room fell silent once more. The men so eager to demand her blood, were now left speechless by the Duchess. It caused Octavian to question the truth himself. Septimus had not spoken of this matter with him. Had Septimus been more aware of his condition than Octavian had assumed?

Volkmar's voice broke the silence, "You condemn yourself again, my love."

Beatrice's face soured at the false flattery. It didn't faze Volkmar as he continued, "You say this is the emperor's wish but where is your proof? Surely he would have let the royal court know of such a decision? You can't possibly tell me the only recognition of something so important is a letter you've provided us?"

Volkmar looked to the others who also weren't endorsing the tale. "As I thought. You see the lies never cease. But should we believe your story, it would defeat itself. You yourself admit the emperor was sick of mind. Delusional, some might even say. So much so that he would choose a child to rule his empire rather than a proven leader?"

Octavian watched as the others nodded at Volkmar's words. He was winning them back to his side he could see, but now, strangely, Octavian almost wished the duke would fail. Octavian looked to Beatrice once more, tears starting to stream down her cheeks. She, too, could see where this would end.

"As you well know, I have not officially claimed any title for myself. Indeed, I am happy to wait if that is what you all choose. But my acts upon the emperor were nothing less than to save this great empire from destruction. As the only acting duke currently in Edonia, I have merely done what is in my right to protect our lands. I hope you can see that, good sirs."

Nodding heads ate up Volkmar's lies and all Octavian did was watch. He could stop this, he realized. It may be too late to change the minds of some about the Duchess, but he could destroy Volkmar in a single stroke. Why didn't he? He wanted to. How he desired to see the smug look wiped from Volkmar's face and yet… This is what he had wanted after all, wasn't it? To see this monstrosity of an empire collapse in on itself. To see it all burn as the men of violence finally turned on one another.

Somehow it had never crossed his mind that truth might also be a victim in it all. That perhaps there were some left untainted by the wretched filth of the empire, and they too would now become its victims. He watched as the small, frightened, marquess shivered in his mother's arms. What had the boy done to deserve the wrath that was about to befall him?

It's not your concern, Octavian, he silently told himself and yet the burden to act pressed him.

"What shall we do with them?" Volkmar cried.

"Burn them!!" A cluster of Varnas guards cried. The chant was picked up by others until it was a crescendo filling the room. Now was the final time to act if Octavian was going to save the boy and his mother, and not just them. If he was going to save the truth. Octavian found himself frozen, unable to act as a retinue of guards moved toward Beatrice, Leo, and Crumwald. The older man who'd served faithfully all his life wilted in the fierce grip of Volkmar's men. Another of the brutes tore at Beatrice's dress partially exposing her. Leo screeched as one guard gripped his arm. Terror filled the boy's eyes as Octavian watched the scene unfold. Watched and did nothing. It was the pattern of his life. Moments of opportunity coming in the blink of an eye as he stood paralyzed by his inaction.

Volkmar strode confidently to Beatrice's side. His final words to her the faintest whisper in Octavian's ears.

"You were supposed to provide me an empire. When you couldn't do that, you could have at least given me a son worthy to stand in my place."

Volkmar paused a look of disdain on his face, "Yet, you took even that from me and left me with this creature." Leo whimpered at the restraints being twisted around him.

"Now, in your final moments just know I achieved all of it… without you."

Beatrice raged against her captor's grip. It was no use. Ten heartbeats later the three of them were ushered away to be burned in the palace's courtyard. Their lives gone forever because of him. Because he did nothing. A firm hand on his shoulder shook Octavian from his stupor. A beaming Volkmar stood next to him.

"We've done it, Octavian! Edonia is ours," he said exuberantly.

"Ours." The words rolled in his mind. He was culpable. He had allowed this. He profited from this. Octavian's eyes met Volkmar's. The joy in Volkmar's expression churned his stomach. The man had just sentenced his own wife and son to death, a horrid one at that, and he had the audacity to smile.

"Yes, friend, we have," Octavian said giving a pathetic grin back.

"Come now, don't let a little death dampen the mood. There will be plenty more to deal out before this is done. I suspect some of the men didn't buy my story. Shantz, that woman almost ruined everything."

Why had he trusted this man? Octavian thought, mortified. *Remember this is about Edonia's fall.* he reminded himself again. He needed a distraction from the turmoil he felt. The strange interruption by Rowan popped into his mind. He turned to asked Volkmar what Rowan had whispered to him moments ago.

"Another concerning matter," Volkmar said, face growing stern. "It's about Thegn Oswald's daughter and another issue of my own making named Mateus."

Octavian had completely forgotten about the young woman he'd helped weeks ago. What had come of her in the midst of all the chaos?

"She wasn't in the palace?" Octavian asked.

"No, it seems she was able to piece together more than either of us could have imagined about The People's Justice. So much so that my men have gotten word of two figures escaping the city together."

"How can you be confident it was them?"

Volkmar stroked his chin thoughtfully. "The leader of The People's Justice is a former forging slave and branded as such. A little coin in the streets has spoken of such a man fleeing with a blonde woman." Volkmar paused, a grimace on his face. "This could stir up chaos, Octavian. I played with fire, I admit, when syphoning weapons to the kingdom of Hunan, but if a forger escapes and joins our enemies... I needn't have to explain the consequences, do I?"

"No, you don't," Octavian said sternly. In his mind however he rejoiced. This could be how the whole empire comes crashing down. Another rebellion from within would tear it apart.

"Good," said Volkmar. "I was a fool to allow Mateus to escape, but there may be an easy solution."

"That is?"

"In order to solidify my ascension to emperor, the leaders of Edonia must be gathered. The war in Hunan should be ending soon. I've been informed of that personally. Even better if the duke and thegn die in the cause. It would leave us with a simple majority here. That is, if you have that new baron in your pocket like you say."

"John of the Wood? I doubt anyone has him in their 'pocket,'" Octavian mused.

"How does that fix our escapee problem?" Octavian questioned.

"Ahh yes, sorry, the grand scale always sidetracks me. At the ceremony I will approach Thegn Oswald. If he isn't housing the traitor himself, then surely his daughter will know where Mateus went. We'll put pressure on the man to reveal what he knows."

The idea of what that "pressure" could be made Octavian squirm. The Lady Juliet was a kind woman. Little had she known what she was wrapped up in by taking that shantz assignment.

"I believe we've talked enough, my friend. Will you join me for the execution? It should be a most satisfying one," Volkmar asked with a sinister smirk.

"There are a few other matters I feel I must attend to." Watching the woman he saw blossom from adolescence and her son murdered in cold blood was anything but satisfying to him. It took all his willpower to restrain his true feelings from Volkmar's penetrating stare.

"Suit yourself, but I will not tolerate that weakness of yours to hold back my ambitions. You understand, don't you?"

"Yes… Your Majesty." The words choked in Octavian's throat. Volkmar turned, wine-colored cape fluttering as he did. The man's thin frame did carry an air of regality, the kind that filled men with dread.

An enraged mob now swarmed around Leo, Crumwald, and his mother. Faces full of venomous intent. Spit and dirt were heaped upon them as a host of guards pushed them forward through the volatile crowd. His mother did all she could to shield him from its wrath, but the ire of the crowd was too strong. Leo found himself squeezing her dress with all his might at each agonizing step.

Why was this happening? Wasn't I supposed to be the emperor? Weren't the people supposed to have loved my grandfather? A heap of excrement hit his trousers sending up a wretched smell. Vomit burned in his throat causing him to pause. One of his father's guards grabbed his arm forcing him forward.

Several steps later the crowd parted revealing the grand court-yard of the emperor's palace. A pyre several feet high was being built at its center. Armored men took stray branches from nearby trees to feed the growing stack. It was a horrifying scene. The once pristine garden Leo so enjoyed was now a foul place consumed by hundreds of angry shouts and stripped away trees. Each face brought to his mind a tale his mother read to him some years ago.

The story was of dark creatures that once lurked in the world, haunting the realms of man. The tales spoke of beasts who were once men twisted by the darkness that consumed them. When he awoke in a cold sweat that night his mother comforted him by saying it was all just myths and legends. Looking at the faces in the mob he wasn't so sure. While they were still human a distinct vileness had overtaken them. Something dehumanizing lurked behind their eyes. As if an external force now controlled the crowd. A small flame burst from the wooden pyre drawing his attention back to the stack of wood. "Mother, what do they intend to do with that?"

Leo watched as his mother's beautiful face turned sorrowful. "It... it is for us, son."

His eyes widened as he stared at the growing flames. "For... for us? I thought I was to be the emperor? I don't want to die, Mother, not like this!" Panic rose in him, and he began to squirm like a wild beast whose leg had been caught in a trap.

"Stop," Beatrice said, her voice kind but firm. For some reason it froze him in place. Her violet eyes met his, they were shaky pools filled with tears. "We will die with dignity. We won't let your father have the satisfaction of seeing us squirm."

"Mother, I don't want to die!" The tears poured down his cheeks as the words left his lips.

"I know, love." She placed a hand on his head and began to stroke his dark hair.

Blurry motion stirred beside them. Leo glanced behind tear filled eyes as Crumwald was ushered forward. His mother's loyal advisor loyal to the end.

"It was a pleasure, my lady," Crumwald said, bowing.

Beatrice gave a wordless smile as she watched a guard drag the man toward the pyre. Shortly after, her time came as a Varnas guard grabbed her arm forcing her to march.

"No!!" Leo screamed in anguish.

"Stop, Leo," Beatrice said behind a growing sob. "Let them see the emperor you could have been."

With those words she was led to the hungry pyre. Two guards moved with warding hands toward the immense heat. With one swift motion they tossed Beatrice into the searing flames. The guards raced away from the overbearing heat, cowards who would push a woman into flames they could not face themselves. Leo watched as fire and smoke consumed his mother. In the midst of the flames something powerful caught his eye. His mother's face was unafraid.

Beatrice stared unflinching out at the crowd. Royal, elegant and defiant to the end.

Leo glanced around him meeting each face. How could they find pleasure in all this? What kind of people were they? Searching, he found his father standing with a host of his personal guards at his back. A look of victory on his face. It made Leo seethe. Without thinking he started to move toward his father, but at that moment his arm was caught. Looking up he met the cold stare of an old family guard. The grizzled face was stone as it stared at him. Within those hardened eyes Leo could see no rescue was coming. This was the end. With a tug of his arm he realized it was now his turn to face the flames.

Cool damp air made the hairs on Octavian's neck stand up. It was an unnerving experience to come back to this cavern alone. No attempt had ever been made without the approval of an emperor. Yet, the emperor was dead, and his replacement remained unaware of all the secrets the palace held. He was dumbfounded the two remaining guards had let him pass. Without a word they had parted letting him through. Fires danced on the dark cavern walls that led the way. With reverence he passed once more through the endless supply of Edonium. Its pure form a light silver sheen reflecting the forge's flames. Bare chested men molded raw Edonium under anvils, singing while they worked.

Octavian stopped for a moment observing their mysterious efforts. White hot metal cooled as it was dipped into a slack tub. Steam radiated from the metal, but it did not turn back to the silvery form it once had. It was as if all imperfections had melted away revealing the pure white blade beneath. A Light Bringer, as their ancient ancestors had called them. A name full of empire propaganda or truth?

He shuffled toward the bare cavern wall where the mysterious library entrance had appeared to him before. It felt irreverent to be here while Beatrice and Leo were being executed, but what else could he do? He felt uncertain he should reveal this place to Volkmar and was already formulating a lie in his head about where the weapons came from. Yet, this place had its own protection. The library remained unrevealed to those who didn't know about it. Why had Septimus shown him this place?

I brought you here to witness it. To see that a place like this can make the legends and the myths seem more possible He repeated the words of Septimus in his mind.

Taking a ring-filled hand, Octavian rubbed the jagged cavern wall. A faint glow sprang to life swiftly forming into the shape of a doorway. Without sound the rock cracked, revealing the faint light from the library within.

"How?" he said aloud.

Ducking, he stepped inside once more taken aback by the grandness of the place. Ancient tomes of countless ages stretching beyond sight.

How could such a place exist? he wondered.

He shuffled forward unsure of what to expect or how to proceed. A patter of footsteps started from a nearby row of books. A petite woman stepped out from between the shelves. Her face was less aged than the woman he'd encountered before. Her clear jade eyes looked at him curiously.

"We weren't expecting visitors," she said not unkindly. "But it seems you have been granted permission to enter. Have you been here before or do you know the ancient words?"

"I... I was here before with the emperor, the late Emperor Septimus," Octavian said trying to hold back his discomfort. *Would she know my role in his death?*

"I see, so his time has come. Are you now the emperor?"

"Me?" he said taken aback. *They truly know nothing in this place. Had Septimus kept them unaware of the entire outside world?*

"I... I am not, but I come seeking the truth."

"The truth? Which truth?"

What kind of question is that? he wondered. *Was there more than one?*

"Men often come seeking 'truth' but what they mean is facts, information, history, but truth is more than these individual things."

Her face was unreadable as she said the words. As if the decades in the place had sucked all emotion from her.

"Let's just start with history," Octavian said eyeing her.

"Which histories?" the woman asked, already moving to find the tome he desired.

"One that speaks of Edonia's purpose."

Without reply the woman began to hum a tune as she perused an adjacent aisle of bookshelves. She along with her tune soon disappeared behind another row of books. Some time passed and yet she still hadn't returned. Octavian could feel his frustration growing. Was this all just a sick joke? Disgruntled he found a seat at the same humble table the emperor had used before. After an hour the woman finally returned with a stack of books higher than her head. She set them down with a thud onto the table. A dense cloud of dust rose into the air catching in Octavian's throat. Wafting away the dust and letting out a hoarse cough he stared, overwhelmed, and in awe at the pile before him.

"I have collected for you the most essential documents of Edonia's founding. Inside should be the various perspectives of the scribes Alitore, Brandt, Afonso, and I believe Ephraim as well."

"Umm... Thank you?" Octavian said, unsure of what else to say. None of those names had any meaning to him.

The woman gave him a satisfied smile. "They are the most well-known ancient scholars on the topic of Edonia's founding, but I can find you more obscure articles if you are so inclined."

"This should do for now," Octavian said patting the books. It was a mistake as another dust cloud caught in his throat.

"I shall leave you to it," the woman said bowing. Overwhelmed and unsure where to begin, Octavian grabbed the first tome in the pile and got to work.

It had taken him hours, perhaps all night to skim through a third of the various tomes. Octavian rubbed his bloodshot eyes as he closed one book among the many in the pile. You could get lost in time in a place like this with no sun or moon to guide you.

I wonder if Volkmar grows suspicious of my absence? he mused to himself. Half a dozen ancient books lay open around him. Their ink-filled pages as old as time itself.

"All this knowledge and I still feel lost," he muttered. He had come hoping for answers, instead he found even the ancients couldn't agree on Edonia's "purpose." Those sympathetic to the empire spoke of the grand uprising against a tyrant. How the men of the east stood fast against the Felled King Maluuk. Those less inclined to aggrandize the empire spoke of its deceit. Alitore, Edonia's largest critic, went so far as to make the claim that Edonia had acted in jealousy and defiance to the one being who could have saved them.

Alitore backed his claim with the idea that Maluuk offered unending life to those who followed him and those who'd rejected this "gift" were only jealous of his power. His final synopsis being that all men seek power and will find any means to pursue it. Even overthrowing life itself. While it was a cynical outlook, indeed, Octavian couldn't help but feel it matched the reality around him.

There was one other obscure view present within the texts. A belief that Edonia was a small piece in a larger purpose. That purpose being the final return of the First King or at least something like him. His supposed return was coined the New Dawn. At its coming one would rise from the fragmented ruins of Edonia. Darkness would swell like a tide for an age, but this ruler would rise to meet it and new life would break out to rescue the world. It was the most fanciful of the tales. Likely just wishful thinking based on the idea of Maluuk's gift belonging to another. Octavian let out a tired sigh as his mind retraced all that he had read. How could anyone be certain they had found the truth from among the rumble of history? A faint light moved between a set of bookshelves to his left. Appearing between them was the aide from earlier. She let out a yawn as she approached the table.

"Still here, huh? Did you get a wink of sleep last night?" she asked.

"Last night?" So, he had studied that long…

"This place can be overwhelming when one first arrives. All that knowledge available and yet unobtainable. Lesser men have gone mad here over the ages." She gave him a smile. "I don't suppose you're one, are you?"

"Perhaps I would be if I stayed here any longer," Octavian said pushing himself from the table. He already knew he'd regret how late he had stayed awake. All that time and still no answers. A sudden weight in his chest fought against his doubt. "I did find answers now it's time to choose which ones to believe."

The strange conviction was right, it hadn't been a total waste. All the historians he'd read had beheld the same events and yet they walked away believing something totally different.

"I suppose I must choose what I believe to be true," he murmured to himself.

"What was that?" the aide asked. "A crazy murmur?" she gave him a playful wink as she said it.

Who was this woman? he wondered. She'd been so emotionless in one breath and nearly flirtatious in another.

Octavian cleared his throat as he moved to leave. "I would like you to prepare another set of volumes for me upon my return tomorrow."

"Of course," the woman said, bowing.

"Find me the early histories of the empire. I'd like to see if they really lived up to their grand claims of a golden age."

The woman bowed again and scurried off as if he was expecting the task to be done right away. Octavian let out another tired sigh before stepping out into the cavern.

"Now it's time to face the empire's new master."

16

JULIET

THE EDON MOUNTAINS set against an auburn sky was their never-ending guide northward. Many a city folk would have gone crazy from boredom after this long on the road. Not Mateus. Every day his expression seemed to carry the mystified wonder of a child at the world around him. Juliet thought this strange until it dawned on her. He'd never seen any of this before. Not the dizzying heights of Edon or the expansive prairies and fields. What would have been the casual view for most was a land of enchantment to this now freed slave. Seeing his wide grin at the setting sun stirred something inside her, that was until his eyes caught hers.

"What? Just admiring my handsome features and rugged form?"

A blush instantly crept up her neck, "I hate you."

"Ahhh I figured. I usually stare longingly at those I hate as well. It's the confusion in their face that really does it for me."

"That's not...!" She decided not to continue. If time on the road with this man had taught her anything it was that he had something clever to say about everything. It was so irritating. Huffing she turned to the crackling fire garnished with roasted game. At least they'd be eating meat tonight. Mateus had mocked her for spending the few silver coins she'd acquired at Hornhall on a cheaply made bow. He'd shut up quickly when she threatened to look for some of her father's men within the city. Little did he know they'd all been shipped off to fight for an empire in whose trust she now wavered.

That was another thing this Mateus was doing to her. She'd never drank the empire's propaganda wholeheartedly but now… well.

"Best not to think about it," she told herself quietly.

Some time passed and the faint remnants of the sun faded behind the Edon Mountains, cloaking the lowlands in shadow. The small rabbit was nearly done and Juliet worked to finish roasting the last uncooked side.

"You never did tell me about your parents," she said breaking the silence between them.

Mateus' gaze was fixed on repairing the threading on a pair of worn trousers in his lap.

"Yea, you see, that wasn't an accident," he said, gaze unflinching from his work.

"It's just you seemed to care about them…"

"Don't all children care about their parents?"

"Yes, well… I mean… uh! Never mind." Why did he always have to act like the most infuriating human being in the world?

Sighing, Mateus put the trousers aside and met her eyes for the first time since they'd sat down, "I suppose you haven't been such a horrible travel companion."

"What's that supposed to mean?"

"It means I'll tell you. It's not a happy tale though. So, I don't know why you're so eager to hear it."

She sat silently waiting for him to continue. Sighing again Mateus' eyes grew distant.

"My father knew the ancient words like all smiths of Edonium. He was third rank among his fellow workers, nothing special. Well, at least among forgers of Edonium. My mother served as one of the grand matriarchs within the emperor's private library. A great honor given only to those most trusted."

"How did they meet? Also, tell me more about this library."

"Well the cavern isn't a big place and the library is quite amazing actually. You don't strike me as a reader though. Don't know if you'd really appreciate it."

Juliet rolled her eyes, "I mean how did they decide they… you know? Liked each other?"

She'd press about the about the library later. He'd likely just deflect to it to avoid the more tantalizing tale of his parents if she let him.

"It's a bit of an odd story, actually. My mother greatly outranked my father as far as status. Many within her ranks frowned upon the union. I grew up hearing whispers about my parents and how my father must have been so 'lucky.' I asked them one day when I was a child why others talked that way about them. My mother simply told me my father's rank as smith mattered little when it came to other qualities. My dad just said she was the best looking one among the bunch."

Mateus let out a weak chuckle as he mused over the memory, "She hit him for that. In reality my mother was one of the wisest and well-read in the emperor's service. Only High Matriarch Anastasia was said to have known more."

"They must have been some incredible people."

"They were. It's funny not once did I ever hear my father complain about mother's rank or status and my mother? She adored her simple old blacksmith. that wasn't a common sight among those in the emperor's service."

"I'm sure you take what you can get when the selection is so sparse." Juliet tried to pull the words back even as she spoke them. "I'm sorry, that was crude…"

"It's fine. It was our life. Not much we could do to change it."

An awkward silence hung in the air as neither of them knew what to say next.

"What was their name? Your parents, that is."

"My father's name was Levi and my mother was Saria."

"Those are lovely. Do you mind if I ask what happened to them?"

Mateus' gaze fixed on the fire. The night sky somehow felt as though it morphed into a dark cloud around him as he weighed her words.

"They are dead and it's my fault."

Juliet choked back the lump in her throat as she could see the pain wash over Mateus.

"One day a note came to my parents. I don't know how but a man with enough influence was able to send a secret message to the forges. In it was a request to betray the empire in order to save it. They discussed for a long time what should be done. In the end my father was unwilling to put us at risk. 'Besides, what could two slaves do about an entire empire?' he'd said. Little did they know I had overhead their conversation. My mother had taught me enough about Edonia's purpose and I knew enough to know what the empire had become. Our lives obviously didn't benefit from the current regime and I believed someone had to do something about it."

"Meaning you?"

"Meaning me."

"And thus, The People's Justice was born," Juliet mused.

"I stole the note sent to my parents and began to correspond with those who sent it. Soon I had someone help me with an escape plan. I only found out after I was freed that the insider within the emperor's ranks was Volkmar or at least someone in his debt. Somehow he was able to map a route from the emperor's quarters for me. All I had to do was go from there and meet up with some contacts in the city."

"Still how did you get past all the emperor's guards?"

"Volkmar helped clear a path. A little coin and being the emperor's son-in-law will do that for you. After I escaped, I found his contact within the city and that's when it all began. Volkmar had another of his contacts funnel the Edonium weapons to us and we smuggled them to Hunan."

Mateus' expression grew angry as he clenched his fists, "When the emperor found out about my escape he took it out on my parents. It wasn't a week later that their bodies were found floating in the Edon Bay by a fishing crew. My parents died because of my betrayal and all I achieved was to help a snake like Volkmar get into power. How could I have been so stupid?"

"Sad tale, kid," came a voice from the darkness. Juliet suddenly felt a familiar feeling of steel on her neck. Glancing down she could make out a weathered hand clutching a dagger at her throat. Her eyes hardened as she prepared to give her attacker the same treatment she'd given Mateus back in Edonia.

"I wouldn't, girl," came a voice behind Mateus. Stepping out of the darkness was a gang of three bandits. Each of them was a grizzly figure with matted hair and missing teeth. A sinister sheen was in their eyes as they looked at her in a way that made her skin crawl. The leader of the crew took another step forward revealing a bowman with arrow nocked and aimed at her.

Five including the one at my back, she thought, taking note of what her next move might be. Bandits had always been an issue along this road, but she hadn't heard tales of them in some time. Likely they'd crawled out from their dens knowing Venhorn's forces were off in a distant land. Pathetic.

"I see you got yourself some restraints there," the bandit leader said looking toward Mateus. He'd agreed to bind himself at night as an insurance of not escaping. She'd liked the man but she didn't trust him, even after his stunt outside Edonia.

"Yea, they are rather uncomfortable I must say," Mateus joked hoping to ease the tension in the air.

The bandit leader eyed Juliet and she could see something captured the man's attention, "That's a mighty fine cloak you got there. Almost Highborn worthy... Where'd you say you were from?"

Juliet fought the panic she felt rising in her chest. If they knew who she was this could turn into more than a simple shakedown.

"She is most definitely Highborn," Mateus chimed in.

"Mateus!" she snarled.

"Quiet now, lass. I want to hear what this nice prisoner has to say," said the bandit leader with a sinister smile. The others with him murmured amongst themselves with a newfound giddiness.

What was Mateus doing?

"Yes, I was a runaway slave as you must have heard earlier. A very important one. She was just on her way to bring me to justice in her father's hall."

"Who's her father?" asked another of the bandits.

"Thegn Oswald if you could believe it. You stand amongst royalty!"

"Mateus… why." But her plea was drowned out by the rising excitement of the fiendish group.

"This could set us for life!"

"How much would a Thegn pay for a daughter, you think?"

"Quiet! None of us make a move until I say," the leader barked. The others grew still awaiting his order.

"First, cut that one free, he's been mighty helpful to us."

The bandit who had held Mateus pulled loose a dagger, sawing away at Mateus' restraints. The bandit leader turned his gaze back toward Juliet. A wicked grin on his face. He stepped forward and knelt in front of her. His breath was foul smelling with a strong waft of ale.

"I've never known the company of royalty before. I wonder, little dove, if you've ever known the companionship of a man?"

Juliet fought back the vomit in her throat. This wasn't happening, it couldn't be happening. She squirmed within her captor's grip but found it only tightened as she fought. Animal-like panic rose within her. She had to escape, had to fight, had to do something. A strange sound came from behind the gnarled face of the bandit leader. He took note of the noise as well, rising to his feet. Only a brief realization was gifted him before an arrow caught in his throat. Shock washed over Juliet at the gruesome scene. Her warrior's mind quickly took over as she realized her captor with the dagger at her throat was now distracted. With lightning speed she twisted his wrist, loosing the weapon from his hand. Not thinking she picked it up, plunging it deep into the man's chest with a feral scream.

A stain of blood spread across the bandit's tunic and his eyes morphed into horrified shock at the fatal wound. Juliet stumbled back gasping for breath. The world darkened at her peripherals. Only a hand on her shoulder brought her back from the abyss. Whipping around she moved with instinct to do the same to her knew pursuer. Instead she met the concerned eyes of Mateus.

It's me, Juls. It's me."

She shoved him away posturing herself in a defensive stance,

"Get away from me."

The other bandits lay dead on the ground behind him. In his hands was her simple bow.

"It's not what you think. I had to get them to trust me. It was the only way I could help. Besides they heard everything, Juliet. They knew who I was."

"What... what do you mean?" she asked, distrust still evident in her voice.

"They'd been waiting to catch us off guard. They heard the whole tale about my parents. You know what kind of reward is out there for someone like me? I couldn't let them live."

"But you told them about me, you..."

"I had to earn their trust. Put their guard down. I was never going to let them do anything to us. Besides all I did was tell them the truth."

The words sank like a rock in her stomach. It was all too much. The smell of foul breath, blood pouring from the man's chest, Mateus, and... and...

She collapsed in a heap, tears streaming down her face. Somewhere in the midst of her cries she felt an embrace surround her. What was she supposed to do with that? Fight it? Run? Instead she let it remain and as she wiped the tears away from her eyes she realized Mateus was weeping too.

"I'm sorry, Juliet. I'm sorry." It was the first time his facade had melted away. The first time she saw who Mateus really was. He wasn't an arrogant, cocky jerk. He was someone with deep regret, loss, and hurt. He was like everyone else in this forsaken world trying to find a better way. Somehow that was more of a comfort to her than any words.

Juliet awoke still amazed to see Mateus slumbering on the other side of the dying fire. It had been nearly a month now on their journey north and she'd finally done away with his restraints. Still she had expected to wake up alone this morning. Rising from the ground she stretched with anticipation at the prospect of reaching Venhorn by evening. It had felt like an eternity since last she saw her family. Nearly three months had passed since she'd first headed south to Edonia. Liam likely had plenty of new studies he couldn't wait to share with her. At that age his mind was like a sponge ready to soak up any knowledge he could find. A smile creased her face at the thought of her chirpy brother scampering around Venhorn's halls. An obnoxious yawn sounded beside her. Mateus stretched a lanky arm into the air as he rose.

"You'd think one would be adjusted to sleeping on the ground after so long," he complained as he worked a kink in his neck.

"We should get going," Juliet said rising to her feet. Standing, she discovered that a host of leaves had found their home on her cloak. With a forceful hand she brushed off the palate of autumn colors.

"What's the rush?" Mateus asked, letting out another yawn.

"The nights are growing chill. Winter will hit us soon, and I doubt a city boy like you would like to be caught out in the wilds."

The truth was she was eager to get home. Not just to see her family either. Being on the road with Mateus had changed her and not just from their night with the bandits. Long days of travel and nights around the fire had convinced her that they must act if the necessary change was to come to Edonia. News had reached them on the road of what had transpired in the capitol city. Duke Volkmar and Head Advisor Octavian had seized the throne. The tales didn't end there either. The atrocities that followed made her shudder. Mateus had his own thoughts on Volkmar as well and none of them good. With the empire beginning to free fall she knew she couldn't be content to just retreat back home and wait. They had to do something, anything, to help bring purpose back to Edonia. Mateus smirked at her as she sat deep in thought.

"Give your mind a break. You just got up and already you're thinking of ways to bring Volkmar and his ilk down?"

"I can't help it. We have to do something."

He rose to his feet, smirk still present. "I could have used you in The People's Justice. Perhaps things would have turned out differently."

"They still can!" she said raising her voice more than she would have liked.

"You're more optimistic than I. I've seen how these rulers respond to change. They rarely like it."

"My father's different."

Silence was Mateus' only reply. He would see, her father wasn't like the other rulers. He was compassionate, a leader, someone who cared for his people. It didn't take long for them to pack up their supplies and hit the road. It was nice having a companion on such a long journey. Sure, she'd had an army with her on her trip south but not a friend. This felt more... well, she wasn't sure. Glancing over at Mateus on the saddle next to her made her wonder. Could he be more than just a companion on the road? The month-long trek had made them close. Endless nights laughing and telling stories around a campfire would bond anyone together. She shoved the thought aside just as Mateus caught her eye. He gave her a playful wink that sent a flush of red sprouting up her neck.

She hated that. Hated how he knew just the right thing to do to fluster her. Wordless, he turned toward the road spurring his horse a few yards ahead of her. The rest of the day was uneventful. Just another trip under the late autumn sun. Frost clung in the air as the last throes of fall began to fade and give way to winter. It always grew cold early in the north, and it would seem this year was no different. Gripping the cloak given by her father, she embraced its strange power to hold in heat. Glancing over at Mateus she could see he was ill equipped for a winter in Venhorn. His light tan tunic was typical of forge workers and had the unfortunate effect of keeping out heat. She thought about offering her cloak for a moment. Just a moment. *I'll let him squirm a little just so he knows how irritating it is,* she thought smugly to herself.

After a few hours more they rounded the final bend of the Edon

Mountains. Before them rested a deep green valley hemmed in with mountains to their left and rolling hills to the right.

"Home," she whispered with frosty breath.

A light dusting descended on the valley before them. Sparkling white gems of winter glistened in the late afternoon sun.

"Snow already?" Mateus snorted with a shiver. "What land have you brought me to?"

He wrapped his frigid arms around his torso as he overlooked their path.

"One not for the faint of heart," she jested. "Come on. Perhaps Venhorn can make a man of you yet."

He gave her a glare but followed as she led the way into the valley below. It wasn't long before the peak of Venhorn's keep came into view shortly followed by the rest of the city. Venhorn was built on an elevated position of the valley floor nestled between a cleft in the mountain chain. Cold stone walls encompassed the city. Roofs made of timber sat with a thin coat of frost that glistened in the sun's light. Buildings both of stone and wood dotted the cobbled streets in a gradual slope. Perched above them all was the keep her family called home. It displayed no grandeur or finery only solid stone and firm timber beams. It was a humble abode for a thegn but she liked it that way. As they approached a farmer from one of the surrounding fields waved as they passed. His toothy grin the warm welcome she was accustomed to in Venhorn.

"Is that man greeting us?" Mateus asked curiously.

"Yes," Juliet said drawing out the word.

"Why?"

"What do you mean?"

"He's a commoner. All of them I've met cower when their leaders pass by or at least avert their gaze. This man greets us."

The question took her aback. Was that how it was in the rest of the world?

"My father is a gracious man. He doesn't lord his position over his people. So, in return they often are happy to see him when he visits their farms."

"He visits their farms?" Mateus stammered in amazement. His eyes didn't leave the farmer even as the man returned to his work of preparing the land for another winter. Drawing near the city Juliet could see two guards standing sentinel at the city gate. Recognizing Juliet they opened the gate with a greeting. Smiling back at them she entered beneath the towering archway, happy to be home once more. Oddly however the streets seemed quiet. Many of Venhorn's city dwellers still crowded the streets but an ominous energy filled the air. Carts pulled by mules clanked on cobbled stone and women chatted quietly among themselves with produce for sale in front of them. All of it likely uneventful to an outsider but something was off. A voice called to her from the crowd as they passed.

"Lady Juliet, how be our sons?" asked a woman operating her booth of carrots.

The war. How could I be so foolish to forget, Juliet thought. She had been so caught up in her own reality that she had forgotten many of Venhorn's sons were on foreign soil dying for the empire. For an empire that may no longer exist.

"They are well, mother," she replied in polite greeting to the older woman. Strangely the woman's face soured.

"And do they still fight for our empire? Eerie news comes from the great city. Ominous, dreadful, news."

So the common folk know... Juliet thought. "We have come to speak with my father about the matter."

"Well hurry and speak then. I don't want my son returning from that foreign land to fight another war at home!" Others nearby began to rally to the woman's dissent in muttered tones.

Juliet nodded uncomfortably as she spurred her mount onward, ready to escape the woman's ire. A few streets away from the scene Mateus turned to her.

"Why did you let that woman speak to you in such a way?" he asked.

"What is a leader if they cannot hear the voice of their people?" she said with more confidence than she felt.

The truth was something very different. Discontent must be festering in the city if the people had grown so bold. Mateus nodded reflectively at the answer. As if he'd never considered that a kingdom actually lived by such rules. Thankfully the keep's gate was just ahead. The reprieve from the occasional darkened stare was a relief she was happy to embrace. The loud clang of the keep's gate shut behind them echoing through the frost covered courtyard. Without the bustle of soldiers prepping for war it felt empty and lifeless. Even in peace time it often served as a practice ground. Now, it sat void of life but for the occasion patrol of guards.

Standing beneath the keep's veranda was her father. His lined and weathered face looked extra weary. As if her month's long journey had really been years. Oswald's grim demeanor broke as his eyes met hers.

"My Juls, you've returned! I heard no word from Edonia, and I had feared the worst!" He wrapped his thick arms around her in an embrace. His grey beard tickled her face as he did. It was only after several heartbeats past that he released her. His gaze fell to Mateus who waited awkwardly behind them.

"And who is this?" Oswald asked curiously.

"Ah Father, this is Mateus. He is… well, I can explain it all inside. We are terribly cold, and I've longed for a hearth's warmth."

Oswald nodded, eyeing Mateus cautiously. Juliet could see her father's gaze fixed on the small brand across Mateus' forehead. The sign of a runaway slave. She had nearly forgotten about the marking in the last few weeks. Her earlier desire for justice and vengeance had turned to a hope of clemency from her father. Seeing Oswald's reaction brought a sudden fear upon her that perhaps she had doomed the young forger rather than saved him.

"Yes, let us speak inside. It seems there is much to discuss," Oswald said in a wary tone.

Deep contemplation masked Oswald's face as he mulled over the news about Edonia. A crack of a log within the hearth resounded within the still hall. The place felt hollow with most of its men gone to war. Juliet glanced toward her mother who waited patiently at her father's side. Liam was off somewhere in the keep most likely getting into mischief without their mother's watching eyes. Mateus still looked mesmerized as he drank in Venhorn's hall. Wrapped around him was a thick bear's pelt to ward off the chill. It made her chuckle inside. If any of the great men of Venhorn had seen him in that at this point in the season he would face their full mockery. She'd let him be though. He did have a certain charm wrapped in the... What was she doing?

I cannot think like that, she chastised herself.

"This is foul news indeed," her father finally said, stroking his chin. The outburst shook away her dangerous thoughts, drawing her attention back to her father.

"You say you had a hand in all this?" Oswald asked Mateus in an accusing tone.

"I founded a movement to help bring change for those who needed it most in Edonia. Volkmar was just a means to that end, or so I thought..." Mateus' voice trailed off with a rare sense of uncertainly.

Oswald eyed the mark on his forehead. "It was good of you to bring him here, Juls. A man like this is a traitor to the empire and deserves to be brought to justice."

Before Mateus could speak Juliet shot to her feet. "That is not why I brought him here, Father. At least not anymore."

Her mother looked at her eyebrow raised. "Then why did you bring him here, Juls?"

Juliet felt her throat tightening as she searched for the words. Why exactly had she brought Mateus here? Not only did he raise up a resistance group within Edonia, he'd also fed weapons to their enemies. What were her parents supposed to think?

"I came here on my own accord," Mateus said calmly. His chestnut eyes met Juliet's for a brief moment before addressing the thegn and his wife.

"I doubt she could have kept me restrained for a month as an unwilling prisoner. No offense," he said smiling at Juliet.

Oswald's face was unamused as he waited for Mateus to continue.

"I accompanied Juliet because I saw in her a faint bit of hope. A hope that Edonia desperately needs right now. It is true I am a slave of the empire, like my fathers before me. Forced to slave away my life within the dark confines of that place you call a palace."

Mateus paused a moment to regain composure. "But it does not mean I wish to see Edonia burn. My whole desire with The People's Justice was to see the real Edonia freed."

"And what is the real Edonia?" Oswald snorted.

"The common folk," Mateus replied. "All the thousands of lives that live in fear and oppression at the whims of a madman. The people who fight and die so that an oppressive regime can stay in power. Those people."

Juliet glanced at her parents. Searching to see any emotion on their face. Her mother's expression was considerate of Mateus' words, seeming to weigh them in her mind. Oswald remained unreadable, his eyes intently fixed on Mateus.

Mateus continued, "Juliet made me believe you were a man who cared for his people, a man that wanted something different for them than a life of servitude to their rulers. I accompanied her here wondering if it could really be true."

Mateus leaned forward meeting the thegn's intense gaze. "I was amazed to see your people upon arrival. All of them were at peace as if their ruler truly did care for them and their needs. I never believed it possible until now."

Oswald's face softened only slightly. "You are still an escaped forger and a keeper of Edonia's greatest secret. If Volkmar finds out you are here and that we are harboring you, we'd have an army at our doorstep."

"Don't you see, Father? Volkmar doesn't know about Mateus. We can hide him away, even change his markings..."

Oswald raised a hand to cut her off. "I don't like your fondness for this man, Juls. It's dangerous."

Juliet felt a sense of dread suddenly wash over her. A look encompassed her father's eyes that she'd never seen before.

"What you've told me of what's happened in Edonia is invaluable and for that I will spare taking your life in haste. But do not think you will avoid judgment when I find how I might best dispense it."

Mateus met his stare with a hardened look of his own. "I know I may have sealed my fate with what I've done, but I can live with my decisions. The question is, can you? Knowing what you now know about this new emperor?"

"Do not lecture me, boy!" Oswald said his booming voice rattling through the hall. A few guards stepped from the shadows, but Juliet's mother waved them off with a dismissive hand.

"He's right, Father," Juliet said, daring to make her voice known. "We cannot let the injustices of Volkmar stand. You know as well as I that he is more sinister than Septimus ever was."

Oswald's temper cooled as he returned to his seat. "What are you suggesting?"

"We send a call to the remaining rulers. We unite under our own council and place a new ruler on the throne. One that will live out a rule that is good for all the peoples of the empire, not just the elite few."

Oswald shook his head wearily. "You do not know these men as I do, Juls. To call such a council at a time like this? It could bring doom on our entire house. Would you have me trade Venhorn for a daydream?"

"I would have you stand for what is right, Father. Even if it costs us."

"Gwen?" Oswald said, turning to his wife for help.

"She speaks truth, Oswald. You were once like her, were you not?"

"I have the scars to prove it," Oswald sighed. "Listen, I received word just the other evening of a coronation for the new emperor. Let me travel to Edonia and survey the situation. Then we can see how we should proceed."

"Father, you'd be walking into the lion's den!" Juliet said, distressed. "We cannot wait for Volkmar to dig his talons into the empire before we act. We must strike while he is still weak and without official status."

"We are weak as well, Juls. We have no army, have you forgotten? With what men would you have me march to dispose him?"

Juliet found her enthusiasm waning. Had she not thought this through? Her father's eyes turned tender as he recognized her inner turmoil.

"You are eager for what is right, and for that I commend you, my dear." His attention shifted briefly to Mateus. "But your youth makes you hasty. I will see what awaits us in Edonia and from there we can decide what we must do."

With that Oswald rose from the table with a yawn. "I think it's time I retire for the evening. I will place a guard in your quarters, Mateus, until your fate is decided. You will remain in this keep until then. Is that understood?"

Mateus nodded, unfazed by Oswald's hostility. Juliet thought of protesting but knew her father's grace had its limits. At least Mateus would stay alive.

"Will you be joining me?" Oswald asked Gwen.

"In a moment, dear. I wish to spend a little more time with our newly returned daughter."

Oswald leaned down kissing her forehead before departing. Gwen turned back to face Juliet and Mateus, her eyes firm. She remained silent until the sound of the door behind her clicked shut signaling Oswald had left the room.

"Your father is a good man, but he is wrong in this matter."

Juliet looked to Mateus who carried the same shocked expression.

"Do you have a plan to call the leaders of Edonia together?" Juliet's mother asked.

"We've discussed how we could have a secret council here in Venhorn," replied Juliet.

Her mother sat thoughtful for a moment. "I can help with this."

"You... you can?" Juliet said dumbfounded.

Her mother gave her a playful expression. "Of course. Doing the right thing is worth it, is it not?"

Juliet stared in amazement at the regality of the woman before her. For the first time in Juliet's life she felt understood by her mother. Not only understood but aligned with a common purpose. Perhaps she had always misjudged her. A pang of guilt struck her. How many times had she been exasperated with her over the years? What missed opportunities and possibilities had passed them by all because of her stubborn ignorance. It was too late to take it back, but they could make something with their future.

"Should I leave you two alone?" Mateus chimed in, breaking the sentimental moment.

Both women stared at him, exasperated.

"I think it's time you go to your cage," Gwen said.

Mateus sighed at the words but rose to his feet as two guards approached.

"I'll make sure you are treated fairly," Juliet said downcast.

"I made my choice, Juls. I can live with the consequence." His face had his typical charming smile plastered on it. She secretly admired how he'd taken to using her nickname. Even if it came from his sarcastic tongue.

"No, Juliet. You can't think like that."

She watched as Mateus was ushered away toward the guest housing. At least it wasn't the dungeon. Turning back to her mother, Juliet's eyes locked with Gwen's.

"Tell me what we must do."

17

JOHN OF THE WOOD

A BLOOD RED SUN BROKE over the horizon of a grey winter sky. Its dull rays peeked in through the keep's window, awakening John from a deep slumber. He let out an annoyed groan as he rolled over in bed. His hand instinctively anticipated to find the warmth of Maggie at his side. Disappointed, it only found bedding. Frost covered windows let in the pesky sunlight that had awakened him. Winter had finally come to the north. That fact alone left him eager to have Maggie back at his side.

"Really, Maggs? How long will this go on?" he complained to himself. Groaning he arose from the bed and shuffled across the room to prepare for the day. He found a newly embroidered tunic made by a local seamstress laid out for him. It was decorated with a sky blue crest encircling a golden sparrow. A common bird, swift and cunning, much like him. That was why he'd decided to take it on as his new sigil. His most coveted possession, however, was the thick winter cloak made of dark leather insulated with the fur of a white wolf. A gift left behind by the deceased baron. Looking over the fine work once more he made for the door, only stopping to wrap Bear Paw around his waist. The object that had given him all this power. Seeing him leave his chambers an attendant rushed to John's side, a look of distress on his face.

"This early and you already have some complaint to bring?" John groaned. It was the part of being a ruler he'd come to detest. The attendant's face was hesitant, but John motioned for the man to speak.

"Lord Bombast, a word has arrived from Edonia," proclaimed the attendant as he swished around the parchment in his hand.

An icy wave of fear washed over John as he took the rolled-up paper. Hiding his nerves he unrolled it, eyes carefully examining each word. It was a summons to the grand city. Emperor Septimus was dead, and Duke Volkmar was calling all the leaders of Edonia to confirm him as their new emperor. Written at the bottom were the words, "Time to answer the call." He didn't need reminding of the promises he'd made to the snake named Octavian. He already had the absence of Maggie for that. More and more he'd grown to wish he'd taken the odds against the Edonian legions.

Don't be a fool, John. They would have wiped you and everyone else out in a matter of hours, he reminded himself.

Maggie would come around eventually. The attendant let out an awkward cough as if waiting for John's attention once more.

"This also came for you, Baron."

The man extended another parchment. This one sealed with a sigil John had only seen in fabled tales. Pressed into the wax was a seven-pointed star. Popping the seal off he quizzically opened the message.

To all who receive this message, your discretion is of the utmost importance. News has likely reached you of the late Emperor Septimus. Do not be deceived. Duke Volkmar has seized the throne by traitorous means. He is not fit to rule and so we have formed an alliance to stand against his reign. You are being called to join our ranks against him. If you will ignore justice in the land, then a curse upon your house. If however you wish to restore Edonia to its ancient glory join us by sending a letter to Farmshire before Volkmar's coronation. Do not try to find us. Burn this letter after you've received it. Do not speak a word of this.

- The New Dawn is coming

"Now this was interesting." John rolled up the parchment tucking it into his belt. "Have you seen Maggie?" he asked the attendant.

"I believe she was spotted leading a hunting party into the northern end of the woods, sir."

"Back to your old life again, Maggs?" John mused. "Prepare my horse. I wish to speak with her at once."

The attendant bowed and rushed to the keep's stable. Soon after, John could see a stable hand lead a jet-black stallion in his direction. Midnight was the name John had given the beast. It was a fine horse bred for royalty. Another gift of the baron John was happy to have received. He mounted the horse with ease. Midnight anxiously tore at the dirt, steam pouring from its nostrils, eager to ride.

"Me too," John said patting its neck. He cracked the reins sending the horse into a bolt. The stable hand jerked back watching in awe as John raced toward Bjønen's gate. A shout rang out from the guards on duty to make way. The wooden gates creaked open just in time for John to burst through. He wasn't sure what had come over him. The sudden desire to be free perhaps? A return back to the days he roamed the woods without a care? Thunderous hooves drummed in his ear as he rounded the city and entered the open plains. Midnight glided northward down the trodden path sending ripples of frigid air across John's cheeks. John couldn't help but laugh at himself. How was he even supposed to find the hunting party in the woods? It wasn't for lack of practice that their forces had remained hidden within the forests for so long.

Looking over the horizon he realized he wouldn't have to. A small band of figures dotted the snow-covered road ahead. Spurring Midnight on, he raced across the bleached field. The surrounding farmland and prairie were a blur of dull color as Midnight galloped ahead at full speed. It felt so freeing to let loose and go. Drawing near, John pulled on the reins causing Midnight to skid to a halt. Six figures were now distinct on the road. Maggie walked among them with Huldwin at her side. The small crew assembled were some of John's closest companions during their runaway days. A faint hint of jealously flared up within him as he heard their laughter in the distance.

"Why had they not invited me?" he seethed.

Dismounting, he led Midnight by the reins the final distance between them. Throwing up a friendly greeting, he was surprised to only receive a half-hearted return from the company. As they approached each held their gaze downward, avoiding his eyes.

"Why do you lot look so downcast? A poor hunt?"

Awkward silence hung in the air as Maggie lifted a bundle of rabbits without a word. Another man pulled back a tarp on a small cart he pulled, revealing a good-sized buck.

What's the matter with them? John wondered.

"I have some interesting news I had wished to share with Maggie. I suppose the rest of you could help me decide as well," John proclaimed. This got a few of them to shoot him a look of curiosity, yet Maggie still avoided his gaze.

John cleared his throat as if declaring a royal decree, "It looks as though we have a decision to make." He pulled the two parchments loose from his tunic handing them to those closest. Waiting patiently, he watched as one by one their eyes grew wide as they read the parchment's contents. Lastly, they reached Maggie who read them with a half-hearted interest. This fed John's fury. How could she not care? Pushing the temper rising within him aside he spoke again, "I know you all were not pleased about our deal with Edonia, but it looks as though we've been given a new opportunity to win our freedom."

"That's not it, John," Maggie said finally looking up at him. "Our problem isn't just your deal with Edonia." The others with her shuffled awkwardly as she spoke. John scanned each of their expressions noticing they agreed with Maggie's words.

"Go on, say what it is then."

Behind misty eyes Maggie spoke again, "It's you, John. You've changed. You say you wanted all this for us and for the people, but it was a lie. We can see through the facade. It's all about you and your quest for personal power. It's always been about that, and we were just your tools to get it."

John felt his face flush as the others nodded silently.

"Has my coming here not disproved that?" John protested.

Maggie wiped a stray tear away. "It will take more than that, John."

"Very well. What would you have of me, men?" John asked pleading to them all.

Huldwin stepped forward. "Abandon the pomp of the baron's keep. Live among the men again. I don't know, be the old, John. The one who was one of us."

John nodded his head toward the small hunting cart. "I have missed this. Perhaps you lot are right."

Unconvinced expressions surrounded him. It would take more than mere confession, John realized.

"I'll abandon the baron's keep starting today. Instead, it will be dedicated to serve all of us. I also pledge to eat the same meals, wear the same clothes, and drink the same drink as you filthy bunch."

A faint smile cracked on the faces of his men, even Maggie's.

"I'm afraid we are going to get drawn into this fight eventually no matter the side we take though. So, I need your help deciding our fate," John said raising the now returned parchments in his hand.

Maggie's face broke into her familiar grin. "Together?"

"Together," John said nodding. As he said it the familiar warmth returned in Maggie's expression that he'd so missed.

"First! We drink to a successful hunt!" one of the other companions shouted. The others raised the cry, and for the first time in a long time John felt that the world had been made right.

John lay still waiting for the dream to fade. Somehow things had righted themselves. Turning over under the thick blanket made of bear fur he felt the smooth skin of Maggie at his side. Dying embers danced in the hearth allowing the frigid winter air to gain a foothold in the stone room. The dwelling wasn't as fine as the baron's keep but with Maggie at his side he didn't care. A fragile peace clung to him now that had eluded him for months. All felt right in the world again. Thoughts of the day came flooding to his mind. It would be a big one, the trip to Edonia would begin as soon as he'd find the desire to get up from bed.

Their plan was simple. Maggie, Huldwin and the others would accompany him to Farmshire to see for themselves if this rebellion was real. Afterward he would keep up the facade of obedience to the empire by traveling to Volkmar's coronation. The plan had risks to be sure but joining this rebellion too early could end in disaster for all of them. *Them* - it felt good to think in those terms again. A yawn broke out beside him as Maggie stretched two bare arms into the air.

"Up already?" she said with a yawn.

"A lot to think about," he replied more somber than he wanted.

This made Maggie sit up. "It's weighing on you, isn't it? This rebellion and the trip to Edonia?"

"That... and other things." His face twisted into a seductive grin. "I missed this, and now I will be deprived from you for a few more weeks of travel south."

Maggie's caramel eyes grew playful. "We best take advantage then."

With a ferocity she leapt onto him. How he'd missed her. Yet even as his world was made right there was a small nagging fear that would not leave his mind. A fear that perhaps his dreams of influence were waning. He didn't like to think about it but if he was honest with himself a small part of him missed the power. On the one hand there was the life of freedom to do as he pleased with those he loved. It wasn't the trappings he'd fallen for when he first became baron. Fine bed chambers and perks were nothing compared to companionship. No this was something different... for something more. He had been made a baron. A higher rank than any man in his station of life had ever risen to achieve. He hated that even as things felt right again he had this ever so faint fear of losing what he'd worked so hard to achieve. So, why did he feel this desperate nagging suddenly? Why could he not find contentment? Maggie's lips parted from him own.

"Are you okay, John?" she asked looking down at him.

Blinking away reflection he stared up at her. "Yes, sorry, like I said there's a lot on my mind."

She gave him a quizzical look but he pulled her into his embrace before she could ask another probing question. He let his mind drift from his confused desires and chose to embrace the moment instead.

Another dire winter sky greeted him as he stepped outside the small stone house. He'd decided to take his woodsmen's cloak and leather armor for the journey south. Hues of forest green and weather-beaten brown were a familiar comfort to his life on the move. Maggie followed just behind him. She wore John's white wolf cloak over a simple brown jacket. Her blonde hair complimenting the look with a tightly woven bun. A host of men awaited them both. Each prepared for the long journey ahead.

"Your steed, sire," Huldwin said ushering Midnight to John by the reins. John took them in hand while extending the other to brush Midnight's neck.

"Think you boys can keep up with us?" John asked with a twinkle in his eye. The men laughed knowing it best not to take his challenge seriously. Another white mare was brought forth by a stable hand for Maggie to use. Snowfall was its name. A marvelous mare bred to race across Edonia's northern plains. With a shouted order from Huldwin they saddled up. A company their size would only need a few days to arrive at Farmshire.

With a crack of his reins John set off. The small pack of woodsmen let out a unified cry as they raced out of Bjønen. The town folk looked on with curiosity as their newly establish baron sped away. John caught their stares smirking to himself. Somehow their confusion and the mystery behind his departure brought him back to the good ole days. Days when he'd been a legendary shadow lurking in the woods. Annoyingly an inner voice nagged at his old passions.

Do you want to be a filthy woodsman forever, John? Shaking his head, he worked to dismiss the thought as if it was a cobweb he could whisk away. While the words faded, the feeling of discontentment lingered in his soul. The adrenaline to start their journey soon faded as the long hours on the road began to take their toll. As the bleak winter sky darkened, they settled down to make camp. Something about a campfire under the open sky surrounded by his closest companions did John's heart well. For a moment it kept his other ambitions at bay. Across the crackling fire he could see Maggie's eyes weighing him. Her stare felt as though it was peering into his mind and examining his inner thoughts. The very idea terrified him. If she knew what he truly was... Thankfully she didn't question him again as they lay together in their tent later that evening.

The next day of travel brought with it the same tedious routines. Long hours of travel under a dusting of snow. Frigid winds from the north swept across their path leaving each man huddled beneath their cloak. There was no song or laughter that night as each quickly huddled under whatever they could find. Heat radiated from the sleeping Maggie beside him. On a frigid night like this it was just another reminder of how much he'd missed her. Unable to sleep John watched the peaceful rhythm of her breathing beside him. He fought the urge to wake her, knowing it would not likely be passion but wrath that he'd evoke.

Turning he stared up at the wind-swept canvas above. *What is wrong with me?* he pondered.

How could someone have so much yet feel so... so... he wasn't sure what to name it. It was like a craving for more when you're already full. Not exactly discontentment but a form of it. He was happy with the woman at his side. His men were loyal to a fault, and he now carried a title beyond his wildest dreams. Still, he wanted more? Closing his eyes again he willed sleep to take him. At long last it wrapped him in its embrace. His eyes blinked open to the pale morning light of winter peeking through the fabric of his tent. With a groan he rose to his feet realizing Maggie had already risen. Fitting on the familiar garb of their woodland days, he stepped outside the tent. Almost all accompanying him had awakened. Some worked to prep for the half day's journey and others still sat chatting over the morning meal. He found Maggie just removing a pair of eggs from the cook fire.

"You want one?" she asked offering him the pan.

"Thanks," John said plopping beside her. Extending frozen fingers he wiggled them in a vain attempt to thaw them by the flame.

"Today's the day," she said, a bit melancholy.

"It is. Time to see if this is an elaborate hoax to flush out traitors or something real."

"If it's not?" she asked. In her caramel eyes John could see a hint of fear.

"Then we fight together to the end."

She looked down as if dissatisfied with the answer.

"What is it, Maggs?"

She let out a deep sigh. "It's just… I'm ready to start something different. To be something different."

He stared at her a mix of confusion and frustration. "Were you not the one who told me I should have stood against Octavian and the empire? Did you suddenly change your mind?"

His voice flared with more anger than he'd intended. Maggie kept her gaze fixed on the ground as she spoke, "When we were separated it gave me time to think. To believe that maybe at the end of all this there could be some kind of meaning. That maybe all our old dreams were about building something completely different. Perhaps it could be a different kind of kingdom. One that strives for some sort of ideals to live by. I don't know, perhaps the idea of a family also…"

He cut her off at those words. "You and I talked about this, Maggie. I don't have a desire for that life, not yet at least."

"It was a stupid thought, John." She rose to her feet dusting off her pants. "Forget I said anything."

Clarity struck him. It was as if an answer long forgotten suddenly arrived. This had always been his fear. The fear of insignificance. To settle down on the farmlands of Bjønen raising a cluster of tiny urchins. A fear that had always been Maggie's desire. He realized now why he'd felt so dissatisfied. It was the pull to a normal life. The thing he'd fought against for so long. He rose to his feet seeing the others pack away their belongings for the day's journey.

Frustratingly, the clarity brought him no relief. It only revealed what he was being asked to choose. Would he sacrifice these people he'd come to cherish in order to be something more, or would he kill that dream to be with the ones who mattered to him the most? A question many had answered with ease throughout history, yet the hunger gnawed at him. Could he truly ever be free of its grip? Unfortunately, another long and dreary day on the road would give him plenty of time to think about it.

As the day turned to evening the town of Farmshire came into view several miles ahead. The flat prairie lands of Venhorn and Bjønen now merged giving travelers a clear view of the surrounding countryside. Farmshire was a simple town that sat partly nestled in the foothills of Kaladin and on the open plains of Venhorn. The disputed territory had been turned into a neutral center for the three northern kingdoms to receive their food supply. It made the humble town vastly more important than other similar places in the north. In fact, it had become the main source of food for many in northern Edonia. It had become deceitfully important. A town full of simple farmers had amassed a fortune all out of the convenience of its location.

As they drew near John could see the wooden spikes of a simple palisade come into view. A coalition of both Venhorn, Kaladin, and Bjønen guards stood watch over the city's defenses. It had been part of the pact the three kingdoms signed so that none could lay claim to the town. It made him wonder what the guards once loyal to Holger would think of their new baron. Passing through the countryside their small band was greeted with an ever-growing stream of farmsteads. The winter left them looking cold and abandoned but John knew better. As the northern cold faded these same fields would be teeming with fresh crops and filled with thousands of farmhands.

A horn blared as they drew near the gate. A cluster of guards stood ready to greet them as the wooden doors creaked opened. Some of the guards dressed themselves with the insignia of the black bear. They gave John a curious expression as he signified who they were. What Huldwin lacked in battlefield courage he made up for with his silver tongue. A carefully crafted story by him let the guards know they'd come to escort the baron on his journey southward to the emperor's coronation. The guards disinterested in staying out in the cold ushered them in with a wave of the hand.

Now their real challenge began. The letter given to John said to return his answer to Farmshire but left no other clues as to where. How was he supposed to join this rebellion if he couldn't find them in the first place? A cold winter's night was beginning to settle in. The orange glow of candlelight flickered to life in the surrounding windows. The snowy cobbled stone road ahead of them sat practically abandoned except for the occasional passerby eager to return home.

"I wondered if this would be a waste of time," Huldwin complained wrapping himself in his cloak with a shiver.

"It's getting dark. We should find a place to stay," Maggie said as a gust of cold wind sent stray hairs dancing across her rosy cheeks.

"What did the letter say again?" John asked beginning to pull it from a pouch around his waist. A high-pitched whistle caught his attention just as he pulled his hand free. In an adjacent alley stood a hooded figure draped in shadow.

"A flair for the dramatic much?" John said turning to face the stranger.

The shadowed form stepped forward into the dying light that painted the street. With a swift motion the hood was thrown back. Blonde hair that rivaled Maggie's fluttered in the wind. Clear sapphire eyes set in a soft featured face met John's. It took him aback for a moment seeing another woman so similar to Maggie. He caught the jealous eye of his lover as she scowled at the woman now revealed before them.

"Did you not read the letter?" the mysterious woman snarled. "It said to send a letter back. Not come here yourself."

Her accent was distinctly from the region of Venhorn, and by the pronunciation of her words the woman was formally trained. John dismounted approaching the woman. He watched as her hand moved ever so slightly to her hip.

"Peace, we come in peace. There's no need for that," John said, eyeing her hand.

"Name is Juliet," the woman said moving her hand away from her weapon's hilt. Her eyes lit with recognition at the blade John carried.

That's right, Juliet. Careful who you threaten, he thought.

"Juliet, like Thegn Oswald's daughter?" Huldwin asked dumbfounded.

"We should talk inside. I have a place." Without another word she turned down the alley, expecting them to follow.

"I don't like her," Maggie said eyeing Juliet as she vanished down the alley.

"Careful, Maggs. Wouldn't want to think you were jealous," John said playfully. She shot him a glare but quickly followed after him. The thegn's daughter led them several blocks until a simple lodge came into view. A small area was afforded for the horses beside it. John and the others quickly tied up their faithful companions before hurriedly escaping the ever increasing cold. Inside the lodge was a large waiting room lit by a flickering hearth. The warmth was an instant comfort after days of exposure on the road. Juliet took a seat at a table with several bowls of soup steaming atop it. A group of armed men stood around her, their faces colder than the air outside. One even carried the brand of a slave on his forehead.

John felt his hand slowly glide to Bear Paw's hilt. Behind him he could feel his men tense at the sight of armed warriors. It was time for this young thegn's daughter to explain herself. She gestured for them to take a seat at the table.

"I apologize if there isn't enough soup. I didn't expect so many of you." Her words gave a hint of frustration at the breaking of the letter's orders.

"You would forgive me for wanting to meet in person about something so… sensitive," John said taking the offered chair.

"I suppose that can be understood."

This Juliet was young, but she sure knew how to play the game, John thought.

"So, what do you have in mind for this… what are we calling it exactly?" he asked.

"Justice," Juliet said sternly. "Volkmar slew the emperor for his own ambition, and we plan to bring him to justice."

"Very noble, but slaying an emperor is no small thing. Before I risk my life and the lives of all my men…"

"And women," interrupted Maggie.

"And women," John said eyeing her. "I'd like to know there is more to this than a grand vision of justice."

Juliet weighed him for a long moment before speaking again, "I don't trust you, John of the Wood. I've heard tales of your tactics. I find them less than honorable, but alas we need all the kingdoms of Edonia if we are to pull this off."

"And how many do you have now?" John asked.

Her expression said it all.

"You don't have any?" He stood from the table in one swift motion. "Don't waste my time."

"Wait," Juliet said rising from her chair. "I was hoping you'd help with that. You of all people should know what it's like to live under a tyrant. Soon all of us will."

John looked at her dismissively. "I thought you said my tactics were dishonorable? Now you want my help to implement them? Because that's what it's going to take. At least with the meager forces you have now."

Juliet grimaced realizing her words were coming back to haunt her. "Things are changing rapidly. News has reached us that Thegn Lucian and most of Kaladin's army has fallen in the taking of Hunan."

"I'm missing your point and how it involves me?" John said taking another step toward the door.

"Duke Arthur is all that remains of Edonia's rulers besides you and my father. He had great sway over the kingdom of Kaladin. If we can turn him to our side, we may be able to muster enough men to stand against Volkmar."

"That's a big ask. Duke Arthur has been a loyal puppet to the throne all his life. It cost him his wife and daughter, and still he bows to the emperor like a loyal dog."

"Bowed, John. He was loyal to Septimus, but Volkmar… He… He strung them up like animals, John. Beatrice and Leo. First, he burned them in the courtyard, and now he has their bodies hung up for all to see," Juliet's voice quivered as she said the words.

"I have no special love for the empire. Not anymore but that is something different. It's a vileness I cannot permit to plague our land," she continued, a fire now burning in her eyes.

John stood stunned. An act so wicked had not been performed to Edonian royalty in a millennia.

"She's right, John," Maggie said. "Shantz, I hate to say it, but she may be right. If Volkmar is willing to do that, we can't sit by and do nothing."

Why, Maggie... he moaned internally. "We need more than hope so what do you have in mind to win Duke Arthur to our side?"

n response Juliet dug into a small pouch at her side. She pulled out an identically sealed letter as the one she'd sent to John.

"All I ask is that you give this to him."

"Why can't your father do that?"

"He doesn't know all that we hope to accomplish...yet."

"Shantz, woman! You know this will make me a marked man, don't you? If the duke doesn't side with our cause, I'll be as good as dead."

"All causes require sacrifice and a little faith," Juliet said still holding the letter extended toward him.

"I'm averse to both, but perhaps I can find a way to deliver it to him without his knowing," John said taking the parchment in hand.

A wave of relief washed over Juliet's face. Curiously she turned to the slave branded man with a smile.

"Thank you," Juliet said turning to John once more.

"Thank me when you get your little rebellion."

Juliet shifted her eyes to the others with John. "You can stay here for the night. Then I suggest we all part ways before more eyes have a chance to see us together."

John nodded and turned to see his men gratefully unload their cloaks in a weary heap.

"Stay sharp," John warned. They gave him an exasperated look, but their demeanor sharpened none the less.

Maggie placed a gentle hand on his shoulder. "Just this small thing, John. Then we can be done with empires and emperors."

"We'll see." The ache inside him told a different story.

238

18

DUKE ARTHUR

LANDFALL HAD FINALLY come. The quiet waves of the Edon Bay lapped against the palace docks. Already the signs of a coronation had begun. Arthur wouldn't be surprised if he was the last to arrive. While the journey northward hadn't required a blade to carve its way forward, it still took time. So much so that the urgent call of the new emperor had taken him ahead of the army by a few weeks. As he surveyed the capitol, he could see much had transpired in Edonia with the absence of its armies. He placed a careful step onto the dock meeting a host of attendances that stood at the ready. In a flurry they gathered around, bombarding him with an endless stream of questions.

"Duke Arthur, so pleasant to have you! How was your journey?"

"Defender of Edonia, is Hunan truly vanquished?"

"Is it true that the thegn is dead?"

"Duke, I must ask that you follow me to prepare for the ceremony."

"Enough!" Arthur roared, silencing them all.

Did these squabbling men have no sense of dignity? Taking several steps forward the host of attendants parted to make way. The man who'd asked him to follow eyed Arthur with scorn.

"I'll return shortly. I wish to see the city so many of my men died defending before I join your little party." Arthur said in a low growl. The truth was different. After a long journey at sea the last thing he wanted was some sniveling aid hounding his every step.

"Emperor Volkmar specifically advised I take you straight to your chambers."

"He's not emperor yet," Arthur said turning his back to the man. The attendant moved to protest but stopped as Arthur rested his hand on Phoenix Flame. Petrified, the attendant retreated back with the others. Arthur let out a satisfied chuckle. He had no intention of using such a weapon on the attendant, but the man needn't know that. Finally left to himself, he forged a path through the large docking platform and onto the palace grounds.

On his return journey he'd heard the hundreds of rumors that circulated about what had transpired in the city. Some claimed a coup had occurred. Others praised Volkmar for bringing Septimus to justice for his war crimes. Wilder claims even spoke of old myths now springing to life again. All of it was just the talk of idle men. He wouldn't know the truth until he saw it for himself. The path ahead led him through a manicured archway of intricately woven vines. Its trail twisted and turned in a disorienting fashion until it finally arrived at the palace grounds.

Edonia's seat of power now towered over him. Magnificent, spired towers and polished white walls decorated with all manner of craftsmanship stood stalwart. The golden dome that capped palace glistened proudly in the sun. Only a few signs of a skirmish remained on the surrounding grounds. All he could detect was the occasional scar on the otherwise well-manicured lawn. It would seem that the emperor's home had quickly returned to form. Perhaps the rumors hadn't been as severe as he'd heard. Bustling life distracted from the remaining flaws as servants worked to bring the finishing touches of the ceremony to life. Arthur paused to watch the last of the decorative wreaths being hung on the perimeter's walls. Volkmar wouldn't hold back for a celebration of himself. Had Arthur expected the man to? The other duke rarely passed on a moment to shine the light on his accomplishments.

Drinking in the scene Arthur found the lonely walk refreshed him with each step. Endless days on a crowded boat and bloody battle on land left him yearning for solitude. The mild climate didn't hurt either. Especially after leaving the scorching lands of Hunan. Winters up north may have left one chilled to the bone but in Edonia the cold was only a mild nuisance.

Rounding the right of the palace he froze in place. Terror and rage flooded him all at once. Swaying gently in the wind hung two corpses above the palace gates. Decorations had been hung as if to include the two remains in the celebration. It was a display of sheer ruthlessness. Without realizing it Arthur had dropped to his knees at the sight. The bodies hanging in the distance morphed. Instead of charred flesh it was the smooth skin and loose blonde hair of his two loves that swayed in the midday breeze. A distant screaming rang in his ears. It grew louder until it nearly overwhelmed him. The sound ripped at his throat leaving it hoarse.

Who was screaming? he wondered in an animal-like panic. Dazed he suddenly realized a mix of servants and attendants had surrounded him. Blinking away his momentary confusion he realized he was on the ground. Why was he on the ground?

"Duke Arthur, I believe it's best you follow me now," The snarky attendant from earlier said offering him a hand. The harshness from their earlier encounter was gone and in its place pity.

Arthur rose to his feet without a word, nodding to the man. Some tried to help him move but he tore free of their grip. He would not be led like a child. Wandering as if in a lucid dream, he followed the attendant through the palace halls. The decorative walls and symbols of power all a blur as he was brought to his chambers. His stupor left him reeling as he realized they'd already reached his room. Observing the humble quarters, he felt nothing but a dull numbness. The sound of a door closed behind him, the attendant retreating as soon as he could.

As he should, Arthur thought. *Who wants to be associated with a maniac?*

Stumbling, he found a nearby mirror placed above a basin of water. Weathered skin and tired eyes stared mindlessly at a thick, scraggly beard that had grown over the last half year. Had it really been that long? A sharpened blade had been provided with the basin.

Likely a less than subtle hint for him to clean himself up before the coronation. He raised the razor to his neck. Dark eyes locked with the ones in the mirror. A sinister thought crept into his mind.

You could end this you know? All this pain it could be over with one...

"No!" he said aloud nearly throwing the razor. Shutting his eyes, he fought the sobs that wished to overtake him. Remembering the technique he'd used in the past he filled his lungs and released them in one strong breath. Gripping the razor with new fervor, he went to work cutting away the scruff. It took time but soon the barbaric looking face was that of a dignified duke once more. He'd even used it to crop the sides of his head. Thick black strands fell to the floor in heaps. Something inside pushed him forward. Now it was the top's turn. Locks of dark hair peppered with grey fell to the floor. Stepping back he observed his handiwork. The sides were cropped nearly to his scalp and a short tuft of hair remained on top. A look he hadn't had since his youthful days as a soldier. The days when his dark eyes still carried a spark of life in them. Peering into the mirror, he worked to will that spark into existence once again. Disappointedly, the jaded, dead eyes remained.

Placing the razor to the side he turned toward the larger tub of water that had been made ready. Steam still wafted from the surface, an invitation he wouldn't refuse. He wasn't sure how long he soaked in its contents, and he didn't care. He allowed his mind to let go for a time. His mind drifted in a sea of nothingness. A solace that was long overdue. It was only when the last button on his crimson and gold trimmed tunic was snapped that a knock came at his door.

"Come in."

The attendant from earlier peered into the room. His face was taken aback by the duke that now stood before him. "Duke Arthur... dinner is ready," the attendant said stammering.

Arthur nodded, accepting the invite. They walked in silence down the marbled halls. This time Arthur drank in every inch of what was around him. Faint remains of battle marred their path, a path cut straight to the throne room itself. They wouldn't go there for the dinner, but as they passed its doors Arthur could see deep gashes and charred markings along the wall. They were accompanied by newly placed rugs that attempted to hide the stained floor.

So there was a fight in the palace, he thought to himself, *and a bloody one at that.*

The attendant led him into the grand dinner room. Already the sounds of clanking plates and silverware could be heard in the hall. As they rounded the corner and entered the room a small gathering of men greeted them. Each turned to the new arrivals. The faces of Thegn Oswald, Octavian, Volkmar, and a man he had never seen before sat at the table. All of them stood as he entered the room. All of them but Volkmar whose face remained focused on the meal before him.

Oswald cracked a smile as he embraced Arthur. "Duke, it has been too long."

"Indeed. How are Gwen, Liam, and Juliet?" Arthur asked.

"Fine. Just fine." Something in the Thegn's eyes told a different story, but now was not the time to press the man. Oswald returned to his seat allowing Octavian to greet Arthur next.

"Duke, I am happy to hear you had a successful campaign," Octavian said extending a hand.

Not the definition I would use, Arthur thought as he took Octavian's hand in his own.

"I'm alive. That I can be grateful for."

"Indeed," Octavian replied. "I would like to introduce you to our newest edition on the emperor's council, Baron John of Bjønen."

"Baron John?" Arthur said taken aback. "I've missed much during my time in Hunan."

Octavian cracked a wry smile. "Yes, you have, my duke."

John stepped forward extending a hand of his own. The young man had a rugged quality to him. Octavian had done his best to dress this John up in a fine garment of green, but the woodsman still shined through behind the fine clothes. Arthur gripped the calloused hand meeting John's gaze. John's stubbled face cracked into a grin.

"Pleasure to meet you, Duke Arthur."

"Same. I think it's good we have a man of the common people's perspective on our council."

John's face slightly twisted at the words. As if the word common had struck a nerve. Releasing his grip John found his place once more at the table.

"Now that all the formality is done, can we get back to business?" Volkmar asked tiredly. His eyes remaining on the piece of steak before him.

You haven't changed, Arthur thought as he sat at the empty seat reserved for him. Unfortunately, it was one designated beside Volkmar. As he sat, Volkmar's eyes rose from his meal.

"Late as usual my old friend. As I was saying before, I believe it's time for the empire to brandish a new symbol. One that speaks of an era on the rise and instills fear into our enemies."

"I didn't know you had been sworn in already?" Arthur said perturbed by Volkmar's audacity.

Volkmar let out a tired sigh. "We all know this is just a formality." Volkmar scanned each man as if searching for any dissent. Arthur noticed the new baron's eyes fix on him for moment. Something strange was hidden in his stare. A curiosity? No, more like pleading?

"I believe you all are in for quite the treat tomorrow," Volkmar said tearing off a piece of steak and plopping it in his mouth. "It will be a symbol that conveys many meanings. The dread of night for our enemies, the hope of morning for our people, and the thing that makes an empire run."

"That is?" Oswald asked.

"Blood," Volkmar said coolly.

An awkward silence clung to those seated at the table. A growing dread killed any appetite Arthur might have had. Looking to the others he could see they felt the same. Each of them sat watching as the soon to be emperor devoured his meal. Eventually Octavian cleared his throat and spoke, "Is there anything you would like to discuss before the ceremony tomorrow? Volkmar has requested your complaints be brought to him personally and not before the people gathered during the ceremony."

Where would I begin? Arthur thought.

"I am curious to know of any documentation left by Septimus claiming you as his heir. I wasn't made aware of such a document, and I'd assume the emperor himself would have made this known to us?"

Volkmar placed his silverware down annoyedly. "I wondered when your hunger for power would show, Arthur."

Volkmar turned his venomous eyes to Arthur as he spoke, "There was documentation found sealed with the emperor's seal itself in his private chambers. I know you have been jealous that he offered Beatrice to me, but Septimus truly did favor me as his heir. So much so that he entrusted me with his own flesh and blood."

"Is that why she hangs in the courtyard?" Arthur snarled. Even as the words left his lips, he knew they were a mistake.

Volkmar's face flushed and a barely contained rage caused his voice to shake, "I saved this empire from treachery and betrayal. The emperor and my own wife conspired to bring us into a war for resources all the while funding our enemy through proxies. I used what the emperor had bestowed on me against him. Should you desire less from your ruler?"

Volkmar met Arthur's eyes and the room melted away. Something behind the man's gaze had changed. Volkmar had always been ambitious, cunning, and venomous but now Arthur could see something more sinister lurked within. Volkmar broke his gaze and the room returned around them. A mix of stunned and ashamed faces surrounded the table.

"I suggest we all get some rest for the day tomorrow," Octavian said rising to his feet.

"Indeed," Volkmar agreed pushing away from the table.

Arthur glanced at Oswald, but the man did not meet his gaze as he stood. Instead he turned a wilted glance in Volkmar's direction. As if he was awaiting another chastisement at any moment. John however, dared to look Arthur's way, that strange pleading still remained as he did. Volkmar passed John and the young baron looked away as he rose to his feet. It was a pathetic procession that filed out of the room. Men who were supposed to be leaders, the best of Edonia, walking with the posture of beaten dogs in the face of a monstrous man. For all his bluster though, the same hopelessness began to take hold of Arthur. Volkmar would become emperor. The sinister politics of the empire had worked their magic once more giving the power hungry the ability to rule the powerless.

Letting out a tired sigh he followed the others out the dining hall's door. Volkmar, Octavian, and Oswald had already vanished from sight but for some reason John staggered behind. He stood fidgeting in the hall as if building up the nerve for something. As Arthur drew near John turned to face him.

"Do you truly think Volkmar is what's best for the empire?" he asked bluntly.

Arthur was taken aback by such a foolish question. A question that would get this man killed. Arthur had generations of royal blood and prestige to protect him from Volkmar's ire. But words like this from a common man? It was a good way to get himself slaughtered.

"I'd be careful never to ask that kind of question to anyone again, especially in these halls. Do you hear me?" Arthur said, leering at the man.

John seemed to wilt at the words. "Yes." The former woodsman sighed before speaking again, "I'm not used to taking part in lavish dinners and jockeying with pompous rulers. I spent my life fighting them."

Why is the man telling me this" Arthur thought.

"Again, not a wise statement to say, ever."

"Like I said, not used to this. Forgive me, duke," John bowed and quickly retreated down the hall.

What was that? Arthur thought, bewildered.

Slowly and full of thoughts, he meandered back to his chambers. Laying his head on the softened silk he let his thoughts consume him. He didn't mind that they kept sleep from his eyes. Anything was better than facing the nightmares that surely awaited him. He wasn't aware when sleep finally got him in its hold. It didn't matter as the relentless nightmare came, like it always did. Gabriella's face appeared before him. Her glossed lips parted in a smile as she tucked back a strand of loose blonde hair. Deep emerald pools looked into his own. There was a longing in them, a beckoning for him to wrap her in his embrace. It was the same temptation he'd always felt in the dream.

Just as his body moved against his will to hold her, she vanished. A deafening scream replaced the serene moment. All was black around him but for a faint light in the distance. Stumbling through the motions for the thousandth time he raced toward the light. It was a cracked door, his bedroom door back in his home of Fenikia. He had been delayed that evening, a soldier of his who'd returned with him from the war in Mascar had gone into a drunk stupor again. Many of them had that problem since their return. The things they'd done and seen had been too much for them to live with. The showers of praise for their heroic deeds still echoed in Arthur's mind. A grand parade had been thrown for the valor of the young duke-to-be and his men. Had it not been for the horrible memories he and his soldiers possessed, they too might have been wrapped up in the praise showered on them. Hailed as the future ruler of Edonia many became disappointed when Septimus' daughter Beatrice had been offered up to another. The disappointment of the people had been a slight his compatriot Volkmar would not soon forget or forgive.

Arthur extended a shaky hand toward the cracked door in his dream. He knew what awaited him. He always did. Yet the dream would not let him escape his fate. All his mental strain could not keep the vision from following its course. His bed chamber was revealed as he pressed his hand against the cold wooden door.

"Duke Arthur?"

The voice startled him awake. The attendant from yesterday stood hunched over him with a frown. Arthur sucked in a breath as he sat up.

"I've laid out your attire for the day. I suggest you get ready as the coronation is beginning soon," chided the attendant.

"What time is it?" Arthur asked, raising a hand to his head.

"Late morning. I suggest you hurry." Without another word the attendant departed slamming the door behind him.

Arthur scowled at the man's back. "He has no love for me that's for sure. Like his master."

Arthur rose with a groan. Inspecting the garments, he found they were tailored perfectly. A fine military uniform strangely colored. It was made of black cotton and sewn together with a blood red trim. A color scheme he'd never seen before at a royal event. Was Volkmar trying to make him a marked man? Begrudgingly he adorned the uniform knowing he had little choice. Wrapping Phoenix Flame around his waist he departed for the palace courtyard. The halls remained empty as almost all the palace's attendants had already gathered for the ceremony.

"I really am late," he mused, passing another set of abandoned corridors.

He followed the familiar path through the palace until he reached the main entryway. A large host had gathered in the lobby, each representing the most important families in Edonia. He was taken aback to see everyone dressed in the same black and red of his own uniform. Servants dressed in similar colors glided across the room offering drinks and appetizers to the crowd. The scene reminded him how much he hated formal events. Gabriella had always managed them so well. She knew the right person to speak with using the correct etiquette. Her bright laughter would fill the room.

"Stop, Arthur," he said chiding himself. "You can't go there."

It had grown harder lately. Years had passed and for a time he'd nearly been able to forget the deep pain that dwelled within her memory. Almost. Something had stirred up those feelings in him again. He knew what it was if he was honest. Being shipped off to another pointless war only to return as an emptier man than he was before. Losing Lucian... It all felt so pointless. All the lives of those he'd loved gone and for what? To keep this going? Glancing over the room he took stock of the pomp and pageantry of Edonia's finest. Lives of thousands sacrificed on the altar of war to fill the pockets of Edonia's noble class. All the while those who give their sons are left destitute.

The sheer hollowness of it all left him feeling jaded. Today, however, hunger stirred within him, not for food, wealth, or prestige. A hunger for something… more. Something beyond what he could see in this room of empty souls. There was a time where he would have been willing to sacrifice anything to obtain the status of emperor. In fact, he had sacrificed it all, and now even the crown itself could not satisfy his longing.

"Duke?" asked a nearby servant. The man extended an arm offering a tray of drinks.

"No, thank you," Arthur replied.

The man bowed politely and moved on to another cluster of guests. "You sure know how to ruin the mood of a party," he could hear Gabriella say to him.

"Indeed, love."

Arthur watched as Octavian stepped before the entry doors of the palace making a pronouncement to the crowd, "The coronation is about to begin. Please find your designated spots."

Octavian hasn't missed a beat in all this, Arthur thought.

The man was the one bright spot that had come from his time in Mascar. A life Arthur had saved among the hundreds he had taken. He and Octavian had never talked about that day. At times he wondered if any within the empire knew where Octavian had come from. The similarities between the Mascarans and Edonians could hide him on the outside. The man had remarkably been able to mask his foreign tongue as well. Yet, resentment had to stir in the man's heart for what had been done to his home and family. Many years ago Arthur had witnessed that resentment himself during Septimus' feast. Octavian somehow suppressed it then and, perhaps, he was suppressing it now.

The crowd began to swarm into place and Arthur felt the pull that he should join in the mindless dance. Wading through the crowd he found his place at the front. It was his unfortunate privilege to stand at the emperor's side as the second highest official in the land. Volkmar appeared from the crowd wrapped in an extravagant robe of black and red. On his head was the emperor's crown and a look of gleeful victory was expressed on his narrow face. Beside him meandered Thegn Oswald and Baron John. Both carried looks of unease as they followed the self-absorbed Volkmar.

As Volkmar passed, he gave Arthur a dismissive nod before settling at the front of the procession. John and Oswald found their
places just behind Arthur. A grim expression flickered between the
three of them as they waited for the ceremony to begin. A horn bellowed out commanding the palace doors to open. Light temporarily
blinded Arthur, but as his vision cleared he could see through frosted
breaths a host that consumed the royal courtyard. Vast tents stood
erected at each corner of the complex. An array of servants armed
with food and drink for all underneath them.

"Wine and dine them until they become used to graveling at
your doorstep," Arthur muttered to himself as he took in the scene.
The next horn blew ushering those in the palace to come forth to
meet the people. Volkmar led them with hands raised in a grandiose
gesture. The rest of them followed like a stream of fine goods lavishly
displayed on the palace steps.

Arthur took his place beside Volkmar. His eyes swaying across
the vast crowd. Some faces shouted with joy, others sat firm, weighing the pompous show, and still others looked fearful of what future
awaited them. As if any second another terror could arise within the
city. Arthur felt the presence of Oswald and John take their place
beside him. He glanced at the new baron, surprised to see that the
young man seemed to enjoy the attention placed on them.

He'll fit right in then, Arthur thought.

Lastly, Volkmar's personal guard fanned out around the distinguished guests who took their place on the palace stairs. Each man
wore a new surcoat over their plated armor. It was the color of midnight and... Arthur squinted looking at the nearest guard. "A blood
red moon?" he whispered to himself in disbelief.

"Good citizens of the empire, I greet you on this marvelous day!"
Volkmar declared to the crowd. A hush fell over the mass as each
desired to hear what their future held with this new emperor.

"It is a new day for the glorious Edonian Empire. One free from
corruption and lack of vision."

Arthur weighed the thousands of faces. Each of them desperate to know what awaited them.

"It is the greatest honor of my life to be presented as your new emperor on this day. I promise you that there will be no lack of vision in my rule. Too long our empire has crumbled little by little under the slow corruption of passivity. No longer. Today I present to you a new future for Edonia. One that makes our enemies tremble and our people proud." Volkmar nodded to the chief guard named Rowan at his side. Arthur could see the Dawn Blade once belonging to Varnas now wrapped around the man's waist.

With a look of acknowledgment, Rowan sent a burst from a horn in his hand. It was the call for all to kneel. Hesitantly the crowd dropped to a knee as two banners were loosed on the palace above. A blood red moon fluttered on a midnight field. It was a haunting symbol. Perfect for the tyrant that stood before them.

"Every era deserves a symbol of its own, and today I present to you our symbol. One that will strike awe and reverence into the nations once again. This is my solemn oath to you!"

With that declaration, the call to swear fealty was given. A murmured chant rose from the crowd.

"From this breath to your last we swear our undying allegiance to you. Rule us well, our emperor. May your reign be long and full of victories. May our swords be sharp and ready to defend. May our hearts be true and loyal only to you."

Arthur felt his lips moving with the rhythmic oath, but his heart wandered elsewhere. They were empty words. Like promises given by a man who has nothing to lose and everything to gain by telling you what you want to hear. The voices of the crowd faded leaving the courtyard in a reverent silence. Rowan stepped forward with Griffin's Dread in hand. Kneeling he offered the emperor's sword to Volkmar. Emperor Volkmar gripped the hilt in his spindly fingers unsheathing the blade.

He raised Griffin's Dread high above him, its blade radiating light for all to see.

"On this blade and by your oaths I declare myself Emperor of Edonia!" Volkmar said for all to hear.

It was strange. It looked to Arthur as though Griffin's Dread shone brighter than usual. He followed a particular beam to the palace complex's gate. The beam of light seemed to rest on two corpses swaying gently in the breeze. Arthur choked back a reaction at the sight. A weight fell on him seeing the Edonium Blade cry out for justice on behalf of Beatrice and Leo.

The last of the horns blew signaling the end of the ceremony and the beginning of the feast. All reverence evaporated as the crowd broke into wild celebration at the food prepared. Revelry overtook any desire for truth or justice. It churned Arthur's stomach. He felt alone in his feelings as countless other royalty dashed to the nearest dining tent. He wished he'd brought Sir William along instead of leaving him in command of the army. At least then he'd have another to share his mood. The eyes of Volkmar met his own as the newly crowned emperor descended the step between them. Volkmar examined Arthur as if searching for something.

"Your army will be returning soon won't they, Duke?" Volkmar asked.

"In a week or so," Arthur replied suspiciously.

"Good. I shall have need of them. Give them the winter months back home then prepare them to return to the city."

"Your Majesty, I don't understand," Arthur said.

"It's time we show the world we are not to be meddled with. The reports say that Ishkar and Kaskar joined with Hunan, is that correct?"

"Yes but their armies were wiped out by…" Arthur's eyes looked up at the banners overhead. As they lowered to meet Volkmar's an eerie knowing passed between them. "By a mysterious army."

Volkmar's lips creased into a sinister grin, "Even better. It will allow you to make quick work in exterminating the vermin's home."

"Exterminating? I beg your pardon, Your Majesty…"

"No, need to beg. It is a command from your emperor," Volkmar said raising a hand to interrupt him.

"I know you're concerned for your men, so I will make sure to see that you run the operation personally. Now, enjoy the feast, Arthur." Volkmar smirked as he placed a hand on Arthur's shoulder. Arthur stood stunned as he watched Volkmar join a group of bureaucrats. One obnoxious man raised a toast as Volkmar took a fine glass of wine in hand.

Another pointless war? Arthur felt the dread consume him. He wouldn't fight another war. He couldn't, not for this man. Just as the anxiety threatened to swallow him another hand clasped his shoulder.

"It seems you're enjoying this party as much as I," Thegn Oswald said releasing his grip.

"The emperor desires we sail for war again when winter ends," Arthur muttered in disbelief.

Oswald's face morphed into a frown. "I suppose he wishes for us to send our own men, too? There is something else we need to discuss, Arthur. Volkmar questioned me about a particular guest in Venhorn. I didn't tell him the truth but I think it's rather pressing…"

"What's with the sour faces?" John asked stepping up beside them with drink in hand.

Oswald shot a disgusted glance at the half-consumed beverage, "We can speak on this later."

Arthur nodded then turned to John, "It seems our new emperor is thirsty for blood already."

John took a swig from his glass. "Aren't all emperors?"

Arthur raised an eyebrow at the brash baron. It was true. How had he not seen it before? In his youth he had been so eager to fight for Edonia's glory, but what glory was there? To bring other's death and desolation? Why did they need to control the world when the one they had was already reeling?

"Come, friend, no need to be gloomy the whole night. Besides, others are watching," John said eyeing a few stray noblemen. "Change may be possible but not if you go marking yourself as a dissident already."

Strange words from an even stranger man, thought Arthur.

"And words like that will double your trouble. Best not to talk about it here," Oswald said shooting them both a glare.

What did they know? Arthur wondered.

"Fine, I will play the part today," Arthur said grabbing a drink from a passing servant's tray.

But I will find a way out, he promised to himself.

John wrapped his arms around both men's shoulders with complete informality. "Come, gentlemen, I know just the tent to start."

19

OCTAVIAN

U NCERTAINTY LOOMED over Edonia's throne room. Octavian found himself where he'd always stood, at the emperor's side. Volkmar sat casual but confident in his new seat of power. The pompous crown glimmered atop his thick black locks of hair. A new robe had been sewn for him made of material black as midnight and that dreadful blood moon as a crest.

"Your Majesty, a display like that will be a bit disturbing for the people will it not?" asked one of the council members in attendance. The man tried to restrain the shaking in his voice to no avail.

"That's exactly what it's intended to be," Volkmar said annoyed.

"Should we really use the word sacrifice? It's so... vile," said another of the royal court.

Volkmar let out a sigh. "Must I spell it out again? I want each and every traitor among the The People's Justice and those loyal to the old emperor brought here. Then I want you to spill their blood until it paints the Edon Bay crimson! The people must know that traitors and corruptors of the new order will not be tolerated. It is a sacrifice, one that must be made if a new Edonia is to be born."

Silence. Octavian examined the royal court. Each of them squirmed under the fierce stare of Volkmar and his request. None daring to raise their voice in protest.

Pathetic, Octavian thought. Quickly after he found a pang of guilt accuse him. Had he not also remained silent in all this? Fighting his conflicting thoughts he quickly excused himself. It was for an entirely different reason he remained silent. What did it matter to him what happened to these men and women? Wasn't his whole purpose to see Edonia collapse in on itself? If he was honest, though, that excuse felt like a thin veil these days. Volkmar had grown increasingly volatile to the point that even Octavian had begun to wonder what was too much. The truth, the thing he wished to ignore at all costs, was he had the power to change all this before it was too late. All he had to do was say something.

No, I've never acted before, why should I now? I'd send this plan crashing down? After all that I have endured? After being so close to finishing this?

"So, it's settled?" Volkmar asked, taking a glass of wine in hand from a servant at his side.

Eleanar, the head of Volkmar's council stepped forward. "As you wish, Your Majesty. We will begin to… gather those who still resist your rule." The man bowed and retreated back to join the other councilors before the throne.

"Excellent. You're dismissed," Volkmar said coolly.

Each of the councilors fled the room as quickly as they could while still retaining some shred of dignity. Their desire to flee Volkmar's presence, however, left them looking weak.

Why did men fear Volkmar so? He was just a man. Could he not be struck down like he had cut down Septimus? Octavian pondered.

"Octavian, there is a matter I would like to discuss before you go," Volkmar said swishing his cup of wine.

"Yes, Your Majesty."

"It concerns the production of Edonium. Septimus died before its exact location could be revealed to me. I tried torturing his old guard, but you know how they are. Loyal until death."

Octavian remained silent waiting for Volkmar to actually ask the question. The new emperor swirled his glass once more, a look of curiosity in his eyes.

"You don't cower to me like the others. I like that about you,

Octavian."

"I did give you this throne, did I not?"

Volkmar's face soured, "No man gave me this. I took it." The emperor slammed his glass down in annoyance. Octavian kept his expression cool, uncaring even, but inside he enjoyed seeing Volkmar squirm.

"Where do they produce the blades? It is my sacred right to know, is it not?" Volkmar asked, all hints of courtesy now vanished.

"Of course. Follow me," Octavian said turning to leave. He could only imagine what kind of expression was on Volkmar's face. The audacity that he had given the emperor an order without fear of repercussion flooded Octavian with an overwhelming sense of satisfaction. A few heartbeats later he heard the patter of Volkmar a few steps behind.

"You may control others, Volkmar, but you won't control me," Octavian muttered under his breath.

He led the self-appointed emperor through the winding halls and down into Septimus' hidden chambers. Several guards stood sentinel in the octagon-shaped room that led to the palace's hidden entryways.

"Who are these men? I didn't order such a guard to be placed in these quarters." Volkmar said as they passed by.

"Some of my own. I assumed you would want to have this place guarded, Your Majesty," lied Octavian. In reality he had placed his own men to keep an account of who went in and out of the emperor's private dwelling. He by all means necessary wanted to prevent Volkmar from knowing the cavern's other secret. Octavian passed through the room Septimus had occupied the last few years of his reign and opened the hidden door to the cavern. A cold blast of air washed over them as the hidden passageway was revealed. With a look of amazement Volkmar stepped forward. "I knew the old man had kept the chamber close but this…"

They journeyed down the damp tunnel until the cavern's entrance was just ahead. Long and slender stalactites loomed over them like teeth ready to devour its prey. The familiar damp stone and still waters brought a similar amazement to Volkmar that Octavian had once felt upon his first arrival.

"So, this is the place? After all these years I finally can see it with my own eyes." Volkmar said in awe. "That shantz, Beatrice, never did allow me to witness this marvel."

I wonder why in the world not? Octavian thought, rolling his eyes.

"This is Edonia's most powerful secret. The source of all her strength," Octavian said moving to lead the way.

The two of them descended the stairway carved from the cavern's side. Occasionally for amusement, Octavian glanced back to witness the rare bewilderment found on Volkmar's face. Reaching the last of the stairs it was Octavian's turn to be shocked. Waiting for them below stood the ancient stewardess he'd met with Septimus months ago.

"Welcome, Emperor," the stewardess said in an aged voice. Her glossy eyes stared past them as if glimpsing something unseen.

"And who are you?" Volkmar asked. The lack of reverence sent annoyance running through Octavian's veins.

The old woman continued, unfazed, "I am grand stewardess of Edonia's house of knowledge. It is my duty to present all new emperors with the secrets of this cavern."

Octavian's pulse quickened. What was this? No one had spoken of such a thing to him. How had the woman known about Volkmar? The questions rushed through his mind as the grand stewardess motioned to the vast chamber.

"In this cavern holds the two greatest powers in Edonia."

"Two?" Volkmar asked. "There is something beyond the forge here?"

"Follow me, Your Majesty."

This was all wrong. She wouldn't reveal the ancient library, would she? If Volkmar knew... Octavian rushed to keep up as the grand stewardess led them through the stacks of Edonium, pointing out the forge to Volkmar. The blacksmiths sang their enchanted song as they stoked the smelting fires. To Octavian's dread she was leading them straight for the library's entrance.

"Here you will find Edonia's greatest resource," the ancient woman said. Her lips barely moved as she whispered out a set of words in the ancient tongue. Soon after, the cavern's wall melted away, revealing the library's entrance.

"What is this?" Volkmar asked gaping.

"It is knowledge beyond compare, Your Majesty, and it is at your disposal," the grand stewardess said waving a hand. Her blinded eyes moved to fix on Octavian.

"It is yours to share with whomever you please. Although very few others beside Edonia's emperors have had the privilege of entering this sacred place."

Volkmar stepped into the space gawking at the endless stream of shelves. "It is sacred, indeed."

His gaze turned toward the woman. "You say it holds knowledge from every age?"

The stewardess nodded. "Records beyond the empire itself, Your Majesty."

Volkmar stood thoughtfully for a moment. "This could change everything." Excitedly he moved toward a nearby bookshelf, picking up a tome. It pained Octavian to see his secret possession now exposed to this man. Turning he found the blinded eyes of the grand stewardess fixed on him.

"I must insist, Your Majesty, that you inform me of those you wish to have access to this place."

"Such a treasure must be guarded at all costs. I can trust no others with something this... marvelous. It would be disastrous for such a place to fall into the wrong hands," Volkmar said absently as he flipped through another tome.

"Then I must ask you to leave," the grand stewardess said turning to Octavian.

It was a betrayal of the most sinister kind. To offer such a gift and then revoke it.

"But..."

The stewardess cut him off, "That was a different emperor's authority."

"Volkmar?" Octavian cried, but the man had already vanished within the vast volume of works.

"I must insist that you leave," the grand stewardess said voice growing firm. A strange aura filled the room. A force that began to expel him against his will. He watched in horror as the endless shelves vanished behind cold stone. Terror filled Octavian at the prospect of Volkmar gaining the knowledge he had come to possession and the knowledge he had yet to obtain.

"No…" Octavian said voice quivering as he placed a single hand on the cold stone. For once in his life he had held true power. A power no one else possessed, and now it was gone. One could only imagine what Volkmar would do with all that knowledge, but that prospect wasn't what haunted Octavian. He realized what he truly feared. A life without power of his own. His whole existence he had lived at the expense of others. First, it was his family taken away by a needless war. Then it was days as a pathetic servant in the halls of lower lords. So, what if he was head advisor to an emperor? All his life someone had held a leash around his neck. His whole life he'd been a tool for others to use. This library, this knowledge, had given him something. It was the ability to search for truth no matter how elusive. It had given him the one thing he'd never had before. Power. And now it had been taken away from him.

20

DUKE ARTHUR

ARTHUR FOUND HIMSELF once more on another dreaded ship. This time, however, its sails would be taking him home. Sir William stood at his side examining a ledger he carried. He likely was going over the pay, transport, and food logistics for the army. At least what was left of it. Arthur surveyed the armada of vessels slowly making their way up the Edon River.

"Less than two thousand men remain," Arthur whispered under his breath.

"Perhaps less than that," William said striking the ledger with a quilled pen. "If I was a vile man, I would try to see the bright side of this."

"Which is?"

"Less payments to make," William replied grimly.

Arthur shot him a stern glance. "Good thing you're not a vile man then."

"There is another matter, sir," William's face turned grim as he spoke.

Arthur knew what he'd say without having to utter a word. "If it's about the bodies of Lucian and Kain…Send what spoils we have gained with Kaladin's returning troops. They paid dearly for this war. The least we can do is give Lucian's people some sort of solace. Make sure Edon's Bane stays with its master as well."

"Shiny trinkets won't do much to cool Kaladin's temper at this kind of loss."

"It's the best I can do. We've all lost too much, William." Arthur found his voice was sharper than he would have liked. The truth was, he was tired. The kind of tired that sinks down into a man's bones and won't let go. Lucian's and Kain's deaths had become another nightmare he'd dreaded every night when he closed his eyes. During the day it was easier to just keep going than to stop and think about their deaths. Arthur moved to apologize to his old companion for the outburst. Without any resentment William had already turned his attention back on the ledger. He grumbled as he let loose a few more strokes of his pen. Arthur let out a sigh, digging two fists into his uniform's pockets. He wasn't sure why he still wore the midnight attire given to him by Volkmar. Perhaps he felt he should play the part until Edonia was far from view. Who was he kidding? Like he could escape the gaze of the new emperor. His fingers fumbled at something in his pocket. A letter? Pulling his left hand free he found a crisp white envelope sealed with a sigil of no house he knew. Pressed into the clay was the seven-pointed star of Edonia's old legends. Carefully, as if it could spring a trap, he broke the seal and opened the letter.

My Dearest Kin,

It has been many years since we last saw one another. Perhaps it is my own doing. The gruesome death of my cousin and your wife has left me unable to face you all these years. Now it seems fate will use that horrid night to bring us together once more. I have stumbled upon the truth of their deaths. Their murders were an inconvenient atrocity to the empire. While our kin desired the truth there were others less interested in its discovery. Despite all the deception I have found it, Arthur, several years ago. I kept it from you in a vain hope to spare you. Now I fear, I must do what I swore I never would. I must use it to bring you to our aid.

Arthur stopped reading for a moment. "You cannot go there, Arthur, it will never end. The nightmares will never stop."

He moved to the edge of the ship ready to toss the letter into the river. Years ago, when all the answers he sought ran dry, he had promised himself to let the truth go. Chasing every dead end and false lead would have driven him mad. The oath he had made was meant to guard him. But after all these years... Pausing, with letter dangling over the murky waters, he drew in a breath. He had to know. Who was he kidding? His mind was practically fractured already. Nightmares haunted his every sleep and the day? It was no different. Familiar heartache crawled beneath his skin. Bringing his shaking hand back from the brink he continued reading.

You see, the hour has come when all Edonia must unite against this traitor, Volkmar. The man who murdered your family. I hired investigators of my own to find out what happened to our beloved Gabriella. They were able to track down the place in which Volkmar hired his assassins. They found a ledger in a sell-swords den showing it was indeed Volkmar who hired them for the job. At first his identity had been hidden in a coded name, but my investigators can be persuasive. After they convinced the sell-swords to talk, we were gifted with a bounty of information. It was you that they intended to kill. Volkmar has always been an insecure man. He feared your growing popularity after the war would see you named next Emperor of Edonia. Your rank and favor with Septimus had become an obstacle to his ambition. Even with his marriage to Beatrice he was never convinced the throne would be his until you were removed. He has manipulated us all to acquire the ultimate seat of power.

I am sorry to do this to you, Arthur. It has taken years for my heart to mend at their loss, and I can only imagine what you must endure each day, but I need you. Edonia needs you. A secret call to the rulers of our land is being sent out. A council here in Venhorn is being held in two months' time from the date of winter's start. I ask not only for the future of Edonia but for the honor of your late wife and daughter, stand with us against this wretched creature and seek the revenge you so duly deserve.

Your Kin,
Gwen

Arthur lowered the parchment, hands shaking. An old rage flooding his veins. A rage he'd not felt in many years.

"Bring me to Oswald's ship, now," he said in a low growl to William. William peered up from his ledger, an expression of concern on his face.

"My duke?"

Arthur shoved the letter into William's chest. "Give the order."

William's eyes hurriedly scanned the note. Upon completion, Arthur could see in his friend's eyes a recognition of what this meant.

"Yes, sir."

The deck creaked beneath them with the churning of the current below. Oswald's face was weary as he put the letter down. Lines of age wrinkled further as he contemplated his wife's note.

"I knew none of this," Oswald said defiantly. "Those shantz women of mine have too much fervor."

"You're telling me you had nothing to do with this note inviting me to Venhorn?" Arthur asked in disbelief.

"It is the truth," Oswald said now beginning to pace. "How many others must think me a traitor to the empire because of these blasted women? No wonder Volkmar interrogated me so much about that wretched blacksmith." The thegn mused quietly to himself.

"Shantz on your reputation right now, Oswald! Did you know about Volkmar and my family all these years and you said nothing?"

Oswald's eyes grew sorrowful. "It was a horrible secret we kept, but it was for the good of the empire. Civil war would have broken out in the land had you known."

"A just war, you mean? And now that viper sits atop the throne thanks to a civil war. Is that good for the empire, Oswald?"

A blush of shame crept onto the thegn's cheeks as he shook his head wearily. "Why must I in my old age face these things?"

"You sowed the seeds of this fruit long ago when you chose deception instead of truth. You're only reaping what you've sown."

The thegn raised his eyes with a sudden fiery resistance. "My hands may not be clean but do not speak as if we all haven't looked away from the truth for some time. We've allowed decades of deception in our land and have done nothing. Edonia lost her purpose long ago."

Oswald shrank, defeated into a nearby chair.

Grinding his teeth, Arthur stepped forward daring to push the man a little further. "So, what? You give up? Time to wither in your old age and leave a corrupt and broken world for your children to clean up instead of you?"

"What can I…" Oswald began before Arthur cut him off.

"Something! Anything but continue lying to yourself that this isn't our responsibility. Gwen may have put you in this position but maybe you needed that push."

Oswald let out another weary sigh. "Perhaps you're right… Return to Fenikia to recoup, then come to Venhorn at the proper time."

"So you will rebel?" Arthur asked.

Oswald's eyes grew sharp. "I have not promised anything. Only that I will see what this cursed beckoning of my wife produces."

It's a start, Arthur thought, temper simmering.

"See you in two months' time," Arthur said turning to leave.

"Safe travels," Oswald muttered under his breath. The weariness slowly returning as he slouched into his seat. Arthur took several steps toward the door when Oswald's voice called out.

"And Arthur, remember, no promises."

"Like I expected anything less," Arthur muttered. Rising to the deck of Oswald's flagship Arthur was greeted by the waiting Sir William.

"How'd that go, sir?"

"We'll see."

William eyed him quizzically but pressed no further.

"Let the men know we can continue our journey," Arthur ordered.

William bowed and barked an order to their ship. The command echoed down the armada and soon a fleet of sails were loosed. It wasn't a few hours later that the stone walls of Fenikia came into view. Banners of white stamped with the proud crimson phoenix fluttered in the wind to greet them from Fenikia's ramparts. Fenikia's ships followed the city's wall north until the first gated port could be seen. With the sound of clanking chains the metal gates lifted sending a spray of water as they went. Men shouted down welcomes from the defenses above, and the sailors gave their own reply. Soon after, Arthur's ship was steered into the narrow passageway. Women and children enveloped the docks, waving banners and tossing flowers onto the decks of the boat. Each of their eyes searched in hope of finding their beloved returned home.

How many would be devastated this day? Arthur wondered. Passing through the narrow channel the port opened into a wide docking space. The whole system had been created to give Fenikia the most secure port in all Edonia. Large enough to house a fleet, it sat in the shape of an octagon within the city's defensive walls. All manner of makeshift stalls had been set up around the docking platforms. Housed within those stalls lay a variety of foods that tantalizingly called to Arthur. How long had it been since he tasted the freshness of a Fenikian meal? He could see in the eyes of his men the same desire stirring their appetite. Above it all was a powder blue sky dotted with puffy clouds.

I am happy for them, he thought drinking in the familiar scene of home. *It's been too long for all of us.*

A slight pang of guilt struck him. How soon would it be before he asked them to offer their lives in service to him again? How many more widows would he make? He shoved the feelings down as he placed a foot onto dry land. William followed close behind barking orders to the other vessels now jockeying for a spot to dock.

"Can you handle this?" Arthur said, turning to his old friend and mentor.

"You act as if I haven't done this for you your whole life," William said chuckling.

"Thank you," Arthur gave a mocking bow.

"Get whatever you need settled within yourself, sir. We will need you in the days to come."

Arthur started to speak and found he didn't know what to say to the man. Locking eyes, he knew words weren't needed. William had walked beside him at every step in Arthur's precarious life. A friend like that didn't need words to know what truly stirred beneath. With another nod Arthur turned toward the road that led to Fenikia's royal dwellings, the road home. He couldn't remember the last time he had walked the streets of Fenikia alone. Relishing the opportunity, he took his time navigating the busy streets. Each domed home he passed was painted in a variety of color. It left the streets with a vibrancy not found anywhere else on the continent of Edonia. The kaleidoscope colors clashed with the uniform patterns of Edonia, or the gothic spires of Varnas. Yet, they had their own form of purposeful design.

As he navigated his way up the winding path home he couldn't help but feel as though so much had changed in the months away. Who was he kidding, though? His life had been a constant journey from one location to the next often in an attempt not to return to Fenikia. Ever since that night, he'd taken every opportunity he could to throw himself into the cause of the empire.

"No more," he said to himself.

The smooth cobbled streets were bustling with the daily life of the city's civilians. It was strange to him how little the affairs of the empire seemed to weigh on his people. Every person that greeted one another smiled here, unlike the cold expressions he'd witnessed in the capitol. Fenikia had been the first to come under Edonia's authority in a time nearly as ancient as the empire itself. Yet, at its heart his home felt oddly separated from its master in the south. In Edonia the concerns of the world could be heard on every street. Fenikia was different. It was as if the city of Edonia strained out the concerns of the Empire and sent the rest upriver.

A retinue of guards greeted him as he approached the palace gate. The wall surrounding his home wasn't made of cold, unyielding stone. Instead, intricately woven iron guarded the place. Each spike was topped with a golden phoenix of exquisite design. It had been Gabriella's idea. She thought it prudent that the people could see into the palace grounds. The idea being that the people could in some way share in the life of their ruler. Cold, impenetrable stone left one cut off from those they served, or so she had said. He wasn't sure about all that, but her smile when the project had been finished was worth the effort.

Strangely enough the people responded well to the whole ordeal. A formal day was even made where citizens would bring flowers to weave around the iron bars. It made a beautiful display. One that his daughter Caiah especially loved. It felt strange to speak her name in his mind. How long had it been now? He knew opening up to the memories even a little might cause a flood of pain to wash over him. But he didn't care, not anymore.

Two guards escorted him across the palace lawn and up its winding path. Reaching the palace doors he was met by two more guards standing at attention. Both took doorknobs in hand at his approach. The iron hinges creaked as daylight flooded into the palace entryway. Inside a servant bowed offering his services as Arthur entered.

"There is no need. I wish for some time to reflect alone," Arthur said dismissing the man with a wave of the hand. The servant bowed, retreating into a nearby room. Arthur inhaled, drinking in the room. Three doors lined its sides. Each leading to a different area of the palace. At the end of the room a white marble stairway awaited his ascent. It housed seven pillars of crimson that propped up a white railing. The banners of his house lined the walls above. Each of them decorated with a white field and a crimson phoenix bursting into the air.

Following the stairs upward Arthur turned to the hall that led to his private chambers. Fenikia's palace paled in comparison to Edonia's, but he didn't mind. What need did he have for all that space? Passing several other rooms, he entered his own. Time had left it untouched. Inside was a room decorated with fine velvet furnishings. White marbled walls streaked with black sparkled in the sunlight. The thin curtains around his bed fluttered in the breeze that entered from a pair of open balcony doors. He couldn't recall the last time he'd stepped into this room. Had it really been since their deaths? A tiny smirk of amusement crossed his lips thinking of the gossip that would soon pass through the palace halls. After taking several steps into the room he knelt near a darkened spot on the velvet floor. Pressing his hand to the spot he began to brush it softly. Inhaling, he allowed his mind to go back to that night.

"Shantz, Alistair, of all nights you had to get into a drunken stupor." Arthur cursed under his breath tugging at his hood. Torrential rain had soaked his cloak leaving him drenched to the bone. It had taken a few hours, but he'd finally gotten the intoxicated soldier safely home. The rain wasn't the real reason his mood had soured. It was the hushed voices and questioning looks he received dragging Alistair home. It happened every time he'd gone out to help one of his old comrades. How could he expect regular civilians to understand? These were his men, his brothers. What they'd been made to do... the thought had sent a shiver up his already freezing spine. Regardless of how it tarnished his image, he felt a sense of duty to those who had fought beside him.

A flickering light from his room's balcony caught his eye as he trudged forward in the midnight rain. It was later than Gabriella usually stayed up to wait for him. Perhaps this evening wouldn't be a total loss after all. A sudden eagerness to see what Gabriella had planned propelled him. The palace door squeaked open as he approached. A sleepy servant stepped forward letting out a yawn.

"Evening, Master," the servant said fighting back another yawn.

"Evening," Arthur said eager to move on from the formality. Sleepily the servant stepped aside allowing him to pass. All was still within the confines of the entryway. Nothing but a small lantern in the servant's hand illuminated the vast room.

"Would you like an escort, master?"

"I can take myself. Get some sleep. You clearly desire some," Arthur said in jest.

"Thank you, master," the servant said with the largest yawn yet.

Arthur took the lantern in hand, stifling a yawn of his own. "Don't let Gabriella see that," Arthur chuckled to himself. Ascending the stairs, he couldn't help but feel an eeriness at the dancing light of the lantern across the marbled walls. It had been a year, but still the palace felt too quiet now that his father had passed. The man had filled its halls with laughter for so many decades. A laughter that would resound in these halls no more. The rain picked up outside, sending an amplified pounding overhead. Slowly Arthur crept toward his room careful not to awaken the slumbering Caiah. As he passed her room something caused him to pause. Her door was cracked open, the thunderstorm likely causing her to flee to their room.

"Come on Cai, I was hoping…"

A muffled cry broke him from the thought. "Was that Gabriella?" His throat tightened.

He felt the rush of adrenaline flood his veins. Reaching for a dagger at his waist, Arthur dashed toward his bedroom door. Thunder crashed overhead resonating with the growing apprehension he felt. He threw open the door with a bang, all rational thought leaving him. He lifted the lantern to illuminate the darkened room. His eyes fell to the balcony doors opened to the storm. Water soaked the velveted floor leaching out as a darkened stain.

"Gabriella?" he said voice shaking.

"Arthur?" came a hoarse voice in the dark. He turned his lantern toward the sound. What he saw made his heart shatter. Curled on the floor was his wife, a circle of blood expanding across her abdomen. Beside her… it couldn't be… He choked on a sob and soon vomit burned in his throat.

"Gabriella!!" he shouted dropping to his knees beside her. The lantern in his hand nearly tilted over as it crashed to the floor.

She raised a limp hand to his cheek. Pursing her lips, she fought to speak but the words didn't come. Arthur watched as the light in her eyes faded. Heartbroken he dared to see the crumpled form huddled beneath his wife. Letting out an uncontainable roar he took Caiah in his arms. Blonde strands stained with blood splayed on his lap. A mass of servants soon entered the room behind him responding to his cry. Each of them stood with horrified expression.

"Get out!" Arthur screamed to the gawking cluster behind him. In silent horror they slipped from the room unsure of what to say. Time passed without meaning, and it was only the sound of dying rain and pale morning light that finally broke him from his stupor. Gently he placed the small frame of Caiah on the floor.

"Master?" asked a servant finally braving to enter the room again.

"Call Sir William and search the whole city for who did this," Arthur said through gritted teeth.

The man nodded in eager obedience before fleeing from the room. Arthur took one last look at his loves now illuminated by the early morning sun. Their faces were hauntingly pale in the dull morning light.

"I will make them suffer whoever they are," he vowed rising to his feet.

He kept that promise. Months of tracking rumors and ghosts had brought Gabriella and Caiah's murders to justice. When it was all said and done the solace Arthur sought evaded him. Watching their murderers tortured and slain like the animals they were didn't bring the satisfaction he so desperately needed. He never found who employed the sell-swords or why they had done what they had. The fading sound of their dying screams took with them any hope of that truth. After all his efforts, he'd come up short. He didn't know how to deal with that reality, so he buried it deep. So deep, in fact, that he'd gone to any means to forget it. All those years he'd avoided confronting that night. Instead, he'd fixed his attention on doing all he could to busy himself from the truth. The truth that he couldn't save them. The reality that they were gone and never coming back.

Kneeling by that stained floor, he let the tears flow. He'd avoided this moment for so long he hadn't thought it possible to find the strength to confront it. Yet by returning to this room, returning

271

to face what he feared the most, he found something. Closure. The solace he sought since their deaths wasn't in avoiding his pain, it wasn't found by inflicting it on their murderers, it was found in confronting it. He wouldn't find them here again. They were gone and, if possible, he had to learn to live in that reality. He knew that now and, somehow, it gave him a hint of peace.

He rose to his feet and opened his eyes. A fresh breeze flowed through the open balcony brushing his face. Its touch like the gentle caress Gabriella had given him as he held her in his arms. In his mind's eye he could picture her. Not as the bloodied tangle of blonde hair and pain, but of her smiling. A ray of sun catching golden locks as she laughed near the ocean with Caiah at her side. It was one of their favorite memories together. The vision vanished as soon as it had appeared. He basked in that forgotten memory. Letting it wash over him, renewing his mind. Over the years he'd worked to push out any thought of them. It had only left him with the memories he dreaded the most, but now he had a past worth remembering again. Letting out a breath he moved to the balcony.

The sun's light was fading on the day, casting the sky in an orange and red hue. Pain still throbbed in his chest at his loss, but somehow it had been transformed. He knew what he must do. A cancer had invaded Edonia. A man who had robbed him and a thousand others of so much. It was time to cut the head off the snake. Not to satiate his pain. He knew the wound he carried would stay with him forever. No, Volkmar must die because this time Arthur had the power to stop him. No matter what it would cost.

21

JULIET

IMPATIENCE GRIPPED HER as she paced in the glow of the hearth's dying light. She really should be working to satisfy its hunger, but she couldn't shake the sense of anticipation knotting in her stomach. Any time now John and Arthur would be arriving to discuss Edonia's future. How could she relax with that in mind?

"You're stressing me out," came the voice of Mateus. He sat reclined by the fire, his chestnut eyes reflecting its dying embers.

Juliet turned to him fighting her annoyance. "It was supposed to be tonight. What if they abandoned us at the last second? What if they were spotted by Volkmar's spies? What if they sold us out!?" She hadn't thought of that prospect until now. She felt her heart sink further into despair.

"Is that what goes on in your mind? Remind me not to ask again," Mateus said with a sigh.

Juliet frowned at him. "How can you be so relaxed when so much rides on this meeting?"

Mateus sat up. His face morphed into contemplation. "Have you considered that maybe it's possible for the outcome you desire to actually come true? I mean look at me. I've even convinced your father not to keep me in chains. Maybe I've lived the life of a slave for so long, but I figure what's the worst that could happen to me now?"

"You clearly don't know Volkmar then," Juliet said poking at the fire with a stick.

"I know the type. Thinks their chamber pots don't smell. Lives with magnificent splendor and majesty. Occasionally kills those he doesn't agree with in a brutal fashion. Am I close?"

Juliet rolled her eyes as she moved to add a few more chunks of wood to the fire. The darkening room fell silent for a time. The hearth's flames grew sending shadows dancing across the hall. She let their mesmerizing trance distract her for a few moments as she continued to wait. It was past midnight, and the late hours of the night began to wear on her. Slowly her eyelids closed as she could feel herself nodding off to sleep. Glancing over at Mateus she could see he already had given himself to its embrace.

"Maybe just a minute," she whispered to herself.

A quiet creaking of a door jolted her to awareness. Across the elongated hall the main door had cracked open. Her father stepped into the room followed by several others. As they drew near her heart picked up its pace. Joined with Oswald was John and the woman named Maggie who'd been with him in Farmshire. Behind them was Duke Arthur himself accompanied by a grizzled man with greying hair. Likely, the Sir William that had served Fenikia's house for decades. Following closely behind was a cluster of other men. Some dressed in the wood folk garb and others in the soaring eagle of Kaladin.

"Arthur did it," she said smiling to herself. The forces of Kaladin had come after all. She turned to her father whose face was now illuminated by the hearth's flames. It was stern. An unaccustomed look that felt strange to Juliet. Another door opened from a side room revealing her mother Gwen in a silky white dress.

An out of place regality to such a secretive meeting, Juliet thought.

She watched her father turn his attention to his wife at her approach. Juliet could see in his eyes the flush of excitement at Gwen's beauty. Oswald quickly buried it working hard to keep a stern tone to his voice.

"Is this everyone you are expecting?" he asked.

Gwen's eyes scanned each face that now stood around the hearth. "It is."

She seemed unfazed by Oswald's mood as she bowed to the

duke. Arthur was a handsome man, perhaps a decade or two Juliet's senior. His squared jaw and chiseled features accentuated his regal station. The jet-black hair and stubble were a common trait of men south of the Edon River. Juliet watched as the duke returned the formal bow to Juliet's father and mother. He stopped however when it came to John. The newly appointed baron seemed to care little about the lack of respect. Although the blonde woman who'd accompanied him looked annoyed by the intentional omission. It was this motley crew that was supposed to unite and defeat Volkmar?

"As you all can imagine this conversation cannot leave this room," Gwen said meeting each of their eyes. All in attendance nodded their agreement.

"Very good. Then I suggest we proceed as quickly as possible. Morning comes soon and with it the prying eyes of our dear emperor."

"What exactly is it you are proposing? Now that you have all of us here?" John asked.

"An alliance," Juliet blurted with impatience at the political dance taking place. Her eyes caught her mother's, who gave a chastising glance.

"As my daughter has so eagerly put it, we are hoping we can come to an agreement about our current situation," Gwen said with a more elegant flair.

"Have you changed your mind on the matter, Oswald?" Duke Arthur asked. "You haven't said a word thus far."

The duke's eyes weighed Juliet's father as he waited for a response. Oswald drew in a resigned breath, "It seems it doesn't matter what I want. For my council is ignored and my authority superseded."

"Oswald, do not act as if you were powerless in this manner," Gwen said shaking her head in frustration.

"Am I not? Here I am the ruler of this kingdom and yet my wife and daughter seem to think they can do whatever they please. Even so far as house traitors to the empire." He stopped, pointing at Mateus who'd stepped back into the shadows at the start of the meeting. "If that were not enough you've gone around all Edonia practically dooming our house on a gamble that we can stand against the might of the emperor."

"This emperor's forces are greatly weakened from the war with Hunan," Arthur said.

"And so are yours," John said. "I agree with Thegn Oswald's concern. Fenikia and Kaladin's armies are a shell of themselves. The bulk of our alliance's forces would be Venhorn and my own. Do you expect us to fight and die for your personal revenge, duke?"

"Personal revenge? This man killed the emperor!" Arthur growled.

"One many of us weren't fond of in the first place," John shot back. "Listen I am here because what Volkmar did to his family is detestable, even for you highborns. But I need assurances that my men are going to make it out of this thing alive. I already have an agreement with Octavian..."

"You what?!" Thegn Oswald interrupted. "You brought this snake into my hall? Who's to say he won't go and report all of us tonight!" Oswald reached for the axe that hung loosely at his hip.

A look of panic flashed across Juliet's face as she turned to her mother. Gwen remained calm, but Juliet could see a small storm of panic stir beneath.

"I believe John was trying to say that the new emperor has already acknowledged his authority in Bjønen, and he would like the same assurances from us," Gwen said placing a calming hand on Oswald's shoulder.

Oswald's face still remained red, but the bluster receded. "Go on then."

John began to speak, but Duke Arthur intervened, "This subject brings up another matter of concern. The matter of authority once Volkmar is removed."

John rolled his eyes. "Of course, the duke is concerned with who gets to be in charge."

Arthur shot him a glare. "How can we give assurances if we don't know who has the authority to give them?"

"I know! Each of us goes on our way and we rule ourselves?" John said with a shrug of his shoulders.

"As if it was that easy," Arthur said rolling his eyes.

"And why shouldn't it be?" John asked throwing his arms out wide. "You want my men to risk their lives so you can rule over us rather than Volkmar? Fight your own bloody battles!"

John turned to leave, exasperated, but was blocked by Sir William who moved into his path.

"Who do you think you are?" John said trying to shove the man aside.

"You haven't heard his offer," William said motioning with his eyes to Arthur.

"I've heard enough of it," John scowled.

"I will make you a duke."

The room grew silent. Juliet watched intently as all eyes fell on the woodsman.

"A fancier title. That's what you offer? Why should I…"

Arthur cut him off. "With all the benefits of such a title. No tax on your lands, exclusive rights to the regions of Bjønen's and Varnas' wealth. Seeing as Volkmar will no longer need it, and the opportunity to be chosen as emperor if I were to pass away before having a male heir. That is my offer."

John stood taken aback by such a lavish proposal. Juliet could see a hunger stir beneath his eyes. Something different gripped Maggie who stood beside him, however. A look of sorrow perhaps?

"In that case, I may be interested," said John with a smile.

"It's madness to offer a common man such a gift," Oswald said dumbfounded. "You would put him before me? Do you think I would march with you under such terms?"

Arthur turned his attention to Oswald. "While I had hoped you would see the common good of this proposal, I did come prepared with another."

"Go on," huffed Oswald crossing his arms. Juliet observed how her father's face looked frail in the flickering light of the hearth. Had he always looked so aged?

"An arranged marriage between Juliet and me."

Juliet felt her body go numb at the words. For a moment the

room started to spin before she found a nearby bench to right herself. Strangely her face fell to Mateus who'd been witnessing the conversation in silence from the shadows. He stood expressionless.

Is he not disappointed? She wondered.

Juliet focused again as the duke continued. "It would place your family directly within the new royal line. Your grandchildren heirs to the throne for generations to come."

Oswald pondered the offer with serious thought. Stepping forward Gwen turned her attention to Juliet. "It should be her decision. She was the one who initiated all this. Let her decide."

The weight of the room's stares now fell on Juliet. Each eye eagerly awaiting what she had to say. How had this suddenly all depended on her? Licking her lips, she fought back the nausea that began to swell.

"I...I..."

"Juls, that is a handsome offer," Oswald coaxed.

"Leave the poor girl alone, Oswald. When did greed have a hold of you so?" Gwen reprimanded.

"All I wish is that our daughter would have what's best for her."

It was all too much. She had wanted to stop Volkmar. She believed all the things Mateus had said about the systems of this empire and now she'd be empress of it? Wasn't that against everything she'd come to believe? Yet, maybe she could bring change...What was she saying?! She'd been thinking about the matter in terms of what it would mean for the empire but had completely overlooked the fact of marriage! Her eyes, unsteady, turned to face the awaiting Arthur.

"You should do it," Mateus said stepping from the shadows.

"Why would she listen to you?" Oswald muttered.

Mateus ignored the remark stepping nearer the fire. "The only way things change is if we are willing to change it ourselves. Now you have that chance, Juliet."

She bit her lip meeting each of their eyes. Eagerness in her father's, pity in her mother's, Arthur's carried a patient yet quizzical look. She brushed past the others meeting Mateus' stare. Something different resided in his. It was a mixture of sorrow, hope, and perhaps acceptance of his fate. It couldn't be love, could it?

"I accept your offer, Duke Arthur," she said, voice quivering.

Arthur's face creased into a weak smile. "Very well then. We can settle the matter when all this is finished."

"I would have it settled tonight," Oswald said gaze unflinching.

"Oswald!" cried Gwen. "Juliet has already accepted."

Oswald raised a hand to silence her. "There will be plenty of bloody battle in the coming days. Duke Arthur may be killed in the process. I want to have assurances that our family will be entitled to what is due to an empress."

Gwen's face remanded vehement but she didn't argue further.

"Tonight?" Juliet found herself blushing at the prospect.

"It's a bit informal for such a marriage, Oswald. I can have things drawn up to put in place..."

"Shy of bedding the lass?" John spouted.

"Watch your tongue," growled Sir William behind him.

Juliet found her gaze drifting to Mateus once more. The man stood shaking his head as the lords of the land bickered over the minutia of Juliet's marriage. A symbol of everything he'd come to hate.

"Enough!" Juliet shouted breaking up their arguments. Perhaps a little too loud for a secret meeting.

"I will seal the marriage with the duke. Can we just focus on how to stop Volkmar?"

Her reply seemed to bring shame on each of them as they stood silently.

"There is one more matter that needs attending," said the representative from Kaladin, making his voice known for the first time. He bore silver plated armor covered by an unmarked surcoat. He was a youthful man with long brunette hair that fell just above his shoulders. Tiny stubble dotted his strong jaw. His green eyes weighted each of the rulers around him.

"I believe it would have been Thegn Lucian's will to abstain from battle. I wish to honor my lord's command. As active captain of his army, I will not force my men into a conflict they don't wish to fight."

"Why did you come then?" asked John impatiently.

Duke Arthur stepped forward to speak on behalf of Kaladin's representative. "Captain Bastian joined me tonight on this condition. He will not force his men to fight, but if we could come to an agreement, he wouldn't prevent them either."

"What's to stop those who wish to retreat from informing on us?" John accused.

"My men are of the highest honor!" Bastian protested.

"A lot of good honor does," John spat.

Arthur raised a hand to stop Bastian from sending his fist into John's face. "Beyond honor, Bastian and I have discussed another group we wish formed from our alliance."

"That is?" Gwen asked.

"One to flee Edonia if things go poorly," Arthur said, tone deadly serious.

Each looked down as if the prospect was a dirty word. Arthur cleared his throat before continuing. "I believe it prudent that we all contribute some of our people to this company. If we fail, I fear what sort of retaliation Volkmar would send our way."

"It seems a wise proposal," Oswald said, nodding.

"How would we decide who flees and who fights?" asked Gwen.

"I leave that up to you," Arthur said. "However, I will only fulfill my oaths if you yourselves join in this fight."

Arthur's gaze fell to John. "Don't worry about me, Duke," John hissed.

"It is settled then?" Gwen asked. All nodded in agreement.

"Tomorrow we can draw up battle plans. I doubt our decision here will stay hidden for long from the prying eyes of Edonia," said Arthur.

"It means we must act swiftly," agreed Oswald.

John stretched his arms high into the air with a yawn. "First can we catch a wink of sleep? I'm no good with tactics otherwise."

Arthur shared an annoyed glance with William. "We will let John catch some beauty sleep for a few hours then convene in private for our plans?"

"I'll have my servants send word closer to the time," said Gwen.

With that the circle broke as others began to join in the chorus of yawns. Each of them drifted off to get the little sleep needed for the day's planning. Oswald remained, clearing his throat as his gaze fixed on Arthur.

"Ahh, yes... Well, where should we?" The duke fumbled over the words showing the first signs that the man could be shaken.

"Juliet, you can show him to your quarters?" Oswald asked.

She nodded awkwardly unsure of how to reply to the strangeness of her father's behavior and the even more dreadful prospect of what was to come.

"Can you take him, Father? I would like a moment."

Oswald's face softened. "Sure thing, Juls." His already aged face seemed to grow wearier by the second. The duke and thegn stepped into an adjacent hall. Arthur paused taking a glance back at her standing by the fading fire.

"Why did you tell me to do this?" Juliet asked to the darkness.

Mateus stepped from the shadows, a look of reservation on his face. "I helped you make the best decision of your life. That's why. If you really believe what I've told you, you'd see that this is the opportunity for you to change this corrupt monster we call an empire. If it can be changed."

"That's not the real reason, Mateus," she said in a whisper.

His eyes grew misty, all the bravado evaporating from them for the briefest of moments. "You live in a dream world, Juliet. I just helped you wake up."

She watched as he turned away leaving her alone in the vast chamber. Perhaps it was time for her to wake up. She wrapped the cloak given by her father tightly around her. Unaware if it was the winter's chill or the coldness of the world that had a hold of her. Knowing the impatience of her father this night, she turned to join him and Arthur. Despondent, she passed through the familiar halls that had taken on a strange foreboding. She caught up with the waiting duke and thegn who stood sentinel by her bedroom door. Oswald's face was a mask of stone beside the ever increasingly awkward duke. Oswald and Arthur exchanged words she couldn't hear, and the duke disappeared into her room shortly after. Wordlessly, Juliet passed her father and reached to open her door. Just as her hand touched the frame Oswald stopped her from entering.

"I'm sorry to do this, Juls. Know that I ask this from a place of love. The world forces us to do things we'd rather not to protect those we care for."

She stopped catching his eyes. "You can lie to me if you want, father, but don't lie to yourself. When it comes down to it, you're like all the other rulers of this horrid empire. You flatter with words and gifts, but at the end of the day all you seek is legacy and power. Not for those you love, no, we are just the means by which you can get them for yourself."

Breaking her arm free from his grip she opened the door. She didn't look back. She had no desire to see the face of the coward her father had become or, more tragic, had always been. Perhaps her assessment was too harsh, but on this evening she felt more alone than ever. Closing the door behind her, she took in the candlelit room. The duke stood, arms clasped behind his back, staring out a window opposite her. He turned upon hearing her enter. His expression broke into a weak smile. His fumbling posture revealed that the moment was as awkward for him as it was for her.

"I don't know if I will ever love you," she said, bluntly.

The Duke nodded as if mulling over each syllable. "Understandable."

"Why did you propose this?" she asked. "It doesn't look as if you have much interest in me."

Arthur's face took on a bemused expression. "Unfortunately, the marriages of the royal court don't often take that factor into consideration."

With a sigh he plopped onto her mattress. "Volkmar must be stopped. I see no other way than the course before us. I will admit this was not my first choice or my second..."

His eyes lifted from the floor and met hers for the briefest of moments before returning. "If it is any consolation, you do possess beauty and the fact that you helped orchestrate all this shows you have a strong mind as well."

"Thank you?" Juliet said unsure of what he meant by his words.

"I'm no good at these things. Gabre... well, never mind."

"Your first wife?" Juliet asked.

"Yes..." Arthur raised his head meeting her gaze. A brief flare of amusement replaced his gloomy demeanor.

"Here I am, supposed to be seducing you and instead I begin to talk about my deceased wife." A faint chuckle left his lips as he said the words.

Surprisingly she found herself laughing as well. It grew and grew until she could barely contain it. She supposed it must have been all the sorrow and anger built up inside her finally being let loose. Like an immense dam finally breaking by how powerless the world made her feel. Tears rolled down her cheeks as she fought to control herself.

"Are you all right?" Arthur asked rising to his feet, face painted with concern.

She waved him back down wiping a tear from her eyes. "I'm fine."

Finding a space beside him she flopped onto the bed. "The world can be so cruel can't it?"

"Yes... yes it can," Arthur replied, his voice trailing in thought.

"Do you promise that you won't be?" she asked.

His sorrowful eyes met her own. "I think I can do that."

"Good." She pulled his face into her own embracing him with a kiss. So much evil ruled their world. Despite it all maybe she could make her own light within it. All that she had to endure, all that she would face, wouldn't stop her from fighting until the last breath to make it mean something.

22

JOHN OF THE WOOD

THE FRESH SMELL OF spring was in the air as John pulled Midnight's saddle straps tight. He hated the awkwardness that hung between Maggie and himself. Their on again, off again, relationship had taken a downward spiral after that fated night in Venhorn. Glancing over his shoulder he could see she busied herself by packing a few belongings inside a saddlebag. He averted his gaze as she turned in his direction. Instead, he fixed on the sight of several dozen banners flapping in the breeze. Each of them bore the same symbol, a golden seven-pointed star on a white field. The Morning Star, the sigil of their rebellion. John wasn't sure why their secret council listened to that strange slave, Mateus, about using it as their distinguishing mark.

I suppose we all like to think there is a golden age coming, he thought.

His motives were less benevolent. The offer of becoming a duke and its perks had been the thing he'd always dreamed of. How could he pass such an opportunity up? If he played his cards right, who knew? Perhaps someday people would call him emperor. That dream would need to be put aside for the moment. For now, his focus was to survive the coming war. Months of planning had led them to this moment where not only the fates of men but of an empire hung in the balance. Somehow, he'd found himself at the center of it all. He only hoped their strategy was half as good as they anticipated.

"Will you really not say anything to me before you go?" Maggie said. He could feel the scowl in her words. Had he mentioned how much he hated this? John turned awkwardly to face her. Maggie was as always beautiful, but he especially admired it when she was in battle form. Blonde braids were pulled back into a tightly woven bun. Her curved figure accentuated by form-fitting leather plate. It was enough to distract him from... Her soft featured face hardened as she noticed his stare.

"John, don't look at me like that. Not now."

What does this woman want from me? he wondered rolling his eyes.

"Was it not you who told me we should join this fight? That it was the right thing to do?" John asked, annoyed.

Maggie's caramel eyes sharped. "You and I both know that's not why you're going."

A gust of spring's wind whipped a loose strand of hair across her face. She wrestled with the rebellious strand until it once again submitted to being tucked away.

She was captivating. Perhaps he should go with her. His mind sharpened again. *No! You've worked your whole life for this moment and you'd throw it away now?*

The inner turmoil felt as though it was wrestling for his soul. What if this was why he'd felt so unsatisfied? What if destiny had been calling him to this moment? Two choices and two lives he wished could merge lay before him. As hard as he fought for both, he realized it never would work. Something told him it was here, surrounded by the frosted mountain peaks and beautiful spring valleys, that he'd have to make his choice for good.

"So that's it?" Maggie asked defeated. "You're going? And me, John? You'd have me left behind to receive the news of your body slain in some mass grave and for what? These highborn's ambitions?"

"You don't know that, Maggs. You talk as though we are bound to fail."

She looked away, not meeting his stare. "I'm leaving Edonia no matter what, John."

"What?!" he stammered. "Why?"

He watched as a stream of tears began to dot the ground beneath her. "I want something different with my life than waiting for a hope that I know will never come. I want a family tucked away in a cottage deep in the woods. Where the beauty of nature and my family is untouched by the corrupt powers of this world. Why can't you see what power does to you, to all of you?! It drives everyone to madness. You desire whatever you fancy and if you can't have it you turn to violence. Now that you have it, you want more. When will it end?"

"Maggie…"

"No, John. No more fancy words and empty promises. If you want a life with me, you know where to find me." With that she swung into the saddle and motioned for her steed, Snowfall, to leave. John watched in silence as Maggie faded from view within the bustling war camp.

"Shantz, woman," he cursed. Angrily he swung into his own saddle. He pulled the reins turning Midnight in the opposite direction toward the command tent. He passed through crowds of men making ready for the coming march. One that would take them south into the heart of Edonia. It was a solid plan by his reckoning. His men along with Thegn Oswald's would march south while Arthur and those of Kaladin would attack the city of Edonia from the east. They'd be able to surround the city and it would cut off any route of escape. Not that Volkmar would retreat by sea. All of them knew the man would rather die than give up the throne. John dismounted finding the command tent already being deconstructed for the long march. Oswald stood pouring over a map with his army's commander, Gudbrand, at his side.

"Yes, I know the path away from the mountains are quicker, but this time of year the roads may be flooded by the spring rains," Oswald said, driving a finger onto a section of the decorative display of Edonia.

"When should I give my men the order to move?" John asked.

Oswald glanced over his shoulder. "We can talk about this later," Oswald said dismissing Gudbrand.

"Within the hour." Oswald's tone made it clear he'd rather have been paired with the forces of Kaladin or Fenikia than John's merry band of fighters. The reality was their army needed speed if the plan was to succeed and the heavily armored troops of Kaladin and Fenikia were anything but.

"Where is that blonde woman of yours?" Oswald asked searching the camp.

"She's joining the others at Edonium Bay," John replied through clenched teeth.

"Hope she's not taking your men with her. Seems she's the one who's got their loyalty."

John bit his tongue knowing if he were to survive all this he needed this man. "Don't worry about my men."

Oswald gave him a wary look but left any further comments to himself. Even at a full march it would take time to get to Edonia. Perhaps Oswald wished their journey to be bearable as well.

"Once we get to the Ironhall, I suspect Volkmar will know of our plan." Oswald said, switching to talk of strategy.

"They may know already, depending on Arthur's army and how stealthy they were."

Oswald nodded his head. "All the more reason for us to hurry. Arthur and his men can't hold out long against Volkmar's forces. At least not in their current shape."

I'm well aware, thought John.

"Very well. I suppose I will check on my men," John said, taking a step toward the camp.

"Fine, just have them ready to march by the hour," Oswald grumbled.

John nodded, happy to be rid of the man. Taking one last look at the old thegn he could see the weight of the moment aging Oswald. It couldn't be easy departing from his wife, children and grandchild on the way. It became apparent to John, even if he was able to acquire both lives he craved it wouldn't ease his mind. Seeing Oswald, perhaps it would only complicate things further.

"No desire for that," John mumbled to himself. He weaved his way through the cluster of beige tents finding Huldwin rallying the men.

"How's it going?" John asked his captain as the rest of their troops broke off into their designated companies.

"Good, sir," Huldwin said wiping away a bead of sweat. "Couldn't ask for a better day or nicer view!"

Huldwin looked up at the towering peaks of the Edon Mountains. It was a breathtaking sight. Spring flowers dotted the surrounding plains in a kaleidoscope of color. John smirked, seeing the childish wonder on Huldwin's face.

"You're a good friend, Huldwin. I haven't always treated you as I should, but you deserve to know that," John said, placing a hand on the man's shoulder.

Huldwin gave him a sheepish smile. "Thank you, sir. I'm... I'm sorry about Maggie."

John followed his gaze northward. "Me too, but she's made her decision, and I've made mine."

John faced his friend. "Now, let's finish this together."

Huldwin nodded eagerly. "Yes, sir!"

There was something about long marches that stole all the momentum for a battle. John had grown accustomed to the quick hit and run tactics they'd implemented in the fight against Holger. This endless marching at a sluggish pace killed any anticipation for combat he might have had. Instead, he found his mind wandering to a soft bed and a warm hearth. Perhaps accompanied by a mug of ale and a fine woman at his side.

"Soon," he said to himself. The stench rising from thousands of soldiers marching made "soon" not nearly soon enough. Their journey had taken them straight south and soon they would reach the Ironhall. A fortress of historic magnitude. Tales told to him as a child spoke of its impenetrable defenses. He'd never seen the vaunted fortress but maybe he could steal a glance as they passed it by. Until then, more marching. The rhythmic patter of thousands of feet was the tune he wished to be rid of forever. Looking ahead he could see Oswald and his men slowing their pace.

"Come on, it's only been half a day's march. They want to stop already?" John complained.

"Something is off, sir," Huldwin said peering ahead. "Do you wish me to go and check it out."

"Fine," John said with a wave of the hand. "Just tell Oswald I'd like to get to Edonia before I'm too old to enjoy being a duke."

Huldwin nodded and spurred his horse forward. Another of John's men by the name Grimwald stopped beside him. He was a scraggly looking man. All beard and toothy grin. A good fighter though, and John would take as many of those as he could get.

"Problem, sir?" asked Grimwald.

"That's what Huldwin is going to find out," John replied.

A strange sound began to rise in the distance just ahead of Oswald's company.

John's eyes searched the horizon but the rearguard of Venhorn prevented him from any clear view. "That sounds like..."

Thundering hooves sounded as Huldwin rushed back to meet them. "Word comes from Oswald's men! It's an ambush!" he shouted.

"Shantz," John cursed. Turning to Grimwald he barked out orders to take formation. Huldwin now returned was ready to implement the command.

"Huldwin, send our quickest scouts south. I doubt Oswald has thought to do so, all things considered."

"Sir?"

John could feel that familiar irritation rising within him. "So, Arthur can know we've been ambushed."

Huldwin's eyes illuminated. "Yes, sir!"

Huldwin could be so dull, John thought, pinching the bridge of his nose.

"Grimwald, tell the men we need to flank whoever is hitting Oswald's lines. Archers first to soften them up."

Grimwald smiled his toothy grin. "Finally, some battle."

Yes, thought John. *Just sooner than we'd hoped.*

Open plains were not his men's specialty. If the enemy had heavy calvary… It didn't matter. Today or tomorrow they'd have to fight. It might as well be today. Drawing Bear Paw from its sheath, John let out a roar. The men behind picked up his cry as they rushed eastward to flank their foe. Rounding Oswald's battle lines John could see their enemy come into view. Two legions of men adorned in black and red surcoats clashed with the front of Oswald's forces.

John lifted his blade, calling his men to follow his lead. He directed them to take position against the enemy's right flank. With another shouted order the archers took their places. The first thrum of arrows released, and John watched as they cascaded into the enemy lines. Some fell to the swarm, but gleaming plate deflected much of the impact.

"Shantz," John cursed drinking in the battle. Holger's men had always been a poor lot. Few armies could afford to equip all their men with finely crafted plate. Not like Edonia at least. This was a different sort of enemy. Slow, yes, but built to withstand arrow fire.

Huldwin turned to him a look of fear pooling in his eyes. "What now, sir?"

"Keep firing!" John barked.

Another wave of arrows descended onto Edonia's forces. Still, no real impact. Coming into view from behind Edonia's swordsmen was a host of archers. Each of them was outfitted with matching chainmail and surcoat. A uniform unit unlike the mismatched one behind John. A sudden wave of darts was sent their way.

"Shields!" John cried.

The few who had them raised them overhead. The sickening thud of bolt in flesh hit like a storm. Screams rang out as men fell to the ground riddled with arrows. They couldn't take another impact like that.

"Forward!" John ordered. Not waiting to see who followed, he dashed ahead, Edonium Blade glistening in the sun. Midnight snorted a gleeful noise as if the beast had been patiently waiting for such a moment. The archers ahead grew large as they pulled bowstrings back for another round of fire. Just as the arrows were loosed, John crashed into their lines. Men flew into the air as Midnight thrust them aside. Bear Paw sang as it cut into flesh. Limb and weapon shattered as the smooth blade sliced through them with ease. The rush of combat overtook John leaving his mind unaware of anything but the thrill of battle. He had no clue whether he stood alone or had a host at his back. It didn't matter, he would not be stopped. Steering Midnight around for another sweep of the enemy he could see most of his men had followed. A trail of strewn bodies littered the field behind them. Too many bodies.

Soldiers roared and steel clashed in a mass of violence. Axe, spear, and sword met with flesh, tearing it asunder in a deadly dance. John pressed Midnight forward to join the fray. Edonia's archers threw down their arms begging for mercy as he approached. John sneered as Bear Paw sank deep into their flesh.

"Mercy for this lot?" he smirked. They would receive every bit of what they had given to so many others over the centuries. It wasn't long before the few remaining archers broke ranks in retreat. Arrows zipped toward their backs cutting down the stragglers. John raised his blade calling his men to reform the formation. That's when he saw doom approaching. At least a thousand heavy calvary revealed themselves on a distance hill. With the signal horn blown John watched as death charged in his direction. Fully armored warriors fixed their gaze on John and his motley crew.

"Spread ranks!" John and his other captains cried in unison. It was too late. Edonia's calvary washed over them like a primordial tidal wave. For a brief flash John watched as his men melted away. Then it was his turn to feel its impact. He was thrown from Midnight, his whole world turning to black. The cold ground greeted him with a pain-inducing thud. Legs of horses swarmed his vision washing all else from sight. Groping in the madness he found Bear Paw's hilt. With strained effort he lifted the blade before him. Its glowing metal shielded him from death and cut down any who dared approach. As the swarm of riders washed away, he slowly rose to his feet with a groan.

In their wake hundreds of corpses lay mutilated and trampled on the field of battle. Men groaned in agony from broken bones and pierced flesh. Dumbfounded, John surveyed his company of men. Barely any remained. A whimper caught his attention. Midnight lay thrashing a few yards away. The proud steed whinnied as it tried to rise to its feet before collapsing. Bone protruded from its leg causing the beast to cry out in agony. John tentatively knelt by the horse stroking its strong neck.

"It's alright, boy," John whispered. He felt the sting of tears in his eyes. Wiping a loose trickle away he loosed a dagger from his belt. Raising the sharpened steel with shaky hand he placed it against Midnight's neck. "Im sorry... I'm so sorry." The razor's edge cut the flesh with ease. John watched as Midnight's eyes grew wide. The beast thrashed wildly for a moment before growing still.

It wasn't supposed to be like this, John thought, looking at the death around him.

Ominous hooves stirred him from his mournful stupor. It was the sound of Edonia's calvary returning to finish the job. Rising to his feet he searched for any way of escape. That's when he heard the retreat horn blowing. John watched as Oswald's men fled in the direction of the Ironhall. All hope was lost in a blink. How had he been so foolish to believe this would have turned out any different? A sudden tug pulled at his shoulder. John swiveled, sword ready to strike before recognizing the bloodied face of Huldwin.

"John, Oswald's falling back to the fortress," Huldwin panted. The man's arm was soaked with blood. A wound likely requiring removal if they were to survive.

If we survive, thought John. "It's no use Huldwin. We won't reach the fortress in time. Not without a horse."

Huldwin cocked his head to a lone stallion a small distance away. Its Edonian master lay dead, leg caught in the reins. The horse paced violently trying to release the corpse. John cracked a wearisome smile.

"I always wanted to see the Ironhall."

23

OCTAVIAN

T HE EMPEROR'S PALACE was dimly lit as the sun set over the peaks of the distant Edon Mountains. It would happen again tonight. Drums beat in the distance from the palace's throne room. A ceremony of the darkest nature. Octavian had feared losing the knowledge of Edonia's greatest treasure. Little had he known a greater threat would rise from that day. Volkmar had taken to the emperor's secret knowledge like a drunk to a pint of ale. He'd spent weeks pouring over the ancient texts. All in pursuit of what? None were quite sure what it was their emperor was so eager to find. They only experienced what such knowledge had driven him to.

The distant drums ceased leaving an eerie silence in their wake. The screams would soon follow. Men whose hearts would be cut from their chests and offered up to… something. Octavian shuttered. Whatever it was that Volkmar wished to accomplish, Octavian had no desire to take part. His guilt felt overwhelming these days. Like an infection that he'd let fester and was now septic. Was he not responsible for unleashing this monster on them all? Had he not been the one to pave the way to the throne for Volkmar?

His frail attempts to remind himself of why felt pathetic. Could he truly justify revenge in place of this? Cries of agony rang out just as the sun slipped from view. Darkness fell over the great city of Edonia, and he had helped make it so. Closing his eyes, he laid in his bed. He strived to take his thoughts somewhere else, but the haunting screams echoed in his mind. Faces of the dead stood like lurking shadows in the room around him. Their condemning eyes weighing his every breath. Even as sleep overtook him, the apparitions wouldn't leave. They watched and watched, waiting for his time to join them. Whatever the future held he knew one thing. He was determined to keep them waiting as long as he could.

"They're retreating!" shouted Aaron to the nearby captains. The chaos of battle died as thousands of men flooded toward the Ironhall. The ambush had all been a blur to Octavian. As a man of the court, the speed of battle was something he was less than accustomed to. Thankfully Aaron was more than capable during such times.

"Shantz," Aaron cursed taking his place beside Octavian. "If they can get a foothold in the Ironhall this battle will drag on for months. Maybe even longer."

"What's the solution, then?" Octavian asked.

Aaron looked at him, eyes narrowing. "A lot of men dying."

Octavian fixed his eyes on the fortress. Already some of Oswald's forces had begun to take position along the ramparts of the vaunted fortress. The rest still streamed into the gates below.

"We could try starving them out, but rumor says they keep the fortress stocked with food year-round. If that's the case…"

Octavian raised a hand for Aaron to stop. "Take the fortress no matter the cost."

Aaron's expression grew grim. "Those are my men. You are asking me to get more than half of them slaughtered."

"Imagine what Volkmar will do to us if we come back without killing these rebels quickly."

Aaron let out a resentful sigh as he cracked his reins. "Shantz, on this new emperor."

Agreed, Octavian thought.

The throne room was empty but for Volkmar and Rowan, his captain of the guard. Rowan looked different these days. His eyes carried an empty gloss to them. As if all the life had been sucked from him. Underneath the black surcoat and armor his skin had grown pale and sickly. Beside him, Volkmar's darkened eyes peered down at Octavian and Aaron from his perched throne.

"Ungrateful peasants. Do they know how this will tear apart the kingdom? Do they not think of what this will do to the people?" Volkmar fumed.

Aaron shifted his glance to Octavian. His eyes saying what Octavian was thinking. How blind had Volkmar become? The emperor stood pointing an accusing finger at Octavian.

"This is your problem. You and your spies couldn't see this coming? Are they blind?"

Octavian strained to keep his gaze from wandering to the fresh corpse-filled alters all around them. Averting his eyes didn't help, however, with the stench of blood permeating the room. He cleared his throat fighting back revulsion. "Your Majesty, the rulers…"

"The rebels," Volkmar snarled.

"Pardon me, these rebels hid their intentions well. My spies didn't find word of anything until last month. Even then nothing so large as an army marching on Edonia was imagined."

It wasn't a total lie. He had only known something was in the works for a month, but as for the scale…

"Do not lie to me, Octavian," Volkmar said eyes narrowing. "Was it not you who used these same sort of lies to help me win this throne? Have you changed your colors again, serpent?"

The room grew cold as several guards stepped from the shadows, swords drawn.

"It seems your usefulness has come to an end," Volkmar growled.

Octavian could feel the desperate stare of Aaron at his side. His eyes joined the countless other dead in the room that haunted Octavian's every heartbeat. He could feel their stares full of judgement, savoring the moment when he'd finally be theirs. Each stained alter within the room called his name, beckoning him to pay his dues.

"How can I prove my loyalty to you?" Octavian asked fighting to push away the apparitions.

Volkmar stroked his chin in contemplation. "I suppose each of the beloved rebel leader's heads will do."

"Issue the troops and we will march at once," Aaron said fighting to keep his voice firm.

"Ahh, but young captain, if my men do the job for you it proves nothing," Volkmar said with a sinister smile.

"You want me to march with just two legions?"

Volkmar's gaze fixed on Octavian. "If this rebel force is as insignificant as you say, two legions should be more than enough."

"It will be done, Your Majesty," Octavian said, bowing. Why was he doing this man's bidding? Then he remembered the eyes watching him, that hated him, hungered for his death. He wouldn't join them. No matter what it cost. Death wouldn't be a mercy for a man like him. Waving a dismissive hand, Volkmar ordered them to leave. Without hesitating Octavian and Aaron turned fleeing the room. Just as the door closed behind them Volkmar's voice cried out,

"And Octavian I wouldn't return without those heads. Not unless you and your men want to join our friends here."

Octavian needn't look back to know who it was that Volkmar spoke of. Whatever the cost he would not join the dead.

Blood soaked the fortress streets. All around Octavian men lay

dead and dying. Every inch of ground they'd taken inside Ironhall paid with blood. These rebels fought with the knowledge that there was no turning back. They had to have known the rumors of what awaited in Volkmar's court. In a way it was a mercy that Octavian's men killed them now. Better to die fighting against evil than to become it. Octavian joined the remaining host of their army up a sloped street until the inner fortress wall came into view. Ironhall had been set into the Edon Mountains in three ginormous rings. Each with its own defensible positions. The remnants of the rebel holdouts were hunkered down behind the last of the blackened stone walls.

"It's like pulling on a tick trying to remove defenders from this place," complained Aaron. The man's silver armor was coated with splotches of blood and more than a few dents.

"Over half my men dead," he continued shaking his head. Any hope of their own rebellion after this was dead. All of it had likely gone just as Volkmar had hoped.

Archers lined the inner defense's wall ahead. The faces of the rebels were battered and stained, yet Octavian could still see determination burning in their eyes. A cluster of Edonian soldiers moved in close using a tortoise formation. Oval shields overhead and in front, they crept in unison toward the defender's iron gate. As a welcome, a swarm of arrows rained down onto the shielded mass. Each arrowhead set alight with flames. As they sank into the shielded formation those made of wood caught fire. Men shrieked as they tossed their protection aside. A calculated mistake as several archers waited to release their darts until the enemy shields had been abandoned. Arrows sank into flesh causing gaps to appear in the formation. Soldiers scrambled to regroup but the next wave of fire chipped away at several more of Aaron's men. Slowly the shielded Edonian's pressed forward until their perilous journey ended at the gate. The front row tossed shields aside at the order and began to hack away at the iron bars.

Light Bringers quickly chipped the metal accomplishing a feat only Edonium was capable of. Ironhall may have been rumored to be impenetrable, but Octavian doubted those rumors were made post-empire. Rebel archers placed before the gate unleashed their arrows cutting down the first line of men who'd abandoned their shields. The next in line took their place working to cut their way into the final defenses. The dance continued until it looked as though Aaron's men would be repelled.

The final cluster of soldiers roared with a valiant effort. Iron snapped just as arrows cut them down. The mass of Edonian soldiers waiting to charge rallied behind the sacrifice, championing the cry of their comrades. Each man broke into a mad dash seeing the end was near and they only had to seize it. All the finery of tactics and generals disintegrated before Octavian's eyes as the two sides clashed in a brutal struggle for survival. Every man fought tooth and nail in a brutal struggle for their next breath. The less armored men of the north gathered in teams, preying on any Edonian soldier who got separated from his companions. Savagely Hacking away they cut each other down with axe and sword. Spears cracked and shields splintered as Octavian watched in awe at the dreadful scene.

Aaron followed his men joining in the fray. His white glossy blade slashed across a fool's chest. Aaron followed up the blow by piercing the back of another unsuspecting rebel. Perhaps it was cowardice that kept Octavian from being enticed to join the fight. He cared little what other men thought of him now. Whatever the cost he was determined not to join the dead this day.

The glow of two Edonium Blades could be seen amongst the brutal scene. Their wielders held up opposite ends of the courtyard. Both of them were familiar to Octavian. It was thegn Oswald who bore the blood-stained face of weathered old man. His expression was that of grimacing pain. With a wild roar he sent his weapon cascading down onto a feeble Edonian.

Octavian turned his attention to the other Edonium Blade wielder. The man known as John of the Wood. The determined and arrogant young man Octavian had met was gone. In his place was a figure of desperation. Each swing of his sword became a reckless attempt at survival. Even still a fool and an old man could easily become their undoing.

Archers from the wall above unleashed a wave of arrows into the chaos below them. Bolts struck down friend and foe alike in a desperate attempt to repel the enemy. Octavian watched as one caught Aaron in the shoulder, loosing the sword from his grip. Still stunned, he never saw the flash of the Edonium Blade that took his life. As if knowing his thoughts Octavian watched as the grimy face of John stood defiantly over Aaron's corpse. The woodsmen moved on as the lifeless head of Aaron tumbled to the ground. Octavian stood numb, his throat dry. Another pair of eyes to haunt him.

Despite the loss of Aaron, the fighting soon turned in Edonia's favor somehow. Seeing that little hope remained the rebels retreated into the fortress' keep. Even John who wielded the most powerful weapon on the battlefield was forced to fall back as men moved to surround him on every side. The keep's entrance slammed shut as the last of the rebels melted behind them. Stepping into the gory courtyard, Octavian knelt beside the headless body of his friend... "friend." It felt like such a strange word in his mind. How long had it been since he had one? Since his life was stripped away decades ago he'd moved from manipulating one relationship after another. All of them had become solely a means to an end. Even this man. Unsure of what to do he placed a hand on Aaron's shoulder paying his respects. The cries of the few remaining stragglers being killed rang in his ears as he rose to his feet.

Scanning the courtyard he could see a group of Edonians clustered around something on the ground. Approaching, Octavian was shocked to find Oswald, Edonium Blade in hand, riddled with arrows. Reasoning for the change in the battle's tide became clear now, as did the irony. It was by Oswald's own archers that the man had finally met his grave. As Octavian observed the aged face of the thegn he could see a look of regret in Oswald's lifeless eyes. Brushing past the others Octavian knelt beside the corpse.

"That's one head," Octavian thought, taking the sword from Oswald's stiff fingers. "Now for the second."

"How would you like us to proceed?" asked one of the surrounding soldiers. His eyes looking toward the sealed door of the keep.

"I think this will work nicely," Octavian said lifting the Edonium Blade known as Iron Fang.

He moved toward the door barring their way. With one swipe of Iron Fang the wood and iron melted away. Two Edonian soldiers pushed the remains to the side and a company of them advanced within the darkened confines. Only the faint glow of Iron Fang in Octavian's hand illuminated the room. From what Octavian could see the space was carved from the heart of the mountain. Heavy breathing accompanied by the clattering of footsteps bounced off the barren walls. Where had they gone? At least a few hundred had to remain of the rebels.

Something caught beneath Octavian's foot. He looked down, examining it. A banner tattered and stained lay beneath his boot. On it was the emblem of a golden star, the sigil the rebellion had taken as their own. The irony made Octavian chuckle. All the knowledge he'd been able to possess still had prevented him from joining the right side. It was too late now, the dawn was dead and he was its murderer. A flickering luminescence whisked away the darkness ahead. It wavered as if weary of shedding its light. Pained cries sounded around Octavian, followed by the thudding of fallen bodies. Panic spread across the Edonia forces as others around them were suddenly picked off.

"Back to back!" a captain yelled above the rise of fearful voices. Men fumbled into formation protecting themselves from the predators lurking in dark. Octavian took a step forward. What was that light? As he drew near, the weak glow revealed a face in the midst of the darkness. It was the woodsman turned baron. A gash across his forehead left a trail of blood streaking into his left eye. His hair was soaked with sweat and his demeanor was that of a cornered animal. The Edonium Blade flickered in his hand. Several brave Edonians saw their chance, rushing at John. Octavian watched as the woodsman deflected the first blow sending the man's Light Bringer flinging across the room. With a quick follow-up, John left his opponent cleaved in two. The next in line dodged John's first swing and nearly struck a fatal blow. With extreme fatigue, John jumped back bringing his sword's edge across the man's gut as he did.

The soldier fell in a heap, voice crying out in agony. Stumbling forward John charged straight for Octavian, animalistic rage on his face. Terrified Octavian raised his weapon to deflect the blow. Nearly closing his eyes Octavian braced for the impact expecting his end to finally come. The voices in his head gasped with anticipation, eager to finally have him in their hands. Instead, the shattering of metal sounded in his ears. He watched in amazement as John fell backward, a broken sword in his hand. Octavian met John's stunned eyes. Strangely Octavian saw no fear in the man. It was more like disappointment. Battle raged around them as the rest of the holdouts broke from the shadows for a final stand. Slowly Octavian moved forward until he loomed over the defeated John.

"You climbed too high, John. You could have remained a baron under Volkmar. Now look at you. What promises did these rebels give you to play the part of the fool?"

John let out a pathetic chuckle. "If you only knew."

A streak of tears began to stream down John's one good eye. The woodsman's stare grew distant as though he was looking far off or lost in a memory. "I'm sorry," John whispered to the darkness around them. Woken from his stupor he faced Octavian once more.

"Beware my friend. Perhaps someday you may climb just a little too high as well."

Octavian gripped Iron Fang. He had to do this. There was no choice. There was no going back. The swing of the blade brought about a strange sensation as it passed through John's flesh, as if the weapon merely passed through water. John's lifeless body slumped to the ground, a pool of blood slowly gathering beneath. Octavian felt another piece of himself fade away. As if each step forward was leaving him more hollow than the last. Pausing briefly, he mustered up the strength to finish the job. Their victory felt different than he expected. There was no sense of triumph, only an empty pit in his stomach.

"Two down," he mumbled to himself. "And two to go." He turned to help finish off the few rebels who remained.

24

JULIET

WAVES CRASHED AGAINST a shell-covered shore. Juliet rubbed the small bulge beginning to form at her waist as she watched several puffins waddle along the coast. Several ships of varying sizes sat eager to depart if need be. She hated not marching with her father's army. All her life she had trained to be a warrior, and now when the biggest fight of their lives arrived, she was here. Glancing down at her tiny stomach, she felt a sudden pang of guilt at her thoughts.

This tiny life is a gift not a burden, she reminded herself. That fact still didn't help brighten her mood. Her gaze moved from the cluster of puffins to the host of people that lined the blackened coast. Men and women from all corners of Edonia had gathered to the humble Port of Edonium Bay.

It was a perfect location to escape the continent if the need should arise. Edonium Bay was about as far as you could get from the capitol. Even if Arthur and the others failed, they would be long gone before Volkmar could reach them. She wondered if the precaution had just been a colossal waste of time. Surely they had enough soldiers to at least match the forces in Edonia. Still, a sense of apprehension hung over the entire group. The plan had been simple. They were to depart if no word had reached them in three months' time. Nearly four weeks had passed since they first departed north, and no word had reached them. The fight for Edonia likely was taking place right now. That thought brought back the bitter feeling of exclusion. She tried pushing it away, but it wouldn't shake. Frustrated, she slumped to the ground.

"I hate doing nothing," she sighed.

"Don't we all," came her mother's voice behind her. Juliet turned to find Gwen smiling with Liam at her side.

She gave her mother an unamused look before inviting them to join her on the beach. Accepting the invite, Gwen and Liam plopped beside her.

"Do you think Father has reached the city?" Liam asked.

"Most likely, dear," Gwen said stroking his head.

"How can you stand to just sit here, mother? After all the hard work you put in to make this happen," Juliet said exasperated.

"That's often how it goes, love."

"Life is cruel," Juliet replied tucking her chin onto her knees.

"Ahh but life also brought you this child, did it not?" Her mother asked. Gwen's gaze turned to the squeaking puffins. Liam clapped as one dove into the frigid water and returned to the surface with a twirl. The little creature had found himself a tasty fish in the process.

"We don't know what life spares us from either," Her mother said distantly. Liam glanced up at her as if confused by the sudden sullen tone. Gwen turned to them both, bearing a warm expression.

"So we must find the joy in life regardless. I know you're frustrated dear, but all of life is inconvenient especially for those who desire more."

"I wanted my life to matter. I wanted to be something, and now when history is being written I'm just another woman who needs protecting."

"You are much more than that, my dear," Gwen said cupping her cheek. "And that child just may surprise you. You never know what impact they will bring into the world. I know I didn't."

Gwen kissed Juliet's forehead as she rose to her feet. Dusting off her skirt she called to Liam. "Come dear, your sister needs time to think."

"Who likes to just sit and think?" Liam asked.

The comment broke through Juliet's sour mood causing her to smile. "Boring grown-ups," she said tussling his hair.

"Well, when you're done being boring let's explore the coast! Mother says there are crabs the size of my head!"

"Deal," Juliet said kissing her brother's cheek.

"Yuck!" Liam cried wiping it away.

Gwen rolled her eyes at the scene. "Come, Liam."

Juliet watched as the two of them strolled back toward the beachside camp. How wrong she had been about her mother all these years. There was a hidden strength she had overlooked. Maybe she had some of that too. Mood slightly lifted, she stood to her feet eager to see if any news had arrived from the south. Hundreds if not thousands roamed the basalt coast. Each of them on a daily search for sources of food. The northern coast was a barren place most times of the year. With so many joining them each day the camp would soon run out of its original supplies. She didn't envy Sir William the task of managing it all.

The faithful companion of Arthur had reluctantly taken the role of leading the contingency up north. Many a night in Venhorn had been spent in argument between Arthur and him. It wasn't until her pregnancy was discovered that William finally caved to Arthur's demands. Steward of the royal family was the title Arthur had given the man. Juliet still cracked a grin thinking of how proud the title had made the grizzled old vet.

Weaving through the camp Juliet spotted a familiar face. The blonde woman who had been John's traveling companion sat on a stool beneath a canopy. She worked diligently on a banner draped across her lap. Juliet could see splashes of emerald and silver woven into the cloth as the woman busied herself with the work.

"Interesting colors. That for house Kaladin?" Juliet asked, stopping by the woman.

The woman glared up at her. "A request by your mother," she said in a thick northern accent. "She saw me stitching up another banner on our way north. She wondered if I might make one for her."

Juliet inspected the work closely. Embroidered on the silvery field she could see the image of a large serpent beginning to form.

"A snake?" Juliet said taken aback. "Why would my mother request such a foul creature?"

The woman shot her an annoyed expression before returning to her work. "It's a leviathan. King of the seas. Your mother said something about an old sigil of her family generations ago. She wanted it made for Liam to know his family's history, I suppose."

Juliet paused observing the menacing beast. Large, scaled fins and sharp teeth curled ready to strike. The woman sewed diligently ignoring Juliet as she loomed over her work. After a time, she paused looking up.

"What do you want, highborn?"

"I'm… I'm not sure. Perhaps a friend," Juliet said taking a seat.

The woman gave Juliet an unsettled look but didn't tell her to leave.

That's a start, thought Juliet.

"What is your name? I don't think I ever caught it in our first encounter," Juliet asked.

"Maggie."

"It's a pleasure, Maggie," Juliet said extending a hand.

Maggie stared at the hand for a moment, unsure if she should take it. "Why would you want to be my friend?"

"I imagine both of our lives look much different than the ones we had envisioned for ourselves, heartbreakingly so. I guess I just need someone who understands that more than anything."

Maggie's expression softened. "I suppose that's not a bad reason."

The two of them sat in silence for a time. Maggie returned to her sewing and Juliet observed her nimble fingers at work. It was amazing what could be created with a simple needle and thread. After some time, Maggie paused leaning back in her chair.

"I wanted a family," she said glancing at Juliet's stomach. "John wanted something else. He always did, and I was too blind and stupid to think otherwise."

"You weren't stupid," Juliet replied. "Love often sees beyond what is reasonable. It's what makes it love, does it not?"

Maggie smiled faintly. "I suppose."

Her caramel eyes looked down at the half-finished Leviathan in her lap. "Do you think they can defeat Volkmar? Is there really a chance any of us get to stay?"

"I don't know," confided Juliet. "Something tells me more is happening here than we know."

Maggie nodded in agreement. "It's like forces beyond our control are driving it all. I just wish I knew where. Whether for good or ill."

"Me too."

Looking out of the canopy across the bustling camp Juliet could see Mateus leaning against one of the ships. His lean figure had filled out now that he could eat more than a slave's portion of food. New vibrancy radiated from him, giving off an air of appreciation for each breath. Juliet supposed that must be true. While everyone here likely had a sense of foreboding, Mateus had been given a new lease on life. Pardoned by Arthur and free to live as he pleased made every step outside the emperor's cavern a new experience to drink in.

Juliet stood to her feet with a faint smile toward Maggie. "I'll come by later if that's all right."

Maggie gave her an approving nod. "See you then."

Juliet returned the gesture then made toward the docked ships. Mateus was busy at work peeling an apple with a knife. Even the small gesture of possessing such an item seemed to bring him joy. His eyes jumped with recognition at Juliet's approach.

"Greetings, my empress," he said with a mock bow. "How can one such as I help you?"

Juliet rolled her eyes. "Knock it off, would you. Besides I'm not an empress yet."

"But you are still highborn," Mateus winked.

Juliet sighed, feigning annoyance. She waited just as Mateus brought a slice of apple up to his mouth before snatching it away for herself.

"Hey! I know you highborns are used to taking what you please, but this is an outrage!"

"It's called taxes. It's how we avoid calling it theft," Juliet said winking.

Mateus shot her a fake frown as he guarded his next slice with care. Juliet's expressed morphed to admiration as she let out a laugh.

Why couldn't it be this man who she would be allowed to spend her time with. Mateus seemed to sense the change of her mood as his face grew playfully serious.

"So, what is it I can help you with?" he asked.

Juliet let out a sigh. "I wish things could be different. For us."

Mateus smirked at the statement. "Ahh, but life often has other plans for us."

"That's what I keep hearing."

"Don't despise the life you're given because it's not as you wish, Juliet. It rarely turns out that way and sometimes it's for the best. I mean, look at me. If life was what we expected I would still be trapped in that damp cave. Think how pale and hideous I would look to you."

"You mean you don't look like that now?" Juliet asked stifling a laugh. "I don't know how you can feel so free. I wish I could take some of it for myself."

"Like my apple?"

"Like your apple," she said smiling.

"Looks like you're needed," Mateus said eyes looking past her. She turned to see Sir William moving at a brisk pace toward them, a concerned expression across his face. As he neared, William shot Mateus a questioning glance before turning to speak with Juliet.

"We need to talk in private, now. I have news from the south. I'd like this to stay a secret for now," William said eyeing Mateus.

Mateus made a motion as if his lips were sealed. "I'm great with secrets!"

"That I know isn't true," William scowled. "If you could follow me." He turned, not waiting for Juliet to respond.

"I suppose I don't have a choice," Juliet mumbled under her breath.

She followed him through the crowded tents until they reached the edge of a nearby tree line. The pine trees were sparse near the sea, leaving them with a good view of the camp and the small dirt road leading into the port. The slight elevation revealed a nearly un-touched coastline stretching as far as she could see. Thousands of white shells lay nestled in coarse volcanic sand as foamy waves of frigid water lapped peacefully against it.

"It concerns your father," William said turning her attention back to the matter at hand. "It seems he and his men were ambushed near Ironhall." William's face grew somber. "It's reported that none survived."

Juliet stood stunned her pulse quickening. "They… they're dead…? All of them?" Another question raced in her mind, "Does that mean we must leave Edonia?"

William shook his head. "If Arthur and his men can take the city, we still have a place here. He's going to need help though. I've convinced a few of the fighting men to join me. Your mother is a wise woman. She can lead the camp better than I ever could."

"Surely Arthur will have marched on Edonia by now," Juliet countered.

"Perhaps, but I cannot…"

A sudden thundering of hooves stopped him mid-sentence. Bolting down the trodden path toward the camp was a tattered and beaten man dressed in the rebel's insignia. His face was dirty, and he nearly fell from his mount at the sight of William and Juliet. William helped hoist the man to his feet demanding news. The messenger's worn voice was tainted with exhaustion and dehydration.

"It's over."

25

DUKE ARTHUR

GRAND EDONIA WITH HER pristine white towers like fingers stretching toward the sky stood ready to face her fate. Arthur exhaled a breath hoping it would release the tempest swirling within. No one was coming to their aid. The task of taking Edonia fell to them alone now. News of Oswald and John's death had spread through the war camp like a plague. Now the thousands of faces in Arthur's army looked to him. Even with the dire news, each of them was willing to sacrifice their life in order to crown him emperor and free their lands from the plight named Volkmar. What could he say to such men? How had he become worthy of this?

"You were born to lead," said the gentle whisper of Gabriella in his ear. The memory enveloped him. They sat on a bench beneath a mighty oak in Fenikia's small hillside. Caiah danced before them, chasing monarchs.

"Father died too early. I don't know half of what it takes to rule these people, Gabriella," he found himself saying.

She placed a comforting hand on his shoulder. "Your father felt the same as you when his time came. All who are given the call to lead do."

Her eyes turned to the playful Caiah in front of them. "You'll inspire the people of Fenikia. You always have."

"But how, Gabriella? The men of the court see me as a youth. What have I done to garner their respect? If anything, I've been a child at my father's table all my life. These men are hungry wolves ready to feast on what scraps are left of his court."

"What about the man you saved in Mascar?" Gabriella asked.

Arthur froze. She had been the only one he'd confided in about that story. Saving the enemy wasn't particularly celebrated in Edonia.

"If anything, that story would only prove my weakness," Arthur said frowning.

"Not for the man you saved," she said leaning back. "Perhaps there is more than one way to inspire. Not as a ravenous wolf but as a humble leader?"

The memory vanished from his mind as he slipped on his helmet. He wasn't sure he'd ever be the man Gabriella had envisioned. Pulling Phoenix Flame from its sheath he raised it high for his army to see. If he could be one thing in his life though, let him be known as the wolf slayer.

"Men of Edonia and the bearers of the Morning Star, I call on you today!"

Each pair of eyes met his own. "We stand alone in this fight. No help comes to our aid this day. Know this. I hold the same fear as you." Curious expressions dotted the crowd at his strange words.

"But despite that fear I stand with you because our hour has come to cleanse these lands of monsters, and we will not shrink back."

Arthur smiled as he saw courage rise within the faces that stood before him. "Today we fight for a better world and the people within it!"

"For Arthur, the true emperor!" someone in the crowd cried. The whole host of the army picked up the cry as they readied for the assault. Siege towers and soldiers equipped with ladders moved into formation. The hour had come to decide the fate of Edonia. A horn blared the order and the weapons of war moved into position around the city's defenses. Shouts to muster courage rang out as men threw themselves at the defenses. Arthur watched in anticipation as the first wave of soldiers came within projectile range. The city's defenses let loose as boulder and arrow rained onto the battlefield. Dismay gripped him as one tower was struck down with ease by an Edonian catapult. Another unit of men came under heavy ballista fire, nearly wiping them out.

"This can't be how it ends."

Arthur's forces lumbered toward the wall until some of the siege towers and ladders reached its ramparts. Soldiers leaped from them in a mad scramble to gain a foothold within Edonia. Swords flashed and spears thrust as each soldier brutally clashed for every inch of ground.

"Men, prepare to advance!" Arthur ordered to the bulk of his forces behind. The captains at his side disbursed issuing the commands to their companies. More towers had reached the walls now unleashing several more squads onto Edonia's defenders. Yet Arthur could see his forces struggled to gain a foothold. "Something must give." That's when movement along Edonia's walls caught his eye. A peculiar frantic motion on a section of wall untouched by his men.

"Was that fighting?" he wondered as he strained his vision. The city's eastern gate burst open in a sudden display of splintered wood and iron. A host of men stood in the opening ushering Arthur's army into the city.

"Had some of his men somehow broken away and infiltrated the city?"

With an exuberant shout Arthur ordered his forces to move at full speed toward the opening. Wind blasted him backward as he spurred his horse onward. As the gate drew near things only became more confusing. Those welcoming them were not soldiers but a mass of disheveled citizens.

"You've come to rescue us, no?" said one stocky man. He wore a dirty brown vest over his tan skin and his hair was the typical jet black of Edonians.

"Yes, and who are you?" Arthur questioned.

"Men sick of dying by the hand of a mad emperor."

The burly figure pointed in the direction of the palace. "The bulk of Volkmar's forces have secured the palace grounds. The forces you see here are just auxiliary units placed to maintain the outer defenses. When we saw your army outside the people revolted."

Arthur couldn't believe it. With Edonia's citizens on their side victory really could be theirs. With restrained exuberance he turned to his commanders.

"Have the calvary enter the city while the foot soldiers remain to help capture the walls. Make sure they take care not to harm the civilians."

The last thing he needed was to slaughter a host of innocents, especially innocents who had joined their side. The men who opened the gate stepped aside to let the calvary enter. Their faces beamed as they watched their liberators passing by. Arthur picked up the rear of the calvary charge, ready to give direction. The streets ahead of them had been emptied of life. Abandoned homes and marketplaces had been left deserted, leaving the city with a haunted feeling in the air. Only the clattering of hooves could be heard bouncing off the narrow passage walls. Moving through the streets with a swiftness only afforded to calvary, they soon drew near to the inner city. A roar of sound was unleashed as they approached. Arthur strode to the front of his unit to investigate. Chaos engulfed the surrounding streets and alleys. Bodies lay littered across the ground as Volkmar's forces slaughtered the city's inhabitants. Shrieks of horror permeated the air as the emperor's men killed indiscriminately.

"Prepare for battle!" Arthur ordered.

With a tilt of his sword his men fanned out, engulfing several side streets. Each leader pressed through the narrow passageways charging at the scattered Volkmar forces. Arthur watched as a nearby soldier of Edonia grew wide eyed before having his head removed. The woman who the man had been harassing scrambled away, now free of the monster. Having no time to stop, Arthur only hoped the woman could find safety in the midst of this mess. Pouring through the streets like a flood, Arthur and his men cut down any who stood in their path. Phoenix Flame sliced with ease through plate and flesh. Arthur savored the feeling of watching these monsters vain attempt to flee from his wrath. Each and every one of them would pay for enabling their master and his wickedness. The narrow corridors began to widen as they cut their way closer to the emperor's dwelling. Still, as the rest of their enemies fell their bodies began to clog the path in a bloodied mass of death.

"Dismount," Arthur ordered regretfully. Following his own order, his skin crawled at the sound of gore squishing beneath his sabatons.

Those around him fought the same revulsion as they were forced to clear a path through the mass of dead. As the men worked to clear a path a nearby soldier began to weep.

"There are woman here, sir. Children…"

"This is an atrocity," whispered another soldier. It was. Images of Hunan flashed before Arthur's eyes. They evaporated only to be replaced by a dreadful night in Mascarda.

Why must he be the witness of such horrendous history?

He continued to wade through the ilk until, at long last, relief came. Those leading the way had reached an entrance that opened into a wide road leading into the palace complex. Arthur raised a hand to halt his men. Lining the palace defenses stood thousands of Volkmar's men. They stood waiting, eager for the battle to come. Below them a mass of bodies had been piled against the wall in the form of a grotesque barricade. As Arthur took in the sight, he could see almost all of them wore civilian clothes.

"Monster…" he growled in disbelief. Men, woman, even children had thrown themselves at the palace in a vain attempt to break in. What could drive them to such foolishness?

"What now, emperor?" asked a nearby captain. *Emperor?* The title felt strange to Arthur. Turning, he examined the palace walls, deciding the best approach. Corpses blocked the gate entrance barring any easy way in.

"How are things behind us?" Arthur asked.

"Word is the walls are being cleared and the men have cut off any route of escape."

"They've made quick work of them." Arthur could see in the men around him an eagerness to do the same to the waiting Volkmar. Adrenaline surged beneath their gleaming plated armor in the form of jittery motion.

"Send a few men back to retrieve ladders." The waiting captain bowed, excited for any task that would move them forward.

"Now to wait," Arthur sighed. Volkmar's men bided their time like menacing statues on the palace ramparts. Their cold eyes peered down at Arthur and his men who remained tucked away in the safety of Edonia's narrow side streets. Sweat trickled down Arthur's neck from the sun looming high above a cluster of ominous clouds. A hush fell over Edonia as the two sides faced one another awaiting the storm of battle to come. It left Arthur anxious as if the city's very stones watched, eager for history to be made. After what felt like hours several squads of men came forward wielding the siege ladders. Each of them lined up in the adjacent passageways readying themselves for a sprint to the wall.

Arthur turned to the captain from earlier now returning with the rest of the army. "How do things fair?"

"Well, Your Majesty," the captain said with a grin. "The walls are ours. Volkmar's men are either dead or captured."

"Very good. Have the men with ladders equipped with shields. The rest of us will follow in tortoise formation to take some of the arrow fire off them. As for you and me, gather some men to help clear a path through the gate."

The unnamed captain nodded before barking out the order to the others. Arthur sucked in a breath steeling himself for the task ahead. Dashing back with eager anticipation, the captain picked up an oval shield bearing the sigil of the seven-pointed star. The symbol that bound them all to this cause. Just as Arthur was about to give the order, a voice shouted from the north.

"Reinforcements!" it cried. Peeking his head out of the sheltered passageway Arthur could see a host marching south on Edonia's main road. Standards bearing the blood red crescent moon fluttered above them.

"It has to be the army that wiped out Thegn Oswald and John, sir," the captain said taking a peek of his own.

Arthur dared another glance risking arrow fire from the wall some fifty yards away. The army drawing near couldn't be measured from the street's view.

"Shantz," Arthur cursed. "Send half the men to stop their advance while the rest of us try to break into the palace."

"Half, Your Majesty?" the captain questioned.

Arthur scowled at the captain's tone. "We can't risk being flanked while we assault the wall. Send half."

The order was sent. Arthur watched in dismay as their numbers dwindled behind him.

It was the right choice, he told himself. Taking the signal horn for himself, he sucked in a breath before releasing the haunting call. Men rushed forward ladder and shield in hand followed by the slower units in a tortoise formation. Arrow fire was let loose from the palace defenses. They came crashing down with screeching fury. Arthur and his company raised shields, feeling the thud of arrows as they hit overhead. Arthur's thighs burned as he worked to keep pace with the other's advance. Another wave of arrows came breaking themselves on their shields. The sound of a stray shot clinked off a soldier's armor behind him.

"Seal the gaps, men!" barked the captain.

"You alright, soldier?" Arthur asked, turning to the man behind him.

"Never better, sir!"

The others chuckled at the remark. It was a kind of gallows humor shared among men of war. The pile of bodies blocking the gate soon came into view just as another round of arrows hit their marks.

"Now what, Your Majesty?" asked the captain eyeing the mass of corpses.

"Two of us need to start tossing the bodies aside while the others hold up a shield for protection."

Arthur dropped his own shield, grabbing a nearby corpse by the legs.

"Sir, let us! Don't expose yourself," the captain cried. Arthur ignored the remark as he worked to move another body from their path.

"Arrows coming!" cried one of the soldiers with them. Arthur stepped under the wall of shields just as a dozen arrows smacked the stone where he once stood.

"Come on, again!" Arthur cried.

Several more now joined him working hastily to clear a path.

"Incoming!"

The arrows came quicker as they frantically worked to move the corpses. Arthur made to step out from the shields before the captain yanked him by the shoulder. An arrow landed where he had planned to place his foot.

"They'll hold back fire until you come out," he said nodding to Arthur.

"Then what are we going to do?" Arthur asked.

The captain ordered several of the men to continue working with their shields in hand. Arthur watched as they deflected fire before removing another body from their path. The warning sounded again, and each man rushed to return to the safety of the group. One of the fleeing soldiers was struck in the gap of armor at his ankle causing him to drop his shield. The enemy took advantage, riddling him with arrows.

"No," Arthur growled. "I won't lose my men this way." He stepped forward ignoring the warning of the captain. Taking Phoenix Flame in hand he sprinted forward. Dozens of arrows loosed in his direction as he did. Several clattered on the pavement beside him and a few hit their mark bouncing off his plated armor. He wouldn't be deterred. Edonium Blade in hand, he launched himself forward slicing through the pile of dead. The sword swiped through them with ease cutting a gory path forward. Arthur squirmed at the feeling of blood and gore flinging onto his pristine armor as he carved a path forward. It didn't matter. The revulsion he fought, the horror of it all, it wouldn't stop him from getting to that monster Volkmar. In blind fury he hacked away until the decorative wooden gate barred with Edonium stood before him. The emperor was no fool to use the material to protect his home. But the design had one simple flaw. Arthur turned to the stone in which the gate was set. Flinging a few more corpses out of the way, he thrust his blade into the wall. Phoenix Flame tore through the plastered stone with ease, sending its foundations crumbling.

Above, Arthur could hear the faint shouts of men as they realized what was happening below. Some of the wall began to crumble sending dust and debris into the air in a thick cloud. Arthur choked, waving away the thick haze of dust. To his relief no more arrows came from the defenses directly above.

So at least that's taken care of, he thought with a self-satisfied smirk.

A gentle breeze arrived sweeping away the dust cloud revealing the company of gawking soldiers. A mix of fear and awe was in their eyes as they stood frozen, mouths open at their proclaimed emperor.

Arthur paused taking note of himself. The crimson-colored armor he bore was streaked with dark red lines. Flecks of flesh, cloth, and hair clung to the steel. He must have looked a monstrosity to these men. It didn't matter, nothing was going to stop him now.

"Come on," Arthur bellowed, motioning them forward with his sword hand. They diligently obeyed, each of them sprinting into the palace grounds at the command. Arthur paused drinking in the scene of battle. Some ladders had reached the wall, but many of the men now dashed toward the tiny opening he had made. Volkmar's men scrambled from the ramparts in an attempt to close the breach. Northward, from what Arthur could see, his forces held steady against the other enemy force.

"Hold a little more, men," he said under his breath. For a brief moment he questioned whether it would be more prudent to join them. "No, if Volkmar falls then this will all be over," he said, convincing himself.

Turning toward the palace he joined where the fighting had grown the most intense. Soldiers on both sides fought for every inch as they littered the palace grounds. Volkmar's reserve of troops within the palace had after all been the bulk of his forces. Their numbers continued to pour from the marvelous structure that sat as the backdrop to the gruesome scene. Assessing the field of battle, Arthur could see another full legion begin to join the rest of Volkmar's men. Battle lines smashed like waves breaking against rock as those bearing the Morning Star and those wielding the crescent moon fought for the fate of the empire. Arthur pushed his way to the front, Edonium Blade held high.

With a downward slash he swatted aside two of Volkmar's men like gnats. Three more melted away with a backward swing of his sword. Men tripped over one another fleeing from his wrath. They would not escape. In a quick flick of his wrist he sent a thrust through a soldier who cowered in fear at his approach. One brave soul moved to block Arthur's path. In his hand was a sword radiating light... The lone warrior's armor was an ebony complexion with a red crescent moon painted onto the breastplate. On the shoulder the man bore an insignia declaring him a knight of the royal guard. All but his eyes were covered with a jet-black helmet adorning raven's wings that expanded from each side. As the two of them drew near a small ring of soldiers formed around them. Men looked on in awe as two Edonium Blades faced off against one another. Arthur moved cautiously in a semi-circle, weighing his opponent.

The ebony armored knight made the first move sending his blade in a downward slash. Arthur deflected the blow shrugging it aside. Seeing an opening he sent a counter at the man's ribs. His opponent leaped backwards barely escaping the blow that would have rent him in two. Arthur could see a small gash trickling blood within the plated steel where Phoenix Flame had made contact. The ebony warrior ignored the cut, pressing his attack. The two swords collided sending sparks into the air. Blades locked, and the ebony knight released his right hand sending it crashing into Arthur's side. The punch surprisingly knocked the air from his lungs causing Arthur to drop to a knee. Looking up Arthur could see the shining streak of a blade descend on him. He rolled, just dodging the blow. The dark knight followed up his attack with a swipe at Arthur's head. The sound of metal sheering off told Arthur the encounter had been nearly fatal. The small trickle of blood running down his cheek made him reassess that thought. But he couldn't die, at least not yet. With a wild shout he moved to send his own assault against the black-plated fiend. The knight deflected the attack, but the blowback caused his own sword to cleave into his breastplate just below his sword arm.

An echoed cry rang out from the warrior's helmet as he steeled himself. Edonium Blades danced, sending sparks flying across the gawking crowd. Arthur felt the full weight of his armor pressing against his sweat-soaked gambeson. Sensing the weariness in Arthur's motion the dark-plated knight heaved all his might into a downward slash. Arthur was sent to his knees upon impact. Sensing the end was near he looked up toward his gloating foe. The brief pause had become the man's fatal mistake. Leaping forward Arthur thrust his blade underneath his opponent's arm, sinking his sword deep into flesh. The knight's body fell limp as Arthur pulled Phoenix Flame free. The heap of dark plate and chainmail crumbled to the grass trodden ground. Arthur took stock of the blade in the knight's hand. The Edonium weapon bore the markings of Raven's Claw, the sword of Varnas.

Could it be? Arthur wondered. He knelt, still encased in a circle of stunned onlookers. Tearing the dead man's helmet free, he was disappointed to find another underneath the helm. Rowan, Volkmar's trusted commander lay lifeless at Arthur's feet. The man's reddish hair was matted with blood and his dark eyes stared upward, void of life. Arthur tossed the decorative helmet aside rising to his feet.

"Another man dead in your place," he snarled cursing Volkmar. The fear-filled circle parted, allowing him to pass. Drawing ever nearer his goal Arthur cut down the occasional brave soldier who dared to face him. It wasn't long before a path cleared to the palace steps. Taking the chance before it vanished, he dashed toward the opening. Climbing to the top of the marbled steps he assessed the battle for a final time. Even with the efforts of his Edonium Blade the tide remained even. Volkmar's men outnumbered his own but the training of a year's worth of war had given Fenikia and Kaladin's men an edge. A pang of guilt stirred in his chest. Deep down he knew he should stay and fight with the rest of them.

"I'm so close..." Only a few steps more and he'd be inside the lion's den. Gripping Phoenix Flame's hilt, he turned to the palace's interior. Large bronze doors of lavish complexity stood at the guard. Years' worth of fine craftsmanship was tarnished in a moment from the swing of his blade. Chunks of metal collapsed to the ground until a size large enough for a man to slip through was made. Arthur ducked into the opening and into a dimly lit room. The only illumination came from a set of vaulted windows. With sword raised ahead of him, he slowly made his way through the palace halls wary of what was to come. Each corner he steeled himself for a trap or a squadron of guards, but none came.

It wasn't until he drew near the throne room that anything seemed amiss. A foul odor suddenly rushed forward to welcome him. He choked back vomit as the stench of something rotten clung to his nostrils. The closer he drew to the throne room the stronger the stench became. Bracing himself, he pushed open the doors to a sight he could only describe as a nightmare. Stone structures lined the room on each side like columns that only reached a few feet above the floor. It was pitch black in the room as all the windows had been covered. The only light came from a strange glowing powder drawn onto the floor. Now illuminated by the open doors Arthur could see to his complete and utter horror dozens of dead piled onto the stone pillars. No, not just dead… bodies mutilated and torn. Some with their entrails exposed. Others were stripped bare, their crumpled frames missing various pieces. One in particular's eye hung loosely from its socket, seeming to watch him as he dared step further into the gruesome scene.

"You like what I've done with the place?" came a slurred voice. Darkness may have prevented him from seeing, but Arthur knew it could only be one man. There was only one creature capable of such evil in Edonia.

"Have you gone completely mad! What is all this?" Arthur roared.

Volkmar leaned forward from his perched throne, his dark eyes strangely replaced with an eerie silver glow. In his hand rested a white bladed dagger. A simple weapon used by Edonia's most common soldiers.

"This was my father's," Volkmar said before pausing to run a spindly finger across the edge. "You know what he said when he gave it to me?"

"Rot in the grave, you shantz," Arthur scowled taking another step toward the throne.

Volkmar looked at him with an amused smile. "No, he told me to seek life for as long as I could. To take as much as my hands could hold. No matter what it cost me." Volkmar sucked in a breath staring at the dagger once more. "It was time he feared. The inevitable end every man faces."

Arthur took another wary step forward. Surely Volkmar had

something planned for him in this horrific room.

"I went above and beyond my father. You see, I searched for a way to remove time. The great enemy of us all." Volkmar bent forward, the alcohol on his breath stronger than the stench of the room.

"He came to me once. Many years ago. Gave me promises even. All I had to do was start a little war. It was simple really. Find a proxy that hated the empire. Give them a few weapons to syphon to an ambitious ruler. Then in the middle of the chaos swoop in and kill our wretched little emperor. It was all so perfect." Volkmar grew contemplative as Arthur placed another foot before the other, rage flooding his veins.

"You think you deserve pity? After everything you've done? Your schemes got Lucian killed! You murdered Gabriella." The tears were streaming now. "My little... Caiah. You... You... I hate you!!" Arthur was only a few feet away now. Raising Phoenix Flame high he readied himself to slay the fiend where he sat.

Volkmar looked up as if seeing Arthur for the first time. "He even offered me his 'gift'. I thought after I'd done all he asked..." Volkmar's expression grew grim. "My boy Leo..." His eyes darted to the stone alters across the room.

"They wait for me you know? Hungry, ravenous things. They've seen what I've done. They know... They know."

Arthur hesitated slightly. The man seated before him was a broken one, his mind shattered by the atrocities he'd committed.

"I was desperate," Volkmar continued in a strange mix of a sob and rage. "I summoned him. I gave him the offerings just as the book said. Why hasn't he come!?"

A wildness overtook Volkmar as he began to thrash violently. Arthur stepped back unsure of what to expect. Volkmar suddenly calmed as Arthur stepped away. He cocked his head as if an idea had come to mind.

"Perhaps he awaits one more... Yes, yes that has to be it. The final commitment. I must prove I am worthy of the 'gift.' Volkmar raised the dagger high overhead. Before Arthur could stop him Volkmar plunged the blade between a sliver in his ebony armor. A gasp of air left his lungs

325

as the cold metal pierced his flesh. Sorrowful realization passed across his face as the anguish of his act settled in. The dying emperor's lips fumbled for words in one last vain attempt. Then with a limp motion he was gone. Arthur stood stunned. Limbs frozen as he stared at the man who had robbed him of everything. Rage churned throughout his whole being.

"Coward!" he screamed. "Coward!" Arthur shook uncontrollably as he fell to his knees. Revenge, just one more thing Volkmar had taken from him. Drained of all his remaining strength he feebly rose to his feet unsure of what to do next. Without thought he moved to leave. Hollowed eyes of the dead followed him as he fled from Edonia's throne. Pacing the Palace's haunted halls, it dawned on him. It was over. They had won. For whatever reason the thought didn't bring him solace. He just wished to rest. To fall into oblivion and never come back. Eventually he found himself at the palace entry. Slipping through the gap he had made earlier he fully embraced having to finish the fight for the city. Instead, he was met with a lifeless corpse-ridden courtyard. It was reminiscent of most fields after battle, only no survivor remained for either side. Screams sounded in the distant as small fires sprang to life across the city.

"What happened here?"

Amongst the scattered remains of the dead two figures approached. One of them a head taller than any man Arthur had ever seen. Everything about his demeanor spoke of regality. His brunette hair was shoulder length and pulled back neatly. The man's slender form gave an imposing posture as it towered over all others. Adorned on his head was a golden crown encrusted with rare gems, some foreign to Arthur. As the two figures drew near Arthur could see it was Octavian at his side. The head advisor's face was different now. Beneath the filth of battle his skin carried an ashen complexion. Slowly Arthur's gaze fell to the shining edge of an Edonium Blade flickering in Octavian's hand.

He had come so far and now here, at the end, he was determined to live and see this through. Battle raged all around Octavian as he cut his way forward with Edonium Blade in hand. It was an unimaginably powerful weapon. No wonder men traded whole kingdoms in hopes of possessing one. It had turned him from a feeble advisor to a feared warrior on the field of battle. Battle lines shifted back and forth as each side raged against another for a foothold. It was impossible to see how Volkmar's men fared in the palace grounds. Not that he cared what befell them. This was about destruction, about watching it all burn down.

He leapt forward cutting down two men who dared to stray too close. Pressing his advantage, Octavian surged forward. Perhaps recklessly but he'd never experienced this kind of thrill in his life. There was no more to lose, no more holding him back. Whatever happened today, Edonia would burn. Men died at his feet and still he worked to add more to the pyre. Time became meaningless as the lust for battle overtook him. All his attention fixated on the repeated motion of the sword and the rhythmic sway of the battle. That's why it took him by surprise when men began to throw down their arms.

"What was happening?" he fumed. The vast host of rebels abruptly turned in the direction of the bay. Octavian squinted, eyes searching for what had captured their attention. Black sails with the dreaded crescent moon had somehow come to dock all along the coast. A panic washed over Arthur's men at the sight. Each of them scrambled away in terror at something… something that was coming Octavian's way.

As the soldiers before him evaporated like mist, a new menace appeared more terrifying than he could have imagined. A mixture of dark creatures streamed toward the two armies. Some of the beasts stood like men while others carried a more animalistic nature. Any who could, fled before the new and horrifying force. While the others around him scrambled to escape in a mad panic, Octavian felt a strange sensation drawing him forward. Gripping his sword he rushed toward the coming foe. A wolf-like beast lunged at him dripping saliva and crimson teeth ready to devour. With a poorly timed swing

Octavian rent the beast in two. The impact almost caused the blade to slip from his grasp. Fumbling he regained control just in time to repel a different kind of monstrosity wielding unnaturally long nails.

Some of the soldiers at his side refused to flee. Octavian watched from the corner of his eye as they stood their ground against their mythical foes. Many fell within minutes against the unending wave of foul creatures. As Octavian slay another of the fiends, a picture arose in his mind. It was the monster in the book Septimus had shown him. The dreaded beast that had once enslaved men. In his distraction a spindly creature with long arms and razor-sharp claws caught him on the side. With a wild swing he was able to end the creature before it could land another blow. The agony from the wound brought him to his knees. A blur of dark motion swarmed his peripherals as the creatures overran the few who remained to stand against them. Octavian felt his vision swimming. It only was able to focus when he noticed a figure unlike any other approach. He was a kingly man dressed in the finest robes Octavian had ever seen. His sharp-featured face was handsome with a confidence built into every fiber. Ancient silver eyes peered down at Octavian with an unexpected sense of pity.

"Pick him up," the regal figure said to a nearby creature who still carried a similarity to a man. The thing obeyed, immediately lifting Octavian to his feet. Octavian's side roared with pain. Glancing down he noticed it was no small amount of blood that streamed from his side.

"No, I'm not ready... I can't face them yet," he shuddered to himself.

The regal figure looked him over as if examining something. "You are Octavian, no?" the mysterious figure asked.

"Yes..." Octavian said hesitantly. The answer brought another jolt of pain roaring across his ribcage.

"You've waited a long time to see this day. So have I," the regal figure said with a smile.

"How do you know my name?" Octavian was feeling weak now. Too much blood was being lost. He needed...

"I know many things about you, my friend. I've been so looking forward to this meeting."

Something about those ancient silver eyes was off-putting. They had a hollowness to them. As if beneath the regal veneer only an empty vessel remained.

"You've unwittingly helped me accomplish something I've waited so long to fulfill."

"You're Maluuk from the histories... aren't you?" Octavian asked coughing up a trickle of blood. He knew he couldn't stand much longer.

Maluuk smirked. "So, you have heard of me? Hopefully the Edonians didn't drag my name in the mud too much."

Octavian fought a mock laugh as the pain of it was too much. "Only that you are mankind's doom."

Maluuk scoffed. "Jealous little rodents, these Edonians. As you've witnessed first-hand they are distrustful of anyone with power. Especially power greater than theirs."

The stories, they really weren't a lie, Octavian thought. "Why come now?" the words made Octavian drop to a knee as his vision grew dim. "No... I'm not..."

"Divide and conquer. It's the greatest time-tested strategy there is. Besides that, I'm a gentleman who only arrives when given permission. You see I am not like the Edonians who force their way on others. I only want willing servants." Maluuk kneeled beside Octavian. "Speaking of which. It looks as though you might be running out of time, friend. Would you like some more?"

A glimpse of sinister intent flashed ever so briefly across Maluuk's haunting silver eyes. Octavian knew who this man, this thing, really was behind the facade. The image from the ancient tome appeared before Octavian once more. The regal figure kneeling beside him was different than the monster portrayed in the stories. Sure, there were those who argued for this Maluuk but seeing the host accompanying this man? Octavian knew this was likely a trick yet, now, after all he had done should he even care? What made him any less of a monster than this creature?

"What can you do?" Octavian asked.

Maluuk's expression turned gleeful. "So much, my friend, and in return from you all I ask is a pledge of loyalty. Pretty generous considering your record."

Octavian breathed in. It would be over soon. His life had come to this. All that he had given and all he had lost just so he could die here in obscurity in this vile city? The ghoulish faces surrounded him in eager anticipation as he felt his life fade. Each of them was a haunting reminder of those he had betrayed or killed. He wasn't ready to face them. When had he ever been? All his life he'd avoided taking responsibility. Why should he start today?

"My loyalty and my life are yours," Octavian said with a gasp. He could feel death's grip about to take him.

"Excellent," Maluuk hissed.

"That's it?" Octavian asked.

"You'll see," Maluuk said with a smirk. A sudden fog appeared around Octavian. Thick black tendrils of smoke seeped up from the ground engulfing him. His body shook as the strange mist penetrated his skin. The feeling of warmth faded from Octavian's body leaving him with a shiver. He watched as his tan Mascaran skin faded to a pale complexion. Just like that the mist vanished leaving him alone and cold with Maluuk. Something was gone, a piece of him he knew he'd never get back. Reaching his hand down toward his side he found the wound had mended. Whatever it was that Maluuk possessed it really had healed him. No, that wasn't the truth. It was an exchange. A life without end but missing what made it matter in the first place. He knew in a moment it had been a bitter trade.

"Rise to new life, my friend," Maluuk said with a gesture of the hand. Octavian stood still in disbelief that what was happening was real.

"A new life deserves a new name, I think," Maluuk said looking Octavian over.

"What do you think of the name Balzara? It's old Mascaran, I do believe."

"It's as good as any," Octavian said stiffly.

"I like that, obedience! I think this will be a very profitable relationship," Maluuk said, placing an arm around Octavian's shoulder.

"Pick up that pesky sword while you still can would you. There is one last bit of business I need your help attending to."

"Duke Arthur, I presume?" the regal figure beside Octavian asked. Arthur leered at the man, wary. "Yes?"

"Excellent!" He exclaimed clasping his hands. "Many call me by the name Maluuk. I was hoping this would be a friendly exchange between the two of us."

"Maluuk, like the ancient legends?" Arthur said dumbfounded.

"The one and only. A bit different than you imagined, huh? Not a monster made of smoke and darkness. At least not to my friends. We are friends aren't we, Arthur?"

Arthur hesitated looking Octavian up and down. "Is this what you do to your friends?"

"Ahh Octavian? He was at death's door. You see, I saved his life. Isn't that right?" Maluuk set a firm hand against Octavian's back.

Octavian's gaze met Arthur's. Sorrow stirred beneath the man's now silver eyes.

"He did," Octavian said in a hushed voice.

"I'd like to offer you the same generous gift, and it is generous considering what you represent."

"That is?" Arthur snarled slightly as he raised his sword.

"You represent the past, my friend. A past where an empire named Edonia existed. A past that is already being washed away as we speak. It's best you join with the up and comer rather than get swept away with the tide," Maluuk feigned a smile as the words left his lips.

"You… you were there in Hunan weren't you? It was your ships that massacred that fleet."

"And the city! Please don't forget that," Maluuk said with a sinister glee.

What fell creature could take pride in that? Arthur wondered in horror. "Did you know my men and I were there?"

"Of course. That's why we're friends, Arthur. I spared you… and you did all this hard work for me." Maluuk's arms stretched as if trying to encompass the city. "Look around you. You helped make this joyous day possible. Without you and this little rebellion of yours who knew if Volkmar would have had it in him to invite me here. You really can't imagine how long I've waited to see this dreaded city burn. It's hard to find servants with that much self-determination anymore."

"You're a monster," Arthur snarled readying his sword.

"To my enemies, I am so much worse than a simple monster, Arthur." Maluuk's eyes burned with a hatred that left Arthur cold. Its potency was such that it threatened to bring him into submission rather than face its wrath.

"But the good thing is, you don't have to be." The sudden malice disappeared from Maluuk, replaced with a welcoming smile.

Arthur shot another glance at Octavian. The man stood silent beside his new master. Cold silver eyes fixed on Arthur mindlessly awaiting the duke's decision. The Mascaran Arthur knew was a cunning, confident man. This… creature before him now was none of those things. Something was missing, as if a vital unseen piece of the man was gone.

"I'd prefer to remain how I am, thanks. I don't like the look of your friends," Arthur said taking a step down the stairs. He held Phoenix Flame as a warding presence between them.

"Pity. I'm afraid that isn't an option," Maluuk said frowning. "But if that's what you wish."

A sharp whistle sounded from Maluuk's lips and a distant murmur answered back. Arthur watched as several foul and disfigured creatures came bursting into the palace courtyard at an inhumane speed. They turned their attention toward Arthur, eyes full of malicious intent.

"I'm sorry you've chosen such a fate, but if one cannot accept progress then one must be prepared to be crushed by it."

The creatures sprung to life lunging at their prey. Arthur whipped Phoenix Flame toward one of the wolf-like creatures causing it to retreat. Another shape in the form of a human but bearing razor sharp teeth and claws moved to flank him. More were pouring in from the street. It soon became an overwhelming number prepared to cut off his route of escape. Arthur darted backward cutting the humanoid creature down with one successful slash. With the monstrosity gone it cleared a path toward the Edon Bay. The host of monsters raced after him, their vile limbs and foaming mouths hungry for prey. Looking over his shoulder he could see the faint glow of a Edonium Blade chasing him as well. Octavian joined the monstrosities in their pursuit.

Arthur pushed down the panic rising in his chest. All around the foul things came, pouring out of every crevasse like a revengeful tide leaving only one avenue of escape. Dark waters shimmered with the light of a reddening sun. With all his remaining strength he sprinted to embrace the Edon Bay's murky depths. Fumbling with straps of armor he began to fling pieces aside knowing their weight would only work to drown him. Hot breath and curses rained down mere inches behind him. The last of his breastplate clattered to the ground causing a howl of pain followed by a crash. He didn't look back, he couldn't look back.

Up ahead was a small path lined with vine covered arches. It led to the training platform and the palace's private docks. Passing underneath them the sound of their dismemberment was only seconds behind. He imagined the manicured garden being washed away by the army of creatures at his back. Breaking free from the path he reached the portico and vast docking platform. A host of the monsters burst from every side closing in on him. Side aching and lungs screaming he pressed forward. Gritting his teeth, he used all his remaining strength to reach a small dock that stretched out onto the bay. Wood clattered beneath his feet as he reached the first plank.

I'm going to make it! he thought, elated. As his arm swung backward he felt the sharp pain of a dozen daggers rip into his flesh. Phoenix Flame fled from his grip and disappeared from sight. Tendons popped as the fangs sank deeper into his flesh. With an agonizing scream, he pulled his arm free feeling the tear of flesh as he did. With a feeble leap he plunged into the impenetrable waters below. Murky depths welcomed him in their embrace, washing away his vision. Darkness. All around him was darkness.

He could faintly feel the stream of blood leaving what was left of his arm. But it was a distant thing now. He was somewhere else. A small light began to roll away the dark until he was no longer floating in water. The bright light cleared into a vision of Fenikia's breathtaking countryside. Birds chirped above in a blooming oak tree. A small blonde girl danced before him humming a happy tune.

"It's beautiful, isn't it?" A woman's voice said.

"It is," Arthur replied sobbing, though he hadn't realized it until then. He knew this scene. It had been his favorite memory. One of the few that hadn't faded from his mind. The sound of the woman's voice beside him was his favorite melody.

"Is it time... Can I finally see you again?" He turned expecting her to vanish from his side. Instead, her warm smile was there to greet him. Her sparkling eyes widened as they met his own.

"It is," she said leaning in to kiss him.

A slight pang of guilt washed over him, "What of the others?"

"Trust me. They are taken care of, love."

He dared to turn his vision toward the oak tree's roots. Waiting with an eager expression was Caiah. She rushed into his waiting arms. Scooping her up into the air they shared an untamed burst of laughter. Lowering her to eye level he spoke the words he had waited so long to say.

"I missed you, little dove."

"I missed you, Daddy."

Gabriella stood resting her head on his shoulder as they all drank in the setting sun.

"Welcome home, Arthur."

EPILOGUE

BALZARA WATCHED AS Maluuk paced gleefully before Volkmar's corpse seated on the throne. "You cannot know how happy this whole day has made me," Maluuk said, letting out a sigh. Balzara stood at attention ready to serve as he always had.

Maluuk glanced at him, eyes serious. "We still have much work to do, my friend."

"Speak the words and I will make it so," Balzara replied stiffly.

"This is going to be beautiful," Maluuk said, placing hands behind his back as he paced back and forth.

"Our first task is to find any of those pesky swords you call Edonium Blades and destroy them."

"Your Majesty?" Balzara asked not understanding. "Would it not be better to wield them against our enemies?"

"I don't have a fond relationship with the things. I'd prefer to be rid of them. As you've seen my army is more than efficient at killing."

That's right. They were made to stop him... Balzara mused. *Perhaps, I can use that later.*

Maluuk gave him a questioning stare before continuing, "On second thought, let's keep one. I may be able to find a use for it. As for the others, melt them in the fires in which they were born and kill the forgers after. I don't want any mistakes on this, understood?"

Balzara nodded in obedience. "Your other orders?"

"We need to make sure no one from Edonia has any ideas of rebellion again. I am charging you with discovering which cities will profess loyalty to me and what ones need removal. Can you handle that?"

"As you wish. One question, master."

"Yes?" Maluuk gave the impression that he was not often asked questions.

"Where will you be going?"

"I have a larger vision than just this pathetic continent." Maluuk paused to stare out a broken window. "My ambitions will lead me elsewhere. There are seeds to be sown if am to see them accomplished."

Balzara contemplated the words, *He means to bring this destruction elsewhere?*

"Of course he does fool," came a voice from within.

"I will make sure Edonia is brought into line until your return."

"Excellent." Maluuk said, gleefully. "I think this partnership of ours is going to be very fruitful."

Octavian bowed in obedience. Was that not what he had been born to do? The two of them made their way out of the throne room passing the altars piled high with the dead. Octavian took one last look at them before facing forward. A sigh of relief left his lips as he did. The haunting faces stared enraged at the prey that had escaped their grasp. That thought made Octavian's lip curl into a faint smile. Stepping out of the palace the view of Edonia in ruins opened up before them. At long last the empire was at an end.

Gulls cawed overhead hungry for any stray fish that had escaped the local fishermen's nets. Juliet watched as her daughter, Saria, played along the white sand beach. A deep ache gnawed at her today. Had it really been a year since her mother had passed away? Long bouts at sea and years of running had taken their toll on them all. Finally, it would soon be over. At least if the rumors proved true. Sir William stood in his dedicated spot a few feet away. His eyes wandered to and fro, always searching for any dangers that could threaten those in his charge. He'd taken his call to steward very seriously. Juliet didn't mind, especially knowing what hunted them.

Liam, somehow already a teen, stepped out of the small merchant's shop behind her. He bore the sigil of the leviathan proudly on his chest. A gesture he'd shown for their deceased mother. The once frail boy now stood nearly as tall as she was. She'd never let him know it, but he may even be able to take her in a sword fight with all the training Sir William had given him.

Where had the years gone? she wondered.

"When does the captain say we can depart? I'm eager to find out if this mystery continent exists," Liam said taking a spot beside Juliet on the beach. He smiled glancing over at the humming Saria who busied herself in the sand.

"They say it's more like a large island than a continent," Juliet said tempering his hopes.

"Whatever it is, I'm eager to call it home if it's all these merchants claim it is. Vast lands untouched by men. Rolling hills, towering mountains, and lush fields? I can picture it now."

"It does sound amazing," she whispered. It was one of the few things she'd allowed to foster hope within her. So much of her experiences had taught her hope was a cruel tool used to control others. Maybe, just maybe, this time it would be different.

"Hey Liam, you coming with me?" came the voice of Maggie behind them. Juliet turned to see the impatient gaze on her face. Liam shot to his feet as if caught.

"Sorry! I got distracted with this merchant. He has live monkeys!"

Maggie rolled her eyes. "I've been waiting over an hour. The others are already at the waterfall, and I don't want to keep them waiting. Juliet exchanged a nod as Maggie met her eyes. It had been a hard few years for them all. Loss and pain hadn't just stayed in Edonia. Not all of it however had been mournful. Maggie had finally found that home she had always desired. It wasn't what she might have expected or the people she would have chosen. As if any of them could have expected the life they now led. Yet, they all had each other and that was enough.

The two exchanged a nod before Liam scampered away to join her. Juliet smiled and turned whistling to Saria, "Come, dear, we should find you some lunch."

"Come on, Mom, it's only been a few minutes," Saria complained. Just as Juliet was going to protest a voice responded for her.

"What if lunch comes to you?"

Juliet turned to see Mateus holding up a string of fish. "So that's what's been keeping you. Here I thought you said you were going to speak with the captain and come right back."

Mateus shot her a childish grin. His darkened hair was greying now, and his once stubbly face carried a thick beard in its place. Their relationship wasn't how Juliet would have envisioned her married life to be, but time and laughter had found a way to bring them together.

"Well, you see, that's exactly what I set off to do, but then there were these fish and Juls, look at them!" He held them up as if he'd found gold.

"I'll start a fire," she said rolling her eyes. "And what did the captain say?" she asked beginning to pick up a few pieces of driftwood.

"We can leave tomorrow."

She dropped the small twigs she was gathering. "It's really happening?" She was unable to hold back the quiver in her voice as she looked up at him.

"It's really happening," Mateus said with a warm smile. He set the fish aside and wrapped an arm around her. They both stared out at the endless expanse of water. So much had happened to them, to all of them. Death, pain, and darkness seemed to follow their motley crew wherever they went, and yet as fate would have it, they were met with a glimmer of hope.

"Now I don't want you to get too eager. It could just be a pile of rocks," Mateus teased as he looked lovingly into her eyes.

"But it will finally be our rocks," she said leaning in to kiss him.

Saria clamored up the beach to join them. Reaching Mateus she lifted her arms in a gesture to be held. Stooping down he swung her up in an excited motion causing her to giggle.

"Again! Daddy! Again!" She cried breathless.

It wasn't a lie they had told Saria. She would never know the man who had given her life. He along with so many others were lost in the tragedy of Edonia's fall. Juliet wasn't entirely comfortable with how little sorrow she felt when she received the news. Edonia's ruins had bought for her a life she would have never had otherwise. It wasn't fondness of becoming her people's de facto leader after her mother's death or desire for adventure. It was this strange little family that had somehow, despite everything, been brought together. Staring at the two people she loved laughing without care made her believe for the briefest of moments that perhaps hope could be springing to life after all. In them she had come to place her hope for a future. Well, that, and a mysterious land by the name of Islandia.

The End

APPENDIX

MUSINGS OF A SCHOLAR

Kingdoms of Islandia Spoilers

I bring to you this day the musings of a scholar. Even after the ancient library in Edonia was retrieved from the city's ruins we have yet to explore even a fraction of their contents. One item of particular interest to me is that of the Dawn Blade, known as an Edonium Blade in the era of the empire. I have come to discovery that Edonium has no special property that should distinguish it from other metals in its raw form. Its only distinguishing ability is that it is able to hold the power of the ancient words spoken over them. Those ancient words being the very essence and language of creative utterances spoken by the First King and the original seven rulers he placed over the world.

Being formed by the substance of creative forces explains why the blades diminish in power with the taking of human life. The words spoken over them are purely a creative, life-giving force. Thus when used for destruction or death the power slowly drains from the metal. It cannot reside in an object of death.

The opposite of creative force is clearly one of destruction and death. This power which we have now come to discover was separate from the figure we know as Maluuk, fixated itself onto him in his betrayal of the First King. Maluuk being one of the original seven rulers however was still granted the ability to access places of power set in place by the First King. I suspect that was this destructive power's motivation was all along. It coveted the ability to create life and so it tried to seize that power for itself through Maluuk. The result was the corrupt and tyrannical reign of Maluuk throughout the ages.

With the creative power of the world seized by destruction all hope seemed lost. Yet, that creative power wasn't done. The forging of the Edonium blades (Dawn Blades) became a response to stop this destructive power by giving men the ability to wield creation in a weapon of man. Another interesting fact unknown to the emperors of Edonia and the forgers of the blades themselves was this. The reason for their success in forging Edonium weapons was do to the fact that in their bloodlines remained fragments of the original seven kings given power from the First King.

By the time of High King Eloy's rule the legends of the First King had all but disappeared no doubt by the hand of Maluuk (and the destructive force that lay behind him). Yet, the vague hope of a "New Dawn" remained within the cultures of men across the world. When Eloy had discovered the prophecies that hinted at a way to defeat the dark power that threatened the world a great sense of vocation came over him. This vocation is what sent him out into the world to find the truth.

Upon his arrival to Edonia he discovered within the city's ancient library the legend of the First King. A tale rediscovered after nearly a millennia. He kept this revelation to himself for fear of Maluuk discovering the other half of the legend lost to time. The tale spoke of a cryptic figure who would come and bare the likeness and power of the First King. This figure would be given a task that could drain Maluuk and the world of his destructive power. The only caveat being that all of Maluuk's power must fall onto this figure. This was the reason Eloy had to keep his gruesome fate a secret for if it was to get out what must be done the cunning Maluuk would have never killed Eloy.

The rest of Eloy's tale is a bit of a mystery. Even upon investigation of the witnesses of his revival I have been unable to piece together how exactly it came about. All that can be said for sure is that something dramatic had happened in which the world would never be the same. Through the taking on of all Maluuk's wrath, Eloy had completed the prophecies of old. While some in the histories who knew the tale mocked such a figure (They would suggest dying as a poor way to defeat your enemies). Eloy had taken them as deeply serious. He was vindicated in his belief and was by all accounts miraculously brought back to life. Not in the same way either. Somehow he had become a vessel far superior to a mere Dawn Blade (As they are rightly named). Just as he had taken on the full force of Maluuk's power, he now bore within himself the full power of creative force that laid the very foundations of our world. Just like the metals in the Edon Mountains, his body had the power to hold within it the full force of primordial creation. This mystery we may never fully understand but it is by that power that Eloy finally vanquished Maluuk and ultimately the power that had given him the ability to destroy and corrupt.

Some may question why the High King waited to vanquish Maluuk at the battle of the Grand Wall. From my understanding it is similar to the reason why all Maluuk's power had to be gathered to strike Eloy down on that dreaded night in Kingshelm. It was imperative that Eloy fooled Maluuk into concentrating his full force at one location to finally be done away with. Again I speak of mysterious I can hardly understand but as a scholar in the age of the New Dawn I suspect there are many mysteries and tales that await discovery. I also suspect we will have an endless amount of time to explore them.

PEOPLE AND PLACES OF EDONIA

Edonia: People and Places of Note

People:

Emperor Septimus: Ruler of the Edonian Empire, Husband of Empress Sofia, Father of Duchess Beatrice, Grandfather of Leo
Empress Sofia: The late wife of the emperor
Octavian: Head Advisor of emperor's court
Aaron: Commander of two Edonian Legions, Ally to Octavian
Mateus: Slave to the Edonium Forges and leader of the People's Justice
Saria: Matriarch of Edonia's hidden library, Mother of Mateus
Wayland: Blacksmith slave of the Edonium Forges, Father of Mateus

Cities in the Edonia Region:

Edonia: Capitol city of the empire
Western Edonia: Growing extension of the capitol city on the western shore
River Watch: Fortification for the northern region of Edonia
West Septem: regional city
East Septem: regional city
Edonus: regional city
Sojourner's Tower: Lookout station for the Edonian Peninsula
Casper Bay: Southern trade route city
Meridon Fortress: Fortification for the southern region of Edonia
Eye of the Shields: Western lookout tower
Northern Watch: Lookout tower for northern Kaskar
Imperious: Central fortification for stability in Kaskar
Forta: Fortification for stability in Northern Hunan
Southern Watch: Lookout tower for Hunan Region

Fenikia: People and Places of Note

People:

Duke Arthur: Duke of the Fenikia Region, husband to the Gabriella, and father to Sylvie
Duchess Gabriella: Late wife to Duke Arthur and Mother of Sylvie.
Sylvie: Late daughter of Duke Arthur and Daughter of Gabriella
Sir William: Trusted Companion and guardian of Duke Arthur's house.

Places:

Fenikia: Capitol of the Fenikia Region and home to Duke Arthur
East Port: Trading town with the region of Varnas
Timber Town: Major timber harvesting town for the empire
Lakeshire: Fenikia's fishing town along the Deepwater Lake
River Cities (South): Trading centers for the northern regions of Edonia

Varnas: People and Places of Note

People:

Duke Volkmar: Duke of the Varnas Region and husband to the emperor's daughter
Duchess Beatrice: Duchess of Varnas and daughter of Emperor Septimus
Leo: Son of Volkmar and Beatrice, grandson to the emperor
Crumwald: Head Advisor and loyal servant to Duchess Beatrice
Sir Rowan: Commander of Varnas' army and loyal companion to Volkmar

Places:

Varnas: Capitol of the Varnas Region and home to Duke Volkmar

Crow's Peak: partially abandoned lookout of Varnas' eastern border
Raven's Port: Trading Center with Edonia and Fenikia

Venhorn: People and Places of Note

People:

Thegn Oswald: Thegn of Venhorn region, husband of Gwen, Father of Juliet and Liam
Gwen: Wife of Thegn Oswald, mother of Juliet and Liam
Juliet: Daughter of Thegn Oswald
Liam: Son of Thegn Oswald

Places:

Venhorn: Capitol city of the Venhorn region
Ironhall: Ancient fortress of Venhorn
Hornhall: Southern trading city of Venhorn
Farmshire (shared rule): Shared farming town of Northern Edonia

Kaladin: People and Places of Note

People:

Thegn Lucian: Thegn of the Kaladin Region
Sir Kain: Trusted companion and guardian of Lucian's house

Places:

Kaladin: Capitol of the Kaladin Region
Stedfort: Regional town
Farmshire (shared rule): Shared farming town with Northern Edonia

Bjønen: People and Places of Note

People:

Baron Holger: Baron of the Bjønen Region
Theodwin: Cousin of Holger, chosen heir of Bjønen
John of the Wood: Rebel leader against Baron Holger's rule
Maggie: Lover and companion to John and his rebellion
Huldwin: Trusted second in command to John's woodland rebels

Places:

Bjønen: Capitol city of the Bjønen Region
Edonium Bay: Northern most port of the Edonian Continent. Once used to transfer the Empire's raw Edonium
Laketon: Bjønen's fishing town on Deepwater Lake
River Cities (North): Trading towns along the Edon River
Farmshire (shared rule): Shared farming town with Northern Edonia

A Special Thank To:

Mike&Ann Brown

For your Incredible Generosity Toward the Kickstarter Campaign

A Special Thank To:

Preston Rosales

For your Incredible Generosity Toward the Kickstarter Campaign

A Special Thank To:

David King

For your Incredible Generosity Toward the Kickstarter Campaign

A Special Thank To:

Jerald Johnson

For your Incredible Generosity
Toward the Kickstarter Campaign

A Special Thank To:

Shane Sentes

For your Incredible Generosity
Toward the Kickstarter Campaign

A Special Thank To:

Randall Fickel

For your Incredible Generosity
Toward the Kickstarter Campaign

KICKSTARTER SUPPORTERS:

Thanks to everyone who helped make Fall of Edonia possible through the Kickstarter campaign. Here is your well deserved recognition:

- Dylan&Emily Blanchard
- Connor&Shianne Fisher
- Ebon&Ranee Carter
- Bill&Mary Campbell
- Argenis&Andrea Matos
- FinsandC
- Todd&Jennifer Jones
- Emily Lynn
- Joe&Amelia Bedwell
- Preston Rosales
- David King
- Zachary Thayer
- Mike&Ann Brown
- Colton&Karlee Lippert
- Randall Fickel
- Nathaniel Glidewell
- Tom&Kimery Lorenz
- Alexander Ourique
- Kevin Hallett
- James&Katie Brown
- Katie Wasley
- Shane Sentes
- Robert Brown
- Zo&Madi Pollum
- Lia Winnard
- Aleda Renter
- Kieran Pritchard

- P.H. Solomon
- Matt&Dana Grimm
- Bob&Barb Van Wyk
- Jon&Valorie Grundmeier
- Isaiah Mattocks
- Andrea Lorenz
- Reagan Lorenz
- Jared& Brittany Lorenz
- Conrad&Karissa Keezer
- Jerry Johnson
- Adam&Katie Olsen
- Matt&Andrea Marlin
- Joey Coons
- Joseph Dindinger

J.J. JOHNSON is the author of the Kingdoms of Islandia trilogy and *Fall of Edonia* novel. He also is a Career Missionary with Assemblies of God World Missions. He along with his wife Vanessa and daughter Kynleigh serves in Botswana, Africa partnering with the national church to empower university students. Jacob has the heart to see students discipled with a deep understanding of God's love and purpose for their lives. He believes that it is only through living life together as a community can we truly be a light shining out into the world.

Ingram Content Group UK Ltd.
Milton Keynes UK
UKHW012132060323
418154UK00022B/87/J